THE ACADEMY OF THE DEAD

BOOK TWO OF THE HAUNTED CREATURES, HAUNTED PLACES STANDALONE SERIES

VERMILION H BAINE

THE ACADEMY OF THE DEAD

VERMILION H BAINE

For information contact; www.authorvermillionhbaine.com

Formatting and Interior Design by Vermilion H Baine
Cover Art by Rashed AlAroka
Cover Design by Vermilion H Baine and @lord.mac_draws
Interior Title Illustration by Kateryna Vitkovska
Interior Scene Illustrations by @lepetitghostcat
Interior Spacer Illustration by @lord.mac_draws

Editing by Vallie O'Hara
Proofreading by Gennifer Ulmen

Paperback ISBN : 979-8-9888144-5-0
ISBN : 979-8-9888144-4-3

First Edition : October 2024
10 9 8 7 6 5 4 3 2 1

The Academy of the Dead is the second book in the *Haunted Creatures, Haunted Places* standalone series.

The *Haunted Creatures, Haunted Places* series comprises multiple books, all set in the same modern, magical world. Each book is a standalone novel and can be read on its own.

Books in the *Haunted Creatures, Haunted Places* series (in order of publication)

The Fey Hotel

The Academy of the Dead

CONTENT WARNINGS

The Academy of the Dead is an adult paranormal romance. Recommended for readers over 18. While this story has a happy ending and some humor, there's darkness sprinkled throughout.

Warnings: strong language, friendship breakup, lying, familial betrayal, complicated and toxic sibling relationship, funerals, loss of family member, eldest son trauma, alcohol use, grave-digging, dark magic, necromancy, violence, swordplay, open door romance, light and consensual breath play, possession, exorcisms, body horror, and insect horror.

THE ACADEMY OF THE DEAD PLAYLIST

Stick Season
Noah Kahan

It Will Come Back
Hozier

Hex Girl
Wynne   Stephanie Beatriz

Waiting On A Miracle Dreadlight, Maiah

Too Sweet
Will Wood and the Tapeworms

Skeleton Appreciation Day Hozier

Magic
Kelly Clarkson

Work Song
Hozier

Necromancin Dancin
Bear Ghost

For the Departed
Shayfer James

Monster
Adventure Time

Rule #21-Memento Mori
Fish in a Birdcage

How I'd Kill
Cowboy Malfoy

Sex with a Ghost
Teddy Hyde

Love Me Dead
Ludo

She Calls Me Back
Noah Kahan

Dedicated to my husband's patience and to those who start decorating for Halloween in August.

CHAPTERS

Excerpt from the 1993 Edition of the Commission of Magic Management's Warnings on Necromancers...

Necromancers are a rare breed of witch, prone to dark magic, hellraising, and general troublemaking. Raising the unwilling dead, of course, is illegal and highly frowned upon. To avoid a sharp finger-wagging, and a fine of 150,000 dollars, all raising of the dead requires the agreement of the corpse being reanimated. The deceased must either agree to be raised from the grave prior to its death, or this may be obtained from a certified Speaker to the Dead.

All American witches suspected of necromancy must attend the New England Academy of the Dead. There are no exceptions.

Liches, of course, are a serious problem in the necromancer community. Though the death witches have an extended lifespan of two hundred years, this is not enough for some. Liches are soulless, power-hungry, undead creatures that will live forever unless disposed of properly. How liches are created is currently unknown. The only known reference was the *Tome of the Undying*, the infamous book of the dead, which has been missing since 1893.

Remember, only purchase hellraising services from certified graduates of the Academy of the Dead.

PROLOGUE

WITCH

Maddox clutched her notecards, her fingers leaving indents in the flimsy paper, but she refused to allow the roaring New England wind to rip her paper safety blanket from her. Hades, whoever came up with the tradition of forcing the Valedictorian to give a graduation speech deserved to be hexed into nothingness.

The academy loomed behind the bored crowd. Maddox swallowed at the sight of the imposing, sharp buildings. From her perch on the ceremony stage, she scanned the main school building and the dorms before settling her eyes on the library. Necromancers were forced to attend the American Academy of the Dead, a college for death witches to learn to control their dark gifts, from the age of sixteen to twenty-two. Those years were a prison sentence that Maddox almost found herself missing.

No, you're just scared. You won't miss him—miss it.

Maddox resisted the urge to clean her round glasses as she squinted at her notes. Her voice struggled to overpower the stormy afternoon, and her failure to be heard killed her already low confidence. It was only her imagination that saved her, that distracted her enough to continue reading her speech. She thought of her academic rival, the warlock she had barely surpassed during their last semester at the academy. Godsblessed *Atticus Blackwell.* Maddox dreamt of him completely defeated and lying prone underneath her hand-me-down black heel. The image both reddened her cheeks and fueled a fire within her.

It would have been better, healthier, to soothe her fear of public speaking by realizing no one in the crowd, save her own family, cared to listen to her.

Maddox's fellow necromancers, a crowd of well-bred, privileged witches and warlocks, all hated her. How dare the daughter of two green witches out-score their bratty progeny!

Maddox fought a scoff and let her farewell and insincere well-wishes flee her mouth. She rushed to return to her seat next to the Salutatorian of the American Academy of the Dead. She struggled across the stage, teetering in her borrowed shoes, and glanced up to see a ghost of a smirk cross Atticus's smug face. For six years, the man had viciously competed with her, and finally, after hundreds of late-night, solitary study sessions, she had emerged victorious.

Sure, some of those nights spent with her nose in books filled with Latin phrases like *"dissect an idyllic heart"* or *"roast human marrow before attempting to use in potions"* hadn't been as solitary as she had wanted. Not after Atticus found her preferred study room, a spot she refused to abandon just because her nemesis would occasionally storm inside, claiming one professor or another said he could copy her notes and would stay long past his welcome.

Despite the enormous crowd, Maddox could hear her family cheer her on, lost somewhere in the waves of bodies. The Abernathys were a full-on unit. Her grandfather, parents, all four of her older sisters, and every single one of her cousins had traveled from the Pacific Northwest just to see her triumph.

This would be their first and final time visiting the prestigious Academy of the Dead. The Abernathy coven consisted of green witches and healers—except for Maddox. Thanks to a great-great-great-grandfather who had a knack for raising the dead, Maddox had spent years amongst her nature-inclined family, watching them heal and nurture while she battled the dark urge for the unnatural that hummed in her veins.

Maddox was a necromancer, a witch with power over the dead and dying. And she was frightfully good at it.

There! Maddox found her family amongst the crowd, wearing jeans and flannels and sorely sticking out from the grimly dressed hellraisers.

She gave her family a shy wave and returned her focus to the graduation stage and her wavering steps. Atticus stood just before she could scoot past his chair and slip into her own. The warlock still had a single, annoying inch of height over her—though she was tall herself and wearing heels. Atticus was lean and unfairly charismatic, and he opened his arms as if he were about to embrace her. Maddox froze before awkwardly placing a single arm around his back, and she resisted the impulse to send one of her four-inch heels through the toe of his black dress shoe.

His touch was brief and completely appropriate, though it still startled her. Perhaps he had matured between finals and graduation.

"Congratulations, Maddox," Atticus whispered with bright crimson eyes that didn't quite match his smile. The flash of red in his iris warned other witches and warlocks that this man was a necromancer. Maddox, despite sharing a magical proficiency with him, didn't have that red-eyed feature. Her eyes were clear and blue. The red of her necromancer's mark, her witch's mark, showed up at the end of her thick, chocolate-brown hair instead.

His sincerity threw her off. Maddox chewed her lip and shrugged. "Thank you."

Atticus, as usual, ruined everything as he continued to open his damned mouth. "I'm surprised you managed to get through that at all. Listening to you practice in the courtyard wasn't exactly awe-inspiring."

"That's *funny*," she scoffed, for once ready with a comeback to his insult. "I found it really helps me focus if I imagine my heel stepping into your chest."

"That's funny." His voice thrummed with his dark laughter. And if Atticus wasn't infuriating enough on his own, the warlock had the nerve to *wink* at her! "I imagined the same scenario last night."

The man was just as horrible as he'd been in class—always needing to one-up her. That lame hug was surely performative. After their finals, Atticus had quickly accepted a teaching position at the Academy. Clearly, he was trying to convey to his new colleagues that he was no longer the cutthroat student he'd been for so many years.

Any other day, Atticus's teasing would have tipped her over the edge. Today, on the stage as Valedictorian, Maddox smiled up at Atticus, her words as sickly sweet as black licorice. "I look forward to never seeing you again, Atticus Blackwell. Goodbye."

That smirk twitched, and his perfect, fine eyebrows pinched together. "What about the librarian position?"

Right, that rumor was still going around. The Academy had a tremendous, multi-level library filled to the brim with North America's most deadly literature—grimoires, tomes, carvings, and scrolls from all over the world. And hardly any of it was properly categorized or even translated. Maddox had been all but guaranteed a position amongst the over-worked library staff. It had been a dream come true to spend her career surrounded by knowledge no other witch would ever see.

It *was* a dream until Atticus had been selected as the new Apothecary professor. While she was sure he deserved it—potion-making had been the one class he always bested her in—Maddox couldn't bear the thought of spending any more of her too-long life near the man.

Maddox felt like a coward, but hid her uncertainty as she informed him, "I withdrew my application."

The class threw their black pointed hats, those that wore them, into the air as the band played Chopin's *Nocturne* in C-Sharp Minor. Maddox turned away from her suddenly pale former rival and, laughing, tossed her hat into the crowd.

She had won. It was time to go home.

CHAPTER 1
WITCH

How many years did it take to recover from academic burnout? To forget that *horrible* moment during their graduation ceremony when Maddox had to look her college rival in the eye and admit to him she was running away?

Maddox hoped five years would be enough.

It *had* to be enough. As cut-throat as the necromantic academic world was, Maddox could not stand another second being apart from it.

Her sister's crate of handmade soap in tow, Maddox pulled along her foldable wagon (leftover from her school days when she toted her study materials from the library to her dorm room) until she found herself on the doorstep of the Refuge on the Moor.

The ivy-covered stone inn had finished repairs from the fire a few winters ago, again looking as imperious and over-the-top as ever. Mimicking a castle, complete with a small, round tower and an arched window, the feyrie innkeepers at the Refuge on the Moor were her family's closest, and only, neighbors. Both families were well-liked amongst the humans populating the nearby town of Fair Harbor, Washington, despite the feyrie innkeeper's notorious temper and the Abernathys' abundant magic.

The Abernathys were a family of green witches. Well, *mostly* green witches. Maddox was the lone exception. Her family occupied a few hundred acres in western Washington, and her grandfather nearly ran their small harbor town by himself. Right next door to the coven's farm was the Refuge on the Moor, an inn run by the folk—the *feyrie* folk.

Maddox waited for a well-dressed brownie to push open the main entrance of the inn for her. The creature's glamour was too weak to stand up against Maddox's magic, and she saw him as he truly was. The brownie's wrinkled face was mischievous, and he hooked a thumb underneath the straps of his moss-green overalls. His skin was a deep brown and mottled like tree bark. The brownie stood only two feet tall.

Pressing further into the inn and entering the foyer, Maddox was relieved to see a familiar face manning the lobby. The strawberry-blonde feyrie at the front desk brightened when she saw what Maddox tugged along behind her.

Maddox couldn't hide her smile as the newest innkeeper, Avalon, ran to the wagon and scooped some of the soap bars into her hands, bringing them to her face to inhale.

"I just want to steal them all." Avalon sighed, trying to choose between the lavender bar and the heather.

"It's not stealing when you paid for them."

"True." Avalon hoisted the soap onto the front desk. "I don't mean to sound rude, but where's Daphne? Usually, she makes the delivery."

Maddox knew why she asked. Daphne was almost into her seventh month of pregnancy and wasn't having the best time with it. Luckily, living on a farm with multiple witches helped Daphne's extreme morning sickness. "She's fine, just resting, but I actually had something I wanted to ask you."

Avalon tapped her chin before brightening. "Bring me some of that cranberry mead your family makes, and I'll be putty in your hands."

"You might want to hear me out first." Maddox grimaced. There were things even tasty alcohol couldn't smooth over. "And Elden should be here."

After Avalon made a quick phone call, the women chatted until Elden entered the inn. The feyrie loomed large and wide-backed, baring teeth that all came to a deadly point. Elden wasn't the type of fey who resembled the beautiful blonde elves Tolkien wrote about. He was dark, deadly, and easily annoyed.

"Maddox," he greeted her, taking a place behind the front desk with Avalon. His accent was a constant fight between American and Irish, something he inherited from his mother along with the inn. "Avalon tells me there's something we can do for you."

Maddox explained her situation calmly, keeping a sweet, wholesome look on her face.

After hearing out her strange request, the fey couple stared at Maddox uneasily.

"I'm not sure how I feel about *the* book of the dead being on the property."

Avalon fiddled with the bottom of her shirt. "As much as we'd like to help, to repay your family—"

"The Tome of the Undying has been missing for over a hundred years," Maddox explained in a rush. "It's just a conference for scholars—"

"*Necromancer* scholars," Elden clarified.

"We're nothing to be afraid of. The Commission prohibits real necromancy, anyway." Maddox put on her best mimicry of innocence and asked, "Are you two *scared* of me?" She ensured her tone remained light, teasing, and hid all her insecurities regarding her deathly magic away.

"No." Avalon laughed. "But perhaps we should be."

"The Commission will have an agent present the entire time," Maddox promised, though it wasn't like she had any other choice regarding the agent's attendance.

The American government's branch responsible for the well-being of magical creatures, the Commission of Magic Management, kept a very close eye on anyone skilled in the necromantic arts. In fact, all necromancers were *required* to attend the Academy of the Dead in the United States. It was a simple, and Orwellian, way to keep tabs on them and watch out for any future problems.

The Commission kept careful logs of all creatures and witches, fey included, but necromancers were especially watched. If hellraisers, the not-so-affectionate nickname for necromancers, delved too deeply into the darker side of their magic, they could become liches.

Liches were granted ultimate power and undead immortality at the cost of their own soul. Didn't seem like a great trade, especially since the Commission wouldn't stop until they put the lich down like a rabid dog.

Of course, there were other reasons the Commission kept necromancers under surveillance. Necromancers lived roughly two centuries. It was just enough time to learn enough dark magic to become a problem.

Two centuries. It seemed like forever, and it wasn't something Maddox liked to even think about. While her grandfather, as the head of their coven, would lead a long life, no one else in the Abernathy clan would. Not until Colter chose someone to take his place. Maddox's eyes suddenly felt too warm. She pushed away the stinging hurt that accompanied the knowledge that she would outlive all of her family.

"It's all theory," Maddox promised. "We discuss what we *think* was in the

Tome of the Undying. Most of it is just shameless gossiping. Not very exciting. But my old professor asked if I knew somewhere that could host..."

Elden rubbed his temples as he considered. "If I say no, you're going to bring your grandfather over here to harass me, aren't you?"

Maddox knew she'd already won. She grinned. "Absolutely."

"Fine." Elden sighed. "I don't have the patience for that old man today. We're at your mercy."

Maddox and Avalon exchanged a quick look, each fighting a smile. Elden could pretend to be a hardass all he wanted, but everyone knew he saw Colter Abernathy as a father figure.

"If it's settled, I have some questions," Maddox said, resisting the urge to tease prickly Elden about his soft heart. "I'm interested in the inn's ability to guard against magic. Having so many witches and warlocks around, it's best to nip any potential magical misuse in the bud."

While Avalon started asking for numbers and dates, Elden began discussing the strengths and limitations of the inn's magical wards and boundaries. Maddox provided all the requested information, feeling drained by the time the innkeepers' interrogation was over. Who knew event planning was such a pain in the ass?

But all this stress would be worth it. If Maddox wanted to return to the strange and unwelcoming academic world of necromancy, this event was a necessary first step.

She would not run away again.

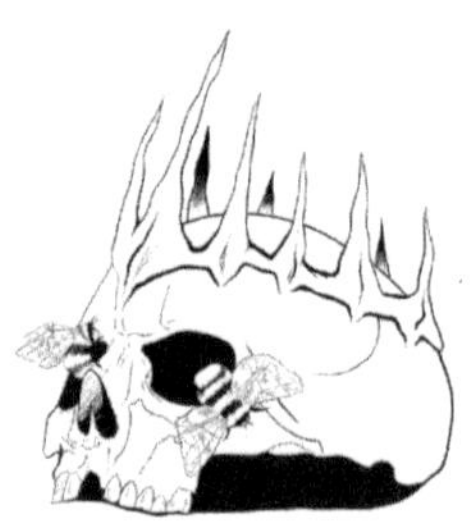

The morning of the event, Maddox kept a close eye on the RSVP list, logging on to the online spreadsheet the inn updated like clockwork. It had been so, *so* nice to just dump all the planning onto someone who actually knew what they were doing. It left Maddox to worry about less important, petty things. Like whether Atticus Blackwell would deign to show his face. He *was* a professor at the New England Academy of the Dead, so she had no choice but to invite him. But the idea of the man being anywhere near her family's farm was sickening. She was certain his presence alone could poison the crops.

Maddox didn't enjoy thinking about the last time she saw Atticus, when she left him behind on the stage at graduation. Her "victory" over him had been short-lived. Maddox had rounded up her extensive family and returned home to do absolutely *nothing* with her new, hard-won education.

It wasn't like she was just sitting around—Maddox worked on the farm, she read, and she helped her grandfather patrol Fair Harbor. Colter Abernathy refused to slow down in his old age. He was Fair Harbor's mayor, the fire chief, and the head of the Abernathy coven. Maddox had no idea how he juggled all those titles, all those responsibilities, even with her help. She and her grandfather spent most days together as Maddox, with all her dark gifts, was spared most of the farm chores that dealt with living things.

This farm life, as rewarding and idyllic as it was, wasn't anything like what she had dreamt of while she studied her ass off to be top of her class.

Maddox missed the tantalizing vanilla scent of old books, of paper cuts slicing her fingertips as she turned pages, desperate to learn more. She wanted to be the one tomb raiders dumped their boring, less shiny spoils onto—the journals, puzzle boxes, and...

She shook her head, forcing herself to slide off her bed and start her morning. Her routine was rigid—as a student, she had always been so wrapped up in her work that sometimes she walked out the door with her sweater on backward.

Such childish mistakes were behind her. Her task list, attached to the bathroom mirror, kept her focused and presentable. She finished with her face scrub and lotion, brushed her hair, and popped in her contacts. The fall weather forced her to shake out a dark green sweater, which she slipped over a black cotton dress and black tights. The ankle boots were her favorite part; black, laced-up things with a slightly pointed toe that she wore on days that she didn't feel very "witchy".

Her last addition to her outfit was a necklace, a small golden bee the only charm on the chain. It had been left on her desk at the end of finals—she'd been so engrossed in her essay section that she hadn't even noticed the gift dropping on her desk. When she had glanced up, she was alone in the room, save for

Professor Boleyn, who beamed at her.

Maddox wore the necklace every day, thankful her professor had given her that small piece of encouragement. Maddox even wore it to graduation, hidden underneath her gown, but she had missed the chance to show her professor. Perhaps she could thank Boleyn for the gift during this conference.

Her sister, Daphne, caught her on the way out the front door.

"Pleeeease," Daphne begged, folding her hands together and batting her eyelashes at her youngest sister. "Can you bring back something sweet from the inn? I heard Lyra made baklava yesterday."

Maddox sighed. It was hard to refuse her sister anything when she was stuck with a bowling ball attached to her front. Daphne was the only one of Maddox's four sisters to remain on the farm. The rest were scattered across the globe, and all were much older than Maddox, so they weren't very close with the baby necromancer in the family.

Maddox nodded. "No problem. I'm sure Lyra will be more than happy to send something over."

It took Daphne several tries to lift herself off the couch, and she batted Maddox's assistance away each time her sister extended a hand. Though it may not have looked like it, while pregnant, Daphne's magic was actually at her strongest. Though it had its downsides. A bluebird flew into the house through an open window, trying to stuff a flailing grasshopper into Daphne's mouth.

"Stop trying to feed me! I have it handled!" Daphne swatted above her head, scowling. "That's the third time today!"

Maddox giggled, helping shoo the bird back outside while fighting back the familiar, shameful pang of jealousy rising in her heart. She loved Daphne—she was Maddox's favorite sister by far—but it was always hard to see her sister succeed where Maddox could not. Daphne was the sort of green witch that left flowers blooming in her wake, and though her morning sickness was awful, she still had a glow about her and around her shining blonde hair. The warmth of the earth enveloped Daphne, flowing out in calming waves that touched even Maddox's dark disposition.

If Daphne knew how hopeless Maddox felt, her sister would probably kick her butt, pregnant or not.

Yet, there was another issue. Daphne's magic was not the only thing Maddox was envious of. The way her sister would express her emotions so freely and could touch others without hesitation...

And the family Daphne was about to bring into existence.

Would Maddox ever find that with someone? Dating terrified her. She had very little desire to be touched romantically, and so she avoided casual dating like the plague and that was, unfortunately, an unskippable stepping stone to finding "the one".

There had only been one person who made her wish to be touched, and that had made her almost desperate for it.

Maddox's cheeks burned in anger at her past foolishness.

Daphne didn't touch her arm, she just pinched Maddox's sweater and tugged. Sighing, Maddox quickly squashed her envy until it died, shrieking.

Maddox rushed a farewell, hurrying out of the house and along the forest path that ran between the farm and the inn. She ignored the tempting blue and purple will-o'-the-wisps that floated throughout the forest on the feyrie side of things.

She glanced back toward home, peering through the branches to give the outside of the three-story farmhouse—a building the men in the family insisted was perfectly level but appeared to be leaning—a once over before moving her gaze to her family's witch tree.

The white, thick tree appeared dead, but her family's magic lived underneath that pale bark. It called to her, despite her necromancy, and she gave her necklace's bee charm a final, reassuring squeeze before leaving home behind.

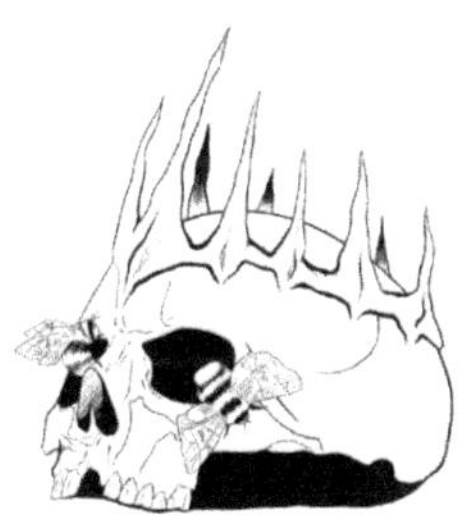

Professor Boleyn lounged in the inn's dining room, sitting with the other guests, and was apparently on her third cocktail when Maddox walked in. The plaid-skirted professor crushed her into a hug that surprised Maddox. She had been the worst definition of a teacher's pet at the Academy. All of her school friends had been tenured and AARP members.

"It's really nice to see you again, Professor."

"*Professor*? You've been out of school for years, Maddox. Call me Angeline." Her former professor pushed up her half-moon glasses, giving Maddox a very obvious look over. She squirmed under the scrutiny. "Mother, how you have changed. I bet warlocks walk into traffic looking at you."

Maddox stifled a laugh. Angeline was being too kind. People didn't mistake her for a beauty. If anything, they saw someone who probably knew far too much about the Dewey Decimal System. Which *was* true, admittedly.

Angeline began introducing Maddox to the other scholars. Some of them handed her business cards, or asked for her resume, and she was embarrassed to report what she'd been up to the last few years. Not. A. Lot.

These people were making *real* discoveries and deciphering dead, magic languages. Last week, she had helped her grandfather trap a particularly unruly raccoon.

Maddox decided to keep the past five years to herself and stuck to what she did best—listen and nod. She pretended her return home hadn't been a waste. At least she had published that article last year in Warlock Weekly—it was the only reason she'd been included in the Dead Literature conference at all.

No, it didn't matter that she had taken a break from this world. Her magic and her knowledge were all that she needed. This conference could be the start of something, and she was determined to make the most out of this opportunity.

And if Maddox needed more than one cocktail to keep the fake smile on her face, and the past empty, dull years out of her mind, then that was what she'd do.

CHAPTER 2
WARLOCK

What a perplexing location for such a prestigious conference. Atticus inhaled the fresh, bracing air and wished for nothing more than to be stuffed back inside an old, dusty library with the threat of lead paint high, instead. Last year's location had been exactly that. Leave it to that perplexing witch, Maddox, to find a way to irritate him before he'd even stepped through the door.

Atticus had never cared for feyries, and he dreaded the thought of spending the next few nights at a feyrie-operated inn. It was exhausting to watch one's language around the fey, forever trying to avoid slipping into some damned bargain with the mischievous devils. And their magic evaded logic—which infuriated Atticus's never-satiated curiosity.

Though it was autumn, there were so many flowers surrounding the Refuge on the Moor that he felt as if he had walked into a perfumery. What overwhelming, colorful eyesores. This flowery addition was the work of a nymph, he was almost certain of it.

He paused before the inn as a large, shaggy black dog stood up. It had been sleeping on the inn's welcome mat until Atticus had stepped out of his car. The dog stalked slowly past Atticus, eyeing him suspiciously before lifting a leg to urinate on one of his tires.

At least that car was a rental.

Atticus smoothed out his expression, and his dark suit, before he entered the hotel and tapped the golden bell on the front desk. A fey woman appeared in the cozy lobby, smiling politely.

Good. He was going to need to turn up the charm as he had neglected to RSVP, hoping to keep his arrival secret from his old classmate, Maddox Abernathy.

"Are you here for the Dead Literature conference?" the woman asked. The answer should have been obvious. Atticus was fully aware he fit every stereotype for necromancers—from the long dark hair, the unsettling crimson eyes, and down to his grim choices of clothing.

"Yes. Atticus Blackwell."

The woman startled at his name. "Blackwell? Like the Apothecary tycoons?"

Ah, his family's reputation proceeded him. His mother's last name always garnered some attention. Maddox Abernathy hadn't been impressed by it, but she had always been unique.

Atticus gave a small shrug. "Yes, though I don't deal with the business myself."

The woman clicked around on the hotel's computer before a stretched, uncomfortable look flashed across her face. A face that was prepared to give bad news.

"You didn't RSVP."

"I didn't? Can you check again?" Electronic devices were hard to spell, but Atticus tried anyway. He frowned as his dark red magic fizzled out on his fingertips. It seemed the feyries had prepared for their witchy guests.

"I don't make a habit of doing things wrong the first time." The innkeeper held his gaze, unfazed as Atticus leaned on the front desk, flashing her his most dazzling smile.

"I'm sure there's *something* we can do about this, hmm? I'm a fantastic guest. You'll hardly notice me." When that failed him, Atticus was fully prepared to flirt his way out of it until the hotel door swung open behind him.

Atticus blinked, fighting against the glamour that encased the giant of a man. Dressed in typical Pacific Northwest fashion, in jeans and a flannel, the man—the *fey*—entered with an axe swinging at his side. Atticus remembered an intimidating feyrie woman from years ago, tall and dark and wild, as he studied the man. The man went behind the desk, kissing the blonde on the forehead.

Thank Hades he hadn't actually tried sweet-talking the woman. If she preferred brutes like *that*, Atticus had nothing to offer her. He was more appealing to the cared-a-little-too-much-about-Halloween crowd. Not to mention what the giant might have done if he had walked in on Atticus hitting on his partner. He doubted the fey would take it as a compliment.

"Let me grab someone that can vouch for you," the woman relented. "And there's a fee."

The behemoth lingered behind, watching Atticus closely. Atticus cast his gaze anywhere else, twirling his ruby-studded family ring until the woman returned with his coworker, Professor Boleyn.

"Hello, Angeline." He noted the iced tea in the professor's hand and sincerely doubted sugar was the only additive in her glass.

"I was wondering if you'd show up. There's a bet going on. You made me fifty dollars." The professor turned back to the fey. "I do, unfortunately, work with this man. He's always one for a dramatic entrance. Please forgive him." Her words were rude, but her tone was teasing.

A hovering, blue-skinned pixie handed Atticus an itinerary for the conference, and he noticed he was about to miss the opening cocktail hour.

That uncontrollable tick, a tremor in his left hand, returned. He shook it out before keeping it clenched into a fist. He left his luggage at the front desk, offering his right arm for his former teacher to link hers through, and let Angeline lead him to the party.

The cocktail hour was held in a pale blue room with arched windows spaced evenly around. The windows were filled with a beautiful mosaic of a winter scene. On one side of the room was a bar made of polished dark wood, and on the opposite side were a few bar tables that his peers were gathered around. He was surprised at the number of attendees—Maddox had certainly drawn a crowd.

Angeline interrupted his scan of the party. "Your old *rival*," she said, using the word like it was some secret joke between them, "is here. I do hope you've managed to grow up some."

"I think I've filled out quite nicely. That's been the general feedback, anyway."

Angeline sighed deeply and took a long swig from her drink. "I see my hopes have been in vain. Good luck, Atticus." She wove her arm out of his and wandered toward where the fey served drinks.

He'd have to be careful with that. One sip of feyrie wine and it'd suddenly become a very different kind of party. He had paid quite a lot for this outfit—he'd like to keep it on for the most part.

The original plan had been to make a few rounds, locate Maddox and keep her in his periphery, before eventually reintroducing himself to her. His plan died the second he glimpsed that unmistakable, bloody hair.

Maddox had changed. Her round, gold-rimmed glasses were gone, and her soft features held onto her fading summer freckles. She'd never worn makeup before—now her lips were stained dark red and her eyes rimmed in black. Only her clothing choices had stayed similar, opting for a dark, neat sweater thrown over a black dress. Though meant to be modest, it hugged her ass in a way that was very much not so.

She used to show up to class with her skirt on backward. What the hell had happened?

Not that her appearance had failed to enrapture him before. It wasn't her lack of eyewear or the makeup she had carefully applied that sent Atticus's heart thudding into overdrive—it was the confidence she now rightfully held. Confidence *not* in her schoolwork—Maddox had always possessed that and deservedly so. *This* was a woman on a quest, her dreams soon to become realities.

And Atticus was *staring*, hopefully not open-mouthed, but his throat had gone instantly dry. He whirled around, ducking Maddox's gaze as she surveyed the crowd and met Angeline at the bar. He held out his hand wordlessly, and a glass found its way into it. A woman at the end of the bar had slid the drink his way, dark eyes finding amusement in his fragile state. She dressed in Western clothing, with a shining silver badge that the Commission of Magic Management required all agents to wear when they worked in an official security capacity.

"You saw her, huh?" The professor had never looked so devious. Atticus pretended he didn't hear her as he downed his glass. Angeline squeezed his shoulder once while she laughed. "I think you're going to have a tough night."

Angeline left him there to finish his glass alone. He waited for the refill before reminding himself that he was a man who could raise the dead and should act accordingly.

He confidently made his way over to Maddox, running through opening lines in his head, working on his smirk, and lightly touched her elbow. She turned around, her faint smile slowly retreating as she recognized who he was.

What can I do, Maddox, to make you forgive me?

He could still get ahead of this. If he started the conversation just right—

Something gold flashed on her chest, stilling him.

"Atticus Blackwell," Maddox said his name as if she were casting a hex.

"What are *you* doing here?"

CHAPTER 3
WITCH

Had Maddox personally invited the man? Well, yes, she had, but the nerve of Atticus to accept it! And she knew he didn't RSVP on purpose, just to give her absolutely no time to prepare for it. For *him*.

She kept her arms crossed, trying to get around her old habit of wringing her hands when she grew nervous.

Atticus's smile, oddly demure and unlike him, quickly quirked up into a smirk. *That* was better. It was *expected*. He raised a glass in her direction. "Hello, Maddox. It appears your prediction at graduation was false. We'll have to suffer one another's presence once again." That same dripping condescension filled his deep tone.

Maddox shook her head and sniped, "It wasn't a *prediction*. It was hope."

Ugh, Atticus made her feel crazy. Always dragging out the worst parts of her—the competitiveness, the absolutely, crushing need to *win*. Monopoly had been banned from the Abernathy farmhouse since she was seventeen. She still didn't know where her grandfather was hiding it.

There were other things, *horrifying things*, that his presence inspired in her, but Maddox would never allow herself to remember those.

Worst of all, Atticus looked to be doing perfectly well for himself. He was a successful professor, his finger directly on the pulse of every new discovery in the necromantic arts. And she was stuck on the farm, gleaning second-hand information from magazines.

Well, her choices were not his fault. She'd been so burnt out after the Academy that withdrawing her application for the school library hadn't been solely due to Atticus's place amongst the staff.

Maddox may have won their little academic rivalry, but she'd been left crushed. Only after years of rest, of praying to her family's witch tree to aid her, was she finally beginning to find her strength again.

Atticus stared at her, still looking down on her despite her heeled boots, and waited for *something*. What, she didn't know, but she was an adult now, no longer the awkward, mousy girl she used to be. She could handle Atticus Blackwell.

She bit down her anger, that biting shame that he drew out of her. Maddox ground her teeth, forcing her breath and heart rate to steady until she could speak without a shred of emotion.

"Thank you for coming," Maddox said dully. "I hope you enjoy the conference."

Atticus blinked at the sudden change in her voice and stepped in front of her as she tried to move away. "I caught your article in Warlock Weekly. It's amazing that you could make such a discovery out here in the backwoods. I checked your findings personally, and I found no mistakes." He slipped a rolled-up magazine out of his jacket, and to her dismay, it was exactly what she had feared. Her article.

So much for her inner peace. "What? You want to point out some inaccuracy or typo? Is that it?"

He flattened out the magazine, handing her a marker. "I was hoping you'd sign it."

"Stop it." How many of those strange feyrie cocktails had she consumed? Maddox failed to recall the number as drunken tears threatened the corners of her eyes. "Fuck you, Blackwell." She clipped his shoulder as she stormed away, regretting that last drink.

For the rest of the conference, Maddox did her best to avoid Atticus, focusing instead on her notebooks and potential job offers. Despite Atticus's upsetting presence, she still felt ready to return to the academic world—just far, far away from the American Academy of the Dead.

Though she sent Atticus every signal to leave her alone, he followed her like a lost puppy. He chattered constantly in her ear, boasting about her former achievements to anyone she tried to talk to. But in his sarcastic, low voice, his words failed to hold any sincerity.

Maddox wished she could allow her natural inability to focus take over and drown out his monologuing, but she wanted to appear determined. It had taken her years—and a few changes in her medication—to shift her reputation from a daydreamer to a serious academic.

It was also why Maddox had burned out so badly.

Atticus's current topic of their one-sided conversation was the London necromancy college, the Royal Necromantic Magistry. They were just as esteemed as the American academy, if not more so. But Atticus knew of the Magistry's every fault and listed them to her repeatedly.

"I really doubt that they sacrifice *children*." Maddox would have to have Daphne brew her something for the headache that accompanied the warlock's companionship.

"I would know better than you. My mother's the Dean."

Maddox already knew that. Cynthia Blackwell had written to her last month listing a few open positions. The Blackwell name made her cringe, but she recalled from her Academy days that Atticus hated his mother.

It made the job offer all the more enticing. She would not, however, tell Atticus anything about it, lest he try to sabotage her somehow.

She wished Atticus would have the decency to have a hair out of place or a single wrinkle in his trousers. But, no, annoyingly, the warlock had wildly transformed from the lanky, short-haired kid he used to be. That dark, wavy hair had grown past his shoulders, and he'd gained some weight as well, just enough to fill out where he had needed to. His beard was short and impeccably trimmed, some grey peppered in despite his youth.

Atticus adjusted a jacket that was probably worth more than the banged-up, hand-me-down Jeep Maddox shared with Daphne. He wore all black, sleek and trimming, aside from the grey sweater he wore today.

He looked like he belonged in a male librarian porno.

Not that she had watched enough of those to—

Oh! "You're making me insane!" Her rageful whisper caught the attention of one of her potential employers to Maddox's dismay.

"Let's take a walk," Atticus offered, standing and presenting his hand to her in front of everyone.

What an asshole. If she refused his deceptively friendly gesture in front of the other guests, it might cost her a job. Maddox accepted his hand, fighting the urge to pinch his palm as they walked outside the inn together.

She shook off his grip as soon as they were out of sight. Her feet started down the familiar path that cut through the surrounding pine forest and hiked toward her family's land. Atticus caught up with her, complaining about his shoes and the autumn mud.

She remained silent, heading toward the sound of the creek that ran partway around the witch-feyrie boundary. The creek narrowed out here, only two feet wide. It was an easy jump Maddox made many a time.

Atticus caught her arm right before she could hop over the invisible, magical border. "Let's be frank with each other," he began, turning her to face him. "What the fuck is your problem?"

His narrowed eyes were a welcome sight. The red lens glasses that he sometimes wore slipped down his nose as he glared down at her. Maddox had never decided if she thought Atticus wore those ridiculous glasses to accentuate the fact he was a necromancer, or if he wore them to hide the true, damning color of his eyes. Add in that condescending sneer and he finally looked like himself.

"*There you are*," Maddox murmured, her own brow furrowing to match his. "It would be easier to list what parts of your persona don't piss me off."

"I have been nothing but kind to you the past few days," he snapped, stepping into her personal space. She held out her hand to stop his approach, her magic ghosting along her skin. "My apologies if I've interrupted your stay in *fucking Mayberry*."

"You know what it's like here! If this place still repulses you that much—" Maddox tried to change the subject desperately, "—then *leave*."

"No."

She couldn't help but whine. "Why? Why are you here, Atticus? You couldn't miss *one* damned conference out of the hundred I'm sure you're invited to?"

His answer nearly drove her to violence. "I came for *you*."

"Liar," she snarled. The urge to drag him over the border, onto her family's territory, so she could hex him out of their county flooded her.

Atticus only nodded. "I'm bringing you back to the Academy, and I guarantee you'll want to."

"How?" She laughed at him, the sound cruel even to her own ears. "What could possibly convince me to spend another minute with you?"

He ceased his over-dramatic buildup. "I have a single page from the Tome of the Undying. One faded page crafted from human skin."

Her stomach dropped, the rush of potential unknown knowledge coursing through her veins. "What does it say? Where did it come from? Who found—" She blushed. Hades below, he had her pegged.

He grinned and continued dangling the bait. "The writing is concealed. A chemical process will be necessary to bring the dead back to life."

She ignored the lame joke. "How can you know that it's from the actual book of the dead? A lot of necromancy grimoires were made from human hide."

"I don't know, but don't you wish to find out?"

Maddox huffed. "I don't believe you."

"That doesn't matter, does it? I *know* you. You'll have to see it for yourself. If only to prove me wrong." He tilted his head, considering her for a long time. "You never let me do anything less than my absolute best. I'll need that for this."

Atticus wanted her there to *support* him? No fucking way. "There's plenty of more qualified people at the Academy. Find one of them to—"

"No. I want it to be you. I know it *has* to be you." Despite the numerous wards the feyries had placed to work against necromantic magic, Maddox watched Atticus's magic, still the color of dried blood, rise like smoke, drift over to her, and caress her skin. She waved it away like it was an irritating fly. Atticus continued, "I can't even count how many languages you can speak, let alone read. You'd truly prefer to stay here? In obscurity? What a fucking waste."

The hex nearly left her lips. She swallowed, fighting a battle inside herself and being unsure of what would emerge as the winner. Finally, she repeated, "I don't believe you."

"Which part?"

She clarified, "You may have found something, but I'll never believe you'd want me to be part of it. This is some kind of trick—"

Atticus rolled his eyes. "I'm getting tired of this, Maddox. This isn't like you. The woman I know wouldn't let anything stand in her way for a chance like this."

You don't know anything about me, you selfish prick. You threw that chance away years ago.

When she refused to speak, Atticus sighed. "Fine. Place a truth spell on me. I'll allow it if it ends this infuriating back and forth."

"The wards—"

He huffed. "Don't pretend like you can't manage a simple spell of truth on a willing participant, even with these damned feyrie wards."

She reached for one of his hands, the left one, but Atticus withdrew from her grasp. "No, this one," he barked, offering his right hand instead.

"It shouldn't matter," she muttered, but Maddox allowed this eccentricity. She rubbed Atticus's palm with her thumbs, working her bright crimson magic into his skin. Maddox despised performing these kinds of spells as she found them to be immoral, but she'd make an exception for Atticus.

She uttered the last bit of the incantation, noticing how his hand twitched as if he had changed his mind. It was enough to make her backpedal until he growled, "Ask your question."

"Okay." She gave him some space, holding her hands on her hips as she demanded, "Do you really think this page is from the Tome of the Undying?"

"Yes." He relaxed, his shoulders dropping. "Now release me."

"I'm not finished." Maddox glared back at him. "Why do I have to be there?"

"I know the work needs you."

The spell was holding strong. Logically, she could not doubt him any longer. The real question was whether she could work with the man, even with such a tantalizing subject. To be the first witch to read from the book of the dead in over a century! Maddox couldn't find a greater purpose if she spent the rest of her life trying.

"And." The word fell like a judge's gavel right before delivering a death sentence.

"And?" Maddox repeated, having nearly forgotten that Atticus was still there.

He blurted, "It's an apology! For chasing you away from the Academy! I never meant for that to happen. I swear it."

She almost relaxed, thinking that this was the worst that was to come. Until the man placed his fist against his mouth, his body shaking, while his red magic swirled around and failed to release the grip her spell held on him.

There *was* more! And he was desperately trying to hide it from her. His outburst of an apology was trying to cover for something else, something he didn't want her to know.

"Maddox, let me go," he pleaded.

"No." *Never.* She stormed forward, ripping his fist from his mouth. Suspicion sharpened her judgment. "Finish what you have to say."

Atticus dropped to his knees, but Maddox mercilessly kept her grip on his arm. Her spell formed a red noose that slipped over Atticus's neck. Maddox used it to force him to match her gaze. "Say it."

"Maddox, *please.*"

She had never seen Atticus so wretched. If there was an ounce less of hate in her heart for him, she would have done as he asked. Would have done what he was *begging* for.

She didn't. Maddox dug her heels in, strangling him with her spell as she repeated her question over and over. What she was doing made her sick. Seeing Atticus on his knees, pleading for the mercy he had denied her in their youth, shattered the passive mask she kept carefully in place. Rage broke through her words, the memory of his betrayal still an open wound in her heart.

Maddox put everything she had into her words. There was power in a name and she, throat raw, shouted his from her broken core. *"Atticus Blackwell, answer me!"*

Her magic coiled tighter around him, squeezing out the truth. "And—and because I want you." The words seemed to deflate him.

"*Want* me? What do you—" She instantly turned red and let his hand go. But the spell kept working.

His forehead hit the earth, giving the impression that he was worshipping her. "I've missed you. I *need* you. I want to see your eyes light up when I unveil that dead language for you. I've never wanted anything more in my life." He pounded a fist against the ground, the violence almost enough to tear her out of her frozen state. "I can't stand being so far from you. If something ever happened to you, I'd crawl into your grave to take my place beside you."

Every word of his confession seemed to pain him. Atticus suddenly scratched at the magic encircling his throat with a renewed, fevered desperation.

Maddox's mind beat against the relentless shockwaves flooding her body, finally thrusting her into action. She fought to undo her spell, bloodying her knees by falling onto the ground beside him. She took his hand and tried to pull her magic out.

The hateful, piercing glare he shot her made her own spell slip away from her. It only took a few seconds for Maddox to regain control, but it was too late.

He was trembling, her poisonous magic nearly gone from his veins, when Atticus whispered, "*I love you.*"

CHAPTER 4
WITCH

S he was certain they both wanted to throw up. Maddox had been seconds too late; Atticus's slack hand was left in her own as her spell finally wrung that final, awful truth from him.

What have I done?

Maddox thought Atticus concealed some trick, some plan to demean her once again. Never, *never*, would she have guessed that he...that he...

There were some things she had always thought she wouldn't do even to her worst enemy, and now she knew she was wrong. Her morality died when her ego was hurt. Hades, he had *begged* her to stop and she—

"I'm so sorry."

"Why?" Atticus jerked his hand away, slowly bringing himself to stand. "Why would you be sorry? You got what you wanted. *You've won.* You've won so completely that I can't imagine you'll ever think of me again. How pathetic I must have looked, kneeling before you and confessing that I—"

"Don't," she pleaded. *I don't want to win like this. I'm so tired of trying to beat you, Atticus.*

"Are you ashamed of me?" Atticus swooped down and yanked her onto her feet. "Don't bother. I can stand your hate, but save your pity."

She avoided looking at him, her guilt-ridden gaze dragging along the ground.

Her refusal to acknowledge him sharpened his tongue. "Congratulations, Maddox. You've won *me*. And what a sorry prize I seem to be."

"Atticus," she began.

"I don't want to hear another apology." He brushed the dirt off his clothing before whirling around to storm away.

What her plan was wasn't clear even to her, but Maddox grabbed his suit jacket to stop him. "That can't be true."

"What?" Atticus looked angrier at that than anything else up to that point. "You won't even *accept* what you stole from me?"

Maddox searched for an alternative answer to his insane admission. "You must be wearing a protection charm or something that counteracted my spell—"

"You are the greatest witch I know! How can you possibly doubt your own spell?" He ran both hands through his hair, eyes wild. "If you believe that, truly, feel free to strip me down and check for yourself! You've already humiliated me once today."

"If you really—" It was impossible to choke out the words. *Loved me.* "—felt that way, you never would have left me. Can you explain that? Will you stop being a damned coward and tell me why I wasn't good enough to be your friend?!"

Atticus was still, a dark shade haunting between two trees. "No, I cannot."

That was all she wanted—the truth and willingly given. How many years would have to pass before he would allow her that? Maddox snarled, "How *else* could you prove it?"

Her challenge darkened Atticus's expression. She *hated* when he looked at her like that, glaring down at her through his lashes with a smirk dancing on his lips. Atticus murmured, "Ever the scientist, aren't you?"

This farce had gone on long enough. "Take it back!" Avoiding the need to stomp her foot like a child, Maddox dared him, "Take it back or make me believe it!"

"Make you believe it?" he cried, tugging again at his hair, his exasperation rising to meet hers. "If you can't trust your own magic, Maddox, what the hell do you want me to do?"

"Kiss me." The words left before her brain could filter them.

Atticus's laughter was startled, almost mad. His eyes bounced from her own and down to her lips. " *What* did you say?"

Maddox shook her head, cocking a brow as she sneered in preemptive triumph. "I knew you didn't mean it. You came all this way just to bullshit me? You—"

Atticus covered the distance between them in three long steps.

Make me believe it, she had asked. There were many negative things she could say about the warlock, but lack of commitment was not one of them.

Atticus silenced her with his mouth, drawing her into a deep kiss. The parts of her hair that she wore down, he twisted his hands into. Not that she had a lot of experience, or any, to draw from, but this wasn't a kiss an actor could pull off. His unbearable want was obvious as he continued, biting her lower lip until the faint, coppery taste of blood hit her senses.

The most unexplainable part of it all was that she kissed him back. Her heart rammed repeatedly against her ribcage, and her magic pooled at their feet as she parted her mouth for him. Was she that desperate for another's touch? At the Academy, it had seemed like everyone had paired up and left her behind to spend her nights alone amongst the yellowing manuscripts. It hadn't bothered her, not at first. She felt very little romantically, and it was her greatest frustration that only Atticus had ever managed to bring out such rampant want in her.

Where the hell was her aversion to being touched when she needed it? Logic begged her to step away, to pull back, but no part of her body was listening as her arms wrapped around Atticus's back to draw him closer.

What am I doing?! Atticus's embrace had wound so tightly around her that it squeezed a breath out of her lungs. At her gasp, the man relaxed his hold, but it was too late. Maddox was able to finally act, pushing herself free from his embrace.

It only lasted a second. More out of breath than she should have been, Maddox panted, "Fuck you," before she reached for him again. Atticus made some sort of relieved, desperate sound as their mouths met once more.

He lifted her, startling her as she quickly wrapped her legs around his waist to avoid falling. He thrust her back against the nearest tree, pressing them closer together.

"How far should we go to convince you?" His mouth moved to her neck, one arm under her thighs, and his free hand began toying with her necklace. "I may not be a good man, but I'll be good to you. And *only* you."

Maddox chewed on her bloody bottom lip—the only thing keeping her silent. While she hated the man, she could not pretend his mouth didn't feel like flames against her skin.

If she didn't stop them, the warlock would have her against this tree, she was sure of it. And, embarrassingly, as overwhelmed as she was, she was only ninety-nine percent sure it was a bad idea.

The threat of things going further shook Maddox out of her stupor. She grabbed one of the ruby studs Atticus wore in his earlobe and tugged on it until he dropped her.

"Fuck!" Atticus rubbed his ear, his lips twisted into a scowl, but his eyes were wide and anxious. "You could have just said something."

"I believe you now. There's no point in continuing." Fucking fantastic. She'd have to live forever with the fact that her first kiss was with *Atticus Blackwell.*

"No *point?*"

"Yes, the experiment is complete. I can't doubt the evidence when it's so...persuasive."

"I'll take that as a compliment."

Her ears burned. She needed time and space away from this man. Maybe he had been, or still was, in love with her. That didn't excuse the way he'd abandoned her during their time at the Academy.

She pressed her hands gently against his chest, flinching at the way his expression softened at her touch. The babbling of the creek in her ears, she shoved him back with all her strength, watching him tumble gracelessly out of the feyries' land and onto the Abernathys'.

The white roots of her family's witch tree shot out of the ground, wrapping up his legs as he tried to scramble away. Thicker, less mobile roots churned up the earth, making room to drag him underground.

"What are you doing? *How* are you doing this?!" Atticus was waist-deep in the ground now, pushing against the dirt to try to pull himself out.

Necromancers had no control over nature. But this was her family tree and generations of Abernathy magic flooding into it allowed her such power. Her grandfather could summon the roots wherever he wished, but Maddox could only call them while on her family's land.

She stood over him, observing him from an angle she'd never been able to try before. One of the roots pressed dangerously against his neck until she called it off him.

"Do you remember in school when we dug up that grave? We found fingernails stuck in the coffin lid. From the inside." She knelt down next to him, taking in his wide eyes as she tilted his chin up with a finger. "I always wondered what it would feel like to be buried alive."

Maddox, thinking it would be the last time, leaned forward and kissed him as he sighed her name against her lips. She sat back, pushing off her knees to stand. "I'm jealous that you get to find out."

With hardly a sound, he disappeared into the earth.

What about Atticus drove her into such darkness? She just told the man she was going to bury him alive! Even though it wasn't true, what could make her say such a thing?

This wasn't right. Maddox was *kind*. She didn't kiss a man and then make him believe she was about to murder him.

She was empathetic, gentle. She had to be to fit in.

Why had she done that*? Am I a terrible person?* It felt like stones were piling, one by one, onto her chest and eventually Maddox would hear her ribs crack under the pressure.

You want him to get over you, her conscience, finally piping up, said. *That performance might have done the trick.*

She wiped at her eyes, shocked at the wetness she found there. Hades help her, what had she done? Maddox slumped against the tree Atticus had pressed her against, her eyes shut as she struggled with her own indecision. She clearly wasn't ready to face Atticus again. She thought the years would have guarded her heart and her hurt against him...

Hades, how long had she wasted time wallowing? Maddox hurried along to the Abernathy farmhouse, struggling to keep her powers in check. There were dozens of farm animals and former familiars buried around the farm. Once, she'd accidentally resurrected her sister's old hamster, and Daphne still hadn't quite forgiven her for it. She didn't want to repeat the incident today.

Maddox's grandfather intercepted her outside the farmhouse. His jaw was set, and he pointed to an impression in front of the witch tree that looked like a shallow grave, just large enough for a man to crawl through.

"Care to explain this?" Colter Abernathy waved a hand, and the roots of the witch tree began shoveling in dirt to fill the hole. Colter rubbed his palms off on his jeans and shook hay out of his thick grey and brunette hair. Maddox rubbed her upper lip until her grandfather took the hint and wiped his mustache free of hay as well. "Or the dirty young man I have sitting in my kitchen?"

Maddox was not about to admit to her grandfather that she had nearly buried a man alive. "The dirty young man is Atticus Blackwell. From my school."

"That was *Blackwell?*" The old druid straightened his back and stomped inside the farmhouse. Maddox kept close on his heels, twisting her hands once before she corrected herself. As surreal as it was, Atticus was sitting at her family's kitchen table, picking rocks and dirt out of his hair while he cradled a steaming cup of tea. Colter stole the cup back and poured it down the sink.

Years ago, she knew Atticus would have snapped at the slight, but he must have realized the strength the older man worked carefully to hide. Atticus ducked Colter's glare and asked Maddox, "Why did you bring me here?"

"I'm bringing him to dinner," she told her grandfather, refusing to look at Atticus. "Have Mom make him a plate."

"You want me to *feed* him?" Colter began sweeping a broom around the table, clicking his tongue at the piles of dirt accumulating underneath Atticus's chair. "I should feed him to the pigs. Or the feyries."

"He's far too bitter for that." Now she turned to Atticus. "Come on, I'll show you where to shower. Unless you want to do that at the inn and risk all of your colleagues seeing you like this."

Atticus sniffed, standing and following her up the farmhouse's wooden stairway to the third floor, complaining the entire time. "That was rather dramatic for you. Normally, we save such theatrics for *my* tantrums." He walked into her as she paused at a doorway. "And!" His fussing never ceased. "You broke my glasses."

"We both know those aren't prescription," she argued, though she felt guilt inching up from her stomach. "Here's the bathroom. Make sure you lock it behind you. No one knocks in this house." Proving her point, Maddox slipped into Daphne's room to rummage through her brother-in-law's closet. She returned with pants and a shirt for Atticus, neither of which he appreciated, and left him to his own devices. "Dinner's at six. See you downstairs."

CHAPTER 5
WARLOCK

All his careful planning had been *wasted*. This trip was supposed to be Atticus's triumph, his chance to prove to Maddox that they could put their mottled past behind them. Instead, his most terrible secret had been stolen from him, ruthlessly wrenched from his lips by the only one he could not stand to hear it.

Disgusted. She had looked sick when the depths of his feelings, his obsession had been laid bare. He loved her. He admired her. He'd *die* for her, and now she *knew*.

Atticus turned the shower as hot as it would go, letting his back turn red from the heat. Even that pain wasn't enough to wash away the feel of her. He shouldn't have touched her, let alone *kissed* her. It was as if being around each other made them both insane. Hades, it had led to Maddox threatening to bury him alive!

He'd believed her, too. She'd distracted him with another kiss to keep him from finding some way around her magic.

Staring, forlorn, at his filthy clothes, Atticus turned to the replacements he'd been given. Wearing flannel and jeans was all good and well for the Abernathys, but on him? He was going to look like a Seattle hipster.

He changed and left his hair down, though it dripped water on his shoulders. Quietly, he wandered the farmhouse hallways, stepping around a gaggle of screaming toddlers, until he found Maddox's room. He still recalled the chipped, lavender paint and the golden doorknob that needed maintenance.

The knob came off in his hand—over a decade later and no one had fixed this? Inwardly groaning, Atticus knocked before slipping inside.

Maddox barely acknowledged him, shuffling things around on her desk and tossing notebooks into a backpack. He let her work without interruption until she fished a small, wheeled piece of luggage from underneath her bed.

"Are you *packing*?" Atticus questioned, unable to stop himself.

Maddox frowned, pointing at the doorknob still in his hand. "Did you break my door?"

"No, I—"

Maddox continued as if she had never expected an answer. "I told you I'd meet you downstairs." She considered him finally, her head tilting as if she could scarcely believe he stood in front of her. "You look like you're about to explain feminism to me."

"Thank you for the clothes," he forced out between gritted teeth. "I don't understand why you had to ruin mine, but—"

An overly obnoxious bell chimed throughout the entire house, the sound of doors opening and closing following it. Maddox left the mess she'd made packing and began pushing him out the door. Her innocent touch was electric. He really was pathetic.

This was his second time staying with the Abernathys, and not one of them looked happy to see he had returned. Exactly what had Maddox been telling them? Only the children seemed to tolerate him, their sticky hands grabbing onto his shirt sleeve and asking him if he could turn them all into zombies.

The answer was yes, with the caveat that he'd have to murder them all first. Atticus opted to remain grim and silent as he sat down at the Abernathys' dining table once more. He had plenty of practice appearing grim, but keeping silent, however, was not a habit he practiced.

The incredibly pregnant woman next to him shooed the children swarming him off to their own plastic table. She stared at Atticus, and he knew he wouldn't be able to avoid dinner conversation any longer.

"Hello, I'm—"

"Atticus Blackwell. We're all very aware." The woman lumped more mashed potatoes onto his plate than he thought a human being could consume. "I'm Daphne, Maddie's sister. I met you last time."

Right, Daphne. There were so many Abernathys that Atticus had given up trying to keep them straight. Daphne asked him if he wanted Brussels sprouts, he declined, and she gave him an extra-large serving.

"You should try everything. You didn't seem to appreciate our food last time."

He cringed. Last time had been his first Thanksgiving holiday without his grandmother. His parents were overseas that year, and Giles had been celebrating with a girlfriend. Which had left Atticus all alone.

Of course, Maddox had pitied him back then, too. She had shyly scrawled her home address on his Apothecary class notes, one of the buttons on her blouse in the wrong place, and told him he was free to show up. Her family was so large that no one would even notice an extra mouth to feed.

Atticus shook off the memory, recognizing the raven sitting on Colter's shoulder. The bird never took its single eye off Atticus. Colter seemed to be doing well, too well, if anyone cared to ask Atticus's opinion. Unlike the other Abernathys that he recognized, Colter didn't appear to have aged a day in over ten years.

The Abernathys' magic had always intrigued him, but he doubted his inquiries would be answered now.

Atticus thanked Daphne for yet another helping he did not want. Not once throughout this awkward dinner did Maddox even look his way, leaving him to suffer her sister's questioning.

"Alright," he finally snapped once the children had left the dining room. "Maddox, can we skip to the part where you explain why I'm here?"

The ridiculously oversized family all stared at him. More than twenty people squished around the warped table, and even more Abernathys were eating at their own homes. Maddox leaned back in her mismatched chair, sipping from a chipped teacup and taking her sweet time before answering him.

Would this be their new power dynamic? Now that Maddox knew the extent of his feelings, she could manipulate him however she wanted. She could, but Atticus doubted she would. Right now, she was just angry and overwhelmed.

"Granddad." Maddox broke her silence and placed her hand softly atop her grandfather's, reassuring the wary look in the old man's eye. Not that Atticus had spent enough time amongst the family to know, but he would bet that Colter Abernathy had a favorite granddaughter, and she was about to make him worry far more than he already did. "I'm going with him."

Colter scoffed loudly, stabbing a fork in Atticus's direction. "I'm going to need a *hell* of a lot more detail than that."

Daphne agreed with the patriarch. "Why would you do that? It's Atticus Blackwell."

What did *that* mean? His family's reputation as necromancers went unrivaled. Other, less kind things *were* said about the Blackwell women and the disturbing trend of madness within, but—

No, he would not think on that.

Maddox remained determined. "I'm going to work with him on a very important, once-in-a-lifetime project. Otherwise, I would not consider it."

Atticus flinched as Colter asked, "Is this dangerous?" When the old man frowned, his mustache only made the glare more intimidating.

Maddox nodded. "Yes."

Colter tapped his fork against this plate, considering. "Is it worth it?"

"Yes."

"Is it worth dealing with *him*?" Daphne demanded, rather ruthless for a soon-to-be mother.

"Unfortunately, also yes."

"I would like to discuss this more tomorrow during our rounds of the town." Colter stood, removing the dessert from Atticus's plate before he had a chance to even try it. "But if you're going, you're taking Edgar. *And* your sword."

Edgar, that was the raven's name! Atticus fought a snort. How on the nose.

Maddox sighed, breaking away from the table. "That will be fun to explain to my hotel and their no pets policy." She pulled out Atticus's chair for him, which he did not appreciate, and brought him back up to her room. While she finished packing her bags, she told him to book them a flight back to Maine.

"And Atticus?" Maddox prompted, her tone tense.

"Yes?" he answered, half-distracted as he searched on his phone for an airline that wouldn't piss him off.

"You were right. You know me a little." Maddox zipped up her carry-on, the golden bee around her neck glittering in the lamplight. "Seeing part of the Tome of the Undying firsthand means the world to me, and I promise not to let our past affect our working relationship. If you don't already regret it, thank you for thinking of me."

In that moment, he realized what their relationship was, and what it never would be, and Atticus wanted nothing more than to stop thinking about her.

CHAPTER 6
WITCH

Diedre, Maddox's mom, helped her load the bed of Colter's pickup with a few coolers filled with casseroles and an assortment of baked goods. Sunday morning was always spent delivering home-cooked meals around the town, stopping first at the volunteer fire station and ending up at the nursing home.

"That should be enough." Deidre slapped a cooler with a sigh. "Doesn't seem fair that your grandfather gets to spend your last day with you and your mother doesn't." Her lips pursed, and her eyes shone with unshed tears. "I don't like what that school did to you. It took you away from me for *six years*. All that stress... It burned you out last time. Do you really have to go back?"

"I was a kid, a teenager, during all that. It's different this time." Maddox wished she could convince herself, let alone her mother. "This is what I'm *supposed* to be doing, Mom. I meant to find a job soon, anyway. This is just a little detour."

"I just wish..." Deidre shook her head. "Never mind. *Please* keep in touch, Maddie. That man, and this book, make me nervous."

"That's enough of that, Deidre." Colter swaggered out of the farmhouse and waved his daughter off. "Let me do the worrying around here. Come on, Mad."

Maddox hugged her mom farewell before hopping in the driver's seat of the truck. Edgar, the raven, settled itself in the backseat and squawked twice.

"What he said," her grandfather muttered, urging her to drive as he buckled himself in.

It was odd how final this moment seemed. Surely, this would not be the last time she and her grandfather would patrol the town together? She would come back, if only for a short while, before launching herself into a new career.

If she could expose the hidden writing and link this lost page back to the Tome of the Undying, Maddox would have her pick of employment.

Even after her unexpected hiatus from the necromantic world.

Colter remained silent, clearly stewing on something, while Maddox left a casserole with the volunteer firefighters manning the phone. The next few stops were with some of Fair Harbor's older residents, those who were unable to regularly cook for themselves. Colter's days were always like this—as the mayor and a general busybody, he was always dreadfully busy. Maddox wondered who would take over for her while she was away. Honestly, though, she didn't want to know.

"I already know that nothing I say will keep you from this evil scrap of paper." Her grandfather scowled, reaching into the back seat to feed Edgar a few unsalted peanuts. "And I wouldn't try to keep you from it, but I have some concerns. Namely about the boy."

Her ego bruised at the insinuation. "I can handle *Atticus.*"

Colter snorted. "I know you can. Though this project will mean you're stuck with him."

Maddox sighed at the thought. "It's unavoidable."

"If you say so."

Defensive, she snapped, "I *want* to do this. More than anything."

"You'll look out for each other?" His question was hesitant as if he already knew her answer.

What an odd way to ask if they'd be careful, but Colter was right to be wary of the project. Necromancer literature was often cursed and guarded. Hellraisers weren't exactly known for willingly sharing knowledge. A book like the Tome of the Undying, even a mere scrap of it, could be deadly. The knowledge it contained could drive a witch insane, or touching the page could lay a hex on the trespasser.

It was going to be dangerous. It was also going to be fun, despite Atticus's annoying presence.

Maddox gave her grandfather the assurance he needed. "I'll be victorious."

Maddox had her parents and her grandfather convinced that this creepy, little field trip with Blackwell was safe, but Daphne refused to give her blessing, which was distressing because they had always found a way to understand each other before.

Daphne stifled a yawn as she entered Maddox's tiny bedroom to see her off. "If this asshole tries to show you a fancy wine cellar, don't go."

"I dueled better than him. Consistently." While Maddox and Atticus had gone back and forth in most classes, he had always been the better chemist and she the far better duelist. "I'm not worried."

Daphne picked at Maddox's comforter as the pair sat on her bed. Maddox wished they weren't too old to listen to pop songs and jump around on the mattress until some adult told them off.

Well, maybe they weren't too old, but Daphne was *way* too pregnant.

Daphne asked, her tone fighting to seem unconcerned, "And are you worried about this *death book* you're messing with?"

Maddox did worry about the potential consequences of messing with the Tome of the Undying, but she and Atticus would surely over-research before even *attempting* to glance at the page.

"We won't rush into this. I might be gone for quite a while, Daphne, and I could miss—"

A pillow smacked Maddox in the face before she could finish.

"If you were about to say you were going to *miss my first birth*, I'll murder you!" Daphne swung the pillow again, forcing Maddox to shield her head with her hands. "You will be there! If I have to suffer through this, you do too!"

"Necromancers are bad luck for childbirth! Everyone knows that—"

Daphne snorted. "I don't know that. And that doesn't make any sense! It's not like necromancers don't have babies."

The pillow onslaught continued, and Maddox took cover underneath her comforter. Muffled, Maddox protested, "It's too much pressure! You remember what happened at the funeral—"

"You're the only one that's hanging on to that. We understand, and you're in control now. I'm not afraid of you, but you should be afraid of me!" Daphne gave the blanket a few harsh smacks. "Now, you *will* be at your niece's birth! You will hold my hand and listen to me yell at Rob for ruining my body. So, tell that rich warlock of yours to keep the private plane running."

He's not mine. "I'll let Richie Rich know," Maddox conceded, realizing Daphne would accept no other response.

Though Maddox's surrender pleased Daphne, the mention of Atticus soured Daphne's disposition further. "I still don't trust him." Daphne pouted. "Why is he trying to get back into your life *now*? He had plenty of time after your little breakup to reconcile—"

"It wasn't a breakup! We weren't dating." Maddox's suddenly warm face was nothing but a coincidence.

"Friend breakups are sometimes *worse* than couple breakups. Especially when you're seventeen years old," Daphne swore solemnly. "I still hope Taylor trips on her wedding day."

Maddox tuned out the rest of her sister's devious wishes for her ex-BFF's wedding and nibbled on her bottom lip. The action stung her already delicate lip, a minor wound where Atticus had bitten her. Her mind refocused on Atticus, on the way he had looked up at her, brought down to his hands and knees by her own dark magic, and confessed that he loved her.

Should she tell Daphne about the truth she had wrenched out of him? Maddox didn't know if she could bear the shame of her heartless actions. How long had she carried such hate for him? Maddox had tended that anger, and yet, seeing Atticus brought down like that—desperate, ashamed, and so very in love—had torn out those bitter roots in her heart. The result was an empty feeling, a sense of loss, and a little relief.

Daphne suddenly laughed. "You know, Atticus is far from my type, but he's rather hot in a definitely-owns-a-cursed-portrait-of-himself sort of way."

"I know!" Maddox shrieked, snatching a pillow and punching it until she felt moderately less frustrated. If there was ever a time to admit to Daphne what she'd done to Atticus, this was it. But Maddox couldn't explain such complicated feelings. Not even to her favorite sister.

Maddox said a final, sad goodbye to Daphne, and she dug her sword out from underneath her bed. It hummed in her hands, its magic still potent through the layers of canvas wrapped around it. She placed the wrapped sword in a solid black case, sealing it with a padlock.

Necromancers dueled with swords, using the weapon to channel their magic more effectively. Most of the other students had swords passed down from within the family. Maddox had to have one forged especially for her.

Grabbing the rest of her luggage, Maddox slowly made her way out of the farmhouse. Most of her family stayed in other houses on the farm, and the rest that lived with Maddox were already working outside. The house was empty and cold, and she moved through it like a ghost.

She found Atticus pulling up the driveway in his rental car, and she threw her luggage into the trunk, noting that he'd moved his bags off to one side to make room for hers.

"I'm ready to go." She sighed, sliding into the passenger seat.

Atticus stared at her, forcing her to turn toward the window so he could not see the tears sparkling in her eyes. Finally, he said, "Okay."

The car lurched forward, stopping so suddenly that her head almost bounced off the dash. "What the hell was that? I want to *leave.*"

"What do you think I'm trying to do?" Another lurch and he parked the car. "Something's wrong. I'm calling a mechanic."

Maddox rolled her eyes, doing a quick tour of the car after she stepped back outside. Just as she thought. One of the white roots from the witch tree was wrapped around the rear axle. "Hang up the phone. My grandfather wants to say goodbye."

Atticus joined her outside, leaning against the car as Colter Abernathy strolled into view, his arrival heralded by his raven.

"I told you to take Edgar," the old man grumped. He placed a cat carrier on top of the car. Getting Edgar into that thing was not something Maddox looked forward to. Maybe she could trick Atticus into doing it for her. "Just tell the airport he's your familiar."

"Sorry, Granddad." She hugged him, knowing she'd miss their patrols of the town. "Can you let the car go now?"

Colter jabbed a finger at Atticus. "Just make sure *he* knows these roots don't end at our border, that they can find him wherever he goes."

"He knows," Atticus said flatly, disappearing back into the vehicle.

One last, clinging hug later, and the necromancers were heading to the airport.

"I feel like an asshole just for sitting here," Maddox complained, slinking down in her first-class seat while other passengers shuffled past them. "Poor Edgar."

Atticus sighed. "I'm sure Edgar is terrorizing the poor dogs trapped with him in the cargo hold. Don't stress about it."

Maddox used her hair to hide her face until everyone had boarded. "I barely slept last night." She crossed her arms, settling into her seat as the flight attendants ran through the safety brief. "Goodnight."

She felt Atticus staring down at her and squeezed her eyes tighter in answer. *Just let me ignore you.*

Atticus huffed. "I can't sleep on planes."

"I don't see how that concerns me." Why hadn't she packed a blanket? Maddox shivered and balled herself up tightly.

He nudged her. "I want to talk to you."

"And *I* don't want to be talked to."

"No, this is important." His honest insistence was almost enough to sway her, but...

Maddox tried, "I don't—"

"I swear, if you don't have this conversation with me, I *will* propose to you on this plane. In front of everyone. With my family ring. And everyone is going to stare at us when you say no—"

Her eyes opened so fast it stung. She gripped his arm in warning. "Ugh, okay! You have my full attention! Please, do not do *any* of that."

"Thank you," he said graciously, as if she had any choice. "I need a promise from you."

"I'm not the one that doesn't keep promises," she countered.

Her words made him blink, but that was all the reaction he rewarded her with. "Once this project begins, once we encounter the page, there can't be any going back. I want to see this through, and if our history has any chance of harming that—"

Him doubting *her* was pure irony. "If I didn't think I could work with you, I wouldn't be here."

"I'll settle for a promise to never drag me underground again. I'm *still* finding dirt on me."

His attempt at humor settled her nerves. She hadn't expected to have such a heavy conversation right at the start. "I promise, but I know a hundred other spells that are far worse than that one. Have you ever heard of a bottomless grave?"

"That sounds...illegal."

"It is." Maddox had spent a lot of her free time after class sneaking into the restricted sections of the Academy library. She continued, "Can I go to sleep *now*? Or is there anything else you need to burden me with?"

Her eyes were closed before Atticus answered.

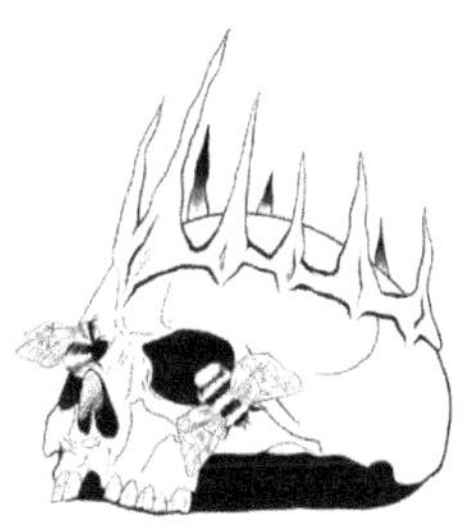

The scent of cardamon and anise filled her nostrils, the aroma clinging to her hair. Maddox inhaled, the combination somehow irritating and ambrosial all at once. She *knew* that smell. It was...

Atticus's cologne, unchanged since college. There was still that odd note of a medicinal bitterness she recalled from all those study sessions trapped with the man.

She shook herself awake, startled to find her head resting against the warlock's shoulder. Maddox straightened herself out immediately, inwardly screaming at the dark spot her drool had left on his jacket. "Why didn't you *wake* me?"

He shrugged, changing the subject deftly. "We've landed. Let's go get your bird and your sword from security."

Edgar the raven had not been pleased with his travel situation, making Maddox feel even more guilty about her first-class seat. As soon as they were outside, she freed Edgar from the carrier. The raven flew a few loops before clamping onto her shoulder.

Parking his Rolls Royce at the airport was not something Atticus would ever do, so they waited for the car to be dropped off for them. Scowling at the extravagance, Maddox snapped a picture of the Wraith to send to her grandfather. A few minutes later, her phone vibrated, and she read the message.

What an asshole. Make him let you drive.

She smiled, missing her grandfather's no-holds-barred sense of humor. Maddox didn't ask to drive as that would have required more conversation with Atticus than she was currently capable of. Maddox zoned out until they arrived at the outskirts of Redhollow, the Academy of the Dead's hometown.

She tapped her hotel address into his navigation system. Redhollow, Maine wasn't a large town—and it was built when walking was a much more common mode of transportation. As long as it didn't rain, and it always rained in Redhollow, Maddox wouldn't have to rent a car to make it to the Academy.

The Home Sweet Home Motel was a far cry from her feyrie neighbor's idyllic inn, the Refuge on the Moor. The flashing vacancy sign was missing more letters than it was left with, and the parking lot was empty save for a couple having an argument in public that should have been saved for counseling. It was so shady, in fact, that Atticus drove right by it, glaring at the motel in his rearview as if its presence was a stain on this earth he personally vowed to wipe clean.

Maddox jerked a thumb back toward the motel. "Uh, Atticus? That was it. Turn around."

"No."

"What do you mean—"

"You're not staying there." He started making turns she did not recognize. "They'll have bedbugs or something, and I won't have you bring anything of the sort into *my* cleanroom."

The Academy was keeping the Tome of the Undying's artifact in one of the downstairs laboratories that hunched underneath the Academy's main library. Though the page most likely held deep, powerful magic, it was older than dirt. Maddox couldn't bear it if it was destroyed by something as trivial and mundane as *bedbugs*.

Maddox started searching for alternative hotels on her phone. Pricewise, the Home Sweet Home Motel was the only place she could afford. But the Tome of the Undying's page was invaluable. She would not dare risk its integrity. Even if it drained her meager savings.

"Okay, it's more out of the way, but I found another place. It's a…" She sighed, already regretting her second choice. "It's a B&B."

"No necromancer worth a damn would dare stay—" He sneered, canceling the new route she had punched in. "—in a *bed and breakfast*. You can just stay with me."

The Blackwells lived in Redhollow—Maddox recalled being able to spy Atticus's massive ancestral home from the Academy's grounds. Maddox didn't care how *convenient* it would be to stay with Atticus. She argued, "No, I will not. Stop this ridiculously vain car! I'll jump out right now." Her hand curled around the handle of her passenger door.

He didn't think she'd do it. Hell, Atticus even increased his speed as if daring her to jump. "You *want* to stay with me."

"Yeah, and why do you think that?" She'd been dreaming of the first hex she'd hit him with for years. It looked like she finally had an excuse to curse him into oblivion.

Atticus continued, unaware of her devious plans for him. "Because my library includes a first edition of Reginald Scot's *Discoverie of Witchcraft*. With his personal notes in the margins."

The hex died before it could leave her lips. "What museum did you steal *that* from?"

"It was a gift from Scot to a great-something or other."

"And I can look at it?"

"Maddox," he sang sweetly, "I wouldn't dare refuse you."

The Blackwell estate loomed on a hill that overlooked the Academy and the town below. It was entirely fenced in, giving it the appearance of a prison rather than a mansion. The mansion consisted of three floors and had large arched windows scattered throughout. The dark, sharp architecture reminded Maddox, oddly, of a church.

The impressive driveway was lined by maple trees on either side. The leaves were bright oranges and yellows, a sight that brought an unwelcome smile to her lips. Maddox loved her evergreen state, but there was no surpassing fall foliage in beauty.

They parked in a garage that sat beneath a modern addition to the home, five other cars already there and waiting. There was even a small elevator that took them up from the garage and onto the first floor of the Blackwell mansion.

The manor's interior was slightly less bleak. Tall oil paintings hung on the walls, portraits of previous Blackwells, all grim and haunting. Atticus may have inherited his father's complexion, but he was a Blackwell in demeanor, through and through.

"Who's this?" Maddox asked, tapping the gilded frame of a rather imperious looking man. His mustache rivaled her grandfather's own monstrosity.

"Dead," Atticus answered without looking back. He pushed further into the house, giving her no choice but to keep following him.

It was so damned dark in the Blackwell manor, causing Maddox's already weak eyes to squint harder. Floor-length curtains blocked off all the windows, casting the manor in shadow. The walls were dark burgundy and covered in filigree that was burnished in peeling gold. The place screamed opulence, but all Maddox saw as she gazed upon the grand staircase, the banister wobbling as they walked up it, was loneliness.

"Be careful if you decide to explore," Atticus cautioned her. "There are hidden passages and rooms that only open during certain moon phases..." He stopped his tour at an old, iron-gated elevator he warned her never to use by herself. "It's easy to get lost in here."

"Hades," she muttered. "I guess I'll have to stop losing my phone all the time. Hey, give me your phone number in case I get *Fortunato'd*."

"Wouldn't *that* require *me* being the one to seal you in my wall?" Atticus questioned but handed his phone over to exchange numbers without protest.

After Maddox added a few rude emoticons after Atticus's name in her contacts list, Atticus led them back upstairs. He pointed out the kitchen, showed her how to find the main entrance again, and brought her to a bedroom.

The room was larger than her family's living room. A huge canopy bed with grey, see-through curtains hanging from the carved wood frame caught her eye. It was easily the grandest room she'd ever stayed in.

"If this is acceptable," Atticus said, after showing her where all the extra amenities were stored in the adjoining bathroom, "then you can stay here. We'll be on separate floors." He marched to the black stone fireplace on the wall opposite the bed, toeing the stacked logs neatly into place before starting the fire with a snap of his fingers.

The crackling fire added to the coziness of the room. Maddox prompted, "And the book?"

Atticus almost smiled at that. "Later. I need to wash off your drool before dinner, and after, I'm going to bed. We'll look at the book another day."

"Tease," Maddox swore under her breath. As she watched him walk away, her thoughts tried to force some logic into her. *I should find somewhere else to stay in the morning. Even if this would save money.*

She had neglected to ask if there was a grant associated with the Tome of the Undying's page. If there wasn't, her trip was going to include a lot of ramen.

After she unpacked a few items from her suitcase, Maddox prepared herself for bed, carefully following her nighttime routine and double-checking each step as she performed it. While she rinsed her face, there was a quick rapping on her door. By the time she reached the door, opening it only a crack to not expose her faded, fuzzy pajamas, Maddox discovered a silver tray with a covered dish, a glass of red wine, and two bottles of water occupying the platter. There was no one in sight as she lifted the heavy, slightly tarnished tray inside her room and plopped it on a small corner table, removing the porcelain lid to expose the steaming pasta underneath.

The wine was delicious, and she sipped it quietly as she regarded the meal. Atticus didn't keep a chef on his estate—he'd been outright insulted when she'd asked during the drive. This meal, unless a local restaurant was brave enough to deliver to the ominous and gothic Blackwell estate, had been prepared by Atticus. Maddox groaned as she tasted the pasta. Yet another thing Atticus could best her in.

His thoughtfulness turned her stomach to lead.

CHAPTER 7
WARLOCK

Atticus knew he was an intelligent man. There was paperwork to prove it. So, why did he insist on making mistake after mistake? When it came to Maddox, Atticus seemed incapable of doing anything right.

Bringing her *here*, to his own home, had been a real stroke of idiocy. She would know, *and hate*, that he had pitied her when he saw the hotel she'd chosen.

With only a single floor between them, Maddox was certain to invade his dreams. Already his magic searched for her; the blood-red tendrils drifted underneath his door and were reluctant to return as he repeatedly called them back.

Maddox would drive him mad. It was one thing to have an impossible dream hidden in your heart. It was something entirely different to have it ripped from you.

Her presence in his ancestral home also raised questions he did not wish to answer. While Maddox couldn't have known that asking about the wall of family portraits would trigger him, he still couldn't banish the wave of nausea roiling his stomach.

He'd learned to be alone, to take care of his empty, echoing house. An outsider, though it was all his selfish idea, would be an adjustment Atticus wasn't sure he was ready for.

When he was a child, his grandmother used to take his hand and point to each family portrait to recite their obituary.

That's my brother, Ezra. The potion he was brewing exploded, taking him away from me. I was only six-years-old.

That's my mother, Matilda. I was seven when she fell from the third floor. And my father—

It went on and on and on. Atticus wished he could forget every gruesome detail, but Theodora had planted each story firmly into his impressionable young mind. The takeaway?

It didn't matter how long necromancers were supposed to live. The Blackwells were cursed to die early. A single accident could leave one all alone. One bad day could turn him into a survivor, just like his grandmother.

And despite Theodora's insistence that she would never leave him, that Atticus would never suffer as his grandmother had, isn't that what had happened, anyway?

Atticus traced the path to his grandmother's lab, hidden away in the humid and deceptively beautiful conservatory, and found his place amongst the supplies. The recipe was still burned into his brain after all these years. Atticus worked on his brew in silence. He had let the stores of his medicine dwindle.

While he concentrated, Atticus heard a soft, familiar hiss. Atticus raised a hand to the overhanging tree that shadowed his workstation. A glossy black viper dropped from the tree onto Atticus's outstretched hand and coiled gently around his forearm.

"Hello, *Venenum*," Atticus crooned. The deadly snake was the form his sword took when Atticus wasn't using it. The viper flicked its tongue, observing the brewing process like it had done a hundred times before.

Atticus recalled the first time his mother had made this potion for him, right before they walked into his grandmother's wake and pretended the casket wasn't empty.

His magic had been just as uncontrolled back then as it was now.

Atticus's left hand wove through his hair, scratching madly at the skin underneath. He could not control this power, nor could he keep this secret. Reddish smoke rolled from his body, flooding the floor of the family apothecary.

His mother tore his hand away, ending the tearing of his flesh. She corrected his slumped posture. "Blackwells are expected to maintain a certain image, Atticus."

His eyes wandered to the stacked, tiny drawers filled with herbs and bits of bone. His grandmother's bench where they mixed potions together was cleared away, every trace of her previous work scrubbed clean. An answer was expected from him. Atticus swallowed, regretting, not for the first or last time, that he had rejected his father's offer to live with him in Dubai. "Yes, Mother."

"Pay attention to how I brew this. You're to take this every morning, do you hear me?" Cynthia crushed an herb with her mother's mortar and pestle. Atticus's brother, Giles, meticulously recorded each step, making a recipe for Atticus to follow later. Cynthia sneered, finishing the concoction with enough whiskey that it had even raised merciless Giles's eyebrows. "The whiskey is only for today. If you can't keep your eyes dry, Atticus, then I suppose I must do it for you."

Atticus fought that memory, only to have Maddox's image take its place, which was almost worse. He knew there would be nothing between them. The fact she stayed in his home proved that. She was not afraid that their proximity would stir anything in her. She was probably glad for another chance to torture him because that was what that kiss had been—torture.

Atticus wished she hadn't kissed him back—now he knew what she felt like, her lips flushed and hungry, and he knew he would never taste that again.

Before he sought her out to help with this deadly grimoire, this Tome of the Undying, Atticus had known he would never deserve Maddox's affection. At best, he had hoped for her forgiveness. And he could have lived with that. What was truly agonizing was living with *Maddox* knowing the depths of his attachment to her.

Atticus returned his gathered ingredients to their rightful places. The potion was perfect—years of working on the recipe had helped its potency, but never the taste. The brew came together, the liquid as black as the void. He poured it into a glass of bourbon, attempting to cut the foul taste with liquor.

While the potion worked its magic, the alcohol leeched away the edge of his emotions, draining his aching heart until the memory of Maddox in his arms faded into a minor burn.

There was no name for his mother's concoction, but Atticus liked to call it *Chameleon.*

Atticus returned upstairs, letting the viper ride along on his shoulders. Atticus swirled his drink around, the clink of ice against glass calming.

CHAPTER 8
WITCH

"There are a few things I should warn you about," Atticus began, his voice grating this early in the morning. His car carefully made its way out of the Blackwell garage and headed to the Academy of the Dead.

Maddox opened her eyes regretfully. Her plan to nap on the drive to the school thwarted, she prompted, "Now what would those be?"

Atticus looked perfect as always, his burgundy blazer striking against his skin. While her wardrobe was better than it had been in school, she didn't feel comparable. She pulled at the hem of her skirt, groaning inwardly at a rip in her black tights.

"The Commission is involved."

She sank into her seat. She had suspected that the government would get involved with such a find, but it was still a letdown to have it confirmed. Even Edgar was upset, squawking in the backseat to voice his displeasure. "Who, and what, did they send?"

"His name's Dr. Lochlan Rhodes. He studied with the Catholic exorcists, but he's no priest. He's...odd."

Maddox pressed, "Odd in a way that's helpful to us or not?"

Atticus was too cheerful for the early hour. "You'll get to judge for yourself soon enough."

It was Sunday, which meant the Academy had no classes. Some students milled about, finishing reports or using the outdoor dueling fields to practice spells. Others clung together, laughing and joking, making Maddox wonder if the school was just as cliquey as it had been during her time as a student.

She kept her grandfather's raven on her shoulder, letting him scope out his surroundings while they walked from the faculty parking lot to the center of the campus.

The Academy's grounds held several buildings. There was a dorm room for the younger students and a second dorm room for the above-twenty students. A graveyard loomed behind the main school building with graves opened and unopened dotting the landscape.

Next to the school graveyard stood over a dozen imposing statues. Each work of white marble was ten feet tall and expertly carved to depict the gods of death. Hades, Persephone, and Thanatos stood together. Anubis, Kali, Hel, Santa Muerte, and many more made up a long line of deities. Not all witches required a patron, a god, to work their magic, but every necromancer did.

Turning away from the statues, Maddox drank in the academy's gothic architecture—she had missed the dark, pointed towers and columns, and the red stained glass windows. The library, their destination today, was its own building, spelled to resist fires and weather. The library was equally foreboding. They walked through the tall main entrance, and they stepped into an open room, the ceiling domed overhead. Bookcases curled around the place, their shelves reaching nearly thirty feet high. Ghostly figures, taking on a vaguely humanoid shape, passed through bookcases and walls at their leisure. Maddox had made friends with most of them long ago, but new memories were hard for ghosts to keep. They'd likely not remember her.

Her breath caught with the influx of smells and hushed sounds—this was her favorite place in the world, despite everything else. Back then, Maddox never thought she would ever see something so beautiful. She and Atticus had spent hours together in that building. Some days as friends, and others, too many, as enemies.

That first school year together, Maddox had thought she'd found an ally, but Atticus didn't let her keep him.

She was being dramatic—Maddox was more than aware of it as she paused and stared at the cases of time-faded books. How different this harsh, competitive environment was compared to the soft, rolling hills of her home, the thriving meadows, and the calm weather. Redhollow, and all it encompassed, was unforgiving—no, it was *challenging*. The first day Maddox had approached those gloomy halls, she had felt like a conqueror. The howling wind couldn't hide the thump of her heart, beating as loud as a call for war on a bloody shield.

Her clothes hadn't mattered; her lack of necromancer ancestry hadn't, either. Maddox had defeated them all. *Alone.* Triumph was sometimes lonesome, but she thought fondly of it, despite the darkness at the edges of her memory.

She cherished those days until she remembered Atticus, ever in the center of her memory, egging her on as if he wanted her to win, too.

Atticus was her dearest friend for such a short time, until he fled just out of reach of her desperate, clawing fingers—always with that sad look on his face. As if he wanted nothing more than to reach for her, too—despite being the one to tear them apart.

They were older now, supposedly wiser and in control of their lives. Without his elitist family goading his heels, if Maddox could overcome her hate and reach for him again, would Atticus take her hand?

It doesn't matter. If he wanted to rekindle your friendship, he would have explained why he hurt you by now. You've waited long enough for something you shouldn't even want.

Several hallways branched out from the central library, leading either to study rooms or smaller collections of materials. Atticus said a brief greeting to the on-duty librarian, trying to keep them moving. The librarian halted their march, blocking them with a sudden downward swing of a yardstick she carried.

"Mrs. Tuttle?" Maddox realized. Mrs. Tuttle had been the master librarian

long before Maddox had attended the Academy. That wasn't too unusual—necromancers lived quite a long time, but Maddox was still surprised the librarian hadn't yet retired. Mrs. Tuttle had threatened to do so every day.

"I remember *you*," Mrs. Tuttle frowned, jabbing her yardstick toward Maddox. "Nosy, and your books were never returned on time."

Deadlines were the bane of Maddox's existence. "I'm sorry—"

Atticus pulled Maddox away, calling over his shoulder to Mrs. Tuttle, "Unless you're going to hit Miss Abernathy with a five-year-old fine, I'm afraid I'm in need of her."

Maddox followed Atticus down a poorly lit hallway and into the faculty laboratories.

The student labs were in the schoolhouse, but the labs where the real work was done were hidden away downstairs in the library. As a student, she'd tried to find them once, as Maddox had spent many evenings alone and wandering the school, but got turned around in the twisting halls below. These Atticus navigated expertly, making her worry that he'd already had a peek at the page without her.

It shouldn't matter to her, not anymore, to be first, but it sadly did.

Someone waited for them outside one of the basement cleanrooms, dressed starkly in a black suit and a white clergy collar.

The man's outfit startled Maddox. She whispered to Atticus, "I thought you said he wasn't a *priest*."

"He isn't," Atticus returned. "He's only trained as an exorcist."

The Catholic church was so overrun with demon sightings and possessions that they allowed men and women to become exorcists without becoming full-on priests. They could perform exorcisms and funeral rites, but that was the extent of their duties.

"Hello, Dr. Rhodes," Atticus announced, taking Maddox by the elbow to bring her in front of him. "This is Maddox Abernathy, the one I told you about."

Dr. Rhodes reached out to shake her hand, grimacing as if he found physical greetings abhorrent but a necessary part of the job. If only Maddox could wordlessly communicate that she felt much the same and spare them both the discomfort. His hair and skin were pale, the green eyes looking down at her the only bright thing about him. He was so much younger than she'd imagined, somewhere around their age, maybe a little older. "The missing piece," Lochlan said to her, releasing her hand quickly. "Blackwell said we couldn't begin without you. Claimed you're the only person who could handle it."

Missing piece? Maddox shrugged, uncomfortable with so much blind faith being placed in her. "I'll do my absolute best and nothing less. It's nice to meet you."

"You may come to regret that sentiment," Dr. Rhodes deadpanned. "You can both call me Lochlan. I prefer it." He left them to return to staring into the cleanroom, looking, of all things, vaguely *excited* to study the deadly scrap of skin. Most Commission men sought solely to contain or destroy such dark magic.

I understand now why Atticus said the man was odd.

"The page is still in the casing the tomb raider carried it in." Atticus tapped on the window of the nearest lab, pointing out a black suitcase sitting on a pedestal.

She found herself drawn to the object, wishing for nothing more than to simply pop that suitcase open and reveal the page inside. Atticus tapped her shoulder after she had stared for far too long.

"It does that. Draws you in." He nodded to the exorcist and started heading back upstairs. "We need to do quite a bit more research about the book before we unleash it. Lochlan will keep an eye on it while we're working."

Maddox fought to keep herself from stepping on Atticus's heels. She was so excited. This would be worth all of that pain, that loneliness, as she had worked her way to the top of the class. Yes, she'd been alone and ridiculed, but even her worst enemy couldn't deny her skill, her work ethic.

But was Atticus ever *really* her enemy? Her memories were confused now, her mind searching for any hidden meaning in all the time they'd spent together in the past. Like how every time he'd shown up in her study room to copy her notes, he brought a drink for her. *A bribe,* he called it, claiming without it she might be tempted to give him a false set of notes to try and tank his grade below hers.

It was always the same drink, too. A special strawberry soda she loved, and that she knew wasn't carried on school grounds.

This confusion would only distract her from their work—Maddox let it go and tried to refocus on the task at hand.

The Academy was greatly unchanged—still proud and impeccably furnished. She ran her fingertips along the brown, prestigious walls as they re-entered the library from the laboratories. They weaved through the main library, and Atticus began unlocking the double doors to the restricted part of the Academy's library, which held the majority of the collection.

"I've always wanted to see the inside," she said, earning her an eye roll from Atticus.

"*Everyone* knows you used to break in at night. Don't pretend otherwise."

She sniffed, unable to come up with anything witty to say.

Atticus set them up in a comfortable study room, much more refined than the one she had spent the majority of her school days hiding in. There was a pair of large, wooden desks, and Atticus pushed them together so the people sitting in them would be facing each other with a few feet of space between them. On one side stood an empty bookshelf, ready for them to store their research while they worked. In a corner, a mini-fridge sat and was filled with fizzy strawberry soda.

"The tomb raider only found a single page?" Maddox wondered aloud. "Is it the only page removed from the rest of the Tome of the Undying or..." She paused her survey of the room, focusing on Atticus. "Could the entire Tome of the Undying be dismantled? What sort of willpower would that require? More than one witch had to be involved. And why would they—"

"There's plenty of time to research the pages we *don't* have later. Let's focus on the one we've got." Atticus cleared his throat. "You know, my grandmother was the head librarian while the Tome of the Undying was housed at the Academy. After she retired, it went missing the following year."

Maddox already knew that—the Tome of the Undying had been the topic of her final Necromantic History paper.

She had researched Theodora Blackwell as well. Atticus's grandmother had lived for two centuries before she hit the end of a necromancer's lifecycle. She must have experienced so many incredible things. Maddox hoped the rest of her life would live up to such a legacy. Rediscovering the book of the dead was a good start. "Did she keep a—"

"A grimoire?" Atticus finished, confidently assuming the end of her sentence. Just like he used to. It was even more annoying that he was usually right. "She did. And, no, you can't look at it. It's against Blackwell tradition to allow someone outside the family to open it. Anyway, it's all in code, and I've only deciphered a few pages myself." He scratched at his beard, a somewhat gaudy, antique ring on his middle finger glinting in the light. She'd seen it before—when they were still friends, Atticus had revealed his family ring was required to read his family's grimoires.

"I would expect nothing less." She claimed a desk and glanced out the window, rain splattering against the pane. "Where was it found, anyway? And which tomb raider found it?"

The Academy kept a few tomb raiders on the payroll. They accompanied human archeologists to their dig sites when dark magic was believed to be involved.

Atticus stopped her interrogation to remove a silver flask from his jacket. Maddox cocked a brow, assuming the worst, before Atticus opened the flask and that bitter scent reached her. He was still taking that medicine? She'd always wondered what it was for, but now was not the time to ask.

"It was found covered in insects and grave dust," Atticus said, sneering. " *Who* found it isn't important," he said with an edge to his words, avoiding her gaze. "As for the where? This page was found nestled inside a ribcage in the Paris Catacombs. It's a little far for a field trip, but I can arrange that if you'd like."

As much as she'd love to see the Catacombs, the page had obviously been staged there. There would be little merit in scouting out the area, though she'd still like to speak with the raider who'd rescued it.

The remainder of the morning was spent gathering anything that remotely referenced the Tome of the Undying. They tucked away a copy of every relevant document into their bookshelf and arranged them in order of most to least useful. Maddox knew there were more books whose titles she could almost recall, but Atticus halted their work at noon.

"This is a marathon, not a sprint," he scolded when Maddox pouted at the interruption. "And you slept through breakfast."

He was right, of course, but that only irritated her further. Before he led her to the faculty cafeteria, Atticus stopped at the study's doorway. He looked at her as if he feared she might bite him. "I suppose we should talk about the money. There are quite a few investors. The Tome of the Undying gathered a lot of interest at your Dead Literature conference."

Maddox felt the relief in her very bones. She wouldn't starve for this venture, after all.

He told her the sum set aside for the researcher's room and board, and she nearly fainted. "I get half of *that?*"

"No, you're getting all of it. I have no need for it." His earlier hesitation now made sense. Before she could snap at him that she didn't care for his charity, Atticus rushed, "If it upsets you so much, just consult the picture you took of my car." He took long strides to the cafeteria, forcing her to jog after him.

"Your meals here are all paid for," he explained, grabbing two wooden trays filled with food. "Get me a black tea."

There was no avoiding it—they would be eating together at work, too. Maddox grabbed his tea and some fruit juice, needing the sugar, and met him at one of the long, rectangular wooden tables throughout the cafeteria. She nudged her tray over to keep a seat between them, only to have it quickly filled by a woman she failed to recognize.

"Hi, Maddox," the woman chirped, her musical voice low in its timber. She had her thick purple braid woven into a neat, large bun on top of her head. A bright yellow bandana was looped around the bun and brought into a bow in the front. "It's been a long time."

The woman's necromancer mark was almost invisible—her lips were dark red and could have been mistaken for simple lipstick. A name flooded Maddox's mind.

"Oh! Gaia Cardenas." Gaia had been another victim of the cruelties of the Academy's social elite. The woman had actually left the school to continue private tutoring as soon as the Commission had approved it.

"Guilty. Except it's Gaia Proctor now, though I'm surprised you even remembered me." Gaia swirled a spoon into her bowl of venison stew and took a steaming bite. "I was hired last year as a dueling instructor. I'm glad Atticus convinced you to come back. He worked so hard to find—"

Atticus coughed suddenly. "Maddox brought her sword, Gaia. She could help with the dueling tournament you're going to hold next month."

Gaia's lips split into a bloody grin. "Oh, Maddox, would you? I would love an extra hand. If you can spare some time away from the Tome of the Undying, I mean."

Maddox was surprised Gaia *wanted* her help. Maybe it was because Gaia had left the Academy before their class began their dueling lessons. Maddox hadn't exactly been subtle with her disdain for her classmates. They looked down on her outside the dueling chambers, but inside them, Maddox enacted her revenge with every lesson.

Her violent behavior was behind her. Maddox nodded. "I'll see what I can do, Gaia."

"Perhaps you could help me in a demonstration?" Gaia nudged Atticus with her elbow, disrupting his meal. "Atticus could even be your second."

Maddox's polite smile faltered. Atticus was the only one who ever volunteered to be her second when she dueled. After the Rowans had made it their mission to put the "green witch" in her place, life at the Academy had become very difficult for Maddox.

If Maddox recalled correctly, Gaia's social difficulties had been because of her dyslexia. It had wreaked havoc on her grades when they had switched from writing in Latin to runes. Something Carol Rowan and her clique had loved to taunt Gaia for.

Gaia and Maddox might have been friends back then, if they'd had enough time before Gaia left to be homeschooled. It would have been nice to have a girlfriend, Maddox thought as the three of them continued to chat cheerfully over lunch. Atticus had been her only companion during their days as scholars, but that relationship had been confusing.

Maddox could sense that wouldn't change now.

CHAPTER 9
WARLOCK

Atticus was almost thankful for the unexpected presence of the not-priest in their study room. It didn't make Maddox's presence at the Academy any less surreal, but it gave them both someone else to talk to.

Lochlan perused their bookshelf leisurely, recording titles and authors in a small journal he carried. The man was supposedly a skilled exorcist—Atticus didn't care to discover if that was true or not. If he and Maddox did their job well, the page's contents would be revealed without any drama or consequence, rendering Dr. Rhodes useless.

"May I ask again who the tomb raider was that brought this back? I have some things I'd love to ask them."

Trust Maddox to ask the one question Atticus would not—could not answer. Not if he wanted to keep the last shreds of dignity he had left in her eyes.

If she ever found out that he had spent the last summer personally searching for the damned artifact, just to tempt her to come back to the Academy...

Atticus could not bear the humiliation.

"Rami Alsharif oversaw the expedition." Technically, Rami had *funded* the expedition, so it wasn't completely a lie to say he was responsible for finding the page.

Lochlan gave Atticus a long, curious glance at his lie. But to the exorcist's credit, he refrained from butting in.

Maddox frowned at the raider's name. "Oh. I've never heard of that tomb raider. Can you help me contact him?"

Perhaps the truth would have been better. Sure, Rami was terrible at checking his email, and his secretary would most likely filter out Maddox's inquiry, but if he actually responded to her...

Hoping to dissuade her, Atticus added, "You can try to email him, but communication is *not* his strong suit."

"I *will* email him," she vowed, returning to her book at last. "We'll need every bit of information we can get. I want to know how the hell that page ended up in the catacombs by itself."

Lochlan cleared his throat, snapping his notebook shut. "There are a few things we should discuss in advance. First, only *one* of you will be allowed to directly handle the artifact. We must have an unexposed party, and I cannot take that position. If things go awry, I may need to handle the artifact or step inside the cleanroom." He grimaced, waiting as if he expected Atticus and Maddox to fight over the honor.

Maddox rose from her desk, her hands fisting at her sides, but before she could argue, Atticus said with a shrug, "Maddox will handle the page. I will abstain."

She stared at him—he could feel her eyes stabbing into the back of his neck. Atticus acted as if he hadn't just ensured Maddox would be the first witch in a century to read from the Tome of the Undying.

The exorcist was not done. Lochlan jotted down something in his notebook and added, "Once Maddox begins handling the artifact, she will need to be observed. This artifact could easily be cursed or could release something malicious. I can act as the observer during the day, but at night—"

"She's staying with me. I'll keep an eye on her," Atticus promised.

"Don't I have any say in this?" Maddox weaved around her desk, planting herself right in front of Atticus. With her hands on her hips and that scowl directed right at him, Atticus felt like he was eighteen again.

"Do you not want to handle the artifact?" Lochlan inquired, saving Atticus the trouble. "Do you not understand the dangers that could be hidden within its words? What we could unleash?"

"No, I do—"

"Do you think Mr. Blackwell unfit to recognize the symptoms of a curse?" Lochlan's pop quiz was devoid of any emotion.

Maddox looked appropriately chastised. "That isn't what I meant."

Lochlan folded his hands together, appearing as if in prayer but cracking his knuckles instead. "I don't like messes. We *will* follow protocol. Maddox is the only one allowed to enter the cleanroom, but only with myself *and* Atticus present on the other side. I have more rules, but I'll compile that into a procedure we will reference each time we approach the artifact."

Maddox sat down in a huff, crossing her arms over her chest. Her navy sweater looked soft, and Atticus wondered how it would feel if he pressed her against the bookshelf. He glanced at Lochlan as if the pseudo-priest could guess his dirty thoughts.

Lochlan remained all grim business. "The Commission has standard procedures for this. I'll consult those documents and tweak them to fit our needs."

Maddox raised a hand before quickly trying to hide the fact she had just acted like a schoolgirl. "Full moonlight reveals things hidden by magic. Can we take the page outside—"

"Absolutely not," Lochlan nearly snarled in answer. "The Commission has made themselves clear. The artifact will not leave the cleanroom until the Commission transfers it into its final display."

Atticus nodded, though he selfishly wanted to take Maddox's side. "I agree with him."

Maddox never could hide her feelings. Her face flushed, but she kept any further arguments to herself.

Lochlan suddenly stood, nodding at them both before leaving the room.

The study room door had barely swung shut before Maddox was back before Atticus's desk. "Atticus, I cannot stay with you that long! It was meant to be a temporary thing—"

"Lochlan is right. If you so much as lay a pinkie on that page, you'll need to be watched. We have no idea what part of the Tome of the Undying we even have. Anything could happen." Atticus rested his chin in his hand, tilting his head as he narrowed his eyes at her. "Unless you'd prefer the *exorcist's* company? He seems like an excellent conversationalist. Handsome, too. You can talk about protocol or, perhaps, you have some *filthy confession* you want the man to hear?"

"Shut up." Maddox sat on the corner of his desk, her pleated skirt riding up a few inches. Atticus struggled to maintain eye contact with her. If she hadn't been wearing tights, he would have already lost that battle.

Maddox leaned closer to him, indignant. "This wasn't...this isn't..." She pinched the bridge of her nose and sighed. "Never mind. I understand why I should be watched overnight. It's just awkward. But I can't think of anyone more qualified than you."

Atticus watched the skin underneath her freckles turn pink after giving him that compliment. He fought the sadistic urge to point out her blush, and said instead, "It was Lochlan's idea. I think he assumed he would be observing me. We can request the Commission to send a female agent if you'd like."

She thought on it before giving a quick shake of her head. "No. If you don't mind, I'll just stay with you."

His heart stuttered at her words. It was disgusting.

"Let's get back to what we're good at," Maddox announced, leaving his desk with a bounce. "Ignoring each other with our noses stuck in books."

CHAPTER 10
DRUIDESS'S DAUGHTER

Twelve years old and Maddox Abernathy's magic had yet to make an appearance. Her older sister, Daphne, had been *six* when a family of bluejays started following her every move. Now Daphne left flowers blooming in her footprints. Maddox had killed a cactus—twice.

Her grandmother had told her not to worry about it, that she had been a late bloomer herself. That didn't ease her worries—her grandmother, Eleanor, was not a witch at all. This was more than late-stage puberty.

Maddox worried she was magicless, a disappointment, *nothing*. And the only woman in her family that she felt safe whispering those fears to, in between bites of homemade snickerdoodles, was dead.

Her grandfather's black cowboy hat hung limp in his hand. Maddox stood uncertainly at his side, staring past the open casket, rather than into it.

Useless, that's what she was. The rest of her family had spent the past week perfecting the floral arrangements and the gravesite while Maddox had spent her time on the phone, delivering the news of her grandmother's quiet passing to relatives she had never heard of.

Her grandmother didn't look dead, the grim thought making Maddox feel guilty somehow. Her sisters and younger cousins had been too afraid to approach the casket. Only Maddox felt strangely calm while gazing at her grandmother's pale face. The mortician had done a good job. She looked like she'd sit up any second and ask what all the fuss was about.

Her grandfather rubbed his red eyes. They were holding the wake at home, in the old farmhouse's large living room, but still, her granddad looked so alone.

The rest of their family lingered toward the back, making small talk and whispering Grandma's medical history to distant relatives.

Maddox focused on her grandmother, something strange welling up inside her chest. Maddox's heart thundered like a drum, and she could almost sense her grandmother's own heart, the organ still and decaying. Her heartbeats reverberated throughout her body, a bell announcing that now was the time for change. Without being fully aware of what she was doing, Maddox stepped right up to the casket, reaching down to touch her grandmother's cold hand. She squeezed the palm hard enough that Maddox felt the sudden, terrifying pulse of life within.

A sickening *crack* and her grandmother sat up, twisting her head to Maddox and then her husband. She moaned, unable to speak through the stitches the mortician had placed to keep her mouth peacefully closed. Maddox fell backward, screaming and crawling away from the casket.

Colter stumbled to his wife, shaking as he tried to ease her back into the casket. Maddox's mother found her, pressing her against her body as she dragged Maddox away from the grasping arms of her grandmother's corpse.

Her mother whispered into her ear, "*Relax*, baby. Relax and let her go."

Maddox sobbed, aware now of what her family had seen. Bright crimson, smoke-like magic encased her, tying her straight to her grandmother. Whatever had just happened, it was all Maddox's *fault*.

"I don't know *how* to stop it!" Maddox finally choked out, wishing her mother would release her and give her some time to think. Maddox was no druidess. She was a *monster*. She—

Colter eased Maddox out of her mother's protective grip. He brushed Maddox's hair while pleading softly, "Maddie, can you let your grandmother go?"

Maddox shook her head, eyes wild. The hazy magic plumed from her, flooding the room. Whatever this was, she had no idea what had caused it to appear or what would make it go away.

Through the red smoke, Maddox saw threads, sharp and gleaming like fishing line, connecting her to her grandmother's body. She caught a handful of the string and yanked, gasping when her grandmother jerked in her direction.

Puppet master. Hellraiser. *Necromancer.*

"No, no, no," she muttered, shoving out of her family's overbearing grasp.

Maddox ran for the exit as if distance could sever her ties to the casket.

The sun was bright, the meadows still filled with wildflowers, and she hated that their farm could still look so picture-perfect when there was evil happening inside.

Each step was harder than the last—the thread tugged at her back, trying to keep her from straying too far from her puppet. She hit the ground with her knees, hugging her chest as she cried. Beneath her, the grass died in a slowly increasing radius.

How could she feel so hollow and bursting at the same time?

It was a family *joke*, their great-great-great-grandfather Jericho being a necromancer. That was so many generations ago—this shouldn't be happening to her.

"I need help," she whimpered, shutting her eyes against the spreading decay she was causing. "Someone help me, please."

First, there was darkness. It was thick, settling on her like a wool blanket, scratching at her skin. The cold was next, and Maddox wondered for a moment if the Winterland feyries had trespassed before she saw the woman.

No, not a woman. A goddess.

And not a goddess Maddox had ever hoped to see.

The woman's warm, olive skin was cloaked in robes of pale grey and lilac. She approached Maddox, her hand outstretched while the rotting pomegranate she held out dripped pulp down her arm. The fruit was dark and dying but smelled sweet enough to tempt even the most wise of witches.

Maddox withdrew into herself—this was not something she wanted. She'd rather be magicless than be...*this*.

Persephone, goddess of spring and queen of the Underworld, did not present herself to green witches. She only approached necromancers, and that was rare. Though, witches only met their patron when they came of age. Maddox was too young to meet her patron. How desperate she must be to meet her goddess early.

The pomegranate's decaying increased, and the fruit became grey, bubbling liquid in the hand of the goddess. It fell in small clumps and killed the plant life below.

Persephone continued her approach, her bare feet coming into contact with the circle of death around Maddox. Her hand, still covered in rotten, bloody pulp, reached out and grasped the nearly invisible strings that connected Maddox to her grandmother. Persephone pulled them taut, and pain erupted in Maddox's chest. The goddess withdrew a small, black dagger and severed the strings.

Relief was instantaneous. Maddox collapsed onto her chest. Hades's wife dropped down to her, a hand on Maddox's hair as she whispered, "You were so lost. I had to come to you now." That stained hand moved to gently, almost motherly, stroke the ends of Maddox's hair. The juice left red stains wherever it touched. The goddess continued, "You are *mine*."

A promise. A threat. The end of everything.

Gone were her dreams of being like her sisters and her mother. Maddox would never cup a broken bird in her hands and release it with its wing mended.

She would heal nothing. She would fix nothing. What a dreary and life-sucking existence lay before her.

When the rest of the Abernathys found her, Maddox was alone. Deidre gathered her daughter into her arms, squeezing her tight. "It's going to be fine, Maddie. We're here. We're all here."

Maddox didn't doubt her family's loyalty, but as she looked at the empathetic and kind faces of her extended family, Maddox only had one thought.

Green witches breathed life *into* the earth, into their children, but Maddox, with every step she took, with every inhale, only stole life from her home.

Necromancers were leeches, destined to live a few centuries. Maddox would outlive them all.

CHAPTER 11
WITCH

Maddox knew it was only a matter of time before someone asked the obvious. She was thankful that it was Gaia who asked it and not one of her former professors.

"I noticed you and Atticus arrive and leave together every day. Is there something going on?" Gaia had caught her during lunch. Maddox had scurried to the dining hall alone, nabbing a small table by a large window so she'd get a perfect view of the dreary school garden. Full of venomous plants, it had been her second favorite study spot when the weather permitted.

Maddox thanked Hades that Atticus had to give a makeup exam during the lunch period. She would have melted if she had to have this conversation with him present. "I *am* staying with him since Atticus has allowed me to be the one to physically handle the artifact—"

Gaia grinned. "Of course, he has."

"Anyway." The interruption made Maddox blink. "The Commission agent wants me watched overnight. So—"

"So, Atticus *valiantly* volunteered?" Gaia wiggled her brows as she plucked one of Maddox's sweet potato fries from her plate.

"I would assume reluctantly volunteered," Maddox corrected.

"Whatever you say."

Maddox's brow pinched together. Did everyone else already know what Atticus had only recently confessed to her? She hoped not. Things were already far too confusing with the pair of them living together.

Maddox fought to find a way out. "You know we're wasting our time talking about a *boy*?"

"Okay, okay! I'll drop the subject." Gaia leaned back in her chair, folding her arms behind her head. "Speaking of the devil, where is tall, dark, and brooding?"

"Makeup test. And that's not dropping the subject."

"Fine! Can you bring your sword in?" Gaia's eyes danced. "I've heard so much about this feyrie sword of yours. I'm mad I never got to see it."

"Sure, but I should warn you..." Maddox winced, pushing the food around on her plate. "The sword's magic is creepy."

Gaia shivered. "All the fey are creepy."

"Gaia, we raise the dead."

Maddox's deadpanned response had them both giggling like schoolgirls.

"Atticus, give me some room!" Maddox used her arms to shield the book she was currently translating, trying to block Atticus's line of sight. "You can read it *after* me."

"I *could*," he agreed, "if you'd stop gasping every time you translate something and then refuse to explain."

Their private study room in the library was too small for him to be hovering like this! Atticus leaned over her, one hand gripping the back of her chair as his long hair tickled the side of her face. If she turned toward him too quickly, they'd practically be kissing.

No, do not think about kissing right now.

Maddox shut the book carefully, resting her elbow on the book as she waited for him to get out of her personal bubble. Instead, Atticus's crimson magic curled underneath the book, pulling it toward him with a quick *snap* of his fingers. Her elbow slid out from underneath her, and her head nearly hit the table.

Atticus, triumphant, gave her a smirk that used to make her blush years ago. Unfortunately, it appeared she hadn't outgrown that. He laughed as he faked a pout. "If you're going to *tease* me, Maddox, you could at least pull my hair."

Her defeat stung her pride, and Maddox could not contain the hot, angry magic leaking out of her palm. The table underneath her hand grew very warm until Atticus lifted her hand free, squeezed her fingers until his own power was enough to nullify hers, and *tsked* as he pointed out with his free hand the burn mark she'd left behind. "That can't be good for the table. I think I might have to give you detention for that, Miss Abernathy."

How easily he teased her. Maddox couldn't decide if she wanted to pinch him or laugh at him. Atticus suddenly looked a lot younger and less gaunt. His grin drew her attention to where she didn't want it to be.

Maddox eased her fingers out of his grip. "Stop making this fun!" As soon as she said it, her stern expression faltered, a smile sneaking its way onto her face.

As much as she hated to admit it, this *was* fun. Fun for two dusty book-loving nerds like them. It was so, so easy to fall back into a pattern with him. Even after their fight all those years ago, Atticus had weaseled his way back into her study room during their last two years at the Academy. It had helped, studying with him, and it made her days both more infuriating and less lonely.

But it was dangerous to relax with him. He could hurt her all over again.

As absorbed in each other as they were, they were unaware that Lochlan stood uneasily in the doorway. He glanced from Maddox over to Atticus, and then back. He looked, if it was at all possible, grimmer than before.

"I prefer to keep things professional," Lochlan announced before he pushed a third desk inside the study room. "I can translate just as well as the pair of you, but I must ask that a certain level of decorum be upheld." He sat primly down at his new desk, folding his hands together as he added, "Please, if one of you bends the other over a desk, refrain from using mine."

Atticus instantly barked out a laugh. Maddox jumped up and fled the room, sure her face would never return to its normal color.

"Lochlan finished the translation for you," Atticus said as he and Maddox entered the Blackwell estate together, their work done for that day, and he handed her a printed English version of the text they had fought over. "I told him any nonsense he may have stumbled upon this afternoon was my fault entirely. He seemed to believe that."

"Well, it *was* your fault," Maddox fumed, snatching the document from his hands. She skimmed the contents before sliding it into her messenger bag. They had wordlessly ridden in his car together from the Academy. She was secretly grateful Atticus had broken their awkward silence. "You live to torment me."

He neglected to offer any response to that.

Maddox glanced outside. The gloomy weather and the sound of distant thunder made it the perfect evening to stay indoors, cozy and warm, with a good book.

Maddox planned to do just that after she dropped her bag off in her bedroom. She turned on her heel, coming to a sudden stop as Atticus clasped the strap of her messenger bag.

"Take a walk with me?" he asked.

Where had that soft tone come from? Maddox waved toward the nearest window where storm clouds gathered outside. "In *this* weather?"

"Yes."

She had *many* good reasons to refuse. "Last time I took a walk with you, you practically attacked me."

"No," he said firmly, "I *kissed* you. And though you asked me to, I shouldn't have done it. I'm sorry." Atticus repeated, "Take a walk with me."

Maddox thought they would simply bury that day in the past. But here he was, bringing it up again and even *apologizing* for it.

Maddox slowly redid the buttons on her coat and followed him back out the door.

Once outside, they strolled through the gardens, their shoulders barely grazing each other's coat sleeves, as they walked on the outside of the small observatory the home boasted.

A long-haired black cat skirted around the home and vanished underneath some hedges. Did it belong to Atticus? He seemed like a cat person.

Maddox spotted a graveyard in the distance and guessed correctly that was their destination. Why had he brought her out here? She raised her face to the sky, scowling up at the rain that gently fell.

"Wait," Maddox blurted, Atticus's earlier apology for kissing her bringing to mind something she was deeply ashamed of. "I need to apologize, too."

Atticus paused, half-turning to glare back at her. "Now? In this weather?" he echoed her earlier words mockingly.

"Yes." Maddox answered without thinking. "I took something from you, and you don't have to forgive me, but I was terrible to you. No matter what happened between us in the past, you asked me to stop my truth spell, and I still—"

"Oh," Atticus interrupted. "You're talking about *that*."

He didn't sound bothered at all. Maddox frowned. "Don't lessen what I did. I was awful. I made you—"

"Made me what? Tell the truth?" The rain increased in volume, as cold and harsh as the planes and angles on Atticus's face as he laughed at her. "Perhaps I *enjoy* you knowing the truth. I've grown tired of hiding."

Maddox stood her ground. She wouldn't let him turn this into a joke. "I hurt you, and I'm sorry. Take this seriously."

The rain splattered against his crimson glasses, and Atticus removed them with a drawn-out sigh. "I see what the problem is. Our relationship has *flipped*. You've done something callously cruel to me, and you can't *stand* being the wicked one."

"That isn't what this is," she argued. "I truly am sorry."

"I think *you're* lying."

Atticus stepped forward quickly, crowding her without warning. Maddox backpedaled until her heel slipped into a newly formed puddle. She would have cracked the back of her head on the crumbling, seven-foot-tall tombstone behind her if Atticus hadn't caught her.

One hand cradled the back of her head while the other caged her in as he pressed his palm against the stone grave behind her.

He smiled insincerely. "Maddox, I forgive you. After all, my revelation worked in my favor, didn't it? *You kissed me back.*"

"You're laughing at me," she cursed.

"No," he assured her. "Never." Atticus moved closer but kept their bodies carefully apart. Maddox had nowhere to go. The towering headstone pressed against her back, blocking her escape.

She set her jaw. "I am *sorry.*" *Be genuine for once.*

"I already answered you. Wait." Atticus craned his neck, his forehead nearly touching hers. The rain grew loud, distracting, but nothing could suppress what Atticus whispered into her ear. "My forgiveness doesn't seem to be enough for you. What could I say, what could I *do*, to give you the moral high ground again? That's what you really want, isn't it? To feel *superior* to me."

She was a masochist. It was the only way to explain why Maddox kept still, halting her breath so she wouldn't miss a single word.

Atticus chuckled. "I dream of doing terrible things to you every night. Does that confession restore your holier-than-thou attitude?" His lips moved away from her ear to hover before her mouth, just out of reach.

This, whatever the hell this was, was out of Maddox's capability to respond to.

"No? Are dreams not enough?" Atticus asked. "Do you need something real to put me back in my place? What do you want from me? You could demand *anything*," Atticus assured her. "If you asked, I'd throw you down on this grave and fuck you right now. Would *that* be wicked enough for you to forgive yourself and return to your lofty pedestal?"

Her hand raised before Maddox knew what she was doing. Her arm swung, but her better nature stopped her palm from connecting with Atticus's face.

Atticus didn't even flinch. He almost seemed disappointed. He caught her hand, amused by her failed slap. "There's no need to hold back on *my* account."

Why did she let him burrow under her skin like that? Maddox should have shut this conversation down a long time ago. Atticus squeezed her wrist, the silence eating at them both. "Well?" he goaded her. "Go ahead. *Ask me.*"

Maddox curled her fingers, her hand still trapped, and flicked Atticus in the forehead. "*What* did you just say to me?" He couldn't intimidate her, no matter how much he'd changed or how much time had passed. Or how nicely his beard had grown in.

Atticus blinked back at her, frozen. Maddox placed her free hand on her hip and scolded him. "Did you *really* just offer to have sex with me in a *cemetery*? Are you binge-reading Mary Shelley biographies again?"

His laughter was off-guard. "Always," Atticus replied. The tension relaxed between them. Atticus no longer appeared towering and seductive. In fact, he sheepishly said, "You should have slapped me for that."

"Maybe," Maddox relented. "But I spent a long time after the Academy trying to let go of my anger toward you. That would have been a step backward."

"How Zen of you. Have you changed that much? You used to want to beat me more than anything." Pushing off the headstone, Atticus whirled around, resuming his earlier path. Though, this time with her hand entwined in his.

Maddox allowed herself to be tugged along, too overwhelmed to protest. *I apologized, he said a bunch of nonsense, and then I almost slapped him.*

Why couldn't they have one *normal* conversation?

She remained silent as Atticus led her through his family cemetery and stopped at a mausoleum. Ivy covered the small building, though the stone itself looked regularly cleaned. Every gravestone they had passed was almost pristine.

Atticus knocked on the tomb's impressive door, each *thump* on the stone accompanied by a quick brush of his magic. Connected to him as she was, Maddox felt his electricity course through her body.

Under his command, the double doors groaned and swung inward, runes carved in every inch of spare space and glowing bright red.

He pulled them both inside, and Maddox wiped her face free of the rain. They fell onto a low stone bench. The seat was cold enough that she let out a small gasp.

Taking up the center of the narrow tomb sat a single coffin. The coffin was grandiose—tall and made of black stone, with small cracks of sparkling white that ran through it like lightning. The epitaph above the coffin was typical and unfeeling—*REST IN PEACE.*

"What do you want to talk about?" Maddox prompted when she could no longer stand the quiet.

"I don't really want to talk at all."

That was unusual. Atticus never *ceased* talking.

Maddox drummed her heels on the floor. "Um, who are we seeing today?"

"That's my grandmother, Theodora Blackwell. She mostly raised me until—"

Unthinking, Maddox squeezed his hand. "I remember."

Their hands were still locked together. In contrast to his attitude in the graveyard, Atticus gently stroked her knuckles with his thumb. It was an absent-minded motion. As if being together like this was a habit.

This was Maddox's entire problem with Atticus. He'd been this way since the day she met him. One minute he was vulnerable and kind, and the next, cruel and wildly unpredictable.

How can you be so heartless when you used to take up so much of my heart?

Maddox's anxiety grew and hammered within her chest, and her magic rose from the floor, a few pale inches of smoke that she could not banish.

She could tear herself away from him, and he would deserve it, but Maddox instead relaxed onto the bench, staring pointedly away from their hands.

"Do you think she'd be pleased that part of the Tome of the Undying has been rediscovered? Or would she call us a pair of fools?" He'd asked for silence, but Maddox needed something to distract her from the warmth of his grip.

"Oh, I'm sure she'd call *me* a fool."

"Oh, sure."

Maddox decided to finally let Atticus have what he wanted. She pressed her lips closed, forcing herself to remain calm and silent, and prayed that her hand would stop sweating.

CHAPTER 12
SON OF A WITCH

"**B**e nice to the Rowans," his mother warned Atticus. Cynthia Blackwell double-checked her pale blonde hair was still tightly in place and tucked her small compact inside her purse. "You ignored Carol during your fifteenth birthday party last year. I don't throw those events for you to hide in the library."

You throw those events to schmooze with the other stockholders, he thought.

Atticus's family ran the largest supplier of Commission-approved potion ingredients. Blackened Salt Apothecary was wildly successful. Most witches, due to climate or time constraints, were unable to grow every single ingredient they needed for their potions. It was a lucrative business, and it kept his family and the Rowans, their largest investor, forever entwined.

It would have pleased his mother if he and Carol got on. Atticus had overheard her and Carol's father, Gavin, speak of a potential match between the two of them.

Atticus sniped between bites of his chef-prepared breakfast, "Carol would dig a grave with the wrong end of the shovel."

Cynthia pinched the fabric of his shirt sleeve. "Atticus, keep such thoughts to yourself or so help me—"

His brother, Giles, appeared in the doorway. "Can we *go* already? Atticus has been to the Academy before. Why does this have to be a big show?"

"Parents always attend the first day, Giles. I won't have Atticus missing out simply because you're embarrassed by your mother." Cynthia shooed her sons toward the garage.

The sight of the rising, sharp steeples of the Academy of the Dead failed to fill Atticus with anything other than dread. He had imagined this day being spent with his grandmother. Theodora was always, without question, the most interesting person in any room.

His left hand ached, and he rubbed his palm until the tremors ceased.

They wove through the crowd of parents and students, heading for the welcome booth. There were a dozen little tables in the Academy's courtyard, a circle of colorful stands representing each class. Cynthia made a beeline toward the Apothecary stand, cornering Professor Gardner, another one of her investors.

Atticus lingered behind. His brother had already vanished, sneaking off to meet up with his girlfriend, no doubt. Atticus had been to the Academy several times and took part in a youth summer research program twice. So, he dodged the tour, vanishing into the glass dome of the Academy's Poison Garden, hoping to be left alone until Family Day was over.

Of course, as his luck was nothing if not awful, Atticus found the garden already occupied by another.

She dressed plainly in jeans and a faded, purple sweater with white lettering and a few cartoonish bees flying around the words. When the girl turned toward him, he could read the words, *Abernathy Farms and Meadery*.

She eyed his clothing as well, her brow furrowing as if she had just realized how little she fit in.

Atticus wanted to turn away but found himself scolding her instead. "Watch yourself. You're sitting next to—"

"Leadwort. I know." She stared at the red leaves in amusement. "Amazing they can grow that all the way up here."

He hummed, surprised the farm girl was knowledgeable in tropical, poisonous plants. She stood with a timid smile dashed across her lightly freckled face. A bee crawled along one of the braids in her hair. Atticus's fingers twitched to shoo it away, but she gently removed the insect before he had a chance to act.

She let the bee fly off her finger. "Are you here to hide, too? My parents are irritating the dueling instructor, I think. We weren't aware I needed a sword."

"For our fourth year, you will." Atticus wondered where the hell she was from if she didn't know that. "Your parents didn't attend the Academy?"

"No, they're druids. Green witches. We're, I mean, they're self-taught." She curled a lock of dark hair around one finger, the ends tinged in red. "I'm the first in my family to be a necromancer. It's been a steep learning curve..." She paused, her face twisting. "I'm Maddox Abernathy. Might have mentioned that sooner."

"Atticus Blackwell." His surname didn't faze her.

"Are you interested in the apothecary trade, too?"

Hades below, didn't she know who his family was? "A little," he replied, just to be polite. "Have you ever heard of Blackened Salt Apothecary?"

"Of course!" She looked offended. "Is that your after-school job or something?"

Laughter rattled out of him, dusty and out of practice. "You really don't know who I am!" What he said next was never meant to leave his lips. "If you don't recognize a Blackwell, why the hell are you talking to me?"

Her head cocked to the side, her round glasses slightly askew. "I don't know *anyone* here. Am I supposed to remain silent for the next six years?"

"No, that's not what I meant."

Maddox's eyes alighted on the worn book he carried at his side. "Is that *Frankenstein*? I almost brought my copy, but I was afraid I'd get laughed at." Her fingers wiggled, but she made no move to grab his book.

Atticus frowned. The worn leather cover was comforting, and more importantly, it was an excuse. He planned to avoid his future classmates and instead spend his time with Mary Shelley, a woman whose gothic dramatics outdid even his own.

"I live nearby," he relented. "I can bring you my extra copy tomorrow, but only if you're not one of those fold-the-corner-over-instead-of-find-a-bookmark types."

"Absolutely not! Anyone who does that should be sentenced to death—" She blinked, her nose scrunching up and pushing her glasses back into their proper place. "I mean—"

It was his second laugh that day.

Maddox stared openly as if she was trying to discern whether his laughter was mocking or genuine. Her choice locked in, she asked, "Have you ever raised a corpse?"

"That's illegal to do outside of class. At least until we graduate." Her question, and everything about this girl, was odd.

"Not even on accident?" she pressed.

"How does that happen by *accident*?"

Before she could answer, a thin, white root burst from the ground, rising a few feet in the air to tap her shoulder. "Oh! That's my mom. I need to go catch up with my parents." She brushed dirt off her jeans and waved a farewell. "See you in class! And don't forget me! I mean, don't forget to bring me that book!"

Atticus stepped away from the doorway, allowing her to leave the greenhouse. As he watched her hurry away, Atticus felt a very familiar magic watching him. He darted his gaze about the grounds until he located his mother in the distance, staring at him while she puffed on her cigarette. She stomped the butt in the grass, and Atticus knew her look, that tight, angry set of her jaw more familiar to him than her smile.

It was disappointment.

CHAPTER 13
SON OF A WITCH

The truck hit a rut in the road, jarring Atticus's pen as he reworded a section of Maddox's Apothecary notes.

"Sorry about that," Maddox's grandfather, Colter, called back to them. The raven, sitting in the passenger seat next to the druid, let out a squawk that made Atticus's ears ring.

Atticus knew he shouldn't be in this truck on his way to the middle of nowhere. His mother certainly wouldn't approve. He *never* should have mentioned to Maddox he was spending the Thanksgiving holiday alone. His parents were both working through the holiday, though his father had offered to have Atticus spend the holiday with him. Atticus had declined, seeing little point in celebrating an old American holiday in Dubai. Giles was spending the day with his girlfriend, not that Atticus actually *wanted* Giles at home.

But Maddox, kind to everyone, wouldn't leave him the hell alone. This friendship between them was new, too new for such a trip. He should have remained at home with his guardian and locked himself in the family library.

"I should warn you," Maddox whispered, stuffing her notes into a messenger bag. "My family is large. And noisy. We don't do Thanksgiving, but we host this end-of-harvest dinner that's chaotic even when things go according to plan."

Atticus couldn't recall the last time his family had been in the same country, let alone the same house. His last few holidays had been spent with his grandmother. He helped her cook, watching her add spices at random, the measurements changing every lesson, and listened to her recount her days as a tomb raider and as the Academy librarian.

Theodora's spice blend was tucked in his luggage. Atticus assumed Maddox would help in the kitchen. Not because she was a girl, but Maddox could never stand by when there was work to be done. She was a terrible teacher's pet. Though, considering how the other students treated her, Atticus could hardly blame her for it.

Her home was just as he imagined it. It looked like the opening sequence for a Hallmark movie. They drove under a tall wooden arch with a sign that swung in the brisk autumn breeze. It read 'Abernathy Farms and Meadery'.

Lavender fields to his right, and an apple orchard to his left, Atticus stared at the sudden influx of technicolor. There was hardly an inch of unused land, and the trees were gorgeous reds and yellows. By this time, all of Redhollow's foliage was a dull, muddy brown.

Colter's truck paused before a white barn. "Get out. I have my own choring to do." The words were gruff, but Maddox seemed unbothered by them. They exited, pulling Atticus's luggage out of the truck bed, and for the moment, they were alone.

Maddox announced, "We have a guest room set up for you. It's small, though."

"I'm not so spoiled that you need to apologize for that," Atticus said with a frown.

Maddox tapped the shiny—and expensive—watch on his wrist, a recent gift from his father. "Are you sure?" she asked, but her teasing tone lifted both of their moods.

She led him to a three-story white farmhouse, pointing out family members as they went. Atticus had to elbow his way past a crowd of people, all of them loud, and most of them harmlessly fighting the way normal families do. Maddox took a wide berth around the kitchen, filled with blonde and ginger women, and led him to the third floor of the home. She showed him a small room, the bedding soft and grey. Dried lavender hung from rafters in the slanted ceiling.

Since he had entered the Abernathy's land, Atticus was overtaken by warmth and light. Their magic felt like a minor sunburn, a lively heat he couldn't cool. Occasionally, Maddox gave off a ghost of that same Abernathy magic, that lifeblood, and her burn always lingered the longest.

Atticus carefully placed his folded clothes inside the small dresser tucked in a corner of the room. "I have one request. Don't leave me alone. I came prepared to help." He handed Maddox the small jar of Theodora's secret spice blend. "That's for you. It's my grandmother's blend."

Maddox opened the lid to smell the contents. "Thank you. You didn't have to—"

"It's bad manners to arrive without a gift for the host," Atticus argued. He plucked another bottle from his luggage, twisting open the child-proof lid and taking a large swig. No matter what he added to *Chameleon*, it still tasted like medicine.

Once the last item was tucked away, Atticus turned away from the dresser. "Okay. Should we help with dinner now?"

"Help with..." She squinted at him. "You want to help *cook*?"

"I can't imagine an extra pair of hands would be unwanted."

"I have a reprieve on chores this weekend since you're here. But...if you really want to..." Maddox was obviously reluctant, but she led him to the kitchen, anyway.

Leaning on the kitchen doorway, Maddox flailed, begging for the attention of a blonde woman who rushed from one side of the kitchen to the other. "Mom! Mom! Mom!"

"Maddox, what!" the blonde woman huffed.

Maddox chirped, "Can we help?"

"We? What—" The woman paused, balancing three mixing bowls in her arms. "That's Atticus? He's skinny."

"Mom!"

"Well, we'll mend that." Maddox's mom laughed, setting two of the bowls down so she could shake his hand with her flour-smeared one. "But we don't make our guests help. I'm Deidre."

"Atticus," he said, though she obviously already knew that. "And I *want* to help."

"You look pale. Here. Eat this." A perfectly ripe peach, which was wildly out of season, dangled before him by another one of Maddox's relatives.

"He needs protein, Heather," another woman said, pointing a wooden spoon at the first woman. "Let him taste the turkey before he passes away."

"He does seem a little ill," Deidre agreed, frowning and emptying her busy hands. "Did the flight disagree with you? Let me see."

Atticus flinched hard when Maddox's mother placed her hands on either side of his head. Her head tilted, and that brow furrowed further. "Atticus, you *really* don't seem well."

Another woman laughed. "That's nothing our food can't fix, Diedre!"

Deidre's look only darkened.

Thankfully, Maddox remained oblivious to her mother's concern or Atticus's slow, rising panic. Maddox snatched his hand, trying to lead him away from the kitchen. "It's going to be like this the whole time," Maddox warned him. "They'll start rubbing tonics into your hair next if we don't—"

Deidre followed them, cutting her daughter off. "Maddie, let's have your grandfather look at Atticus. He's not feeling well."

Maddie? Atticus wondered how Maddox would retaliate if he tried that nickname on her. It would be safer for his health, which was already in question, if he looked for another. "I'm feeling fine," Atticus protested, wishing Deidre would leave him be.

"It will only take a minute," Diedre said, her tone quite motherly and matter-of-fact. She placed a hand on both teens' shoulders and pushed them outside of the house and toward a large barn.

While her mother went inside the barn, leaving them to wait, Maddox asked him, "Are you *really* okay? If you need to go to bed, that's—"

"No!" Atticus snapped. Damn these nosy green witches. No backyard tonic could help him. Why couldn't they leave it alone? "I don't need anything."

That outburst silenced further inquiry. Maddox kicked at the ground until her mother and grandfather emerged from the barn.

"Let me see the boy, Diedre, before you ask for a diagnosis." Colter did not appear happy to be dragged from his chores. "Atticus? Let me see your eyes."

Could he refuse without raising suspicion? Atticus doubted it. Though he told himself there was no way the old green witch could know what was wrong with him, he still couldn't keep his left hand from trembling. Holding Colter's gaze—it took everything he had not to waver under the scrutiny.

"Leave these kids alone, Deidre. The boy doesn't need one of our tonics."

There was something in the old man's eyes that haunted Atticus. Something all-knowing. He cringed, unable to take the staring contest anymore.

"Okay," Deidre said, though she seemed unconvinced. She turned Maddox around by her shoulders and pointed at a blonde girl struggling with a very large picnic basket. "Go help your sister."

Atticus was pulled along again, this time led by Maddox. "Come on," she beckoned him. "You can meet one of my sisters."

"How many are there?" he asked. He felt Colter's eyes linger on the back of his neck.

"I'm number five and the youngest."

Atticus nearly choked on his next breath. "*Five?* Do they not get cable out here?"

Her laughter disappeared some of his previous worry.

They met up with the girl, and she groaned in relief. "Here. You can take this over to the inn." Maddox's older sister, Daphne as she revealed herself to be, thrust a picnic basket into his arms, and Atticus staggered under the weight. He saw an insane number of pies, bread, and jam jars inside the basket. "Have fun with that, Herbet West."

Daphne's reference was accurately funny, but Maddox didn't laugh, so neither did Atticus. Maddox scowled at Daphne and led him away from the farm.

As they cut through a thick patch of forest, following a narrow footpath, Atticus asked, "Your neighbors run an inn?"

"Oh, heck." Maddox suddenly stopped, and Atticus bounced off her back. She whirled around, face pale. "I forgot to mention our neighbors are—"

A tiny bridge, spanning over a clear, bubbling creek, was now in sight. At the other end of the bridge was easily the tallest woman Atticus had ever seen.

The giantess glimmered, magic moving across her body like firelight. It took his eyes a moment to adjust, but when they did, he saw black armor and a greatsword that peeked over the woman's shoulder.

The woman grinned, sharp teeth drawing every ounce of Atticus's attention. "Hello, Maddox. I've been waiting for you."

Fey! Maddox was bringing gifts to a *feyrie*. Of all the foolish things for that confounding girl to do! Was she trapped in a bargain with this skyscraper of a woman? Maddox tugged at the basket, and he clung to it, pulling it back against his chest.

"Atticus, give me—" Maddox overpowered him, yanking the gift out of his grasp. She presented it to the feyrie. "Happy harvest, Ashling."

"Thank you. Our guests will appreciate these." Ashling looped her arm through the basket's handle. "I've nearly completed your sword, Maddox, but I'm afraid the enchantment has taken a life of its own. It will give you a hard time."

Maddox worried her lip. "I'm not really sure what that means but thank you."

Ashling glanced behind her, whistling and calling forth a large, black dog who padded forward, tongue lolling out of its mouth. "Would you bring Hob back with you? The beast has been whining all morning. All that food you have cooking over there is driving him mad."

"Sure. The kids love him."

The dog was oversized and terrifying as well. Atticus remained silent and grey, refusing to speak in front of the fey, until Maddox grabbed his hand and led him back to the farmhouse. The woman on the bridge watched them until they were no longer within eyesight.

He exploded into a rant. "Why are you giving a *feyrie* gifts? And those teeth! I've never heard of such a thing." Atticus crossed his arms, Maddox's amused expression annoying him to no end. "Answers. Now."

"Ashling is a redcap—"

"Redcap! The psychos that dip their hats in blood?"

"Yes. But she wasn't even wearing a hat today, so I think you're safe."

Atticus shook his head. "This is *funny* to you?"

"A little." Maddox veered off the footpath, heading away from the farmhouse. The dog kept to the path, bounding toward the scent of turkey and pie. Maddox offered Atticus a small shrug. "Our neighbors are feyries. They run an inn. Sorry, I forgot to warn you. We're so used to them, I didn't even think."

She lived so close to the fey, and Maddox didn't seem at all concerned. "You shouldn't accept anything from them. You can borrow one of my swords. My mother would hardly notice."

"I have it handled," Maddox said with a scowl that was intense enough that Atticus changed the subject.

He asked with a slight pout, "Is the dog just a dog?"

"A Black Dog. Capitalized."

Atticus kicked a rock, and it skipped in front of them. "Perfect!"

They ended up in a meadow, grass knee-high and wildflowers still blooming. He guessed living with a family of green witches ensured the foliage remained spring-like throughout the year. Nearby were a few wooden boxes, and he heard the buzz of honeybees flitting about.

Maddox spun around, shoving him backward, and Atticus fell. Before he could snap at her, Maddox landed beside him, the top of their heads nearly touching.

"What the hell was—"

"Shh. Look." She pointed above them, shielding her eyes from the dim sunlight. A swarm of bees gently flew above their heads, moving in a lazy loop. The insects formed a circle, bumbling a few turns before flying off in search of nectar. "I like to imagine that I'm making them do that, but I'm not." Her kind voice became sad, disappointed.

"Why did you invite me here?" It had to be asked before he went insane.

"You said you'd be alone during the break." She reached back and poked his head. "And you're my only friend back there. Why did you come?"

Atticus couldn't think of anything to say that he felt comfortable with her hearing.

"I'm sorry my mother was being nosy." Maddox sighed and the concern—the fear—in her voice was touching and unwarranted. "My family thinks they can mend anything—which might explain the state of my wardrobe."

"It's fine," he whispered, knowing all too well he was not something that could be mended. It would be better to throw him out and start fresh with something untainted.

Atticus and Maddox set the dinner table. He placed plate after mismatched plate on the long, rectangular table. Just how big was her family? He turned to ask Maddox where the silverware was and found she was missing.

Women suddenly fled from the kitchen, shrieking as that black dog ran through the room and chased what appeared to be a reanimated dead rabbit. Only Atticus ignored the chaos, watching as Maddox snuck into the kitchen, shaking his grandmother's spices on what remained of the turkey.

Though those spices really needed to be roasted, the act knitted Atticus's brow and hollowed out his chest.

Blackwells did not make friends—they made mutually beneficial connections. But, perhaps, Atticus had escaped that family cycle.

CHAPTER 14
WITCH

Despite the rocky start to their research, Atticus and Maddox eventually found a rhythm as they studied every reference they could find. Which was shockingly sparse. For a library that used to house the book of the dead, there were few references to be found.

The Tome of the Undying was believed to have had thirteen authors, and since they couldn't yet read what was on their single page, there was no way to know which necromancer had penned it. The contents could be useless...or extremely deadly.

Some of the authors had descended into madness before even finishing their section. They could unveil the chicken scratch of a lunatic.

It took three weeks, but soon Atticus and Maddox felt they had enough information on the Tome of the Undying to begin taking samples of the page. Lochlan was less convinced, but agreed to a small test sample, as long as his extensive procedure was followed to the dot.

While the men set up the rest of the laboratory, Maddox slipped into her cleanroom gown, a white, stuffy suit that covered her from head to toe. Before she could slip the hood on, Atticus slipped a twine necklace over her head, tiny bundles of various herbs tied to the loop. It covered the bee necklace she wore daily and, not for the first time, Atticus fingered the small, gold charm.

"I don't understand why you have this." He let the charm drop.

"Why?" Maddox fumed. "Does my cheap jewelry bother you?"

Atticus's brow furrowed. "It wasn't *cheap*, but I guess that explains why you're wearing it."

Lochlan stepped between them, thrusting her head covering in Maddox's face. "Put this on. You're losing focus."

Maddox swallowed her argument. She *was* acting unprofessional, but what had Atticus meant by "it wasn't cheap"? Her stomach dropped.

She hadn't witnessed who had left the necklace on her desk during her final exam. She had only assumed from Professor Boleyn's Cheshire grin that she had been the one who…

Every day! Maddox wore that blasted thing every single day, and worst of all, now Atticus had seen her wear it.

Lochlan had prepared a checklist for her, tasks that he dictated needed to be completed before she entered the cleanroom and interacted with the Tome of the Undying's page. Most of the tasks involved a quick study of her current mental health, and a few involved Atticus placing some wards over her. Atticus's magic stuck to her skin like invisible, dried blood, and Maddox rubbed her arms self-consciously.

At least the procedure gave her something else to focus on. She circled each item, performed it, and then marked the task complete with an X. Lochlan read the list aloud, waiting for her to confirm verbally that each step was performed.

"I'm satisfied," the exorcist announced, stepping out of the way of the cleanroom door. He moved to a keypad, punched in a code only he knew, and the door slid open.

Maddox waited for the door to close automatically behind her. Once she was sealed in, she pressed inside, approaching the locked and heavily warded briefcase that contained the supposed Tome of the Undying's page. She unlocked the case with a key the head librarian stored for them. This ensured Lochlan wouldn't be able to access the artifact without the Academy's knowledge.

Her breath halted—Maddox slowly opened the case, staring longingly at the flattened sheet of human skin nestled within. The only problem was that the page was completely blank.

There must be some way to unveil the writing Maddox was certain was hidden from sight. Or, as Atticus had guessed, a chemical process might be necessary to reveal the text.

Someone knocked on the glass viewing window. Maddox peered over, watching Lochlan lower his hand. He spoke into the intercom system. "Take the sample and get out of there."

She nodded, removing a small vial and a pair of scissors from the pouch around her belt. *Snip!* Maddox cut a small section of the page and deposited the skin into the vial. She twisted the lid shut and her tools went back into the pouch. Slowly, she closed the case, locking it again, though something prickled at her mind, urging her to open it again.

On this side of the cleanroom, safe and contained in the magically protected space, was a microscope. Maddox placed the sample in a slide and set it on the stage, clipping it in place. The eyepiece of the microscope was actually outside the room where the artifact was kept. The glass had been cut to allow this intrusion. With this, Atticus would be able to examine the sample without exposure. If he needed anything physically done to the slide, Maddox would have to enter and perform the task.

Lochlan's plans and procedures were tedious, but Maddox was thankful for his attentiveness.

Her task complete, Maddox made her way to the exit before longing tore through her chest, a yearning like she had never experienced. What she wanted, Maddox didn't know, but she knew she would draw blood to get it. Anything to end this over-bearing emptiness she *had* to fill.

Maddox tripped as she stumbled to the cleanroom's door. She needed to escape the artifact's influence and quickly. She pawed at the inner keypad, mashing the button for the timed release. Through the hazy glass, she saw Lochlan directly on the other side, waiting to cleanse her of any lingering dark magic.

The keypad screen went dark. The lab had completely lost power. This artifact would not release her willingly.

Oh, no.

She felt the darkness leaking out from that singular page, but Maddox refused to look back. She sank slowly to her knees, pinching her eyes shut while her own magic curled protectively around her body.

Fingers, too long and thin, clamped down on her shoulder. The hand, Maddox half-believed, was only a hallucination. She used her own magic to shake the weight away from her body—real or not, she wanted that pressure gone.

It was hard not to lean into the dark magic reaching for her. Maddox's curiosity begged her to open her senses to it, to discover its intent. But with any necromancer artifact, it was all too easy to learn too much. To learn something mind-breaking.

An ache threatened to split her in half, rising from her lower belly. Pressing her forearms against her stomach, Maddox screamed, "RESET THE

BREAKER!"

She could hear the men scrambling outside, catching a few heavy *thuds* that did not sound like they were locating the breaker panel. Hades, what were they doing out there?

A voice, low and sultry, whispered to her from behind. If she listened carefully, she'd be able to translate those words. If she did that, she and everything she was would be gone.

Maddox covered her ears, but, as she expected, the voice was speaking directly to her mind.

This feeling hurt—her ribcage felt as if someone was trying to pry it open and expose the inner workings. Maddox felt hollow, but she also felt something she wasn't used to. She never wanted like *this*—it was what kept her apart from other people.

Persephone, help me.

The *whoosh* of an electric door cut off the artifact's whispers before Maddox could apply any meaning to them. Someone caught her underneath her arms and dragged her out of the cleanroom.

Only when she heard the cleanroom door shut again did Maddox open her eyes.

Lochlan knelt before her, his perfectly coiffed blonde hair out of place. She glanced over his shoulder, awed by the inky black magic that filled every atom of space in the cleanroom.

Three minutes. Maddox had only been near the unprotected page for three minutes and her heart raced as if she'd just finished running a marathon. Lochlan's fingers rested against her temples while his thumbs lifted her chin. He checked her eyes, staring into them so long that she began to flush under the fierce attention.

Maddox turned her face away from the exorcist, meeting Atticus's wild, red-eyed stare. Blood cascaded down from his nose. What had *happened* out here? Atticus returned her gaze so fully that the terrible hunger the artifact had inspired in her grew more painful until she placed her focus on Lochlan.

"Well?" Atticus barked, his voice sounding off with his damaged nose. "Is she clear?"

"This will feel a little uncomfortable considering your magical proclivity." Lochlan spoke softly, murmuring a few lines in Latin, and Maddox felt a warmth flood her. Small flickers of flame appeared where Lochlan laid his hands on her, white and so bright that her eyes watered. He wasn't lying—it was *very* uncomfortable, a heat that raced underneath her skin. Perspiration beaded on her forehead.

Eventually, the fire faded, and with it, the pain.

Lochlan helped her stand. "There. You're clean."

"Wow, and I was barely in there." She laughed, cutting the silence. "I wonder what the hell that page says."

Lochlan moved toward the keypad, fingers hovering over the buttons. "I need time alone to cleanse the room. I don't want either of you exposed—my attempt to clear the room of the artifact's influence may piss it off."

"Let's both go outside while the good, little exorcist works," Atticus snarled.

"Good idea." Lochlan shrugged, turning away and tugging on his own cleanroom suit. "I'll call you once the artifact is...the simplest term is 'asleep', and after I have placed the appropriate protections on it. If I don't reach out in thirty minutes, please return here and check on me. And, Atticus?"

Lochlan may have been an unusual specimen of a Commission agent, but his disapproving tone betrayed his true allegiance—his allegiance to the Commission. To the safeguarding of dangerous, dark artifacts.

"You are *never* to enter the cleanroom, even if you fear for Maddox's life. Don't make me remind you again."

CHAPTER 15
WARLOCK

Insanity was not a far stretch for a Blackwell, but this was the first time Atticus had felt his mind slip so far into that always-waiting black pool.

Maddox was in danger. And it was *his fault*.

Such thoughtless action was new to him—his magic welled up inside him, sending large tendrils that banged against the glass of the cleanroom.

Magic and electricity rarely mixed, but Atticus had found himself before the cleanroom door in an instant. Sparks flew from his fingers, painful and red, and he tried to power the door just long enough to get inside. The cleanroom door, upon a loss of power, failed-shut to contain whatever dark artifact was being stored within.

There was a flare of light from the keypad, but his triumph was short-lived once he remembered only Lochlan knew the code.

He would have resorted to beating through the glass with his bare hands had Lochlan not stopped him.

There was a loud click as Lochlan reset the breaker. While Lochlan punched in the code, covering the numbers from Atticus's view, Atticus kept close to the door and waited for his opportunity to enter.

Lochlan suddenly understood the warlock's plan and ceased typing in the code. "Only *I* can enter, Atticus!" he snapped, pushing Atticus aside. "You'll ruin the experiment if you—"

The exorcist's words meant absolutely nothing. Atticus snarled, "*Shut up* and open the fucking door! She's not going to last against that thing!"

"Disperse your magic," Lochlan ordered, his tone cold and commanding. "Stand aside."

Atticus's magic was no longer smoke-like—it was more corporeal than it had been in years. It was almost a liquid, and that should have scared him, but with Maddox in danger, he couldn't care about anything else. The red offshoots of his magic threatened the integrity of the cleanroom's glass and the lab outside of it. But he could not call it out of being. No Latin turn of phrase would make his magic obey him when his heart screamed at it to tear down those barriers separating him from Maddox.

My fault. My fault. My fault. My fault. My fault.

Lochlan's collar was in Atticus's hands before logic could reel him back in. "*Open the Hades-damned door.*"

And *that* was when Lochlan gripped Atticus by the back of his neck and drove his nose down on Lochlan's forehead.

Tears flooded Atticus's eyes, turning the exorcist into a blurry version of himself. The man was stronger than Atticus would have ever thought. Atticus stumbled backward as he watched Lochlan enter the cleanroom and drag Maddox's body away from the artifact.

All those theatrics were for naught, he thought grimly. Maddox was rescued not by Atticus, but by the exorcist.

Now Atticus and Maddox were shooed outside while Lochlan properly contained the artifact. With a sample in place, there was so much more work to be done, and Atticus felt too exhausted to muster any excitement for any of it.

This was all a mistake. He'd brought a bomb to the Academy, and he dropped it right into Maddox's eager hands.

Nothing is worth this.

"Wait." Maddox caught his arm, halting Atticus's absentminded march out of the lab and back to the library above them. "Let me see your face. Did Lochlan hit you?"

"Head-butted me." Atticus only half-turned, shielding his nose with his free hand. "I'll be fine."

"Blackwell, only *you* could piss off a priest enough to make him *head-butt* you." Maddox chuckled lightly, gently removing his hand to study his nose. She was quick and emotionless—her bedside manner flawless. "I don't think it's broken—just bruised. If I were one of my sisters, I could mend this in an instant."

"If you were one of your sisters, you'd leave me to suffer."

Her smile was soft, unsure. "You're right, but I meant that I'm useless here, while the rest of my family—"

"Your magic is different, not less." He immediately cursed himself.

Maddox's gaze snapped up to his, her eyes narrowing as uncertainty and embarrassment overran her features.

"You..." she began, rubbing her neck. "You don't need to do that. I haven't been very nice to you."

"You were *always* nice to me," he argued, a short laugh escaping him. "Even after...our fight, you were still the kindest person in our class. Sure, sometimes you *tried* to be mean to me, but it was like a toothless dog trying to bite."

"I didn't mean when we were students." She frowned. "I meant recently. I meant when I dared you to—"

If she brought up their kiss, Atticus wasn't certain he could keep his despair from showing. He raised a hand to stop her. "Let's take a break from anything relating to the Tome of the Undying. Perhaps you'd like to practice your swordplay before you make a fool of yourself in front of Gaia and her students?"

"Make a *fool* of myself!" Maddox abandoned their previous topic entirely, her brow knitting together.

"I doubt you practiced your swordplay back in Mayberry."

"I don't live in Mayberry!"

Atticus shrugged as if it didn't matter. "I would even bet that *I* could disarm you easily."

That cold warning flash in her eyes was familiar. If rekindling their rivalry stopped Maddox from discussing their kiss, what Maddox *must* consider her *mistake*, then Atticus would gladly do so.

Once they were back at the Blackwell estate, the pair planned to change clothes and meet up on the second floor. Atticus made a quick detour to the conservatory, finding Venenum in one of its favorite trees. Dropping down from a branch, the snake wound around his neck as Atticus climbed upstairs. This level consisted mainly of bedrooms, but at one end of the floor was a dedicated sparring room. Once inside the dueling chambers, Venenum came down from its perch, sliding down Atticus's arm where the viper twisted and changed until it returned to its sword form.

Atticus tested the shining blade, giving Venenum a few practice thrusts. The Blackwell's rapiers were a little heavy for his taste, but the weapon, dark as midnight and with an edge Atticus kept carefully honed, was beautiful.

He recalled Maddox's sword well. Necromancers carried rapiers to help focus their spells, though in a modern society, there was little need for such force. Maddox's blade was unique—the hilt crafted with the bones of her great-great-grandfather, the only other necromancer in her family. Her blade, always gleaming a deep red, had defeated them all. Considering who the blacksmith had been, that terrifying feyrie giantess, Atticus hadn't been surprised that Maddox had dominated them.

"Hades, I forgot how exciting this can be," Maddox said as she entered the room. She carried her sword over to the countertop that lined one wall of the mostly empty room. Setting the blade on the counter, she carefully unwrapped it to reveal the human bone hilt and red humming blade.

Keeping his attention on her sword and not the athletic black leggings she wore was a battle in itself.

Her grandfather's raven hopped from her shoulder to land next to the sword. It squawked at Atticus as if to say, "Game on."

"So, what's the bet?" Maddox moved to the center of the padded floor, sitting down to stretch out her legs. She grabbed the tip of her black boots and leaned forward. The entire room contained wall-to-wall mirrors, and Atticus was presented with multiple, and flexible, Maddox Abernathys.

Atticus looked at the ceiling for a beat. "I propose nothing monetary."

"Duh." Maddox stretched forward even further, her forehead touching her leg. "We currently stand inside your *mansion*. The stakes aren't quite the same for you as they are for me."

"If I win..." he mused, tapping at his chin. "If I win, I would like you to cook dinner tonight."

His answer startled her, but Maddox shrugged it off quickly. "Well, that's not really a *prize*, but I accept." She sprung up from the floor, moving over to her blade. Maddox held a hand over the edge of her sword, using her magic to temporarily dull the edge.

Atticus copied her spell over his own blade before showing her where he had a few armored gloves, face guards, and chest plates stored. The sizing wasn't perfect, but it would do for a "friendly" match.

"No magic whatsoever," Atticus decided, and Maddox nodded in agreement. "Don't mar my pretty face, and I'll spare yours."

He stepped, blade in hand, into the fighting ring. His face guard hid his smirk. "Now, Maddox, what can I offer *you*?"

CHAPTER 16
WITCH

What did Maddox even *want* from Atticus? Why had she insisted on placing a bet?

Because there must be competition between you two, always. It's safer. It keeps your mind from wandering if you're focused on beating him.

This duel was nothing but a distraction from their project. The *Tome* deserved her focus, not Atticus Blackwell. Even though the man seemed starved for her attention, for Maddox to puzzle *him* out instead of the Tome.

Shaking off her distracting inner monologue, Maddox followed Atticus to the middle of the sparring room, her blade feeling heavier than she remembered. It had been far too long since she had wielded her sword, and the damned thing wouldn't let her forget it.

The hilt flared with a dull heat, just enough to feel uncomfortable as she adjusted her grip.

Did you miss me, my dark little witch? Or were you perfectly content letting me gather dust?

That voice she couldn't blame on her muddied stream of consciousness. Her blade, her feyrie-forged blade, carried with it a personality Maddox had always failed to control.

The point of her blade dipped to the ground, suddenly feeling like it weighed fifty pounds. Oh, good. The thing was pouting.

Maddox hissed, "Aegis! Cut it out!"

The sword ignored her and now Atticus had a single brow quirked in question. Trying to cover her odd actions, Maddox blurted, "If I win, you must answer whatever question I ask."

"I don't care to play Truth or Dare with you again." Atticus wasn't happy with her choice, but she would stand by it. She could think of nothing else. He sighed, drawing it out rather dramatically. "Only one question?"

"Yes. That's the bet—take it or surrender now and spare yourself the humiliation."

Her sword, Aegis, rumbled in Maddox's mind. *I recognize that snobby voice.*

Maddox was grateful that the blade could only speak to her telepathically. She didn't want Atticus to know that an inanimate object was insulting him.

Is that Blackwell? Remember, his left hand is weak. Are we allowed to kill him yet?

If Maddox had known beforehand that the blades her feyrie neighbor forged had a habit of developing their own personality, she would have just ordered something off Etsy.

She doubted Atticus's blade ever gave him any backtalk.

Atticus was already in position waiting for her, and Maddox mirrored his stance. Aegis took pity on her and lightened its weight. Once her sword was in a "ready" pose, Atticus announced, "Begin!"

The ring of their blades meeting cleared Maddox's mind of all distractions. Though her muscle memory had faded, Maddox was more than able to keep up with her former rival. Atticus was testing her, each of his thrusts a mere tease. He was going to regret his insulting mercy.

This duel was more dance-like than their school-day face-offs. At the Academy, Maddox had always been so angry, so ready to prove herself, but now she failed to call up that former aggression.

"What the hell is wrong with you?" Atticus barked, his next attack nearly breaking through her defenses. "It's like you haven't picked up your sword in years."

Because she hasn't, Aegis growled. *She left me in the dark. In the dust. Just like her magic.*

Maddox swallowed her shame and said nothing. They exchanged a few more blows before Atticus pulled back.

He held out a hand to signal a break, and when Maddox lowered her sword, he tipped his mask up to stare at her. "Are you fucking with me?" His snort was abrupt and shocked. "I know it's been a long time since we sparred, but..."

"Is this some ploy to get me off-guard?" Maddox demanded.

Atticus snapped, "When was the last time you touched that blade? Be honest with me."

"Be honest? That's rich coming from you."

He had no patience for her stalling. "*Answer me.*"

"Our final exam," she breathed, hating him for his attention to detail. "Are you satisfied?"

"Satisfied?" Atticus sneered. "What has *happened* to you?" He sounded angry, but sad, too. "I understand leaving the school, *leaving me*, but why would you lock such a powerful, fucking beautiful part of yourself away? When you fought, you were like a goddess."

His grief-stricken compliments brought her shame forward, the burning heat of her guilt spreading from head to toe. "Put your fucking mask back on!" Maddox ordered. She held her position, her sword raised, and waited for him to comply. Atticus let his mask drop back into place and matched her stance, her energy.

Their swords tapped once, and the fight resumed.

Maddox couldn't deny she *was* out of practice. Her unused muscles ached and strained, no longer working on mere memory. And she felt painfully slow and clumsy.

That didn't mean Maddox was going to let Atticus win.

She didn't believe she was even capable of it.

His next failed thrust gave her an opening as he retreated. Maddox sprung forward, planting her boot into his chest. He staggered backward, but that was all.

He's heavier than before. Give us some more effort, little witch. When did you get so damned lazy? I'll tell Ashling if you don't get your head out of your ass.

"I forgot you liked kicking so much," Atticus snapped, a touch out of breath.

"No changing the rules *now*, Blackwell." Her swordsmanship had never matched well with the other necromancers. Her teacher had been a feyrie who'd been taught to *kill*, not to show off.

And Maddox had gladly adopted that ruthlessness.

She allowed her next overhead swing to bounce off a little too much as Atticus deflected it. Her sword ricocheted off his blade, connecting with her helmet. It stung like hell, but through the pain, Maddox saw Atticus falter and lower his weapon.

She charged, and his graceful steps turned into a frenzied backpedal. After a few more connections with her sword, she sent his blade flying away from him.

Further off balance, he was unable to stop her as Maddox ducked forward, reaching an arm underneath his thigh and lifting upwards until they both tumbled to the ground. She would not underestimate his weight a second time. Their backs both hit the floor, but Maddox recovered faster, standing and kicking down on Atticus's chest.

His gasp was pleasing to her ears. Maddox dropped and straddled him roughly, tearing off his face guard and pushing up the edge of her blade until it kissed his throat.

"You didn't make a *mistake*." Atticus scowled, letting his head fall back against the floor. "You tricked me."

"Of course." She removed her face gear and shook out her hair. "You make it too easy."

"Remove your blade. I've no desire for a shave."

Maddox relaxed the blade against his throat an inch, but that was all she gave him. "Perhaps I miss your clean-shaven look," she teased, and, before she realized what she was doing, Maddox let her fingers stroke his jawline, his beard tickling her skin.

There it was. His eyes traced her movement, flashing with that strange, reluctant longing. There was no telling how it happened, but Maddox suddenly found herself on her back with Atticus on top. Atticus had picked up a new trick, something her ego hadn't seen coming. Aegis cursed her in some feyrie tongue. Maddox didn't understand a word her blade said, nor did she try to. Her attention was all drawn to the man hovering over her.

There was no ignoring that they were both so different now. She had always remembered Atticus as a lanky twenty-year-old, confusing and mercurial. Now, with his weight bearing down on her, she could no longer ignore the man—the stranger—he'd become. Her throat was suddenly dry, and when she swallowed, Atticus's gaze snapped to her own.

"How dare you, you wicked thing." His smirk was mirthless. "How cruel you are to tease me, knowing what you know."

Her guilt returned. "I—"

"If your younger self could only see you now—" His eyes, uncovered, sparkled with mischief. What a jerk. She realized Atticus was *enjoying* this. "—how disappointed she would be."

If only he knew that a few years ago Maddox would have been shamefully delighted to be in such a predicament. She knew a half-dozen different ways to escape him and was confident she would succeed, but Maddox didn't move. She let his weight warm her while she glared, waiting.

"Is this how we'll go on?" Atticus asked, one hand taking her wrist and squeezing hard until Maddox, a hiss of pain escaping her, released her blade. "I want you, and now that you *know*, you'll use it against me? You hate me and I deserve it, but I didn't think you were so heartless."

Properly chastised, Maddox cut him off. "I'm sorry. I knew if I looked hurt, you'd freeze. That was shitty of me." She would not apologize for her more recent transgression—for touching him. Maddox didn't feel capable of discussing it without revealing more about herself than she wanted Atticus to know.

That tight hold on her wrist faded. Maddox almost missed the pain. Atticus would not look back at her until she placed her hands softly on his chest, this time with no intention of pushing him away. Maddox continued, now truly apologetic, "When we're in competition with each other, it's like I'm a different person. I don't think about how my actions might affect you." It was easier to admit such things as an adult.

Her revelation seemed to burn him. Atticus scowled. "I never wanted that."

"I didn't either," she snapped, her old hurt flaring with a vengeance. Maddox soothed it down and added, trying to lighten the dark, vulnerable mood, "I'm clearly out of practice. Perhaps we should make a habit out of this. My sword would appreciate it."

Atticus had tied his hair back before their sparring match, but now some strands escaped to fall across his brow. His expression was dark as he agreed. "We should. It would give you an excuse to get yourself under me. You seem to be enjoying it."

Maddox used her left leg to lock Atticus's right ankle against her side and used her other leg to roll them over. Besides a rough exhale at the switch in positions, Atticus didn't look uncomfortable at all.

She felt him relax underneath her, which shut up whatever witty retort she'd been about to serve him.

"You know," Atticus began, his eyes narrowed. "When you accepted my proposal—" Hades, Maddox wished he'd use a different word. "—I thought your true intention in joining this project was to find a way to get back at me. To punish me."

"Still a narcissist, I see. I don't make my life decisions based on you." This conversation was headed in a direction Maddox didn't think she was ready for. "I want this project to succeed, that's all. I don't want to punish you."

"But you could," he countered, his voice dropping nearly to a whisper. Maddox had to lean forward just to understand him. "You could punish me so easily."

"How?" The word left before Maddox could think about the ramifications. Her curiosity always got the best of her, and Atticus confused her still.

"By looking at me like you remember what we used to be. I've caught you once or twice already."

She sniffed. "I never—"

Atticus struck her with a laugh. "Oh, you have. And it fucking *hurts*. But I think you can do better."

Get off him. End whatever the hell this is.

"After all this time, you still think you know better than me," she snapped. "Enlighten me, Atticus. How can I destroy you better?"

"Touch me."

Maddox hoped he would mistake anger as the reason for the red that flushed her cheeks. The memory of the warmth of his jaw underneath her fingertips was really to blame. "I already did that today—"

He cut her off almost desperately. "*Not* like you hated me. If you touched me like *that*, Maddox, I would unravel."

Memories of past duels with Atticus quickly came to mind. She had never lost a duel while at the Academy, and every time she faced off with Atticus, she had walked away wondering why he seemed almost pleased to have her blade at his throat.

Was he a masochist? Maddox slid her hand up his chest, her palm resting against his throat. "Like this?" She was new to such things, so she kept it superficial, merely pressing her fingertips lightly into his neck.

Atticus hadn't expected her to play along with his game. His eyes widened as he purred, "Yes, yes, you're *perfect.*" He squeezed her thighs, demonstrating the pressure he wanted from her.

Maddox complied without thinking, increasing the pressure on his throat until he softened his own grip. Her hands should have been shaking. Physically, maybe she appeared in control, but on the inside, Maddox was coming undone.

He was pinned underneath her and at her mercy. Atticus was allowing her to punish him in all the ways she secretly wanted.

Maddox suddenly relaxed her hand, releasing his constricted airway. "I'm not sure how to..." she began, twisting a lock of her hair until she felt the pain in her scalp. "I mean, I'm not confident I can do this safely."

"Would you like me to demonstrate?" Atticus breathed.

The silence between them was heavy, stifling. Maddox nodded before logic could stall her. "Yes."

His magic snapped into existence, curling around her shoulders and pulling her to the floor. Her back hit with a soft thud against the padded surface, and Atticus was on top of her before she could catch her breath.

His hand slid up her body, starting from her stomach, slipping between her breasts, and stopping at her neck. He applied pressure to the sides of her neck, leaving the front rather stress-free.

"Keep off the front," Atticus lectured her, his voice deeper and more authoritative. Maddox could imagine him as a professor easily. "Apply pressure to the sides, go slow, keep your eyes on me, and I'll let you know if we need to stop."

"Okay," she managed, waiting for him to free her.

Atticus's weight remained, and his lips twitched into that smirk she loathed and loved. "Oh, Maddox. If you truly wish to punish me, you'll have to work for it."

Infuriating, she thought. *Inevitable,* she realized.

Her magic slowly rose, materializing around her body until she thrust all her power at him. Atticus fell to the floor, her magic pushing against his chest to give her time to straddle him again. Some of her magic trailed up his body to pin his wrists down. Maddox vanished all traces of her magic, except for the power trapping his wrists, and caught Atticus's throat just as he taught her.

His eyes lit up instantly. Atticus could barely manage the words as he gasped, "Maddox, I love you."

Maddox knew what he wanted her to say, and she did. "I hate you," she returned without feeling.

He relaxed, but whether it was from her words or her now-loosened grip, Maddox couldn't guess. Atticus sighed. "I know."

She didn't want him to *agree* with her. Maddox repeated herself, but this time frustration laced her words with poison. "I *hate* you."

"That's better. Say it again," Atticus demanded. His magic fought with hers until he managed to slip one of his hands free of her spell. Atticus gripped her wrist, the one pinning his throat, and locked it in place. "Say it again and kiss me."

The room was dead silent, save for Atticus's ragged breath. Part of her wanted to listen to the kind, quiet parts of her that begged her to stop. But the rest...

She *wanted* to give in. To feel his fire again. Despite what it would cost them both in the end. If she gave him this, it would determine the rest of their relationship. Their dark, demented dance would continue, leaving no room for anything more. They would hurt each other until one of them broke.

Well, she thought. *How much more fucked could things get?*

Maddox stole what little breath the man could catch. She kissed him, one hand on his throat and the other tugging his hair until it came loose. She threaded her fingers into it, angling his head to deepen their kiss.

Atticus, after he recovered from his initial shock, was frantic. He broke his other wrist free so his hands could dance all over her body until they settled for grabbing her ass to pull her against him.

Maddox broke their kiss, her face aflame. Atticus gave her a two-handed squeeze before gripping the back of her neck and guiding her down until he could kiss her throat.

His words tickled her as she grew more and more sensitive. "Do you have any idea how *crazy* you make me? There doesn't seem to be a fucking thing I can do about it, either."

That's right. Atticus's feelings for her were something he was ashamed of.

His teeth rested against her skin as he reminded her, his voice husky, "You forgot to say it." Maddox shivered as he slid a hand underneath her shirt and ran it up her spine. Why was it only *his* touch that did this to her? His hands wandered further as he said, "I want to hear you say it while my hands are all over you."

What was she supposed to say again? She was trying not to think for once and couldn't recall—

I hate you.

"No." The word fled her mouth, her better nature finally speaking up.

Atticus's touch immediately vanished. His eyes were wide and vulnerable as he watched her expression, searching for where he had gone wrong.

She rushed to clarify. "Let me explain. I don't want you like this," Maddox admitted, covering her face with one hand. "I *missed* you. I missed my friend."

" *What?*" Atticus suddenly sat up, and Maddox snatched the hand around his throat away, curling it against her heart. "Why would you miss *me?*"

She'd wondered that herself. Their friendship ended so long ago. It wasn't logical to feel anything for him anymore.

How Maddox longed to simplify what she felt for him. If she could gather all those past and present emotions and jam them into a single box labeled "I hate Atticus", oh, she gladly would. But she was not raised to think so black and white. Her family prized empathy above all else and gave second, third, and even fourth chances.

Maddox could not hate him because she understood him.

And Atticus had known her once, and that was what hurt the most. If he asked, if he *explained,* Maddox would forgive him. Surely Atticus must know that?

But he hadn't explained or asked to be forgiven, not once since he turned away from her. Was a momentary blow to his pride too great a cost for her forgiveness?

What was she worth to him?

Atticus silently waited for her answer, and that pissed her off. Even if Maddox could explain why she missed him, now was not the time. *Enough.* If this continued, Maddox knew her emotions would get the better of her and they'd either sleep together or she'd cry. And she wasn't about to risk crying in front of Atticus.

Maddox got up quickly, pushing down at his chest to aid her momentum. "Haven't you taunted me enough?" she cursed, bending down to retrieve her sword. "Aren't you sick of it?"

Atticus coughed. "I'm sorry. I was out of hand." Maddox heard him suck his teeth, and when she could bear to look at him, she saw his skin was flushed as well. "You won the duel, so I'll answer your question." Atticus remained seated in the middle of the room, rubbing his temples.

Gods, she almost forgot about their stupid bet. The situation reminded her too much of the day in the feyrie woods when she had stolen his truth from him. Maddox shook her head violently.

Maddox moved over to the counter where she had left her sheath. While she put her sword carefully away, ignoring Aegis's complaints, she explained, "No, Atticus. I cheated. The win should go to you, but you'll regret it. I haven't cooked anything more complex than scrambled eggs." How surreal it was to suddenly discuss dinner as if nothing had just happened, or almost happened, between them.

"I..." He lifted off the ground and brushed off his workout clothes. "I can teach you, if you have the patience for it."

Her laugh escaped and spooked them both. "Do *you* have the patience for it?"

"I just need time to get used to it again."

He used to cook with his grandmother—she remembered that now. "Okay, I'll shower and meet you in the kitchen?" Maddox hated how her voice sounded—unsure and too high-pitched.

He nodded, letting her leave the room first.

Maddox waited for Atticus, poking around in his kitchen cabinets and avoiding the temptation to run back up to her room. Edgar hopped around on the kitchen island, something Maddox was sure Atticus would hate. She shooed the bird off the counter, opening the kitchen door that led outside to let Edgar free. The black cat she'd spotted earlier limped inside.

"Oh! Are you supposed to be in here?" she fretted, but the cat ignored her. Maddox told herself that if the animal was crouched right outside the door, waiting for such an opportunity, surely it belonged to Atticus?

The cat was matted and far too thin. It stopped at Maddox's feet, curled its tail around its body, and fell asleep. Maddox bent down to stroke the animal, running her hand up and down its back before she realized the cat wasn't breathing.

You've got to be kidding me.

She heard a door open and close somewhere in the house, spurring her magic into action before she could think. Red traces of smoke coiled around the cat before slipping through its nostrils. The now resurrected cat drew in a deep, though shaky, breath and jumped to its feet. It shook its coat out, sending hair and dirt everywhere, before the cat slipped out of the kitchen and further into the home.

If Atticus didn't have a cat before, he now had an *undead* cat. Either way, she wasn't going to admit her possible mistake to her archrival.

Well, I guess we aren't rivals anymore. We're supposed to be on the same team. Maddox rubbed her wrist, examining the purple fingerprints Atticus had left while disarming her. The sight of his marks on her skin made her ache, but not where she should have been aching.

When Atticus finally showed, he looked as uneasy as she felt. What was this fluttering happening in her stomach? Hunger, perhaps?

"I'm not sure what to make," Maddox admitted, trailing behind him as he went to the sink to wash his hands.

"Why don't we make something familiar? What's your favorite thing your mother makes?"

Every meal her mother made sounded too simple to say in front of Atticus. Everything he cooked belonged in a restaurant she couldn't afford.

"I don't know. Steak? Potatoes? We're not very complex when it comes to food."

"We can do that. I'll keep it basic since you're new to this. Don't make this into a *competition*. It's okay if it doesn't come out perfectly the first time." Atticus began tapping on his cell phone. "We'll have to wait for the grocery delivery to arrive, but it's early. There's plenty of time."

Maddox joined him as he leaned against the kitchen island. "I just wanted to say again, I'm sorry about cheating. Here I am living in your house, eating your groceries, and I still pulled a dirty trick like that. I need to leave our past in the past. I—"

"You make me sound so innocent." He shifted uncomfortably. "Really, I'm not so altruistic. I have some selfish reasons for asking you to stay here."

She always focused on the wrong thing. "Asking?! You practically kidnapped me," Maddox complained. *What other reason was Atticus referring to?*

He clarified, "I couldn't keep you here if I tried. Though, if your cuisine is as pathetic as you claim, perhaps I know the reason you're still here."

"Yes, yes, we finally found something you're better at than me." Maddox rolled her eyes, pretending that fact didn't annoy her at all. It did, though.

Atticus smiled. "I think we could find a few other things. I'm an excellent dancer, for example."

"Okay, two things." Dancing was something Maddox did alone, never with a partner. That involved far too much physical contact. "Though I've never seen you dance, so you could be exaggerating your skills."

"If we decipher this page, I'm sure the Academy's benefactors will throw quite the event for us. I can prove myself to you then."

How would he prove it? Let Maddox stand back and observe as he danced with another, or would he demonstrate his ability as *her* partner? Maddox refused to linger on the thought, and silence returned between them.

Atticus never could allow a moment of quiet to pass. He jumped topics quickly. "I should tell you, we're not working on the artifact tomorrow. I have class all day, and Lochlan thinks we should take a break after every interaction. Especially you."

Something illogical inside her wanted to argue. Maddox squashed it down, asking quietly, "Would you like me to describe it to you? The page?"

Those reddish eyes looked very warm. "Please."

Maddox gave a very detailed debriefing of the page—what it looked like, felt like, what it even smelled like. Not good, was the answer to that last one. Atticus drank in every single scrap of information, his eyes never leaving her own.

"Atticus." She hadn't removed her necklace since discovering its origin, but she had slipped the bee charm underneath her shirt. "You bought this necklace for me, didn't you?"

"Yes," he admitted sourly. "I wanted to give it to you face-to-face, but I was a coward."

Maddox nodded, playing with the gold chain. "Would you like me to stop wearing it?"

"You *still* want to wear it? Knowing now that it came from me?"

"It's..." How should she say it? "It's been a good luck charm for me, but

I'll stop if it bothers you."

Hades, she wished he would allow her this small, metallic comfort. The tiny weight against her collarbones shouldn't have been as significant as it was, but...

"No." Atticus shrugged. "It's fine. I know it doesn't mean anything to you."

But that wasn't right. It did mean something to her, even though she had assumed another person had given it to her. If she had thought critically on it at all, Maddox would have realized that, of course, Atticus had been the source.

CHAPTER 17
WARLOCK

"**Y**ou recall the deal the Commission made with you?" Lochlan asked, cornering Atticus in the lab outside the cleanroom. "Don't forget, while you study that sample, to think about how to destroy it as well as decipher it. Of course, I want to know what it hides, but we must be able to contain it at all costs."

Atticus didn't care for being supervised. "I read the terms before I signed. I don't need the constant reminders." Atticus wished Lochlan would take a vow of silence.

"See," the exorcist said as he frowned, his tone sharp, "I don't think that's true. You and Miss Abernathy seem to have something *personal* going on, and it puts me on edge."

His concern irked Atticus. "Don't be so dramatic. What you're insinuating couldn't be more wrong."

"We aren't playing with some basic grimoire here!" Lochlan pointed back at the cleanroom that contained the artifact. "That page was able to affect Miss Abernathy, and we haven't even *read* it yet. If it infects her badly enough, I'll have to take her to the Commission's main office, and we all know what her chances are of making it out of there."

What went into the Washington D.C. Commission of Magic Management office rarely came back out again. Atticus dropped the notebook he'd been scribbling in and took a quick step toward Lochlan, red smoke curling around him.

His magic did not seem to frighten Lochlan—it only confirmed something for him. "All I am asking for here, Mr. Blackwell, is that when I say we're done, you side with me. No matter what Miss Abernathy might ask of you. With her exposure, her opinion may be influenced by—"

"I understand." Atticus didn't care to think about that possibility—that Maddox might be cursed by that small scrap of paper. It would mean he was directly responsible for it. That he had dragged her back here to suffer, just so he could be in her proximity once again.

Selfish. Foolish. A better man would have asked Lochlan to take the page back to the Commission now—unread.

Atticus had realized what sort of man he was a long time ago.

He raised his hand like a boy scout. "We'll proceed with caution and stop altogether if we need to. You have my word."

Lochlan squinted at Atticus for a long time, as though his lie hadn't gone undetected, before the Commission agent quickly left the room.

Atticus had to be *very* careful as he tested the sample. Even separated as it was, the tiny piece Maddox had cut off still radiated power. He kept it contained, using Maddox whenever he needed something done to the sample.

Though Lochlan had warned Maddox against being in the lab while Atticus worked, to minimize her exposure, she visited often. She made herself as useful as Atticus would allow her to be, giving him someone to bounce ideas off and making coffee. What she really wanted was obvious—access to the sample.

It was the only thing Atticus could deny her.

Atticus ushered her to the door. "No, you cannot look. You agreed to five minutes, and it's been seven. Leave."

Maddox whined, "Your watch is fast."

"If you knew how much my watch *cost*—"

"Oh! Fine!" She stomped out of the lab, but not before she took a theatrical swig of his coffee—as if that would keep him from drinking the rest.

Ten minutes later, Maddox came back, but this time Atticus had locked the door. She rapped on the small viewing window until he looked up to see her sticking her tongue out at him.

A week passed and Atticus burst into their assigned study room to find Maddox standing before the bookshelf, her fingers grazing the edges of the shelves with boredom.

Atticus announced, "I think I have a solution." She stilled, turning her head and waiting for more. Atticus smirked. "I just finished the first batch of chemicals. We should be able to reveal what's on that page."

Maddox ran at him, placing both palms against his chest as she shoved him back out the door. Atticus backpedaled until his hip hit a library cart. "Maddox, slow down! Lochlan wants to wait until Friday. We have to prepare you to be in the cleanroom for that long."

"He wants to *wait*? What for? Does Father Blondie have a hot date tonight?" Maddox hunched forward dramatically.

"Impatience is quite becoming on you," Atticus teased.

Maddox gave his tie a quick yank. The action was altogether too friendly for their usual antics, and it brought an embarrassing amount of heat to Atticus's face. "It's only Tuesday. I'm going to be bouncing off the walls until Friday," she whined. Atticus could think of several ways to work out her anxious energy. He also knew if he voiced such naughty suggestions, he would meet the end of her blade.

"I think Lochlan is ill. The man didn't even shave this morning. Quite unusual." He tossed his car keys to Maddox, and she caught them easily. "Anyway, I have the perfect distraction. Gaia wants our help this afternoon with her dueling tournament. Go get your sword from the house—and don't make me regret letting you drive my car."

"One question." Maddox grinned, holding the keys behind her back. "How attached are you to your paint job?"

While Atticus watched Gaia fawn over Maddox's sword as she blushed underneath the compliments, he wished regret would cease churning his insides. If his teenage-self had been more attentive to the other students around him, he might have intervened more when the Rowans targeted Gaia during her first semester. Perhaps she might have stayed at the Academy, instead of leaving to be homeschooled. Maddox might have had a friend. A *friend* would have been much better than a *rival*.

But his teenage years had been a fog of grief—and the after-effects of the *Chameleon* potion had taken him years to adjust to.

Atticus lingered on the outskirts of the gymnasium, letting Gaia and Maddox lead the dueling lesson. Both women's faces were flush with excitement as their swords clashed in a few testing strikes. Most of the students remained enthralled with the battle—only a few worried about their own upcoming duels, and Atticus helped them perfect their grips and stances.

A few of the other professors sat in the bleachers, sipping cups of coffee or tea as they placed bets on which student would emerge victorious. Angeline wiggled her fingers at Atticus when he caught her eye. The betting was all her idea, the mischievous woman. At least it distracted her from pestering Atticus about his relationship with Maddox.

The reluctant object of his burdensome affections wandered toward him during a break amid the tournament. Maddox sipped from a small cup of water, glistening and flushed. She had always been most attractive to him with a blade in her hand—it was why he always volunteered to be her second. Otherwise, when he dueled her, he always found himself...*distracted.* Not what he wanted to be when pointy things were involved.

"The student body..." Maddox began, gesturing towards the students who were laughing with each other in a singular mass. "I don't see any outcasts."

He shrugged. "There are issues, but Gaia, Angeline, and I have tried to keep the usual cliques from reforming. It's constant work to battle the prejudices of their parents."

"But you're still trying?"

Atticus didn't wish to discuss his current success when all he could think about was his past failure. "We're still trying. In a few decades, who knows? Maybe what happened to you and Gaia won't ever happen again."

She bumped her shoulder against him lightly. "That's wonderful, Atticus. I mean it."

He didn't want her admiration, not about this. "Better late than never, I suppose."

She circled to stand in front of him, a hand resting on the sheathed sword at her side. Her grin was crooked, beautiful, and unearned. "What's wrong? I thought you loved being praised."

It was too easy to let his mind run away with that, with the daydream of Maddox praising him, but Atticus brushed it off. "Only when it's deserved."

CHAPTER 18
SON OF A WITCH

Summer—the heat, the humidity, the painfully bright rays that tore at Atticus's sensitive eyes...

He hated all of it.

Atticus would have preferred to stay at the Academy throughout the summer, but it wasn't allowed. Instead, he was stuck haunting the empty halls of his family estate, counting down the days until his third year at the Academy could begin. And counting down the minutes until his older brother left the estate, taking off down the drive with a car that was much faster than what their parents should have trusted Giles with.

With his brother gone, Atticus only had to wait for his appointed guardian, a rather unobservant man named Mr. Thomas, to make his daily trek to the graveyard. This wasn't to tend the graves, as Atticus did that himself—it was to smoke unseen by the estate's security cameras. Atticus didn't care what Mr. Thomas did out there, it gave Atticus an opportunity.

Dragging the corded telephone into his bedroom, shutting the door, careful not to unplug the cord in the process, Atticus dialed Maddox's home phone number from memory.

He prayed anyone other than her grandfather would answer.

Colter Abernathy rumbled through the phone, "Is this Blackwell again?"

"It's for book club!" he blurted, pinching his leg at the crack in his voice. "Is Maddox there?"

"She's still choring. Call back in—"

There was an unseen struggle and static plagued his ears until Maddox huffed into the phone, "I'm here! Don't hang up!"

His relief was embarrassing. "Did you finish the book?"

"Did I finish the book? Are you kidding me? Of course I did."

He relaxed, opening his freshly annotated copy of *Pet Sematary*. "Your grandfather isn't going to listen in on another line again, is he?"

"Probably. Just start talking about the book and he'll get bored."

Atticus looked forward to their daily chats more than anything else currently going on in his life. Summer crawled by with snail-like speed but having something consistent in his life helped him feel less alone. He'd been unsure whether this could work. He knew he asked a lot of her, and Maddox hadn't pressed him when he made her promise to wait for him to call and never call him herself. Of course, he'd offered some excuse about his brother sounding too much like him and claiming that Giles would try to embarrass her if he answered the phone first.

It was lame, but Maddox had simply agreed.

He wasn't used to things being simple.

Maddox kept her promise not to call, but her family wasn't aware of Atticus's strange stipulation. Her grandfather called the estate a week before the start of the school year.

"This is about Atticus?" Giles drawled, his voice deepening at the end of his sentence. "Yes, this is his father. Call me Rami."

Atticus backtracked through the second floor, following his brother's voice, until he found Giles in their mother's study, a phone pressed to his ear. There was a wicked, yet playful grin on Giles's face as he nodded along to whatever was being said on the other end of the line.

"Who are you talking to?" Atticus demanded as he reached to pull the phone cord out of the wall. Giles gripped the back of his shirt and hauled him back before he could kill the phone.

"Oh, you *loved* having Atticus stay over?" Giles sounded unbothered as Atticus tried to wrestle the phone out of his hands. "I'm sure he had a great time—that trip is all he blathers on about."

That holiday trip to the Abernathy farm had been a secret from the rest of his family, except for his out-of-the-country father, who had happily paid for the plane ticket for Atticus to visit his friend. Giles knowing about his connection to Maddox Abernathy wasn't ideal, but what he really worried his brother would find out was—

"Atticus seemed *sick* to you? But that was years ago. I assure you, he's fine now." Giles's grin wavered as he gave up trying to physically shove Atticus off him. Magic the color of river clay materialized and wrapped around Atticus's ankles. One good yank sent him to the floor, his chin connecting with the hardwood.

That wasn't enough for Giles. His magic continued pulling on Atticus, dragging him out of the study and along the hallway floor until he reached the top of the stairwell. There the magic stopped tugging, though Atticus hadn't expected the mercy, and pinned him to the floor instead.

Giles emerged from the study, the phone nowhere in sight, and knelt next to his little brother. His fingers tapped on the floor thoughtfully. "I thought this could be good for you. You having a little girlfriend. Something to keep you from spending your days in the cemetery." Giles allowed the magic to relax only enough to let Atticus lift his head. "Necromancers that spend all day around corpses eventually spend their nights with one."

Atticus gagged. His brother could be rather vulgar, especially after their mother had left for her new career in England.

"I'm trying to look out for you," Giles continued, pinching at his fine brow. Atticus hated that they looked so alike—he could see himself in Giles when this cruelty emerged—a genetic gift from their mother, no doubt.

"I don't need you—"

"*Listen*, little brother." Giles's words were accentuated by a sharp tug of Atticus's hair. "I don't care who you fuck, but make sure it's someone who doesn't notice your...*oddities.*"

"It—it isn't like that between us!" Atticus spat, pushing desperately on the floor.

"How can you not see that's worse?"

The magic pinning Atticus to the floor released all at once. Atticus rolled to his back, chest heaving as he regained his breath. "Just leave me alone."

"Wish that I could." Giles sighed, rising to stand over his younger brother. "But I don't think you'll let me. I'll fill you in on the conversation I just had. Those green witches, they know something's wrong with you. Your friend keeps them updated. They want to *help*. As if the Blackwells would ever need anything from them."

When Atticus made to sit up, Giles forced him back down with a quick kick to his shoulder. "As long as you're friends with that girl, they won't stop picking, won't stop asking the wrong questions. You need to take that far more seriously than you are."

That was enough. Atticus shoved Giles's foot away and scrambled to his feet. "I can handle this myself."

"You're lucky *I* answered the phone and not Mr. Thomas. He'd rat you out to Mother. I'm Cynthia's favorite son, so trust me when I tell you...you don't want a Blackwell woman's attention. I *thought* you learned that lesson once before."

Though they were close in age, Atticus and Giles never spent much time together. Giles was always busy—extra dueling lessons, business classes at the local college, internships at Blackened Salt Apothecary. Atticus had always thought Giles didn't notice him at all, but when Atticus watched his brother now, he saw the cold logic in his eyes. There was no denying Atticus took up some space in Giles's mind, and there would be no reasoning with him now. Atticus was in danger, and there was a very simple solution.

Lamely, Atticus said, "I'm her only friend." *And she's mine.*

"I know that old man's type. He won't leave it alone. And once you're found out, do you think he'd let you around her ever again?" At his wince, Giles laughed. "*That's* what gets to you? Being separated from your little girlfriend? You *should* be worried about..."

Even Giles wasn't sadistic enough to say it aloud.

Giles adopted a new tone, something quiet and hesitant. "Have you gotten any better at controlling your symptoms? If that old man pesters you again, could you hide it?"

Atticus knew he must truly be pathetic in his brother's eyes if Giles was offering him another chance. What he wanted to say and what the truth was were two very different things.

"No, I don't think I could hide it. Not from Colter Abernathy."

Giles clicked his tongue. "You can't go back to that farm. As long as you stay here—" Giles gestured to the fading walls that surrounded them. That *imprisoned* them both. "—then you'll be safe."

Atticus nodded. "I understand."

This was a mercy Giles would not extend a second time. Atticus waited for his brother to leave before calling his magic to gather into his palm. It swirled, a cyclone of red smoke, yet still in his control. He thought briefly of Maddox, and his magic turned to a sickly liquid, drops of blood flowing freely from his palm.

Each droplet hit the floor and hissed like acid.

The first semester had flown by with Maddox at his side. After three years of friendship, Atticus felt Maddox knew him better than anyone ever had—or ever would again. This knowledge didn't help his resistance to sleep.

Atticus spent most nights staring up at the flaking ceiling of his dorm room, the twin bed's springs digging into his back. Despite the discomfort, he rested better at the Academy than he ever did at home.

His eyelids grew heavy, soothing the tired itchiness of his eyeballs. Tonight, his dreams did not drag him back into his past, but instead sent him teasing images of his future. They showed him lies.

Atticus woke painfully panicked, sweat running down his brow and his clothes sticking to his skin.

The floor of his dorm room held several inches of what looked like blood, but Atticus knew it was something much worse.

Dropping off the bed and wincing at the squelch of his feet hitting the wet carpet, Atticus crept to the door and peered into the hallway. This was *bad*. The liquid had seeped underneath his door and formed a river of magic that ran toward the girls' side of the dorms.

Atticus did not have to guess where the dark water led. Maddox's room was the second stop he made every morning, right after he hit the coffee truck parked outside the school grounds. The human who ran the truck didn't care if a rogue zombie or two passed him by as long as he continued to profit off the sleep-deprived students.

Maddox's door was unlocked, a bad habit she'd learned from her family. Atticus pushed open the door slowly, the unoiled hinges protesting with squeals.

Her room was flooded with his viscous magic, that blood-red, tainted sorcery defying gravity and inching up her bedframe.

It was going to do as he secretly wished when he allowed his heart to wish at all. It would consume her. Ensnare her. Make her forever *his*, no matter the means.

His selfish magic was too focused on its accidental task. It did not pull back when Atticus demanded it to stop. When he begged it to.

"Shit, shit, shit!" Atticus tore at the roots of his short hair before running down a few doors to Giles's most recent girlfriend's door. He rapped on the frame quietly, despite his swelling anxiety.

Natalie answered his call, rolled her eyes at the state of him, and pulled Giles out of her twin bed. His brother mumbled curses as he half-dressed and met Atticus at the door.

Giles fought an angry yawn. "Someone better be dead."

Atticus didn't say a word, only pulled his brother down the hall by his arm. Atticus stopped them before Maddox's room, reopened the door, and waited.

Giles stared for only a moment, the incriminating scene drawing out a strangled curse. Atticus's magic had made it to Maddox herself, that blood wrapping around and staining her skin. His magic crept up her walls and coated her ceiling.

"What the fuck is this?" Giles hissed.

There was no other explanation. Though it was horrific, Atticus confessed, "I love her."

"That isn't what this is. Stop it now," Giles whispered, eyes wide. "Fucking right now—"

"Do you think I'd come to you if I hadn't already tried?"

Giles read the desperation in Atticus's plea and tore Atticus from the scene.

Giles half-dragged Atticus through the Blackwell family cemetery, leading him to Theodora's tomb. Dawn was approaching—if anyone noticed what was happening in Maddox's room...

Giles's hand shook as he pressed it against the door to the tomb. Magic spidered from his stretched fingers and the door swung open.

"Don't leave me in here all day," Atticus pleaded before Giles threw him inside. The magic wards inside the mausoleum flashed and flickered so brightly that Atticus was blinded for a moment. The wavering wards were a sign that Atticus was completely out of control.

Giles didn't answer for a long moment, unable to stop watching the stone coffin that held their grandmother. Finally, he said hoarsely, "I think, until you get this under control, you should sleep here. I can bring a cot from *her* old tomb raiding supplies." Giles refused to say Theodora's name even now. "You really could have hurt that girl. I think you know what you need to do."

The doors slammed shut, and Atticus laid on his back next to Theodora's resting place, staring at each rune his family had carved into the tomb to prevent graverobbers.

The runes glowed softly, a dim pink in total darkness. They were created to drain magic, to weaken a trespassing necromancer. Giles had activated the runes before leaving. It was the quickest way to fix Atticus when he lost his grip on his magic.

He prayed to Hades—each plea ignored as they always were—that Maddox was okay. He prayed she slept through the entire ordeal.

Atticus understood, finally, what he *had* to do. Until he was skilled enough to completely mask his symptoms, Atticus could not risk the company of someone who actually cared about him.

He dreamt that night of Theodora's laughter.

CHAPTER 19
WITCH

On Friday morning, three solutions sat before her. Maddox's anxiety rose as she looked from one small vial to the next. Atticus claimed she could apply the solutions in whatever order she desired, that one bottle wasn't more likely than any other, and still, she worried.

She so hated getting things wrong.

Her cleanroom gown felt stuffy, despite the cool weather, as she slid her legs inside the pants. October was almost here, Redhollow's temperature had plummeted, and the skies were the same dreary grey she remembered.

While Atticus slipped a lanyard with the key for the artifact's case over Maddox's head, Lochlan made for the electric keypad. Without turning to acknowledge him, he ordered Atticus, "Get out. Your actions during Maddox's first encounter with the artifact prove you can't be trusted inside the laboratory right now."

In the library, the exorcist and necromancer got along surprisingly well, but Atticus was not used to being bossed around in his own lab and it showed.

"No." Atticus folded his arms and readjusted his glasses. He'd replaced them as soon as they had returned to Redhollow. "Absolutely not. Exorcist you may be, but you need a necromancer with you—"

"I *need* someone I don't have to knock sense into at the slightest hint of Maddox being in danger." Lochlan pointed toward the exit, his stance unyielding. "I won't have you ruining this experiment, Mr. Blackwell. You failed to follow protocol. Leave."

Atticus ran a hand over his face in a way that Maddox suspected was attempting to hide the flush blooming on his skin. "Fine. I will remain outside, but I will be watching the security feed. If something goes wrong and you aren't handling it, you'll be answering to me."

"Turn your ass around," Lochlan snapped, holding his palm up as a barricade.

Atticus's eyes widened, his brow furrowed, but he set his jaw and whirled around. His white coat whipped dramatically behind him as he exited, drawing Maddox's eye. Atticus had always looked his best in a lab coat. *Stop ogling him!* She bit her cheek until the pain helped her refocus as Lochlan ran through the entry procedure with her.

Once she stepped inside the cleanroom and the *whoosh* of the automatic door sealed her in, Maddox felt that same overbearing longing she had the first time she encountered the artifact. She doubted increased exposure would strengthen her immunity to it. Each time she stepped inside this room, she was less and less prepared.

Lochlan rapped on the glass, reminding her of her task. Maddox nodded and placed the three vials on the workstation inside. She unlocked the artifact's case and exposed the worn paper to the air.

Black, oily magic hissed as it gathered around the paper. She glanced about the floor, catching herself too late. That buzzing and the sound of scuttling insects she heard must be another one of the artifact's tricks.

Which author had penned this particular page? She internally ran through the list of suspected authors, a rather incomplete list as the book had vanished over a century ago, along with, suspiciously, most references to the text. That longing she had endured, horrific and unending...she could not tell if one author was more likely than the others to have caused it.

Maddox swiped the middle vial, bringing it over the page to test a corner of the scrap. The vial's stopper included a small brush, which Maddox used to apply a smooth wipe across the left-hand corner.

There was no adverse reaction, so she waited a few more minutes before placing some of the solution where text would most likely be hiding.

"Nothing," she announced to satisfy Lochlan's curiosity. For an almost-priest, the man was shockingly interested in darker texts.

As she walked back and forth between the artifact's case and where the vials were stored, Maddox thought she heard a second pair of footsteps, lagging only a second behind her own. She quickened her pace.

The next vial's contents burned like acid when she applied it to the page.

Oh, Goddess. If that acid spread any further, the artifact would be destroyed. Maddox fumbled to fix it.

Her actions were graceless, but at the sight of the slightest possibility of a mistake, Maddox's lonely school years came rushing back to her. She had to be better than all of them—had to prove herself all over again to those pretentious assholes. If she ruined this page, their last chance to understand the Tome of the Undying, Maddox would not survive the shame.

Her shaking hand slipped into the spreading acid as she tried to cut off the damaged corner. She felt a slight pinch in her finger, almost like a bug bite, but ignored it as she removed the acid-touched portion. Nothing mattered more to her than preventing further destruction.

Her finger ached. Should she stop? But there was still one vial left. Maddox side-eyed the exorcist. Lochlan seemed calm. He hadn't yet noticed her panic.

Maddox couldn't risk being forced off the project—this was her last chance to achieve her dream. If she wanted back into necromancer academia, she couldn't fuck up her first project.

Yes, something inside her agreed. *You've been missing something these past five years. You've been living as a shell of yourself. The real Maddox, the complete Maddox, needs this project to go perfectly.*

A void sat heavily in her stomach, a reminder of how broken she was. She let the emptiness sit and stew before clearing her throat. Maddox would keep going. After all, there was only one more vial left to try.

By this point, her hope was squished thoroughly. Maddox still applied an even brush of vial three's solution, but Maddox felt nothing until a rust-brown swirl appeared upon the skin.

She froze, her fingers shaking despite her best efforts, and gently applied another small streak of the solution.

A frenzied scrawl appeared, and Maddox released a shriek of joy. Lochlan slapped a hand against the glass, glaring at her with a furrowed brow. He must have mistaken her yelp for fear, and Maddox waved a hand at him to communicate that she was fine.

Only when she ran for the cleanroom workbench and pulled out a notebook and pen did Lochlan understand.

It was tedious work—applying a little of the solution and then pausing to recapture the scratchy text by hand. Cameras rarely worked on artifacts of this nature—at best, the picture would turn out blurry, and at worst, the camera itself would become cursed. Interesting, but not helpful.

As Maddox wrote, that humdrum of insects only increased. Her body itched terribly as if something small and many-legged was crawling under her skin.

You can't make another mistake here, she scolded herself. Even the tiniest misprint could ruin everything she and Atticus hoped to achieve. Maddox did her best to ignore the phantom insects swarming her body and kept writing.

Once she was absolutely certain she'd copied down each letter precisely, Maddox locked the artifact back in its case. Lochlan had overloaded her with protective charms and spent an hour muttering Latin over her this morning, so Maddox hoped the aftermath of this encounter would not be as painful as the first. At least there were no disembodied hands grabbing for her or dark promises whispered into her ear.

Maddox escaped the room, notebook in hand, and slumped into a desk chair. She tore the hood off her head and cast it on the ground.

Lochlan locked the cleanroom again and headed straight for the notebook. Maddox pressed it against her chest, her eyes narrowing. "I want Atticus to see it first," she snapped, wondering where this sudden passion came from. Lochlan only nodded, and after placing that holy flame against her heart for a few moments, he left to retrieve Atticus.

Atticus burst into the room a few minutes later. Maddox tried to hand him the notebook, but it was as if Atticus couldn't even see it. He strode right up to her, knelt between her knees, and stared into her eyes to check for any foreign entity within them. He did not touch her, but he was oh so close.

Maddox suddenly understood the phrase *"I could eat him up"*. She *wanted* him, a wildfire of longing but—if she was being honest with herself—not entirely new. Though, this time was different. It was out of her control. She longed to consume *everything* Atticus was. She wished to hold it inside her palm, admire the complex, confusing beauty of it, before she squeezed her fist tight and kept it for herself.

No, she didn't want to harm Atticus. Maddox only wanted what he'd stolen from her. He kept her from being *complete*. Atticus had ripped her apart and taken vital pieces of her heart away. These torn shards lived on within him, whether he wanted it or not, and now she wanted it back. Even if she needed to peel it from his skin or scrape it from his bones.

Maddox stared at her hand, trying to guide her thoughts away from such violence. She froze, her last breath catching in her lungs painfully. There was a breach in her glove. At the very tip of her index finger, there was a hole with the edges curling as if burned.

The acid. She hadn't been as careful as she'd thought. Her finger pad hadn't escaped unharmed, either. There was a small red burn on her skin, red flesh visible. Had she bled on the artifact? Even one drop of blood could prove fatal.

Show them. That was logical, procedural, but Maddox instead tore off the glove and remained silent. She could not say why. She fought to bring it up, but the words vanished before they could leave her mouth and eventually, she could not recall what she even wanted to say.

Something's wrong. Very wrong.

"I think," Maddox whispered, her head tilting forward and hitting Atticus's shoulder. She felt invaded, and it took all her willpower not to burrow her face into Atticus's chest. "I think I might need another round of that damned holy fire."

"Doctor!" Atticus shouted, catching her before she could fall any further. He tugged down the zipper of her cleanroom suit, letting cool air inside to brush her skin.

Lochlan's sneer was audible. "Mr. Blackwell, you have a habit of treating everyone around you as if they work for you. I assure you that's not the case with me."

"Blame my mother."

"Something your therapist hears often, I presume."

Maddox fought to join in, her thoughts growing more and more disjointed. "Does...does Atticus strike you as a man who's going to the right amount of therapy?"

"Tease me later, Maddox." Atticus held her by her shoulders, keeping her from falling further into him. "For now, focus and let Lochlan work."

"So you *do* know my name," Lochlan huffed, walking over to place a hand atop Maddox's head. The exorcist's heat was unbearable, and Maddox chewed her lower lip until the pain could no longer keep her grounded. A small whimper escaped her as she fought against the artifact's shadowy remnants of power. She was being attacked from the inside.

"Hang on, Maddox. Just a little longer," Atticus promised.

"It wants something," she whispered, though the words were not her own. "It wants to be *whole.*"

Lochlan abandoned his current tactic. "Atticus, help me lift her onto the table!"

She was no tiny thing, but Lochlan didn't seem to need any help hauling her onto one of the silver metal tables. Maddox lay back, staring up at the pristine, clinical ceiling. The rest of the Academy was artful, gothic. Only the labs were modern and bland.

"That thing wasn't so obvious in its attempt at possession this time," Lochlan said. He placed both hands on either side of her face, and she twitched at the pain. It was much too hot, this flame of his. It worked its way down her body, burning out the artifact's haunting essence, and burning Maddox, too.

Atticus slipped his hand in hers, and Maddox dug her fingers into the back of his hand until he let out a quiet exhale. When her vice-like grip lessened, Atticus murmured, "Keep squeezing, Maddox. Work out the pain on me. It will never bother me."

Tears slipped downward, dripping into her hair. The holy fire didn't bring forth this shameful release of emotion—it was the way Atticus looked down at her. His crimson-colored lenses couldn't hide how wide his eyes were, how terrified. For the first time, Maddox realized why he wore those silly things. Blackwells were famously the only necromancers whose hellraiser mark showed up in their iris. As much as he liked to boast about his mother's lineage, he was still hiding it behind those glasses.

"Why, Atticus?" His open concern was barbed wire around her heart. "Why did you leave me behind? I could tell you didn't want to, but you wouldn't take it back."

To his credit, Lochlan completely ignored them. His chanting never ceased, never paused. The flames licking at her soul didn't either.

Atticus's other hand cupped the side of her face. Maddox didn't tense at his hesitant touch. She *welcomed* it. Atticus muttered, "Oh, *Maddox*."

It wasn't fair. Wasn't fair that Atticus felt he could whisper her name like that. "You left me! You were my best friend, and you abandoned me!" Her fingernails scratched into his skin, and she didn't care that he jumped because of it.

"You'll never know how sorry I am—"

"How can I? You didn't explain when we were seventeen, and you certainly haven't clarified anything now! You've only made things more confusing!" She sat up, refusing to let him go. "How *dare* you, Atticus! How dare you look at me like that!"

Atticus appealed to Lochlan for help, but Maddox threaded her other hand into Atticus's hair and forced him to hold her tearful gaze. "You made me *hate* you, and I am so tired of it." Her hand fell away from him, laying limp in her lap. "I'm exhausted."

"She's clean," Lochlan interrupted quietly, stepping away. "I can sense only her personality."

Atticus commanded, "You better be absolutely fucking sure of that."

Maddox continued to slump into herself. "I'm so tired," she whispered, her vision beginning to fade.

Lochlan said, his words cutting in and out, "The thoughts, the emotions inside her all appear to coincide with her own."

The last voice Maddox heard was unfamiliar and quiet, but clear.

That's right. We feel the same, don't we?

We've both been torn apart.

CHAPTER 20
WARLOCK

There was an emptiness inside Atticus, a hole that had been torn into him at a young age. Maddox's words stretched the scar tissue, threatening to split open the poor job he'd done mending that gap. Atticus caught Maddox and gently laid her back down on the table. Though it was clear she was asleep and not in any more danger, he watched the slight rise and fall of her breath for several minutes before he spoke.

"What the *fuck* happened?"

"What typically happens when one attempts to understand the book of the dead," Lochlan replied, his tone making it quite clear he was tired of Atticus's constant accusations. "Whatever dark magic lingers on that page has a goal and craves a body to accomplish it with. This is Enchanted Artifacts 101."

Atticus had never taken well to being spoken to like he was a fool. He bristled, but after weighing his options, let the slight slide. "Are you *certain* that she's clear this time?"

"No, I am not." Lochlan placed his hands behind his back and considered Maddox with an intensity Atticus didn't care for. "My particular method for rooting out demons or other possessors is a mixture of psychology and religion. I can sense different emotions and personalities in the host, and I use that to find the demon. But I can't sense anything in Maddox that isn't something she believes."

Atticus questioned, "If that's the case, why are you worried?"

"I'm not sure." Lochlan tugged his notebook out of his jacket pocket and flipped through it. "I think I should monitor Maddox overnight. The Commission—"

"I don't give a shit about the Commission," Atticus said, his magic gathering around his feet. Lochlan watched it without interest. "But you may observe her, if that's absolutely needed."

"I think it is."

It was terrible, this urge to gather Maddox into his arms. Atticus sighed. "I think we should ask for help moving her."

"Between the two of us—"

"Oh, I'm sure both of us working together can lift this unconscious woman and throw her in the back of my car, but how will that *look*?"

For once, the exorcist appeared like the fool.

Lochlan flushed. "Ah. I see. What do you recommend?"

CHAPTER 21
WITCH

This was not her bedroom or Atticus's guest room. Or any place Maddox even remotely recognized.

She rubbed her face, pressing her fingers into her eyes. When Maddox opened them again, she still recognized nothing and there was a small dark patch in the corner of her vision. Though, as she tried to focus on it, it faded.

A few blinks and the blur was gone.

Maddox took stock of what was going *right* in her life. She was comfortable, whatever bed she'd been placed in was soft and warm, and a nearby oil diffuser made the room smell a little too much like eucalyptus.

Sitting up with a groan, Maddox admired the soothing sea-green walls of the room and ran a hand over the soft, hand-stitched quilt. It was very homey. A wicker basket filled with worn, well-read books sat in one corner of the room, and hanging over the doorway were bunches of dried herbs. Homesickness hit her stomach like a hunk of lead.

This must be a witch's home, but whose?

Without warning, a man dressed in dirty navy coveralls stood in the doorway watching her. His outfit reminded Maddox too much of a horror film her sister Dove let her watch way too young.

She shrieked. The man in coveralls shrieked, and Gaia ran into the room, shoving the man out of her way. "Maddox! Are you okay? What happened?"

A few, but not all, of the puzzle pieces fell into place. Maddox was in Gaia's house, in her guest room, and that man was not about to power walk his way to murdering her.

"I assume that's *Mr.* Proctor?" Maddox asked with a sheepish grin.

Mr. Proctor shifted from one foot to the other. "I'm Rick. Sorry about startling you. I heard you moving around, and I was just checking to see if you were awake so I could tell Gaia."

"It's fine..." Maddox hoped Gaia would hear her silent question and continue their conversation in private.

She was in luck. Gaia shooed off her husband, assigning some kitchen task to him, and sat on the corner of Maddox's bed. "I bet," Gaia began, "that you have some questions."

"Uh, yeah. How did I even get here? Also, before I forget, you have a lovely home."

"You've only seen one part of it, but thank you. You may change your mind when you see the state of the garage. Or my craft room." Gaia pulled a duffel bag out of a closet. "These are some of your clothes, and yes, *I* was the one to grab them for you. Atticus refused to step foot in your room at Chateau Blackwell."

Maddox wasn't surprised. "Well, he knows if Edgar caught him rifling through my panties, that bird would peck his eyes out."

Gaia laughed a little too loud. "I'm relieved you're in such good spirits. You scared us earlier. Atticus brought me down to the laboratory after you passed out. He asked if you could stay with me for a few nights."

"What the devil for?" Maddox feared she was being rude, but she hated when plans changed. And especially without her say so.

"Dr. Rhodes wishes to observe you overnight, and Atticus was quite insistent that you would not want to be around him when you woke."

Maddox couldn't find the right facial response and opted for a blank stare. Gaia was obviously curious about what had happened in the lab, but it was bad enough that Lochlan had witnessed her emotional outburst—that another person knew something that happened a decade ago still hurt her so.

She barely remembered what she'd said to Atticus, only that she'd made sure it hurt him.

Something Gaia said earlier finally registered. Maddox paled. "Wait...Lochlan is going to observe me overnight? Does that mean he's *here?*"

"Maddox," Gaia swore, holding a hand over her heart solemnly. "I promise this slumber party will be the best slumber party ever. This single night will heal all of our teenage trauma. There will be popcorn, movies, and boy and girl talk. But unfortunately, there will also be a man dressed like a priest. And I don't think he's going to strip for us."

"Are you trying to ruin this sleepover?" Gaia threatened Lochlan with a throw pillow as he sat primly on her couch. "Who's actually allergic to chocolate?"

"What do I gain by lying about that?" Lochlan scoffed.

Gaia narrowed her eyes. "You irritate me."

"This may surprise you, but that is not my goal, just a happy coincidence."

Maddox helped Rick pick out a sheet, two blankets, and a pillow for Lochlan to use later. The Proctors only had one guest room, so Lochlan had volunteered to sleep on the couch.

Now that she'd had time to adjust to her new sleeping arrangement, Maddox was excited about the slumber party. Though Lochlan was doing his best to tone down the *party* and focus on the *slumber.*

"Maddox needs rest," he reiterated as Gaia finished reading the grocery list for the sleepover festivities out loud. "She doesn't need margaritas."

"Please speak for yourself," Maddox countered, grabbing the list and adding a few more snack foods. Gaia handed the list off to her husband, and he left for the local grocery.

Next, the girls rearranged Gaia's living room to better suit the party. They pushed the couch against a wall and carried in nearly every pillow and blanket in the house to make a nest on the rug. Lochlan mostly stayed out of the way, scribbling in his leather notebook from his perch on the couch.

"For the love of Hades, at least take off the dog collar!" Gaia pointed at the white strip tucked underneath his black shirt collar. "You're killing the vibes."

"Fine," Lochlan said, surprising both Gaia and Maddox. He grabbed a small, wheeled carry-on and headed to the bathroom. When he returned, he wore a simple grey and white baseball tee and black sweatpants. "This is all I have. I don't want to hear any more complaints concerning my attire."

"It's worse now," Gaia whined. "Now he's attractive."

Maddox had to agree. With the black clothes and white collar, Lochlan was rather unapproachable. In civilian clothes, for lack of a better term, he seemed less severe, less washed out. His white-blond hair almost took on a honey glow—one good tousle of that perfectly gelled hair, and he'd have a lot of unwanted attention.

"Then stop looking at me," Lochlan snapped, covering his face with his book. "If Maddox's head starts spinning around in circles, *then* you may interrupt me."

They left him to his journaling. Maddox and Gaia piled blankets on top of themselves, and once Rick returned from the grocer, he served them an unhealthy charcuterie board of chips, dips, cheese, and candies.

The whir of the Proctors' blender became a familiar sound as Maddox and Gaia sipped margaritas. Maddox was just beginning to feel a buzz after they finished their second *Scooby-Doo* movie.

Gaia clicked the television off, and while sipping her drink, announced, "It's girl talk time!"

Maddox was eager, hugging her knees to her chest as she waited for Gaia to continue. She had plenty of sleepovers with her older sisters, but never with anyone outside her family.

"First kiss!" Gaia pointed a peanut butter-covered pretzel rod her way. "Maddox goes first!"

Maddox's stomach dropped. Her throat went dry. *Just lie,* her logic screamed at her, but every thought flew out of her head as Maddox remembered that day in the woods. How Atticus had crushed her body against his. How wild and deep his kisses were.

He'd had her enraptured, her pleasure overpowering her self-control or her fear of inadequacy. She had *wanted,* and that was the most terribly amazing part of it all.

Lochlan eyed Maddox over the top of his book, one brow quirked. *Do you want out of this?* he seemed to hint.

Maddox nodded while she dug underneath the blanket-pillow nest for her cell phone.

"My first kiss was part siren. She tried to drown me after." Lochlan stood, leaving his book behind on the couch. He sat down next to Gaia, who now hung on his every word.

Maddox opened her latest text message from Daphne and keyboard-smashed while appearing to pay attention to Lochlan. A few seconds later her phone rang, and Maddox held it aloft triumphantly as she accepted the call.

"Sorry," she lied and rose from the floor. "It's my sister. She's pregnant—I have to take this."

Maddox raced to the guest room, locking the door behind her and jumping on the blanket-free bed. "Thank you, Daphne," she said into the phone. "You saved me."

"I'm glad your 'pregnant sister' could be of some use. Of all the adjectives to describe me—stunning, graceful, all-powerful healer...and you pick *pregnant.*"

"Sorry!" This time Maddox meant it. "Thank you for calling so fast. I'm at a sleepover, and I got asked about my first kiss." Before Daphne could declare Gaia her enemy forever, Maddox rushed on, "She doesn't know. She didn't mean anything by it."

Daphne took a pause as if she'd needed time to reroute her anger. "It's not a big deal, anyway. If you wanted to tell them that you don't feel attraction very often, I'm sure... Wait. Who the hell are you with right now?"

"One of the teachers at the Academy. She used to be in my class before she was bullied into homeschooling."

"So, she's not on my murder list?"

"Nope, not Gaia."

Daphne's tone settled down. Maddox heard that sharp intake that normally prefaced Daphne saying, *well, I suppose I should get back to it.* Maddox didn't give her the chance.

"Can we do a video call?"

"Oh!" Daphne sounded happy. "Yes, of course. Let me find an empty room and call you back."

Maddox drummed her heels against the mattress as she waited. Once Daphne's glowing, smiling face was on her phone screen, Maddox burst into tears.

"Maddie, what's wrong? What did Blackwell say to you?!"

"It's nothing like that." Maddox sighed, wiping the inner corners of her eyes dry. "It's... It's... I *want* him."

"You want him to do what? Sorry, Cousin Leigh's kids are screaming downstairs. I'm about to lose my mind."

Maddox thought she was ready to admit this, but an out was presented and she took it like the coward she was. "I want him to apologize to me. For dropping me out of nowhere."

"He still hasn't apologized?" Daphne shook her head. "I thought, since you left with him to work on this evil book, that he at least—"

"He's said he was sorry, but he hasn't explained! How can I accept his apology if Atticus isn't man enough to give me a reason?"

"Why do you think that is?" Oh, here was Daphne the therapist. "While you think on that," her sister continued, "let me ask you something. Did you have any tequila at this sleepover?"

"Yes."

"Even though it always turns you into a crying mess?"

"Yes."

"Sounds like good decisions are being made."

Maddox laughed, regretting that third margarita while also planning to have another. "Wait until you hear all of it! I'm living with him!"

Daphne dropped the phone, and it bounced and slid, judging from the changes on the screen's image, underneath a dresser. Daphne shouted from off-camera, "WHY ARE YOU LIVING WITH HIM?!"

Maddox moaned, knowing her decisions were indefensible. "He cooks! It's free! He said my hotel would bring bedbugs into the cleanroom! I wanted to! I don't know!"

The phone slid into the light. Back on camera, Daphne's hair was no longer perfect and straight. Daphne yanked on it repeatedly as she asked Maddox question after question about her living arrangements and scolded her for not letting the family know where she was actually staying.

"What is going on with you?" Daphne sighed.

How could Maddox condense it in a way her sister could understand? She cried, looking away from her phone, "I told you already! *I want him!* I want Atticus to give me a genuine apology, and then an explanation, and then I want *everything.*" Her breath caught in her chest, threatening to burst her lungs with the pain. "I want to forgive him, and I want him to believe it. I want him to kiss me again."

And there it was. The secret sickening her stomach—or that could have been the alcohol—but Maddox felt relief all the same.

Daphne had gone very, very quiet. "He kissed you?"

Maddox felt like she was out of her body as she answered. "I put a truth-seeking spell on Atticus after he told me about the book of the dead project. I couldn't trust him, and I took something from him he didn't wish to give."

"Maddie, what was it?"

Something else must have replied, because how could Maddox say something she couldn't believe? "He loves me, and how he must *loathe* that he does. You should have seen his face, Daphne, when I ripped that confession out of him. I never thought he hated me, but in that moment... How could he feel any other way?"

"He doesn't hate you. You can't hate and love someone."

"Really? I think I can." Maddox stared dully at the phone screen. "I've known there was something wrong with me, but how damaged must I be to want someone who hurt me like that?"

Daphne looked lost for a moment, but those years of training to be a therapist took over and she gave an answer as perfect as she was. "Maddox, you need to stop worrying about what other people feel. If you want to forgive him, you don't need to feel guilty about it. If you want him, then that's what you feel, too. At one point, you two were nauseatingly close. There's no shame if you miss that, but you absolutely have to talk to him."

Daphne gave her time to answer, and when Maddox said nothing, she went on. "He might assume you'd never accept his explanation for what he said and did to you. He might think you don't want to even hear it. If you want answers, then say something. Yes—" Daphne rolled her eyes as Maddox opened her mouth. "—you shouldn't have to be the one who brings it up, but if this is what you want, you need to work for it. You need to try."

"I'm afraid I'll hear the answer, and I won't be able to forgive him. I don't want to lose him again."

"You know what Granddad would say to you right now?" Daphne prompted.

The sisters said in unison, "Cheer up, the worst is yet to come!"

"Right." Daphne nodded, seeming far wiser than a thirty-year-old ought to be. "But if he really does love *and* hate you, you can't be in a relationship like that. You need to walk away. Do you understand?"

"I...understand."

"And the same goes for you. If you hate him, don't put you both through that. You have a lot to think about. I would suggest no more tequila, but I have a feeling you're not going to listen to that."

Maddox gave her a mischievous, though weary, grin. "Nope. Definitely not."

When Maddox re-entered the living room, another movie was softly playing, and Lochlan was asleep on the couch. Gaia patted the ground where a sleeping bag waited for her.

Gaia poked Maddox's knee. "Is your sister okay?"

Maddox nodded, turning a little pink at her earlier lie. "She's good. Just haven't checked in recently."

"Do you want another margarita?" Gaia handed Maddox a glass. Though it was dim in the living room, Maddox could see Gaia biting her lip in worry.

Gaia murmured, making sure her volume didn't disturb Lochlan, "I'm sorry about earlier. I didn't mean to embarrass you. I never attended any sleepovers, so I was basing everything off movies."

Maddox waved it off and took a long gulp of the strawberry-flavored drink. "That's okay. You didn't know that—"

"I wouldn't want to admit Atticus was my first kiss in front of Lochlan, either. It might make the rest of the Tome of the Undying project awkward."

Numbness returned to Maddox's limbs, the glass nearly slipping out from her fingers. "How the hell do you know about that?"

Gaia blinked at her intensity. "It was just a guess. I wasn't around after our first year at the Academy, but the man keeps a picture of the two of you in his classroom."

"He has *what*?"

"A picture of you. And him. It sits right on his desk for anyone to see. You're holding a trophy, I think."

He kept that? During their fifth year at the Academy, they had entered a potion-brewing contest together and won. The contest had been held in Salem, and their hotel rooms had been right next to each other.

It was the first night Maddox had felt any sort of attraction, lying in bed and knowing Atticus was only a few feet away, a flimsy door the only obstacle between them.

It had ached but in a pleasant way.

"Anyway," Gaia said, filling the silence Maddox left behind. "Teenagers do silly things all the time. I would know—I teach them how to play with sharp objects. You shouldn't be embarrassed if your teenage hormones acted up and you two made kissy faces at each other."

"Oh, right." Of course, Gaia didn't know about their *actual* first kiss.

"But I think Atticus thinks about it A LOT."

Maddox was grateful for the darkness. This conversation was beyond embarrassing. "Thank you for your input, Gaia. And the margaritas."

"You're welcome, but I think we're going to regret the latter."

They did regret the margaritas. The following morning, all of them headed out for a very late afternoon brunch, where Gaia and Maddox moaned and groaned with their heads on the table of a very cute café. Maddox couldn't even eat a second bite of her pancakes, and she'd shoved them to Lochlan, who ate a ridiculous amount of food.

Gaia glared at him. "Fuck you. Where does all of that go?"

Lochlan swiped her bacon. "I'm a runner. I run it off."

Maddox wanted to pinch him for being sober and enjoying running. "I second that 'fuck you'."

Maddox was meant to stay another night with Gaia, but Lochlan gave her the okay to resume her normal activities and neither of the women could handle round two of their sleepover.

Instead, after a long afternoon nap back at the Proctors' place, Rick drove Maddox to the Blackwell estate, whistling at the gothic, spiky architecture that waited for her in the already fading light. A brilliant orange sunset made the mansion appear as if it were bleeding.

"Call me if you start getting haunted!" Rick shouted as he drove away.

As hungover as she was, Maddox didn't think she'd care if she did.

CHAPTER 22
WITCH

Would she be able to find Atticus's home apothecary? Maddox wondered as she staggered inside the Blackwell estate. Her head throbbed and her stomach still threatened to empty itself despite there being nothing left to heave up.

She really didn't want to have to ask Atticus to brew her a hangover remedy. Lochlan already had to hold back her hair that morning—her pride couldn't take much more humiliation.

At least Gaia had been just as bad off.

The Blackwell estate was always eerie, but this evening it was terribly silent. Maddox trudged along to her room, praying she wouldn't run into Atticus before she could shower. The warlock was nowhere in sight, and Maddox made it to her room unscathed. While Edgar watched her with a disapproving eye, Maddox dropped her duffel on the bed, undressed, and stepped into her gloriously large shower.

Clean and feeling a little less like hot garbage, Maddox followed her after-shower routine flawlessly. She braided her hair loosely, and threw on a pair of cotton shorts, a comfy sports bra, and an old flannel she didn't bother to button. At the Academy, she wouldn't have worn such obviously hand-me-down clothes, but she refused to be hungover *and* uncomfortable.

"Atticus!" she called throughout the halls on the first floor. "I need to brew something! Where do I go?"

There was no answer. Maybe he'd gone out? The man wasn't a complete hermit—it would be silly to assume he'd be waiting at the door for her like a codependent canine. Or maybe Atticus simply didn't want to see her after their rather one-sided fight in the lab?

The estate was too vast to keep blindly searching. Atticus had even mentioned the estate hosting a ballroom at one point—a room Maddox had yet to even glimpse. She could get lost if she wasn't careful.

Maybe he was outside? Visiting his grandmother's tomb? Maddox toed on her sneakers, walked out the front door, and was barely able to recall the quickest path to the Blackwell family cemetery.

She pulled her flannel shut against the autumn wind. That howling and cutting force drowned out nearly every other sound. Maddox was halfway to the mausoleum when she heard three knocks clear above the gusts.

Maddox froze, the stone walkway in front of her suddenly seeming impassable. She could not take another step forward, as if her heels were glued in place.

Three more knocks rattled through the air before Maddox flushed and turned back towards the mansion. In one of the large windows stood Atticus, staring back at her through the glass.

She felt silly. That rapping was just Atticus trying to call her attention. The estate inspired her imagination to run wild. The house fit in with every standard gothic horror novel setting. Maddox counted the windows on her way back inside, ensuring she'd know which room Atticus was holed up in when she re-entered the home.

She found him in a tidy study with the lights dimmed to the lowest setting. Atticus sat at a desk, his head tilted strangely, as if he could barely keep it upright. His glasses lay on the desk, folded next to an opened whiskey bottle.

Maddox almost overlooked it—the glossy, black snake coiled around the desk's antique lamp. She'd met Venenum before, back at the Academy. There were rules against carrying swords through the school outside of dueling lessons, but Atticus liked to carry Venenum around in its snake form.

Venenum opened its maw and hissed. Its head turned toward the upper part of the study's bookshelf. The black cat Maddox had let inside hissed back, crouching inside the shelf.

"Venenum, love, leave Maddox's mangy cat alone." Atticus cracked one eye open as Venenum slithered through the eye socket of a mounted human skull atop his desk. The viper vanished inside the skull completely.

Before reason could catch up to her mouth, Maddox asked, "Who's the skull?" She peered closer at it. "And why does it have a mustache and angry eyebrows drawn on it?"

"That's my Great-Uncle Thaddeus," Atticus moaned. "And he was being loud. Like you are right now."

Maddox drew her attention away from Thaddeus. "Are you okay?"

"Okay? I hoped you wouldn't see me in this state. I *thought* you were staying with Gaia another night," Atticus said, rubbing his temples. "You aren't supposed to be here."

Her hangover brew was no longer priority number one. Her own comfort paled in comparison to the uneasy state Atticus seemed to be in.

"How much have you had to drink?" she asked softly, leaving any judgment from her tone. After all, Maddox had lost count after margarita number four just last night.

Atticus's whiskey glass was nearly empty, a small bit of brown liquor staining the melted ice. His head dropped on top of his desk, the only cluttered space in his otherwise pristine study.

The black cat jumped down and landed on Atticus's desk. It strutted across the surface to Maddox, scratching at her shirt sleeve. It needed to be brushed desperately.

"Why did you let the cat that eats my garbage *inside* my house?" Atticus muttered. Maddox paled. Oh, dear. She'd been feeding that cat for days now, certain it belonged to Atticus. She didn't even want to think about where it was going for its bathroom business.

"Jinx isn't yours?"

"You already *named* it," Atticus grumped, sitting up to rub his eyes. "Why would I have a cat *and* a deadly snake in the same house? Seems ill-advised. Worst case, one of them goes missing. Best case, they have a mouse-hunting competition, and if I wake up *one time* with a dead rat on my chest, I'll—"

Jinx launched off the desk, cutting short Atticus's rant. Atticus leaned back in his chair and watched the feline vanish into the hall.

Atticus's eyes sluggishly followed Jinx's escape. "Did you know that cat is dead?"

"No, I haven't really examined her. I-I've been respecting her privacy," Maddox lied.

"*You* reanimated it, didn't you? You can't fool a seasoned liar." Atticus shrugged. "It explains why the cat is so drawn to you. You are familiar magic, and now you've got yourself a *familiar.*"

Maddox frowned. Necromancers didn't have familiars. That was more of a nature-inclined witch thing, but she didn't care to start an intellectual discussion on familiars while Atticus could barely sit upright.

What to do about the cat would have to be a conversation between sober Atticus and less-hungover Maddox. What the warlock needed now was rest. Maddox pressed the back of her hand against his forehead to feel his temperature until Atticus swatted her away.

He sniffed. "Don't pretend to care. I know I'm the villain, and you are the kind and beautiful heroine. We don't need to prove it anymore, do we?"

"You forgot forgiving," Maddox whispered, pulling the whiskey bottle away and stashing it in one of the many bookshelves lining the study.

"*What* did you say?" His words weren't slurred, but they were still unsteady.

"Kind and, um, beautiful, *and* forgiving," she repeated.

He squinted at her. His anger cut her as he laughed. "It cannot be that easy."

His laughter stirred up that old loathing again, but Maddox did her damnedest to ignore it. No, not ignore it. She was tired of burying it, only for it to rise again. She wanted to let it go. She wanted to understand.

"Tell me why you left me behind. Please."

Her request stunned him. Atticus dropped his head back on the desktop, covering his face with his arms. "That's the only thing I can't do for you, I'm afraid. Ask me anything else."

How much longer could she keep throwing him a lifeline? How many more times would Atticus reject her friendship? Her rage boiled, and it seeped into her words. "If you *still* refuse to explain, why bring me here? Why tell me that you...you..." She could not say it, could not fathom it. Maddox knew his childhood had been lonely and unsteady, and she'd always thought his family had been the reason he'd so viciously denied her all those years ago...but if he wouldn't speak of it, what was she supposed to do?

"I *brought you here* to work on the artifact and nothing more." Atticus would not meet her eyes or lift his head. "This...is more difficult than I ever imagined. You weren't meant to know the extent of my feelings for you. You don't deserve that."

How could Maddox convince him his confession no longer bothered her? As they were now, adults aware of their childhood shortcomings and mistakes, it was easy to be around Atticus. Maddox only wished Atticus could feel that same serenity.

Let me forgive you. Give me anything, Atticus. I'll take whatever you have to offer.

"It will become easier," Maddox tried, moving forward to rest her hand atop his head. The urge to run her fingers through his hair was brief but strong. "When this project is done, and I leave—"

Atticus sat up quickly, startling her. His gaze was merciless and burning. Without his glasses covering them, his irises were hypnotic. "If I thought distance could end this horrible longing, then I would gladly reside in Hell to spare you my unwanted infatuation."

What's a girl supposed to say to that? Maddox swallowed, her hand falling away from him before Atticus caught it. He pressed her palm against his cheek for a moment before turning his head to kiss her wrist.

He sighed. "You must think you could never hate me more than you already do."

When was the last time Atticus had slept? The dark circles under his eyes seemed permanent.

He released Maddox's hand with a deep chuckle. "If you ever found out what I dream of doing to you, you might hate me even more than *I* do."

Maddox shrunk back. She shouldn't have been pestering him like this. It wasn't fair to ask him for a rational explanation for the cruel, irrational behavior of a teenager. Especially not when he was clearly drunk.

Walk away, Maddox. You don't need the last word. You don't need to win.

"How you must *hate* what you feel for me." He'd rather live in Hell than live with loving her? She covered her face with both hands and murmured through her fingers, "How inconvenient I must be! How *disappointing—*"

He rose so quickly out of his chair that it turned over on its side with a *clunk!* Atticus's voice was raspy as if he'd spent the day sobbing or screaming. "You have *never* disappointed me. You have always been better than I deserved, and no one will say otherwise ever again. Not me, and certainly not you."

CHAPTER 23
SON OF A WITCH

It was their third year at the Academy, and Maddox still carried the copy of *Frankenstein and other Tales of Horror* Atticus had lent her that first day of school.

She bore it like a shield, clutching it to her chest as they walked from class to class together. It was as if she subconsciously understood that around Atticus she'd need any armor she could get.

It had to be today.

Last night, Giles had replayed, over and over and fucking over, a voicemail left on their home machine. It was Colter Abernathy, offering again to help Atticus with his illness.

Why did they care about him? Let him rot. This *kindness* was ruining everything.

Atticus and Maddox normally ate lunch in the Poison Garden, away from the other students, but today, Atticus suggested they eat in the courtyard with everyone else. He didn't want to ruin their sanctuary in her eyes.

Maddox looked uneasy but agreed.

Atticus thought about running. He needed to vomit. He wanted to tell her everything. Instead, Atticus kept walking until he reached the center of the courtyard and locked eyes with his brother. There had never been mercy in Giles's heart, and that hadn't changed now.

No, this couldn't be blamed on Giles. Atticus had come to the same conclusion his brother had—the Abernathys were too observant, too kind, and their attention was dangerous. And Atticus was equally dangerous to *them*.

The blame, the guilt, could only be lain at his feet. Just a few nights ago,

Atticus had nearly...had nearly...

He'd spent every spare minute he'd had brewing sleeping tonics. *Anything* to keep him from dreaming of Maddox. He'd kill his dreams permanently if it would keep her out of harm's way, but nothing helped. Nothing spared him from wanting her and from his magic working on its own to satisfy his hunger.

Atticus would hurt her if this continued. It was too much. Her family digging into his health, his dreams that turned quickly into nightmares... Atticus was sleeping in a fucking crypt, for Hades's sake.

Yes, this was the only way. He had to cut her off completely. If he ignored her, his magic would stop hunting her down while what remained of his morality slumbered. Perhaps if Maddox *hated* him, she would be *safe.*

This would have to wait until after they ate. Atticus knew her—if he ended things before lunch, Maddox would be too upset to eat. His hands shook as he placed half of his sandwich on her tray.

"*You* need to eat something," she protested, trying to return the food and giving up when he kept moving his tray out of her reach. "I can tell you've been losing weight. Which reminds me, Granddad wanted to know if you're coming for the harvest dinner."

Of course he does. Colter wants to diagnose me.

"I think my dad wants me in Dubai this year," Atticus lied. Well, it wasn't a lie, really. Rami wanted Atticus with him, but permanently. He wasn't happy Cynthia now worked in England and had left their sons with a guardian.

"Oh, that's good," Maddox said, though her tone held some disappointment.

She ate, he drummed his fingers, and the school bell rang from its high tower and made him jump in his seat.

"Wait." He grabbed her wrist as she tried to leave with the other students. "Let's sit a few minutes more. We have study hall next, anyway."

The courtyard cleared out until only Atticus, Maddox, and Giles remained. Maddox peered over Atticus's shoulder, scowling at his older brother.

Frankenstein sat on the table, and Atticus stared at the familiar, faded edges where the cloth cover peeled away.

"I don't think we should spend time together anymore."

Maddox didn't move her gaze away from Giles. "I disagree."

Atticus's left hand ached, but nothing helped it anymore. No poultice dulled the pain. "I don't *want* to spend time together anymore. That—that's what I meant."

Her back straightened, and she finally looked at him. Atticus could feel her eyes, hot on the top of his head, as he stared down at the table. Maddox laughed, but it was shaky. "Why are you saying this? What did your brother say to you?"

"This is my decision."

"Liar." The word was emotionless and accurate. "Those aren't your words."

"I'm saying them. It doesn't matter who planted them—what matters is that I agree."

"Take them back."

It was an order, and though Atticus had never wished to refuse her anything, he only shook his head. "Maddox, don't follow me. Don't talk to me. Don't even *think* about me anymore."

He stood, and Maddox was at his back instantly, her hand fisted in his shirt. "Wait. Atticus, please. You're the only one that doesn't hate me here. And I—I *care* about you."

His command wasn't enough—of course, it wasn't. His reluctance was obvious, and no one knew him better than Maddox.

She anchored him in place, and Atticus couldn't look back at her. His brother was ahead of him, waiting and blank.

If Atticus didn't do it now, he never would. *This* was the only thing he could control.

"That isn't my problem anymore," he snapped.

Her insistent tone faded. "*Problem*? What are you talking about?"

"Don't ever touch me again."

She released his shirt. Maddox pleaded, her tone edging towards begging, "Don't do this. What did I do wrong?"

Children weren't supposed to be subjected to what Atticus had been. They weren't supposed to be allowed to make mistakes with such lasting consequences.

"I'm tired," Atticus lied, wishing he could think of some other plan, anything other than this. "I'm tired of carrying you. Sick of having to explain every little nuanced thing about being a necromancer."

Her anguish melted into fury. "I didn't realize I was such a pain."

"No, you didn't. Because you're *never* paying attention to anything. You just assume I'll fill you in later."

She winced, her sorrow returning. "I'm catching up, though."

"*Because* I have to drag you along with me. If you were on your own, you'd fail. You can't keep track of any deadlines, and you're constantly daydreaming through class. If you didn't have me to babysit you—"

"I get it," she muttered. "That's enough."

"I *hope* it is. I've had enough of repeating myself to you."

He kept walking, and Maddox remained rooted in place. She didn't call him back or chase after him. Though he hated himself for doing so, Atticus looked back at her for just a second.

The courtyard's landscaping, every stalk and leaf and root, was brown and curled and dried. Maddox surrounded herself with death.

Later, Atticus found the borrowed copy of Frankenstein stuffed in his locker. As he flipped through the soft-edged pages, a note fell out.

She must have forgotten it was in there—it was the only thing that made sense.

Thank you for being my friend.

After that ordeal, Atticus only wanted to hide himself away. He returned home to the Blackwell estate, blindly trudging through the empty halls.

His brother didn't give him the chance. Giles strutted into Atticus's room with his usual swagger. Giles's intrusion grated on Atticus's already-fragile nerves. Atticus had hoped to avoid Giles—at least for today, and if Giles had any decency left in him, he would have allowed Atticus that much.

"Get out." Atticus was in bed, and now he turned on his side toward the wall. He felt Giles's weight on the edge of his mattress and scowled. "I said—"

Giles never needed an opening—he always made one. "You did the right thing, though you did it poorly. I almost thought I'd have to step in and deal with her."

"Don't you have online college tonight?" Atticus protested.

"I took the test early. I'm free, and we're going to get you out of this damned house." Giles stood up and gripped Atticus by his ankles. One tug and Atticus hit the floor, flailing.

"I'm not going anywhere." Atticus stood and shoved Giles toward the door, but that did nothing to dissuade him.

"Look at yourself." Giles *tsked.* "You need a drink."

"I'm seventeen, and I have no desire to watch you drink. Now, leave me alone." Atticus gestured grandly toward the door, but Giles didn't move an inch.

Instead, Giles pulled an ID card out of his pocket and waved it around. "Seventeen is old enough for a beer or two, and you can pull off twenty-one. Don't be difficult."

"Haven't you done enough?" Atticus left his room, marching down the hallway as Giles chased his heels. "I want to be alone!" Atticus knew one place Giles would never follow him—Theodora's tomb.

Before he could escape outside, Giles spun him by his shoulder. "What I've done is *protect* you!" Giles shoved Atticus's chest hard. "That's *all* I ever do! I'm the one who has to remind you to take your medicine when you're too wrapped up in whatever fantasy world you and that redneck escape to. And you don't even like me for it."

Atticus stumbled back another step, and this time there was no physical reason for it. "Why do you care if I like you? *You hate me.*"

Giles blinked, his fingers tracing the scar that ran down his eye to the corner of his mouth. *Fencing accident* was the lie they told. Another second and whatever emotion Giles had been toying with was gone. He shrugged. "You've trapped me here with you, Atticus, and that *does* make me hate you. You've made me your jailor. Night after night, I do my part to help you, and all you care about is some girl. Fine. Fuck you. Do whatever you want next year, and the year after that, and the year after that—"

Atticus covered his ears. "Shut up!"

"I'm leaving as soon as Dad secures my job with Blackened Salt. After that, you're on your own. *Forever.*" Giles stepped off to the side, his smile an open wound slashing across his face. "Maybe you hate me, but I think you hate that

I didn't let you just give up even more."

Atticus could only stare at Giles. How long had Giles felt this way?

"She'll forget about you. Eventually," Giles said sternly. It was as close to comforting as he'd ever get.

Atticus's next steps were slow and unsteady. He passed Giles by and walked out of the house, zombie-like, until he reached the family graveyard. Theodora's tomb was silent and familiar.

I'm all that you have.

How right Theodora had been.

CHAPTER 24
WARLOCK

"**Y**ou need to go to bed."

Maddox hauled Atticus away from his study and his whiskey and led him, shockingly, to her room. Atticus leaned heavily against her, his arm draped over her shoulders. Was he as drunk as she believed? No, but Atticus didn't particularly wish to tell her how few drinks it took before he was a lamenting, hopelessly romantic mess.

His weight didn't slow her down. She was strong, always had been, and...

Beautiful, even when her freckled nose was scrunched up in fear that he was about to pass out. Or throw up.

She kicked open her bedroom door and dragged him inside. Maddox set him on the bed before she dropped to her knees in front of him.

He couldn't form a single, coherent thought as she untied and removed his shoes.

"Lie down," she ordered, and Atticus obeyed, his mind still restarting.

Maddox left him there, and he heard her moving inside the bathroom. When she returned, her old gold-rimmed glasses sat crookedly on her nose. After setting a glass of water on his side of the bed, Maddox climbed into the other.

Now his brain was overclocking. "What are you doing, Maddox?"

"Sleeping."

He let that sit, his disbelief stalling his response. "Okay. What am *I* doing here?"

"Drinking water and *then* sleeping." She lifted one of the extra pillows and pushed it against his back until he rolled on his side. "There. Sleep like that. Wake me if you need anything."

She wanted them to share a bed? There wasn't a chance in any hell he'd able to sleep knowing Maddox Abernathy was mere inches away.

"I—" he tried.

"Whatever it is, it can wait until morning. I'm still hungover from last night. I fell off Gaia's back porch and puked in her hedges. Lochlan had to hold my hair for me." She shifted around, yanking the blanket a little more to her side. "I'm only telling you this because I feel sorry for you, and you should know that we're both embarrassing drunks."

It didn't make him feel better. He only felt jealous that Lochlan had been there for her, and wasn't that crazy?

Hades, he was so tired. Whiskey was a lullaby he knew too well. Atticus fought against it, but eventually, he drifted off to sleep.

Waking up in Maddox's room filled Atticus with sudden and blinding terror. Had he slept-walked in here? She was going to kill him, and he—

"Good morning," Maddox said, sitting up to rub her sleepy eyes underneath her glasses. Her flannel had been discarded in the middle of the night, leaving behind only a black sports bra. "How are you feeling?"

"A bit of a headache, but fine otherwise." He tried to slide out of the bed, wanting to leave before he said something more insane than he had the night before. Atticus remembered offering to live in hell or something equally melodramatic... Hades, but he was a mess.

Maddox pulled at his sleeve, yanking until he stopped trying to leave the bed. "Wait. Please talk to me."

Atticus knew what she wanted from him. "What is there to talk about? I told you, I can't give you the reason—"

Maddox grabbed his shirt collar and pinned him to the bed by it. He'd dreamt of such a scenario, but not under these circumstances. "Let me go."

"It was because of your family, wasn't it? Just answer that for me, and I'll stop asking. I promise."

This desperation in her voice... Where was this coming from? Surely Maddox didn't care that much?

Atticus steadied his breath and imagined what advice Angeline would give him now.

His answer came out as a sigh. "*Yes.*"

Maddox startled, stunned she received an answer. "Because I wasn't good enough for you?"

"No, and never think that again." Atticus held back his anger by biting the inside of his cheek. *It's not Maddox you're angry at.* "That's all I can tell you."

She released his clothing, but he remained prone on the bed with her towering over him. Maddox ran a hand through her dark, wild hair and only made it more tangled. "Atticus," she murmured, her fingernails scratching at her neck. She was nervous, and that made him *terrified.* "Atticus, just fucking ask me what you're most afraid to know."

He shielded his eyes with a hand, wishing he could hide more of himself from her. "I don't deserve to ask that."

"What you think you deserve is irrelevant here. What I think you deserve is what matters." She was shaking as her hand cupped the left side of his face. He leaned into the touch, eyes shut tight. "I want to give this to you so badly, but you have to ask."

"Maddox—"

"I'm tired! Haven't I waited long enough? Can't we move past this? All the energy I spent trying to be better than you, all that time spent hating you... I want to be *done.*"

Her voice broke. She still cared that much? What had changed? Just weeks ago, she'd buried him alive, and now she was begging him to accept her forgiveness.

Atticus had brought her into the Tome of the Undying project to make up for what he'd done to her. She was meant to be in academia, and he'd ruined that by trying to be close to her again. He *knew* that she had withdrawn from the librarian position because she'd learned he had accepted a job as the apothecary professor. She couldn't stand being close to him again, so she left. Maddox had withdrawn from their world, and it was all his fault.

He had righted, as much as he could, his mistake. Maddox was doing what she loved again. Atticus didn't deserve anything else.

She leaned down to touch her forehead to his for a moment. He couldn't move. When she withdrew, Maddox's words were gentle, but cut him down mercilessly.

"Can you do it for me? Atticus, can you give me what *I* want?"

His magic was no longer out of his control. His life, such as it was, could change.

Atticus could only whisper it. "Can you forgive me? Can you understand that I can't explain? It wasn't a thoughtless act—it wasn't a *whim*. You were my only true friend, and I hurt you, and it aches still. I wished you hated me, but I could tell you never really did. You were always waiting for that explanation, and I can't give it to you."

Not a moment was wasted. Maddox's words were clear. "I forgive you."

He stopped breathing for a moment before his guilt overwhelmed him. "Fuck! I want that more than anything."

She repeated, "Atticus, I forgive you."

Burning tears raced down his face as her words started to sink in. Maddox fell back from her kneeling position on the bed and opened up her arms. Atticus only stared dully back at her until she tugged him over. He buried his face in her shoulder while her arms wrapped around him.

"I forgive you, and I want to be your friend."

"Stop." Her skin still held a hint of lavender, even after all those weeks being away from her family farm. Each one of his trembling breaths drew it in. "I ignored you for *years*. I saw how you waited for me. Hate me, Maddox."

"No." One of her hands stroked his hair, and the other rubbed his back in small, slow circles. Maddox acted like being together like this was the easiest thing in the world.

"Do you want to be my friend again?" she asked, her lips nearly kissing his ear. "I want to be yours."

"I loved you, and I still hurt you."

The circle she traced on him paused for a few beats. "I'll tell you I forgive you as many times as you need to believe me."

His voice broke as he said, "I want to be friends again, but I still—" There was no truth spell loosening his tongue this time, but the words tumbled out, anyway. "I still love you, Maddie. How can we be friends if I feel that way?"

Maddox softly pushed him back so she could look into his eyes. Without his rose-tinted glasses, Atticus felt exposed. He'd only ever heard her family call her by that name, but he'd longed to be that close to her one day, and *Maddie* had slipped out.

Her brow furrowed and relaxed. "We take it one day at a time. We go slow." She drew him back into her embrace. "Let's start up our book club again."

He laughed, her words unexpected.

She pouted. "I'm serious."

"I know. It's just surreal." Being forgiven was already unbelievable on its own, but she really wanted to be friends again? And being tucked against her shoulder was almost healing.

But this wasn't *friendly*. The way she quieted his anxieties with her touches, the way she held him tight... This went far past "friendship". A weed of hope sprang from one of the cracks in his heart, and he tried his best to smother it, to dig up the roots.

Weeds were always persistent things, thriving on the barest of nutrients and the harshest of conditions.

Don't you dare think about it. Be grateful she forgave you, grateful she'll even look at you. Don't make more out of this than it is. Pity.

Atticus attempted once to untangle himself from her, but she only clutched him tighter. "Stop moving around! It's cold!"

He relaxed against her, drinking in her scent greedily. "Are you just using me for my body heat?"

"Yes. Your house is very drafty." Maddox pulled the covers over them.

"By the way, I don't think Venenum appreciates you allowing a stray cat into my home." Atticus plucked a cat hair off his shirt and frowned.

"In my defense," Maddox protested, one of her legs shifting to move over his, "you are a very stereotypical cat person."

Maddox, as unique as she was, was still an Abernathy. Even Atticus knew the Abernathys loved collecting pitiful things. There would be no getting rid of the cat now that Maddox had spoiled it.

It was hard to care about something so trivial with their bodies pressed together. Did Maddox really want to sleep like *this*? With him half-crushing her? He was lean, but tall, and worried his weight might be uncomfortable. Then again, Maddox was tall herself. Perhaps this *was* what she wanted? He couldn't find the courage to ask for clarification. "I'm sorry," Atticus said, though he was losing track of all he was sorry for.

"Go back to sleep," she hushed him. "We'll talk more when we wake up."

Atticus didn't want to wake up. He knew once he did, it would be the last time he ever woke up with Maddox. He would mourn that hour spent resting in her hold.

"Ugh," Maddox moaned, squirming out from underneath him. "I need to brush my teeth before I go insane."

She tiptoed to the bathroom, and Atticus knew it was over. As he placed his shoes back on, Maddox called, "I'll meet you in the kitchen. I'm making pancakes."

"A mess is what you're going to make," he argued and left the room before she could find something to throw at him.

Atticus chewed somewhat dry pancakes, grinning between bites. Maddox sat next to him at the kitchen island, her bouncing, anxious leg knocking into his own. He didn't mind at all. He soothed it with a hand on her knee, and Maddox left her own on top of it. Now, he was forced to eat with his left hand, which was tricky, but Atticus didn't mind that, either.

"Let's pick out something for the book club," Maddox decided while she helped him with cleaning the breakfast dishes. "Sundays are made for reading."

He agreed but grabbed her hand when she took off in the wrong direction. "Where are you going?"

"To your study. I thought I saw two copies of *Dracula* on your shelf."

"You know that's not our main library, right?"

Maddox pulled Atticus against her, the front of their bodies pressed together as she took his collar into her hands. This yanking him about by his shirt was becoming a habit of hers, and Atticus loved it. Maddox was tall and strong—he'd dreamt of being thrown around by her often.

"Take me there immediately."

Maddox was a whirlwind, and her laughter joined his as Atticus watched her explore the Blackwell library. Maddox ran between aisles, bouncing from section to section with Jinx following loyally at her heels. It was obvious to Atticus that the cat was Maddox's familiar, though he doubted she would ever believe it.

There was an incredible amount of plant life in the library. While Maddox and most others of their kind killed every plant they touched, Atticus had quite the green thumb for a necromancer. Potted plants were carefully arranged on top of bookshelves, the vines trailing down nearly to the floor. The room was two levels, and the second level had a huge arched window with a cushioned bench. Atticus imagined Maddox laying out on the bench, her nose in a book, and her limbs stretched out and dangling over the side.

Her racing down the aisles was tailed by their feline friend. The black cat's fur was thick, but glossy—Atticus did not doubt the dinner portions Maddox saved went straight to that spoiled creature. He didn't really mind having a cat, and he doubted he had a choice now, but Venenum would need help adjusting to a new housemate.

Once Maddox tired herself out with her wandering, Atticus found her in the science fiction section, brushing the spine of her old copy of *Frankenstein and other Tales of Horror*.

"What about this? It's about time for a reread." Maddox began to carefully slide the book out.

His words trembled as much as his fingers did as they pushed the book back into the shelf. "Let's save that for later." Sweat beaded his forehead. "I feel like something a bit more modern."

"Sacrilege," she scoffed but started checking the shelves for something less dusty. What she presented to him next was horrific.

"Oh, Hades. I don't even want to know who brought that in here." A shirtless man winked at him from the cover of Harlequin Romance, and the book looked disturbingly well-read. He thumbed through the pages with a wince. "There's only one copy."

"You can read it to me," she teased.

"You don't want that. You're turning red just looking at the cover."

She sniffed. "I am not."

He cracked open the book and nearly snorted. "I don't think you can handle the amount of times 'heaving bosoms' is in here."

Now she really seemed offended. "I said I can handle it."

Her response was rather short, and Atticus feared he'd made another mistake he didn't understand. Needing a distraction, he read a passage aloud while adopting a poor imitation of a British accent and watched Maddox's reaction carefully. "The duke triumphantly sheathed himself to the hilt inside my quivering and moist—Hades help me, they did *not* just use the word 'moist' here."

Maddox ran from him and the novel, shouting back at him, "Just grab those copies of *Dracula* I mentioned! Also, never say 'quivering' again!"

CHAPTER 25
WiTCH

Translating the page was going about as well as retrieving the writing had gone.

On the bright side, since they no longer needed to handle the artifact, the threat of possession was no longer hanging over Maddox's head. Maddox thanked the gods for that. She didn't know how much more of Lochlan's holy fire she could survive.

"It's nonsense," Maddox whined, pushing away from her desk in their study room. Staring at what she had copied from the page was useless. They'd already tried every language that made logical sense, tried many that didn't, and still nothing was working. She feared the page was in code, and that could take *years* to break.

"Perhaps the page contains knowledge we're better off not knowing," Lochlan said, flipping through his text listlessly. "The Tome of the Undying held the key to creating liches. Though, I never understood the appeal. Necromancers live so long as it is. Why trade their soul for immortality?"

"We breathe life back into the dead," Atticus drawled, standing and crossing behind Maddox's chair. His fingers dragged across her shoulders, his nails scraping her skin. "Necromancers always long for what's forbidden to them."

Maddox hoped Lochlan hadn't seen Atticus touch her, but judging from the exorcist's obnoxious snort, she knew Lochlan had.

Atticus retrieved another book and set it open on the desk. He sneered at the state of it. Pages fell out of the binding, and Atticus carefully collected them into a sad stack.

Maddox itched to repair it—maybe Atticus would help her with it after they were done torturing themselves for the day? Bookbinding was yet another one of her nerdy hobbies.

Atticus surprised her with his next question. "When was the last time you made an offering to your patron?"

"It's been quite a while..." Maddox winced. She used to pray to Persephone daily and twice before exams. Her altar back home was a minuscule, unworthy table stuffed in the bottom of her closet.

"Let's make an offering together," Atticus suggested. He looked to Lochlan who was already shaking his head.

"I'll keep working here," Lochlan said. "I'll only get in your way."

"Maddox, let's try it," Atticus decided. "Perhaps our patrons will pity us enough to aid our venture." He slipped his glasses back into place, letting them fall from where they had perched on top of his head.

Atticus's eagerness was unsurprising. He'd always been consistent with his offerings to his patron. As for Maddox, ADHD did not make for a diligent disciple.

Atticus's idea was worth a shot. Maddox's patron was Persephone, while he followed Hades. Making an offering together would surely please the married gods.

On the other hand, Atticus was always happy to distract from the translation. He drew Lochlan and her both into long, though interesting, discussions any time they took his bait. It was almost as if Atticus didn't care about the project at all.

Maybe he *didn't*. They only possessed one small piece of the Tome of the Undying. He had nothing to prove like she did.

If she wasn't so exhausted, it might have bothered her.

Maddox was about to stand when Lochlan tilted a paper so she could see some cramped writing. Atticus was slipping into his coat, the movement obscuring his line of sight.

Hang back and speak with me. Alone.

What could Lochlan need to tell her *alone*? There was no use overthinking it. Maddox already knew her curiosity wouldn't let her deny the request.

Maddox stood, turning to Atticus. She said carefully, "I'll meet you outside in a few minutes. I have to use the restroom."

Atticus nodded and left. As soon as the warlock's footsteps fell silent, Lochlan met her eyes. "I don't really understand the relationship between you two, but I thought I would warn you. I've caught Atticus working on the translation without us."

"I've worked on it alone, too," she countered, though why was she defending Atticus at all? "That's not a crime."

Lochlan clarified, "After you both leave for the day, sometimes Atticus comes *back*. If I enter the room, he stops his work and tries to distract me with his monologuing."

"You brought this up for a reason," Maddox said, feeling chills despite the overheated room. "Well?"

He paused for a moment, scrutinizing her before he spoke again. "His grandmother was the last person in charge of the Tome, and now Atticus is working on the first piece of it found in over a century. What I'm saying is, I think he knows more than he's letting on."

She crafted her response carefully. Lochlan was, after all, a Commission agent and not her friend. "All of our names are on this project. Why would he not share information?"

"I don't know, but I think we should be cautious." Lochlan coughed uncomfortably. "Despite our personal feelings on the man."

Oh, Hades. What did he mean by *that*? Maddox nodded. "I understand. Thank you for telling me."

"You're welcome, and good luck."

Maddox waved a farewell and escaped the library as quickly as she could without getting yelled at by Mrs. Tuttle. She found Atticus outside the library and struggled to mimic the small smile he gave her. They walked together through the grey courtyard, dried orange and brown leaves crunching underneath their steps.

They stopped in a large field, bare of trees and covered with tall, waving grasses. A large red circle was painted on the grass, a ward the groundskeeper maintained. They entered the circle, the harmony of the outdoors falling silent inside the warded space. Here, inside this spell circle, their magic would not harm anything outside the boundaries.

Atticus followed the circle, checking the strength of the painted wards before heading to the center. He removed his burgundy jacket and tossed it outside the wards, leaving him in a plain black collared shirt and black waistcoat. Atticus unbuttoned his cuffs and rolled his sleeves to his elbows before presenting both hands to her.

Maddox placed her hands tightly in his. There could be no letting go once they began.

Offering their power, their will, started slowly. The two necromancers' magic appeared as a waist-high red fog. The fog grew thicker as more magic poured out of them.

Maddox bit her lip. This was about to get tricky. She pushed some of her power to Atticus, running electricity down her right arm, to their entwined hands, and into his body. Atticus gasped and matched her level of power, letting her magic flow through him and mix with his own. He sent their power back to her through her left arm.

She repeated the process, allowing their electricity to flow faster and faster as they combined their magic. The air above them filled with static. The sky grew dark, and a storm appeared above them. All this was expected.

Atticus intoned, his voice loud and rasping, "Goddess and wife, queen of below, we offer back what was given to us. God and husband, lord of below, we—"

Maddox hadn't seen Atticus work such complex magic in a long time. He really was such a powerful warlock.

If I'm not careful, he could easily overwhelm my magic.

Their electricity was no longer contained in their bodies. Some of it escaped, forming lightning that spiraled around them. If one of them overpowered the other, the weaker one would be electrocuted.

Lochlan's suspicions broke through her concentration. Another thought—illogical, traitorous, and wrong—hit her.

Atticus could kill me.

Before she could call it back, Maddox doubled her power and the sudden burst interrupted Atticus's spell.

"Too much!" he snapped, wincing. Perhaps it was simply a reflex on his part, but Atticus's power jolted her body, threatening to overtake her.

Maddox released more magic in return, and they both nearly broke apart as the electricity looping through their hands became agonizing. She might have forgiven Atticus, but she couldn't force her magic to trust him.

"Maddox." Atticus's voice was soft but pained. "You're upsetting the balance. You need to back off."

"I—I can't," she realized. Fear ate away at her logic, and her magic was no longer in her control. Lightning shot from their bodies, crashing against the invisible ward that surrounded them like a bubble. The sound of magic hitting the barrier made her ears ring.

Atticus squeezed her hands hard, digging his thumbnails into her skin. "Focus. Let it *go*, Maddox."

If this kept up, this escalating back and forth, they could both explode. All because Maddox couldn't reign her magic in.

She shouldn't have attempted this. She should have told Atticus the truth—that since she had left the Academy, not only had she neglected to pick up her sword, but she also hadn't uttered a single spell.

Maddox had been too tired, too angry, too *heartbroken*. Burnt-out.

I forgave him! I can trust him! Her argument failed to gentle her survival instinct. Fine. This was her fault. Maddox would break the circle the next time their magic passed into her body. While it would certainly destroy her in the process, Atticus would be safe.

Maddox tried to yank her hands away, but Atticus anticipated her sacrifice. Atticus crushed her hands and screamed, "DON'T YOU FUCKING DARE!"

Flashes of light revealed the anguish in Atticus's eyes. He caught her off-guard, charging forward and taking her to the ground. They fell awkwardly, their grip on each other still tight, and Maddox hit her back in the compacted dirt.

Air left her lungs as she cursed. Atticus straddled her, pinning her hands to the floor.

"Enough!" he shouted over the storm. "I can't take anymore. *Please.* I won't let anything happen to you. If you slow down your magic, I promise I won't let mine overpower you."

Promises, promises. Just another promise he'd break. Maddox was panicking, adrenaline choosing her path for her.

"Maddie, please! I won't hurt you again. I swear it." He was desperate. Atticus tugged their joined hands and brought the top of her hand to his lips. "I won't hurt you. Never again. I'm in control. If you just let go, I can match you. I can control it now."

A tear dropped from on high, hitting her cheek as it slid down it and hit the floor. *Atticus's tear.* It was enough to bring her world rushing back into focus.

Maddox drew in a single, shaky breath and drew her magic back inside her, too.

Atticus's power lowered with hers until the spell extinguished itself. He let her go, standing and pulling her to her feet. Maddox stumbled once, hitting his chest, and there she stayed, panting.

A few seconds passed, and Atticus haltingly wrapped his arms around her. The fog and the storm they'd conjured faded away as she returned his embrace.

"*Never again*," Atticus repeated, nearly crushing her against him. "The *things* I'd do to keep you safe, Maddox. You wouldn't like me if you knew even a fraction."

"I'm sorry," she murmured into his chest. "I meant it when I said I forgave you. I just—"

"It's *okay*," Atticus reassured her. "Your mind can forgive, but your body remembers. I understand if it takes time. We should have started by blending our magic for something small. Not for something like this."

She felt pathetic, always relying on him to soothe her. How long had they stood together like this? Why did being in his arms make Atticus feel like home and a stranger all at once?

He dropped his hold on her, but they remained close. "Can I say what an incredible storm we made together? What beautiful darkness."

"You're always so poetic." Maddox laughed.

"Perhaps I missed my true calling," he agreed. "I'll spare you a sonnet, however, as you've just been through an ordeal already." Atticus nodded back to the school. "Did you know Fred still works that coffee truck in the courtyard? Let's get you a hot cider before we go home."

CHAPTER 26
WITCH

Maddox was on her own for a few days, using the free time to recover from that nearly disastrous spell. She couldn't decide if the feel of Atticus's power running through her was more memorable than the panicked, overbearing warmth of his arms caging her.

She spent her time wandering the library, searching the card catalogue for more references on the Tome of the Undying. Ten times Maddox found a reference in the system, but when she found the corresponding bookshelf, the text was not there. Once or twice could be a coincidence. But this was looking like sabotage.

Someone had stolen the Tome of the Undying. Had they stolen all the major references to it as well? Destruction of library property made Maddox grind her teeth in suppressed rage.

While Maddox searched for another missing reference, Professor Angeline Boleyn tracked her down.

"How much longer can the project afford to keep you on?" Angeline asked, helping Maddox straighten the stack of papers she'd finished perusing.

Maddox frowned, still mystified by the business side of the research project. "Atticus takes care of all that, so I'm a little in the dark."

Angeline cocked her head. "My experience tells me if you can't figure out what that page says soon, you'll have to dump the project or find a job to keep the lights on while you keep working unfunded."

How amateurish. Maddox hadn't considered that. She had no bills since she was staying with Atticus and he kept her fed, but how long could she impose on his hospitality? Hades, she needed to think about the future.

It was difficult to look ahead when all Maddox thought about was making every day with Atticus count. They'd spent years apart, and she worried that outside the Academy, Atticus's life had been rather lonely. Or he'd been living the life of a rich bachelor and spending his nights the *opposite* of lonely.

That got under her skin, and Maddox couldn't pretend that she didn't know why.

She liked the way things were—mostly. She and Atticus had started taking their lunch in the Poison Garden again. Though this time, Lochlan and Gaia joined them. It was cozy. They all liked the same books and were interested in darker magic, but there were enough differences between them all to never dull the conversation.

Maddox wanted that friendship to last. She had to be very careful not to ruin it, not to push too far. They were making progress, her and Atticus. Not with uncovering the page's writing, but with each other. Though things were still fragile. One crack and they would split in two.

"Well, you've given me a lot to think about," Maddox said, hoping to end this frustrating and eye-opening conversation.

"Not yet, I haven't." Angeline slid a folder her way. "There's a position opening for a librarian, and this is the letter of recommendation I wrote for you all those years ago. I've tweaked it a bit. It should suffice."

Maddox's eyes misted as she read the opening paragraph of the recommendation letter. It was almost the same as she remembered. "You've kept this for five years?"

"Yes. Maddox, please use it this time."

This was the first time Maddox had visited Atticus's classroom. It wasn't much different from what she remembered when Professor Gardner had run the student labs.

One half of the room had whiteboards spanned across it. Atticus's careful handwriting danced everywhere, and against the opposite wall was the teacher's desk. Everywhere else was filled with cabinetry and tall tables with sinks and burners.

Atticus's desk was clean, apart from a coffee mug and a single photo frame. It was just as Gaia said. When Maddox lifted the frame, she found her twenty-one-year-old self again. In the picture, Maddox lofted a small trophy, her glasses askew, while Atticus stood next to her. He ignored the camera, staring at their interlocked hands as she raised them together in triumph.

She had barely set the frame back on the desk when Atticus walked in. He startled, pausing in the doorway and shuffling the papers in his hands. "Have you made any progress with the translation?"

He sounded hopeful that she had not. Maddox shook her head, shrugging. "Not at all, but Professor Bol—Angeline had something interesting to say."

"About the project?"

"Yes, but she mentioned something else." Maddox sat on his desk before jumping back up. Atticus might not be pleased to have her butt on his desk. "I wanted to ask your permission before I took the next step."

"The next step?" Atticus echoed, pushing further into his own classroom.

"A position in the library opened up. I want to apply, but I wanted to ask you about it first."

He stilled, a few of the papers falling out of the stack in his hands. Maddox doubted he noticed. "Are you..." His voice failed him, and Atticus tried again. "Are you asking me to leave?"

"*Leave?*" Maddox gathered his fallen papers and took the rest from him. Placing them on a nearby lab table, she took his hands in her own. Lately, she had gotten away with touching him like this, even in front of Lochlan. Maddox wondered if he thought it was simply friendship and nothing more. Did he have any idea what she was trying to work toward?

She smiled. "No, I just wanted to ask if you'd be comfortable with me working here. It's not temporary like our current project, and I—"

Atticus laughed like he had the first time she'd met him. It was loud and shocked and free. His hands snapped around her waist, lifting her and spinning her around in one smooth motion. Maddox panicked, her hands clamping down on his shoulders for support. She couldn't recall the last time she'd been picked up like this.

"Stop! You're going to throw your back out!" she howled.

"I won't and wouldn't care if I did," he huffed but settled her back on the ground. Atticus removed his hands from her, sticking them into his pockets. "Of course you may apply. I can provide a recommendation if you—"

"Angeline still had the original one she wrote for me." Maddox smoothed her skirt down, hating how warm her face suddenly felt. "And after that, I don't think your recommendation would be very impartial."

At least there was some red dashed across his cheekbones as well. "Right. That wasn't very professional, was it?"

"Do you need me to answer that for you?"

Atticus didn't seem nearly as sorry as he should have. "So, we shall remain coworkers."

"Don't worry about me overstaying my welcome in your home," she said, recalling the second planned part of this conversation. "I'll find lodging elsewhere. I'll start looking today."

"Now, what would you do that for?" He hunched, the light hitting his glasses in a way that made him impossible to read. "Lochlan said you needed to be watched."

She had her argument ready. "We're no longer handling the page directly. Am I to be watched until the end of my days?"

"If it was needed, I would not hesitate."

Oh, Hades. How were they going to work together when he kept saying things like that where anyone could hear him?

Maddox answered, "I think we're going to make HR very tired."

CHAPTER 27
SON OF A WITCH

ONE YEAR BEFORE ATTICUS ENTERS THE ACADEMY

Once, the Blackwell estate crawled with relatives.

At least, that's what Theodora had told Atticus. He never saw the estate in its prime. Since his parents' divorce, it had only been the four of them.

Atticus didn't see his mother very often. Cynthia went abroad often and when she was home, Giles and his bright, capitalist future held all her unwanted attention.

His brother wasn't any better than their mother. Giles mostly ignored Atticus, still angry that during the divorce proceedings Atticus had chosen to stay with their mother. Why Giles was upset over that, Atticus didn't know. Giles could have lived with their father. It was his right to choose his own path. Atticus had once questioned why Giles had echoed Atticus's decision, but Giles had only replied with, "Because you're a fucking dipshit."

So, it was Atticus and Theodora against the world.

Atticus preferred it that way. It was simple. They read the same books, and Theodora loved to spoil him. He enjoyed sitting in on her secret parties, where her old friends—a group that was dwindling year by year—brought her stolen artifacts to examine.

Those séances and gatherings were becoming less frequent, though he didn't mind. It meant he and Theodora could spend more one-on-one time together.

At teatime, Theodora ushered him into her office, pouring them both a cup of tea and pushing a tray of cookies across her desk to him. Atticus happily took what his grandmother still called a biscuit.

She clicked her tongue, tucking her pale hair behind an ear. "How is your brother treating you?"

What an odd question. Atticus choked on his cookie. "Giles barely acknowledges me."

"And your mother is busy looking for employment in England," Theodora mused.

"She's *what?*" Atticus asked, leaning forward in his chair. "Are we going with her?"

"I don't think she intends to take either of you with her. Not even your brother." Theodora offered another cookie which he refused. "You could live with your father, I suppose, but that would leave the estate empty. There's been a Blackwell watching over the home since we left England. Can we let *four hundred years of legacy* die so easily?"

Theodora often spoke like this, casually hinting at her nearing death. It could happen any day now. Necromancers led long lives, but she had reached the end of hers.

She tapped on the desk to get his attention. "I don't have much time left. I've left the manor to you, Atticus, and I know how lonely this home can feel." She cringed. "I spent many years entirely by myself. The solitude was better than watching our family taken from me, one by one. Blood has seeped into the bones of this house, and it is still *thirsty.*"

Atticus reminded her gently, "It's not anyone's fault, what happened to our family. It's just bad luck."

"Bad luck?" she seethed. Theodora stood, striding to the bookshelf to pull her grimoire from its place. She let it drop unceremoniously on the desk and pointed to the family tree sketched inside. He knew what was coming, but Atticus flinched, anyway.

Theodora spoke each word with venom. "Exploded. Crushed. Drowned. Plagued. How much bad luck could one family have?" She shook her head, shutting her grimoire with a *snap.* "We are cursed. Except for me, but I can protect you."

This used to be something Theodora *joked* about, but lately she seemed utterly convinced. Or at her age, she no longer cared to hide her illogical, non-conforming thoughts.

She lifted his chin, her nails scratching his tender skin. "You won't leave me, will you?"

"No." The answer was easy. He'd been trained well.

"And I..." Her nails left his chin to stroke his hair. "I will *never* leave you."

CHAPTER 28
WITCH

While Maddox wanted Atticus closer and for there to be no more lies between them, she still tiptoed through his house like a burglar. She combed through his family library, taking out a few texts on the history of the Blackwells. These texts she shoved in her disorganized messenger bag and kept them hidden until she headed to the Academy on foot. Alone.

The library was quiet, but dawn was just breaking. Few students were as determined—or desperate—as Maddox had been during her school days. For what she was doing, she was grateful for the solitude.

"It's not like I'm investigating *him*," Maddox argued with one of the Academy's ghosts. "I'm merely trying to...investigate his favorite relative."

She sighed, shivering as the ghost, bored with their conversation, passed through her and left the study room.

Maddox let go of her guilt. Somewhat. She flipped through the Blackwells' handwritten histories, noting any mention of Theodora.

"If I had access to Theodora's grimoire," Maddox grumbled, "this would be so much easier."

"Are you stalking Mr. Blackwell?" Lochlan's dull, matter-of-fact tone made Maddox screech. He winced at the sound before pointing to the book in her hands. "I can't see why else you'd be studying his family history. If you're stalking him, I'm obligated to report you."

"No, I'm not *stalking* him," Maddox snapped, one hand pressed against her pounding heart.

"I'll need more explanation than that," Lochlan insisted. He sat down next to her, tugging her book over so he could read. "Let me guess. You've noticed the missing references, too."

"How'd you know?" Maddox asked. She let him steal her book away, knowing there was nothing useful in it.

Lochlan scanned the text as he answered. "The Commission suspected Theodora from the start when the Tome of the Undying was initially reported missing. They investigated a century ago, but..."

"What happened?"

"Theodora Blackwell was *incredibly* wealthy." Lochlan rolled his eyes. "The investigation's initial findings have officially been declared lost. Hmph. Typical government operation."

Maddox dropped her voice to a whisper. "I think Theodora may have stolen other texts from the Academy of the Dead's library. I just don't know what for."

"You don't think Atticus will let us dig her up and ask?" Lochlan inquired thoughtfully.

"No. He loved her dearly. I don't think he'd let us disturb her rest for an *interrogation*." Maddox stole her book back from him and placed it into her bag. "This was a waste of time."

"Maybe not. We share our suspicions, so perhaps we can work together." Lochlan waited for her to protest, and when nothing came, he continued. "These possibly stolen references...perhaps they are still on the estate. I could help you find them."

"I've checked the Blackwells' personal library and every study I could access. If the books are still there, they're well hidden and possibly warded."

"A necromancer's magic leaves behind a stain. It's difficult for me personally, but I *can* detect it. If the stolen texts are hidden through magic, I may find it." Lochlan, despite her barely knowing the man, seemed trustworthy. He was definitely honest. Sometimes *too* honest.

Maddox gave in to her curiosity. "Okay, I can get you inside, but I'd rather not tell Atticus."

Lochlan nodded. "I'll follow you."

Maddox buried her guilt and, once the sun went down, she snuck Lochlan inside the manor through the kitchen entrance. Jinx entered the room to investigate, hissed at Lochlan, and immediately vanished to run down the hall.

"She's new to being an inside cat," Maddox explained. She gestured about the room. "Well? Feel anything?"

"Actually, I do," Lochlan said, and then his head snapped to the left. He pointed to a door with an amused expression. "What's behind there?"

Maddox shrugged, yanking at the handle until the warped door swung free. "Looks like a cellar."

"Then down we go."

Lochlan led them downstairs, a white ball of flame cupped in his palm to light their way until Maddox found the light switch. They found themselves in an impressive wine cellar with many branching tunnels.

Without a moment's pause, Lochlan started down one of the cramped tunnels and left her to hurry after him. Maddox chased his heels until they stepped into an echoing open room.

Lochlan's nose crinkled. "This place has been wiped."

"Wiped?"

He nodded and walked around the empty, circular room as he trailed one hand along the wall. "Like when someone uses bleach to cover a crime, magic can be scrubbed away as well."

This grew more complicated by the minute. Maddox laughed nervously. "Maybe we're researching the wrong mystery." Lochlan didn't laugh with her.

As Lochlan continued to circle the space, Maddox walked into the center of the room, her feet stopping on the round metal grate below. Digging out her phone, Maddox turned on its flashlight and peered into the darkness of the drain.

Maddox pointed to the grate, beckoning him over. "Can you cast some light down there? I thought I saw something."

He approached, summoning again his bright fire before letting it float down into the drain. "It looks like bone," he mused. "I'm not sticking my arm down there to find out, though."

"Move back," she ordered, squatting to lift the grate off the drain. Maddox dropped to her knees and dug around in the filthy drain until her fingers grasped something solid. She pulled it out, shaking dirt and muck from its surface.

"Disgusting," Lochlan sneered. "And definitely human bone."

"It's not just a bit of bone!" Maddox nearly laughed in her excitement. "It's a key!"

That caught his attention. Lochlan brought his light closer to the key, illuminating the bone cylinder and the black writing carved into it.

A voice, magically amplified, sliced through the air. "If you're here to rob me of my wine, at least let me help you pick out a good year."

"*Atticus*," Maddox and Lochlan said in unison.

Maddox stuffed the cylinder into her jacket pocket, racking her brain for an explanation. Nope. Nothing. What could she say when Atticus inevitably asked why she and Lochlan were squatting in his cellar?

Her worrying came to naught. As Atticus cautiously entered the room, Lochlan announced, "We came here to snoop on your family."

Atticus halted his approach, squinting at the pair of them. Maddox's hands fisted in her hair. She stuttered, "Lochlan, *why* would you—"

Lochlan shrugged. "If I lie, I have to confess. The local priest made me say *fifty Our Fathers* last time. I'm not risking that again."

Atticus crossed his arms and chuckled. "Lochlan, if you wanted to know about me, all you had to do was ask. I *love* talking about myself."

"That wouldn't have helped," Maddox said, wincing. "We think Theodora may have stolen references from the Academy library, namely those that covered the Tome."

"Oh." Atticus scratched his beard absentmindedly. "She probably did."

"You admit that so easily," Lochlan huffed.

"My family runs a billion-dollar business. Do you think any of them would hesitate to just take what they want?" Atticus shrugged, stepping backward out of the room and motioning them to follow. "I hate this room. Come upstairs.

Lochlan, you may as well stay for dinner."

As they followed Atticus up to the kitchen, Lochlan murmured to Maddox, "He took our spying a little too well."

"Maybe what he has to hide is somewhere else," Maddox whispered back.

Atticus patted his kitchen island, motioning for them to take a seat while he cooked. Maddox broke the silence quickly. "If you knew your grandmother stole Academy property, why didn't you tell us?"

Atticus tasted a dish before he answered. "I've scoured the estate many times over since her death. Anything I found that belonged to the Academy, I returned years ago."

"So," Lochlan drawled, "this project is fucked."

"Not necessarily. Not yet," Atticus amended. "I made a few calls, and Japan's Grim Academy has a package on its way to us. It should arrive in a few days."

Oh, thank Hades! Maddox blurted, "What did they send?!"

"Copies of every reference to the Tome—no matter how brief—they have." Atticus grinned. "There's no need to thank me—"

Lochlan interrupted him coldly. "No one should thank you for doing *your job.*"

"I'm feeding you, trespasser. Be nicer to me."

As Atticus turned his back to them, focusing on the stove once more, Maddox exchanged a worried glance with Lochlan.

What was the real mystery here? The Tome of the Undying or Atticus?

CHAPTER 29
WARLOCK

Just as Atticus had promised, after a few anxious days of waiting, Japan came through. The Japanese Grim Academy sent photocopied references concerning the authors of the Tome and even translated some copies into English for them as well. Not to mention, Japan provided something even more invaluable—handwriting samples of each of the thirteen writers.

They spent all morning unboxing the files. Lochlan kept Maddox from tearing through the papers like a wild animal and logged everything they received to check his notes against the shipping manifest.

"Japan's records *are* so much more thorough. It's almost embarrassing how little our library has." Maddox squinted at the piles of files Japan sent before coming to a decision. "We have to go back into the cleanroom!" Maddox declared, slamming her hand on the desk that the three of them were crowding around.

"You mean *you're* going back in," Atticus clarified, folding his arms.

"Of course she does." Lochlan was impatiently waiting his turn to read Japan's excerpts. "She's following protocol, and I agree. Getting another up close encounter with the artifact could help us."

Atticus rolled his eyes. "Because last time went so well!"

"What choice do we have? With these handwriting samples, we can compare this to our paper. But I'll need another look to be sure." Maddox sighed, passing the documents off to Lochlan. "If we can learn which author wrote our sample, we'll have a better idea on how to translate it."

"No."

Both Maddox and Lochlan glared at him. Lochlan laughed coldly. "Who do you have less faith in? Maddox or me? Who do you assume is going to fail?"

"Yes, Atticus." Maddox leaned back in her chair, teeth nearly bared. "What right do you have to control what I do?"

You're going to lose her again if she faces that cursed thing.

Atticus couldn't stop himself. He ducked his head, silently willing his voice to remain steady. If Giles knew what he was about to do... Atticus promised, "There's another way."

The words were a betrayal to one long dead. Atticus removed his family ring and gently took Maddox's left hand. He ignored Lochlan's awkward cough and slipped the band onto her middle finger. As Atticus murmured a spell, the ring glowed, a short and overwhelming flash of heat, but Maddox swallowed the pain silently.

"This ring allows the bearer to read a Blackwell grimoire. You'll need it to read my grandmother's notes."

"What good will those do?" Lochlan watched them from a distance, sneering Atticus's way. Atticus took no offense—though the exorcist liked to keep them both at arm's length, Atticus knew Lochlan hated to be left out.

"My grandmother, after she retired as the Academy's master librarian, helped dismantle the Tome of the Undying and scattered it across the world. Her grimoire is the best reference regarding the Tome." He couldn't look at either of them.

"*Why* would she do that?" Maddox gasped, her hand covering her mouth with a slap.

"I would like to say Theodora felt it was too dangerous to remain whole, but I think she and her friends wanted to keep certain knowledge to themselves. They split it up between them."

Lochlan dropped into a chair, rubbing his temples. "Are you fucking serious, Mr. Blackwell?"

He was back to *Mr. Blackwell.* That wasn't a good sign. Atticus continued, "Theodora has a way to break the Tome's code. I've already tried it and had no luck, but maybe Maddox will."

Atticus lifted Maddox's hand once more and softly kissed the ring. He hoped she would believe that was only another part of the ritual.

He hoped too much.

CHAPTER 30
WITCH

The trio moved their research team to the Blackwell estate. Though Lochlan protested the decision for many reasons, the one he brought up the most was the *cat*. Jinx hated Lochlan and seemed to take pleasure in sneaking up on the man and brushing against him as if it knew about the exorcist's disdain for felines.

Maddox refused to get involved; she couldn't be distracted by a rivalry between a cat and a grown man. She'd just ended her own rivalry, after all.

She helped Atticus set up a workstation inside the Blackwell library. After that, the warlock promptly left her and Lochlan alone with his grandmother's grimoire. And Maddox was *pissed*.

What else was Atticus hiding in these damp halls? She could hardly concentrate on Theodora Blackwell's grimoire, but as she was the only one who could read it, Maddox focused on it until her eyes burned.

This grimoire belonged in its own exhibit. Two centuries of knowledge, all of it logged daily since Theodora was eight-years-old. Maddox had thought her own ledger meticulous, but this filled her with shame.

The front of the grimoire held private details on Theodora's life. Her family tree was beautiful—the calligraphy a work of art. Maddox noted the dates of Theodora's many siblings, shocked that they had all died so young. Under each deceased's name was a brief explanation of their death. Experimental accidents or genetic illnesses were mostly the causes. Mental health issues had claimed some. Theodora was left alone at an early age and raised by a governess.

What a morbid childhood.

Maddox moved on from Theodora's gruesome family history, pushing past to details on the Tome of the Undying. She felt her ire rise. Atticus could have saved them *weeks* of work if he had come forward with this at the start.

She was so irritated with the tall, grimly handsome man, that Maddox wasn't even pleased when she found the section she needed in Theodora's overly detailed notes. Each author of the Tome of the Undying was listed, and there was a summary of what aspect of the dark arts their section covered.

Most importantly, Theodora recorded where every single section of the Tome was once hidden. Though, there was an issue. Next to each location was Atticus's careful handwriting, noting that the page was either missing or destroyed. That left only the section they possessed, which Atticus had circled in red ink three times.

How long had Atticus been searching for a piece of the Tome? This looked like *years* of work. It was as worrying as it was impressive.

Maddox pushed thoughts of Atticus aside and studied every tidbit of information on their page. She learned it was penned by Warlock Kaspar. He had traveled all throughout the Middle East, notorious for leaving behind cursed artifacts in whatever village he inevitably fled.

Theodora had even provided a sample of the warlock's code, and if Maddox could make sense of it, *she would win.*

Maddox pushed the grimoire away from her, rubbing her eyes. She wanted a break, but Lochlan was on the edge of his seat, waiting for her to share what she'd found. The words were dull and made her throat sore, but Maddox recounted to Lochlan everything she'd read. He recorded the details in his journal while Maddox excused herself from the table.

The kitchen was her first stop. She grabbed a water bottle from the fridge and sipped it half-heartedly. This wasn't like her—this stalling. But the more she considered Atticus's situation, the repercussions of revealing to a Commission agent that his grandmother had helped destroy necromancy's greatest resource, the more she understood why he had kept it a secret. It was unfair to expect him to expose his family that way. Maddox honestly didn't understand why Atticus had revealed it at all. Would the Commission punish Atticus somehow? Would a fine suffice or would there be harsher consequences?

No, if Giles was the same as she remembered, he wouldn't let his family's name be dragged through the mud. He'd find a not-so-legal way out of this mess.

Logic was annoying. If only Maddox had been raised to be a little less understanding, she wouldn't be so irritated now. Yes, Atticus had technically lied, and by doing so prolonged this project, but what choice did he really have?

Atticus's study was shut. Maddox rapped on the doorframe a few times and waited for an answer.

"Come in, if you must."

How friendly. Swallowing her initial reaction, Maddox cooled her temper and entered the room. The first thing she looked for was the whiskey bottle she'd confiscated from him earlier. It remained in place, the liquor level about the same.

This time, he wasn't lamenting over his desk. Atticus lounged on a dark green settee, his legs stretched across the cushions. Maddox swung his legs off the couch to make room for her to sit next to him.

He jolted when she gently rested a hand on his knee, so she quickly removed it.

How to begin? "Atticus, why did you tell us what your grandmother did?"

"That..." He sank into the couch, side-eying her. "That isn't what I thought you'd ask."

"It doesn't make sense. You're risking your family's reputation. We can't know what Lochlan will report to his superiors, and I—"

"Don't you *know*?" He faced her, hands clamped around his knees. "I brought this damned artifact into your life, so if something were to happen to you, it would be my fault. Maddox, I've been manipulating you this entire time." He stood, now pacing a death march into the study's ornamental rug. "I knew Theodora hid sections of the Tome away, and I led the expedition myself."

"You went *in person*?" The image of Atticus scrambling amongst bones and underground silt, raiding the Paris Catacombs, contradicted with the impeccably dressed man before her. "I thought someone else led the expedition? Rami?"

"You mean my *father*? Rami Alsharif?" Atticus's pacing paused, and he spun in her direction. "He was happy to fund the trip, not that I needed it. I just wanted someone else's name on the paperwork to hide that I..."

Embarrassment flooded her expression. All those years Maddox had known Atticus, and she had *never* learned his father's name? Was she that self-absorbed? Though, in her defense, Atticus liked to drive the conversation away from his family at the soonest opportunity.

"You did this all for *me*." How long had Atticus planned this venture?

Atticus seemed embarrassed for a moment, his desperation now plain for her to see. Atticus swallowed down his shame, eyes narrowing. "The extraction wasn't clean. I crushed skulls with each step, breathed in that same corpse dust, but I would do so much worse for you."

Maddox believed him. She hoped she'd never have to test the limits of his promise.

Atticus rubbed his tense jaw. "You deserved to accomplish your goals. You worked so hard, you struggled, and all of it alone." A sigh escaped him, but his guilt remained. "You were gone so long from our world. This project gave you a chance to return. I planned all of it. I gathered a team, got funding from my father just to lessen my part in it, and I made sure some other warlock extracted the artifact so I could keep my hands clean and work on the translation with you."

The extent of his trap chilled her blood. "You lied to me."

"Yes. Many times." Atticus withdrew into himself. "But I had to try."

Was it pity that fueled his actions or something else? "You didn't think I could be happy there? Back in Washington?"

"I did. I just..." He shrugged. "If you were happy, you would have easily rejected me. Hell, you would have *laughed* at me. But if you were as desperate as I feared to return to our world...I had to give you that chance."

She went to him, rising from the couch and reaching for his arm, but Atticus shook her off. He flopped down on the middle of the couch, gripping the edge of the settee as if it could ground him in his spiral. "I purposefully brought this cursed thing to you, and it has hurt you. I can't allow it any longer." His chin raised, his voice loud and steady, Atticus continued, "I don't doubt your strength, and I never have. I simply understand the limits of mine. Maddox, I'll do anything to keep you from entering that room. Even if it makes you hate me again. I am weak, and selfish, and a coward, but I am something much worse. I am in love."

She gave him a few minutes' respite before Maddox crossed the few feet between them. "You say that as if it's the worst thing you've ever done to me." Maddox straddled his lap, one knee on either side of his thighs, and faced him. His breath was too fast, and she could do nothing for him but wait for it to settle. "Could you ever love me without guilt hanging on every declaration?"

His response was too quick, no space of breath betwixt the words. "We're about to work together. You can't speak like this to me. I'll never get over you if you..." Close as they were, it was hard to avoid each other's gaze, but Atticus was doing his damnedest. "Maddox, I don't understand where this is going."

She lifted his chin with two fingers, her brow quirked and her voice soft. "Don't you? You're far more experienced in this sort of thing than I am."

"I don't know what 'sort of thing' you're talking about!"

It was soft and unsure—a kiss unlike any they had shared before. Maddox wasn't unsure about *Atticus*—it was her skill that made her anxiously tremble. When she'd kissed him all those times before, it felt more like they were fighting. There was no time to second guess herself. She had thought she was punishing him.

She didn't want to punish him anymore.

She just wanted him.

Maddox needed her ill-tempered, sharp-tongued magician, who dressed too fine and thought Mary Shelley and her gothic dramatics were a perfect role model.

She held his face in her hands, running her thumbs over his almost gaunt cheeks. Her kisses were exploratory, slow, and though Atticus was gently returning her kisses, something seemed wrong.

When she pulled away, Atticus only stared at her, lips tight and brow pinched together. He reached up and removed her hands from him, his head slowly shaking "no."

Her cheeks reddened, and though it sent panic coursing through her veins, Maddox was glad to hear Lochlan shouting down the hallway, "Did you find Atticus yet? Can we finish translating this cursed thing?"

Maddox scrambled off Atticus's lap, refusing to look back at her failure. For all Atticus's well-worded, romantic confessions, he really just wanted to get over her. And that made sense. They were to be colleagues—anything more between them would get messy.

But if it was so logical, why did it hurt so fucking bad?

Luckily, Lochlan made things easy for her. He bossed them all back to the library and together they worked on the translation while Atticus sat at the head of their table. He didn't say a word, only watched Maddox and Lochlan translate while he frowned.

After yet another dead end, Maddox was about to stab her pencil through her notebook when she muttered, "No fucking way." Maddox hauled her overstuffed messenger bag on top of the table and violently threw items aside.

"Your bag is full of garbage." Lochlan leaned away from her, using a book to block any debris tossed his way.

"It's full of garbage and *this*!" Maddox triumphantly held out the bone key that she and Lochlan had fished out of the scummy drain.

Atticus tore the key from her, scanning the carved writing on the cylinder. She barely recognized him. All color had drained from his face. "Where was this?" Atticus demanded. He tossed his glasses down on the table, the meal frames clattering against the wood. "I haven't seen this in *years*."

What was this attitude? Maddox sniffed. "In your cellar. It fell down the drain, or it was stashed there." She reached forward and took the key back. "Give me a few hours with this before you take it from me."

He seemed happy to let her steal it back, though what else he felt was a mystery. Atticus kept glancing at the key and rapping his knuckles on his forehead.

Lochlan moved to the other side of the table, dropping a stack of papers in front of Atticus. "Organize these," he ordered.

Normally, Atticus would have protested. Now, he took the papers and shuffled them nervously, though the task seemed to alleviate some of his stress. Lochlan gave Maddox a sharp nod, taking a seat as he watched over the warlock.

Maddox returned to work, but only because Lochlan was a doctor and specifically a psychiatrist. If Atticus was dealing with something he was unwilling to share, Lochlan could handle it. Even if Maddox wanted to throw down her notebooks and work on the puzzle that was Atticus instead.

It was difficult, but Maddox used the key to get a rough idea of the page's meaning. Though it would take a few more days to get an exact picture, she could see where she needed to go.

This key was something Theodora had stolen from the Academy or somewhere else, or it was something Theodora had created herself, perhaps using the missing references as a basis.

"It's instructions," Lochlan summarized, leaning in so close to Maddox they were touching. Maddox doubted he was aware of it—he was so focused on the page that even his pupils had dilated, a large void that overtook the green.

Maddox agreed. "It describes something called a parasitoid." She read aloud for Atticus's benefit, but he was hardly paying them any attention at all. She continued, raising her voice, "It's a simple being that can be bound to a magical object. Or to a magical *creature*."

Only now did Atticus acknowledge her, his face grim and shadowed. He stared right through her, the intensity pinning her in place like a dried insect behind glass.

"Considering how the artifact attacked me, I believe the Tome of the Undying held such a parasite. Maybe as a type of protection?" Maddox theorized. "But when the book was torn apart, surely that would have destroyed such a simple thing?"

Atticus accepted the rushed partial translation when she offered it. Her words caused him to fade back into his earlier gloom.

Lochlan rose from the table. His voice was clear, authoritative. "We've been at this all day, *and* we skipped lunch. We should rest for a few hours before dinner."

Maddox couldn't have argued even if she wanted to. With today's work complete, there was nothing left to keep her from hyper-focusing on her romantic misstep. She slid Theodora's grimoire back over to Atticus and turned toward the exit. "I'm going to my room."

Lochlan waited for Atticus to respond, and when the warlock remained silent, Lochlan said, "I can text you when dinner's ready, Maddox."

Maddox only nodded to the exorcist, rushing out of the library before the bile churning her gut made an appearance.

Once in her room, Maddox opened a window, and Edgar flew in after a few moments. She ran her fingers over the bird's feathered head as she replayed her mistake. Atticus's ring glinted as she stroked the corvid—she had forgotten to give it back to him. Damn her absent-mindedness. Maddox wanted to throw the antique band across the room, and she couldn't say why she contained her rage.

He never said I love you without a dash of regret.

She pressed her thumbs into her eyes. The urge to scream "*loser, loser, loser*" into her pillow returned. Maddox hadn't felt like this since the Academy—when nothing mattered to her besides doing her best. She laughed at her own lie, spooking the raven at her side.

She didn't care about doing her best. She needed to be better than everyone else. Only total victory could give irrefutable proof that she belonged.

Love isn't like a test, she scolded herself. *You can't do it perfectly, no matter how much you try.*

Maddox flopped back on her bed, eyes dry and wide as her brain worked overtime to find every flaw in herself and her actions and tried to fix the lacking person she was.

CHAPTER 31
WARLOCK

Maddox had kissed him.

Atticus was now absolutely certain she was possessed.

Even if he hadn't caught that flicker of a shadow in the corner of her eye, that tender pressing of her lips to his would have been proof enough she wasn't in her right mind.

Could you ever love me without guilt hanging on every declaration?

What a ridiculous question—of course, he couldn't. His sins—*his lies*—ran a mile long, and he had to be bullied and pressured and begged to unravel just a small part of the tangled web he'd woven.

Jinx dove between his legs, crying for attention. Atticus lifted the cat into his arms just to have some quiet to think. He ignored how calming the warm and annoying ball of fur could be.

"I bet you were outside eating my trash for months before you tricked Maddox into letting you inside," Atticus complained. Jinx yawned, revealing those feline fangs. "You're lucky that woman has a soft spot for pitiful things. And that Venenum listens to me."

A small piece of that damned page had latched on to Maddox, and Atticus didn't know if it had happened during the first or the second encounter. Not that it mattered. The shadow, the *parasite*, was still weak, but every day it remained in Maddox, it would only grow stronger as it fed off her magic.

The worst part of it? He couldn't tell Maddox about his discovery. That parasite was biding its time, trying to remain unnoticed. If it became aware that its cover was up, it might try to jump hosts, or take over the body completely, or kill itself—and that would take Maddox with it.

Hades below, she would hate being kept in the dark. Atticus thought of his patron with a grimace. Not that the Lord of the Underworld had ever helped him before, but it might still be worth making an offering if Hades would help Maddox.

Atticus had to get Lochlan alone soon. Together, they would find a solution. All Atticus needed was for Maddox to stay put and underneath his watchful eye. Currently, that was easily accomplished. They lived and worked together, and as long as Maddox's interview went well—and it damn well should—they would stay together.

He could keep her safe, the exorcist would find a way to do his job properly and destroy the parasite, and Maddox would forgive his lies—again.

That last hope seemed the most futile of all.

"Exorcist."

"Hellraiser." Lochlan eyed Atticus with a grimace. Atticus had requested that Lochlan arrive for dinner early, and judging from his attitude, Atticus hadn't done so politely. Lochlan grumped, "I'll forgive the rude text you sent if you make this quick."

Atticus pulled Lochlan out of the dining room, across the hall, through a tall door, and into his family ballroom. He waved a hand through the air as if that would clear over a decade of dust. "We need to talk about Maddox."

"You're not about to *confess* something to me, are you?" Lochlan leaned away, frowning. "I'm not that kind of priest, and even when I explain that, people still burden me with their disturbing secrets."

"I believe Maddox is showing signs of possession."

Lochlan relaxed for a moment before tensing, his back snapping straight. "What evidence do you have? I've sensed nothing, and I've been far from slacking."

"She's not acting like herself, and I saw a shadow in the corner of her eye. It was only a flicker, a weak pulse, but I swear it was there."

Lochlan tapped his chin. "A shadow isn't much to go off of. I will, of course, test Maddox again, but if its successfully hiding from me, I'll need more information. More symptoms."

Atticus searched for anything else before he answered. "Maddox kissed me."

Lochlan squinted at him for a long time. "And that's *unusual* for you two?"

"Our relationship is complicated. It's my fault, obviously, and it started when—"

"Stop!" Lochlan waved his hands in front of him frantically. "That sounds like a confession, and I don't hear confession! If absolution is what you're after, find a real priest."

"I know there's something wrong! I know what I saw." Atticus scratched his beard, sure more grey would soon meld with the black. "I'm not trying to say you aren't skilled or you made a mistake. Maddox is my only concern here. I *saw* something hiding away in her. We need to remove it without it realizing that we're on to it."

That seemed to be enough to get Lochlan to stop asking questions. Lochlan nodded grimly. "If you truly believe this, Atticus, I'll look again."

"Thank you for taking this seriously," Atticus said.

"That's my job." Lochlan sighed. "I can ask the Commission for another exorcist, but they keep us busy. It might be months before they can send someone, and there's no guarantee they can even help us."

Atticus slowed down Lochlan's planning. "Just give me more time. Maddox can remain under my observation. There's no need to *escalate* things."

What Atticus was hinting at made Lochlan pale. "I agree. Let's save the Asylum as a last resort, and I want to confirm that there's even anything to worry about. No offense."

The Asylum wasn't an official name—that didn't look good on a pamphlet. The Commission kept, for lack of a better term, a prison for magical beings that were possessed or otherwise couldn't control themselves. Rehabilitation was its claimed purpose, but few that ventured inside ever returned.

Atticus would pull it apart brick by brick before he ever let Maddox step inside that hellhole.

"Let's get back to the kitchen," Atticus decided, leading the way back. "And say nothing of this—"

"To Maddox," Lochlan finished. "You don't need to explain possession to me."

Taking a seat at the kitchen island, Lochlan referenced the journal he kept while Atticus cooked. He had opted for something he knew well. The majboos was nearly done when Maddox walked in.

"Maddox?" Atticus abandoned the rice, sweeping over to her. She seated herself next to Lochlan, absentmindedly reading over his shoulder.

"Yes?" Her attention remained on the journal.

"May I—may I have my ring back?"

She seemed to tense, but Atticus must have imagined it. She tugged off the ring and dropped it into his waiting palm, careful to avoid contact. "Here."

The metal was cold and heavy in his hand. He didn't want it back, but he needed to consult Theodora's notes to help Maddox. Theodora was responsible for tearing apart the Tome of the Undying and scrubbing most of the Academy's references of it, but he suspected her grimoire might hold enough information to give Maddox a fighting chance.

Or maybe not. As a child, Atticus had believed Theodora to be infallible, a paragon. Someone who always possessed the answers to all his problems.

He'd been wrong.

CHAPTER 32
WITCH

The translation moved quickly thanks to Theodora's key, but now Maddox was stuck doing the project write-up by herself. Atticus and Lochlan both claimed they had other, more pressing priorities and left her in the Academy library to continue the work alone. She understood why Atticus wished to avoid her after her foolish pass at him, but she hadn't expected Lochlan to abandon her as well. *There.* Just one more read-through of the translation and Maddox could put this project, and all its disappointments, to rest.

An excerpt of Warlock Kaspar's section of the Tome of the Undying. This portion contains some text that was too damaged to read and some text that has been translated into modern necromantic terms.

—my colleagues call it a useless leech, but I believe my parasitoid could be useful with a strong host. It is small, simple, but so are insects and an infestation can be a fearsome thing. Not to mention, since this creature is so simple, so single-minded, it can be stored within an object if the object is embedded with enough magic to sustain it. If it's allowed to feast on a living host, however, it will not go back to an inanimate object again.

This "parasitoid" can only be imbued with one purpose. This is where my colleagues deem it weak, a waste, but I know much can be achieved with a warlock's single desire. And weakness means it will be underestimated.

(illegible text due to the artifact's age)

—once the parasitoid has leeched enough energy to reveal itself, it will act on its given directive until the host has perished or its aim has been achieved.

Maddox read over her work, her listless heart not excited in the least. A few weeks ago, revealing such knowledge would have sent her into a frenzy, but now she could only gather mild interest. She remained distracted by a man she'd never understand, and maybe it was better to realize that today than years from now.

You should have learned your lesson years ago.

It certainly didn't help her mood that her interview for the open librarian position hadn't gone exactly as she had hoped. The current head librarian, Mrs. Tuttle, had muttered to herself throughout the process, and, ominously, she had ended their interview with, "The library ghosts have told me all I need to know about you."

Maddox, though she knew she was qualified, left worrying that her five-year absence had doomed her chances. Or her former failure to return her library books on time.

If that was the reason, well, that wasn't fucking fair. Maddox was better at regulating her lack of focus now. Human medicine had its uses.

For the third time that day, Maddox checked her email for a job offer *or a* rejection. The outcome mattered less and less to her—she just wanted this painful waiting to end.

Could she finish the write-up at home? And by home, she meant Fair Harbor, *not* the Blackwell estate. Maddox tired of seeing Atticus daily—it only stung to see him ignore her again. He buried himself in work, but he refused to share this new enterprise with her, though she suspected Lochlan was involved.

You should have been happy with what you had.

The voice sounded a lot like Aegis, but Maddox knew it was coming from her own cruel logic.

Her writing swam in front of her eyes, the words too blurred to mean a damned thing. Sleep evaded her, despite the brew she'd mustered from the Blackwell laboratory, a room she'd finally discovered in this maze of a house. Atticus used the estate's attached greenhouse, a large, jungle-like room covered wall to wall with green glass and black iron bars, for his home apothecary. He had such unexpected ingredients for a household apothecary, but Maddox ignored the oddities as Atticus himself was an oddity.

Rest wasn't an option anymore—Maddox was swaying on her feet. Gods, she felt so drained lately. Maddox started the march back to the Blackwell estate, her shoes covered in mud by the end of it.

Once inside, she saw Atticus's study was lit from within. She walked past the room softly, praying she didn't disturb him. What Atticus wanted from her was clear. Space. She might have ruined what they had barely rebuilt, and that had to be the source of her insomnia.

The right answer here was to leave it alone.

Back in her bedroom, Maddox's phone dinged, and she checked the notification out of habit.

We regret to inform you...

She let the phone clatter to the floor, the quickest way to get the email summary out of her sight.

The job wasn't hers. A job she had fought for, and she'd managed to fuck that up, too. What had she done wrong? The interview wasn't perfect, but had she lost focus at some point? She thought she had it handled.

Maddox needed darkness. Her magic swarmed the room, billowing clouds that extinguished every source of light bleeding into her room.

The simple magic took much more strength than it should have, but Maddox ignored that thought as the frustrated scream she'd been swallowing escaped.

CHAPTER 33
DRUIDESS'S DAUGHTER

The days when Maddox had no classes, she didn't speak a word. If there was no teacher to call on her, Maddox had no reason to use her voice. Atticus still ignored her, and Maddox preferred that to the random times he seemed to stare at her in that haunting way of his.

"Just two more years," Maddox muttered, her voice hoarse from disuse. She was twenty, no, today she was twenty-one, and all it meant to her that she was a little closer to graduation.

The door to the study room she had permanently booked in the Academy library swung open. Maddox tensed, not wanting to be seen by anyone. She'd sprinted to the library immediately after practicing with Aegis, her rapier, in the school gym. Students weren't supposed to bring their swords anywhere except to and from the gym, and Maddox hated to ruin her perfect record.

She relaxed after she discovered her interrupter was none other than Atticus Blackwell, the very reason she had sprinted back to the library to study. She was slowly gaining on his top mark, and every *second* of studying counted if she hoped to overtake him.

At least Atticus wouldn't snitch on her for having her weapon in an unauthorized space.

Maddox pointed at the door, refusing to let Atticus have the first or the last word. "Get out."

Atticus continued moving into the already cramped study room. As he walked, he traced the edges of the single rectangular table in the room until he was inches away from where she sat. He sat on the tabletop, pushing a soda, strawberry flavored, her way.

What was Atticus doing? Did he need to borrow her notes? Maddox scrunched up her brow, waiting for clarification.

"Happy birthday," he said with a smirk.

She felt lightheaded, and she curled her fingers into fists to regain some feeling in them. What she feared had finally happened. He was mocking her, just like the others.

Action kept her frustrated tears at bay. Maddox stood and, in one swift motion, grabbed Atticus by the collar and threw him down on the table. Aegis was in her hand before she could think about repercussions, and Maddox brought the blade to his throat.

"What the hell kind of foreplay is *this*?" Atticus snapped, and he seemed deeply unsettled. *Good.* Let him be the one not in control of their emotions for once. "If you wanted to play rough with me, you could have just asked nicely."

She searched her heart for compassion, for *reason*, and found none. "Fuck you. You should have kept ignoring me."

"Maddox," he breathed, shirking from her blade and paling when she only pressed the edge closer against his skin. "I didn't come here to fight."

"You just came to be an asshole, then?" She left her blade where it lay. This was how she liked Atticus best—at her mercy.

"No! Hades, can you put your sword away? I'm here to help you."

"I don't want anything from you." *But I am keeping that soda.* Maddox knew she needed to let him go, but that didn't mean she had to be nice about it. She sheathed Aegis and snatched Atticus's burgundy tie, yanking him back into a seated position. "Now leave."

He rubbed his neck, frowning. "I came here to make an offer, and I'm not leaving without saying my piece."

Atticus always made things difficult. Maddox gathered her notebooks and pens in a huff. "Then *I'll* leave."

"Wait." Atticus caught her elbow, halting her. "I know you're entering the Salem Cracked Cauldron Brewing Competition."

Typical. All Atticus wanted was to suss out his competition. "That's what you barged in here for?" She tore out of his grip. "Are you trying to convince me to quit?"

Atticus straightened his tie and snapped, "I'm *trying* to convince you to work together."

She laughed in his face. "Why would I work with you? And why would you want to work with *me?*"

Atticus shrugged. "It's simple. You're the smartest person I know. Blackwells *always* win the CC Brewing Competition. Doesn't it make more sense to team up?"

"It makes absolutely no sense," she returned heartlessly. "I despise you."

"It'll be an ensured victory," Atticus countered, sliding off the table and rushing to beat her to the door. He blocked her exit with an arm, barricading the doorframe and coming way too close to her personal bubble.

"I'll take my chances." Maddox refused to move another step. She stuffed her books into her messenger bag and waited, glaring up at him.

"If you win this competition, no one can say it's unearned. Think how it'll look on your resume." He lingered, rubbing his chin thoughtfully. "I'll let you keep throwing me around. You seem to enjoy that, but I draw the line at involving your sword."

"What kind of woman do you think I am?" Maddox blushed, biting her lip while she twisted her hands together painfully.

"The best," he answered. "I'll even let you use my Apothecary notes for the next exam. If you join me in this, Maddox, it'll save me a lot of hell from my mother."

Why, why, why! After years of overlooking her, why was Atticus focusing his attention on her *now?* She was almost free of them all. It would be the best course of action to refuse him, to avoid getting involved with him again.

So why was she tempted?

Ah, if they joined forces, she'd have someone to talk to. Even if it was only temporary.

Atticus sensed her inner turmoil. "Just give it some thought? Maybe if we win, you'll let me study with you again."

"I—I don't want to be your friend again."

His eyes narrowed. "I wasn't suggesting that."

"Oh." Maddox played with the strap of her messenger bag. "Okay. Good. If that's really the case—"

"It is."

"—then let's work together for now." Though she hated to admit it, even internally, Atticus would be quite the advantage. His potions were always perfect, effortlessly so. Maddox had to put in hours of preparation before every potions lab just to keep up with him.

Atticus held out a hand to her, and Maddox shook it after a prolonged sigh. "We have a deal?" he asked.

"I shook your hand, didn't I? If it's good enough for a feyrie bargain, it should be good enough for you." Maddox eased out of the study room and hurried back to her dorm room.

They won. Maddox fled the Cracked Cauldron Brewing Competition's crowd, her heart only settling once she had her back against the door of her hotel room. She desired victory above all else, but she hated what came after. Ass-kissing and insincere congratulations.

Whatever. It was over, and Maddox had the trophy to prove it. It even had a cute little cauldron on top of it, and it bubbled and smoked noisily.

The Academy had accidentally booked Maddox and Atticus in adjoining hotel rooms. Maddox heard Atticus return to his room through the thin walls.

The competition had taken hours, and so had the judging. Worst of all was the banquet where they were asked to speak a few words about their victory. Hades, she was thankful that Atticus loved talking. That in itself was worth teaming up with him.

That and he looks damned good in a lab coat.

Maddox tried to shake the image of Atticus out of her mind. She wasn't used to feeling such things—Maddox knew she fell somewhere on the ace spectrum, but she was still figuring out where she fit. Daphne was confident that Maddox simply needed a strong emotional connection to feel sexual attraction, but Maddox worried that her feelings weren't so easily explained. After all, she had only felt such longing a few times, and they all had one unexplainable common denominator.

Atticus.

"Am I toxic?" Maddox whispered to herself, dragging a hand down her face. "Am I only into him because he hurt me?"

Maddox squirmed on the bed before slamming her palms down on the mattress and pushing herself off. She stalked up to the flimsy door that separated her room from Atticus's and knocked.

Oh, gods. Why had she done that?

Maddox heard nothing from Atticus's side. If she only stayed quiet, she could pretend she had never knocked at all—and she was knocking again.

"Atticus?" she said softly, pressing her ear against the door. "Are you in there?"

He was walking around in there earlier; she was sure of it. Louder this time, she repeated, "Atticus? Can I come in? I—I want to see you."

How pathetic she was. Maddox held her breath, listening and cursing her rapid heartbeat for the distraction it was.

Would he let her in? Would he answer?

Another breath and another and still not a word from the other side.

After a few agonizing minutes, Maddox slowly inched away from the door, her stomach unsettled. Why was she so *embarrassing*? Of course, he would ignore her. He wanted her to win this competition and nothing more.

Fine. It was better this way. Maddox had simply gotten caught up in the excitement of working and triumphing together. She didn't need Atticus. She didn't need anyone.

She only needed to win.

CHAPTER 34
WARLOCK

"**M**addox finished the write-up. I sent a copy to the Commission. They're pleased there were only minor issues."

Atticus seethed at Lochlan's words. Minor issues? Maddox having some parasite latched onto her magic was no minor issue. Atticus let his nasty retort stay festering in his throat. There was no point in agitating Lochlan—the man was working as hard as Atticus was. Though it had so far been fruitless, Atticus still appreciated the effort. Any other exorcist would have dragged Maddox to the Asylum by now. It was strange that Lochlan had yet to even suggest it.

"I have news," Atticus said as he eased Theodora's grimoire shut. He stood and cracked open a window—his study was stuffy. "It's not particularly helpful, but Theodora has instructions for a brew that would remove the parasite, though it would only work if there was a willing secondary host."

"No." Lochlan gripped Atticus's shoulder and pinched hard when he was ignored. "That's not an option."

Atticus tried to keep his tone light to avoid suspicion. "Relax. We don't even *have* a willing host—"

"Don't bullshit me. I'm sure you're already stocking the ingredients for it, but this isn't something we should attempt. Maddox has been successfully fighting against it so far. We can't know if you'd do half as well."

"I *might* be better suited for it," Atticus countered.

Lochlan scoffed. "Unlikely. Promise me you won't do something so stupid."

Atticus let the insult slide. "I'll keep looking. Have *you* found anything?"

"I've tried everything I've trained to do. I don't know if it's because Maddox and I work for different deities or..." He trailed off, which was unusual for Lochlan.

"We still have time." Atticus motioned to his laptop and pulled up an email from his father. "I should also mention that Blackened Salt's R&D department is throwing a gala for us. Here, at the estate. They, and my father, were the primary backers for the project. Didn't seem like we could refuse a celebration."

Lochlan groaned. "I feared that might happen. I was hoping not to be here for it."

"Not one for parties?"

"I'm not one for people, regardless of the setting."

Atticus smirked. He had no problem hogging all the glory. "I can handle all the speeches and grandstanding. You just stand there and look like a buzzkill—yes, just like that."

Theodora's grimoire had little to say about possession. It recommended consulting an exorcist and if that was unsuccessful, kill the host.

That cutthroat old woman, Atticus cursed. Besides the potion, which would allow a safe transfer of the parasite from one host to another, there wasn't anything else Atticus could think to try. He wanted more than anything to ask Maddox for help, which was the one thing he could not do.

How was this thing avoiding Lochlan's holy fire? Like a damned cockroach, it survived everything they had thrown at it. He knew the Catholic exorcists were better at expelling their own demons. The monsters necromancers made were sometimes resistant to the Catholic methods.

Artifacts were often cursed or booby-trapped. But they had an exorcist on hand, a privilege Atticus had paid dearly for. This shouldn't be a problem, but the parasitoid was so neatly mixed in with Maddox's own dark power that Lochlan couldn't even locate the thing, let alone expel it.

Maddox would be better at this than me. She can mend far better than I can, even if she refuses to see it.

Atticus walked aimlessly for a few minutes before he realized his feet had led him to Maddox's room. He could hear sad, girly music on the other side of her door and winced. Perhaps this wasn't the best time to interrupt her.

Maddox's bedroom door swung open, exposing Atticus lurking outside. Fantastic. As if he needed help to look like a stalker.

Maddox blinked at him, turning down the music on her phone. "Yes?"

"Hello, Maddox." He could not speak her name without tasting the memory of her lips. Atticus cleared his throat. "You heard about the gala?"

Maddox laughed dryly. "Yes, and I can't believe you're *hosting* it, and so soon! This house needs to be dusted and aired out and I don't know what else. Will two weeks be enough time to prepare?"

"I'm hiring people for all that. Don't give it another thought." He waved a hand.

She still seemed displeased. "Well, I have a lot of work to do. This is all last minute. My family is attending, and I have to figure out where the hell they'll all fit."

"I apologize for the poor timing. My father hasn't had an excuse to visit in years, and he wants to be with me for All Hallow's Eve." Atticus wedged his foot into the small open space of the door, keeping Maddox from shutting him out. "How many are coming?"

"My parents, my grandfather, Daphne and her husband, *and* the triplets."

He'd forgotten that her eldest sisters were triplets. Atticus hadn't met them yet, but if they were anything like Daphne, they surely hated him. "They can stay here. I'll let the cleaning crew know they need to make ready... How many rooms would they need?"

She was hesitant. "Well, they would like six, but you don't need to go to all that trouble—"

It would be a lot of trouble, and it would be terrifying to have so much of her family in his house, but if her family stayed elsewhere, Maddox might join them. And he wanted her under his roof and under his watch.

"It's no trouble."

"Liar," she countered, but she sounded...lighter? As if he'd actually managed to lift some weight off her shoulders.

Atticus attempted to cheapen what he was doing for her, uncomfortable with her gratitude. "I need to repay your family for feeding me twice now."

"And now you're going to *cook* for all of them, too?"

"Of course. They haven't witnessed my better qualities yet."

CHAPTER 35
WARLOCK

"They're early!"

Atticus jumped as Maddox broke into his office. He swept his latest book into a desk drawer—he was reviewing a possession case study and didn't want to tip off her parasitoid. "Who's early?"

Maddox pulled out his chair for him, making him frown. "My family! They drove since Daphne isn't allowed on planes, and evidently my grandfather drove like a madman to get here."

His stomach dropped. "Are they already in Redhollow?"

"They're ten minutes out. They stopped at the airport to pick up my other sisters."

Atticus groaned. "They are all arriving at once?"

"Unfortunately." Maddox seemed as nervous as he was. "I need to shower *now*. I had a little accident in your lab, nothing major, but do not look until I can hide my—*clean* my mess. Can you greet them?"

"*Alone?*"

"Please?" She pouted her lower lip, widening her eyes, and Atticus could only sigh and wave her off.

While Maddox ran to her room, Atticus trudged to the manor's grand entrance. He could hear cars idling outside, and with some under-his-breath swears, he stepped out to meet the Abernathy coven.

The first Abernathy he saw was Daphne, hands on her knees, as she vomited onto his driveway.

Her husband rubbed her back and offered soothing words while she cursed his existence. Atticus took a step back—not because of the steaming vomit, but because wild magic rolled off Daphne. The grass around the drive grew several inches—the grass that had just been mowed. Dandelions began sprouting as well and while Atticus appreciated the plant for its medicinal uses, he knew his landscaper would not be pleased.

The Abernathys had driven two cars, and three blonde women, probably in their mid-thirties, nearly fell out of the old man's red truck. They stretched and yawned for a moment before their sights narrowed on Atticus.

He swallowed, preparing his hello before they swarmed him.

"What a creepy house!" One sporting a blonde undercut walked past him to stare at the black steeples of his home. The triplets all had drastically different hairstyles, but he knew he'd never keep them straight, even with such obvious differences. "Is it haunted?"

Was she actually wanting to know? Atticus shrugged. "I'm afraid I'm the only wraith that haunts this home."

Another triplet laughed. "Daphne was right. He *does* talk like a penny dreadful come to life."

"No wonder Maddox puts up with him—she can be just as creepy," the last triplet agreed.

They introduced themselves as Dove, Amber, and Poppy. Atticus wondered if it was rude to ask them to wear name tags. Maybe he could get away with it at the gala.

"Maddox texted!" Daphne held a hand over her mouth for a second before she continued. "She says 'leave him alone'."

"We've barely even started!" Dove, he thought, giggled and walked into the manor.

Her sisters followed behind, and Atticus thought he should follow, too, before Colter Abernathy shouted at him. "Help me with this luggage, Blackwell!"

Atticus raced to the back of the truck, and Colter began hanging duffel bags on him without a word. The situation felt less awkward when Maddox's father and Daphne's husband, Rob, walked over and were subjected to the same treatment.

Atticus staggered inside, showing them their rooms, and one by one luggage was removed from his person. "Please take a moment to rest," he panted, rubbing his shoulder with a wince. "Dinner's at six o'clock. Someone will be by to collect you, and we can have a proper tour after we eat."

While Theodora was alive, the Blackwells kept a butler and a few maids. Atticus had hired a few temps just until the Abernathys went home. He could barely handle the home with all the rooms closed up—with everything open, he would drown without help.

Would the Abernathys notice Maddox's unwelcome guest? As Atticus worked in the kitchen, preparing the evening meal, he could not shake the phantom presence of her lips. They'd kissed before, an angry battle of lips and teeth, but this had been different. Maddox had been warm and soft and—

What if that cockroach had nothing to do with her kiss? What if Atticus had rejected *her*, and not some parasite's trick?

No! Though Lochlan doubted there was anything tagging along in Maddox's body, Atticus was so certain that he had seen something. *Wasn't he?*

Once he finished cooking, Atticus let a pair of temporary maids serve the food while he rejoined the group. The head of the dining table had been left open for him, which placed him next to Maddox...and Colter.

Atticus waited. He waited for the worst, for the dinner to be awkward and tense. For the food to be criticized. For anything other than Colter Abernathy thanking him for his hospitality and struggling to find some common ground with which to keep a conversation going.

The raven had returned to Colter's side, perching on the back of his chair while they ate, waiting for scraps. Atticus didn't doubt the bird was a spy for the old man.

Colter failed to find a good, mutual topic and resorted to bragging about his granddaughters. Dove, the eldest of Maddox's sisters, designed and built prosthetics, and Atticus even surprised himself with how long he spoke with her on the subject.

He kept the tour after dinner short, and afterward, he watched Maddox and her sisters all pile into the same room after bidding him goodnight.

Sweat beaded on his forehead and he wiped it with a handkerchief. Those women certainly were going to talk, and he fled the hallway before he overheard them say anything about him.

CHAPTER 36
WITCH

Three seconds. Maddox lasted three seconds under her sisters' keen gazes before she burst into tears.

"Good Goddess," Dove moaned, jumping out of the way as Maddox ran to the bed.

Maddox buried her face into the pillow, not caring if her mascara ran all over Blackwell's damned silk pillowcases. She heard Daphne defend her childish behavior.

"Hey! She's been through a lot! That Victorian ghost of a man confessed he loves her—that would throw anyone off."

"It isn't just that," Maddox argued lamely. "Well, that's part of it, but I'm screwing everything up." She flipped over on her back, sniffling. "I didn't get the job."

"What job?" Amber pushed Maddox over so she and the other sisters could perch on the side of the bed.

Maddox had yet to speak her failure aloud. This confession made it real. "I applied to be a librarian at the Academy, and they rejected me."

"Why the hell would they do that?" Poppy played with her new eyebrow piercing and scoffed. "Didn't you just crack some *National Treasure* level secret for that place?"

"I don't know."

"They didn't give a reason?" Dove asked.

"I didn't read the email. The subject line was more than enough."

Daphne *tsked*. "Maddie, you have to open the email."

"Why?" Dove stood, reasserting her position as eldest, even if it was only by a minute. "Fuck that place. Maddie shouldn't work there, anyway. I'm sure it's as cliquey and snotty as it was when you were a student."

"It's not." Maddox tried to face away from her sisters, but Amber and Poppy locked her body in place. "I don't know how he did it, but it's different now." Her voice dropped into a whisper. "I really wanted to work with him."

"I think I should mention..." Daphne grimaced, holding a hand against her stomach. "Maddie has a crush on our esteemed and spooky host."

Her sisters' pitying sighs stung Maddox's pride. She didn't care for her feelings to be so trivialized. "I think I'm in love with him. Maybe I always was." She sat up so quickly that Amber startled and fell off the bed. "Is *that* what's wrong with me? Is that why I don't feel attraction to anyone else? Maybe I need it to *hurt* to have any interest. Maybe I'm broken."

"I doubt that's the reason," Dove decided, reaching over to flick Maddox on the nose.

"If anything," Daphne offered, "I think you have a hero complex, Maddie. You're taking our family motto a little too seriously. Atticus needs mending— it doesn't take a psychologist to see that man had a terrible childhood. Look at how he stands."

Maddox hoped they were right about her. She wrung her hands together until Poppy gently held them apart. Her sister rubbed her knuckles with her thumbs while Maddox's chin sunk down to her chest.

"He doesn't want me, anyway. I tried, and he rejected me, too." At Maddox's revelation, Daphne gave her an incredulous glance. *Yeah, it doesn't make sense to me, either.*

"Well, fuck that fickle fuck. Fuck that school. Fuck it all." Dove pushed Poppy aside and tore Maddox out of bed. She straightened Maddox's posture and lifted her chin. "All that's left is this party, right? Once that's over, you can come home and start applying to a place that will appreciate you."

Amber sprung up from the floor. "Don't worry about a thing, Maddie. We're here. Let's take you shopping for this gala."

Poppy agreed, bouncing from one foot to the other. "Yes! Let's make her evil hot!"

That idea went over very well. Each sister began chattering and offering outfit suggestions as they played with Maddox's hair and looked through her makeup. Maddox couldn't help but feel overwhelmed at their support, though she should have expected it. She laughed, wiping away her tears while Daphne looked up a few witch-owned boutiques.

It was insane the amount of work the cleaning crew did on the estate. Maddox was certain they had some magical help. She had seen a few brownies, a type of feyrie that was known for being tidy, among the workers. But it was still impressive how the manor had transformed over the course of a few days.

Maddox had yet to see the grand ballroom where the gala was to take place, but she wanted to save her first look for the actual party.

Stepping around the cleaners while they finished the last-minute details, Maddox handed off her shopping bags to Amber to take up to her room. Her outfit for the gala showed a little more skin than she was used to, but with her sisters hyping her up, Maddox had felt confident rather than exposed.

On her way to the kitchen, she noticed her grandad sneak inside Atticus's conservatory. Maddox ran after him. Atticus was very particular about his garden.

Colter strolled along the Blackwell's greenhouse, inspecting each plant and either nodding or muttering about some needed improvement. Maddox tapped his shoulder and handed him his credit card back. She said with a wince, "You might regret lending this to us."

"No, I won't." Colter placed his card back into his worn, handmade leather wallet. "You deserve to let me spoil you at least once."

She knew when her grandfather had more to say, so Maddox sat on a black wicker chair and waited him out.

"He's a talented gardener," Colter admitted. "Better than you."

"Well, his family runs the largest apothecary in the world. I imagine at one point they actually had to get their hands dirty." Her tone was unkind, and it didn't escape Colter's notice.

Maddox was sure what would come next—Colter would start questioning her admittedly absurd decision to stay in Atticus's estate with him. But he surprised her.

"The boy still seems...unwell."

Did Colter mean gaunt? "He's always been thin. Atticus doesn't eat very much, which is insane with the way he can cook." Maddox hated complimenting him, but it was the truth.

Colter gave her a grunt in return. "I would still keep an eye on him."

"He's a grown man. He doesn't need me to watch over him," Maddox snapped, though her words failed to convince Colter or herself.

Her grandfather's hand weighed heavy on her shoulder. Did he know about what went on between her and Atticus? Probably. It was foolish to think the triplets would keep Maddox's private life private.

Colter just gave her shoulder a squeeze as he said, "Let's spend some time in the actual outdoors before it rains again. You look like you need some fresh air."

Fresh air, for Colter at least, had to wait. Lochlan entered the greenhouse and stood before them, blocking their way. "May I interrupt you, Mr. Abernathy? I wish to discuss the gala with Maddox."

"It's Colter, and what do you think you need *my* permission for?"

Lochlan coughed twice. "My phrasing was...regrettable. Maddox?" He nodded her direction and Maddox pushed up from her chair with a groan.

They stopped for their coats first, Maddox's an obnoxiously purple puffer coat while Lochlan wore a grey peacoat devoid of any personality. Once outside the manor, Lochlan stopped underneath a cluster of bare trees, the best windbreaker available.

"I have a gift for you," he said, dropping something into her hands. It was a miniature bottle of hand sanitizer. "This damned party. Everyone's going to want to shake our hands, despite the fact it's flu season."

She sighed, sharing his disdain for unnecessary contact with strangers. This was a small gift, but Maddox knew it meant Lochlan thought of her enough to know some of her dislikes. Maddox said, while thinking of ways to pay him back, "I, at least, have my sisters to run interference. What are you going to do?"

"Hope my natural charm keeps people away."

"Just hang out with me and my family. You're blonde—you'll fit right in. Even more than I do." Maddox only hoped her family would refrain from quizzing Lochlan about which vows he did and didn't have to take. Maddox squeezed the hand sanitizer bottle in her pocket, waiting for his answer.

"That would…be nice. I know I'm not very extroverted, but your energy is nice to be around. As long as I'm not expected to make chitchat." Lochlan removed one of his gloves and held out a hand to her. "I'll join your entourage, but can I check something first?"

She slid her hand into his without thinking. "What do you need from me?"

"Could you cast a prolonged spell for me? It doesn't need to be extravagant."

When would these tests end? Maddox held up her other hand and, after whispering a few Latin words, formed an orb of red light. It floated before her, and she concentrated on controlling it. It was an entropic spell and would drain the life out of anything it touched, so Maddox was careful to keep it floating safely above their heads.

While she worked on the spell, Lochlan let his white flames lick the palm he held as he stared into her eyes. It was the most uncomfortable ten minutes of her life.

"That's enough," he said, releasing her hand. "I just wanted to see if your magic remained unaffected by your encounters with the artifact. All seems well."

"I didn't know that was under debate," she said carefully, stuffing her hand into her coat pockets. "Any other surprises, Lochlan?"

"Wouldn't say this is a surprise, but if this gala includes dancing, I don't dance."

"No one is surprised by that."

CHAPTER 37
WARLOCK

Glass shattered in the room underneath him. Atticus sat up, glancing about his darkened bedroom like a madman before catching himself. With his house full of guests, that noise could have originated from any of them stumbling about in search of a midnight snack.

Or it could have been the disheveled, devious cat Maddox had rescued from his garbage can.

Atticus nearly let himself fall back asleep. But worry, and a lot of irritation, kept him awake. It was possible to become lost in the estate in the daylight—it was almost a certainty at night. The Blackwell home was designed that way.

The noise seemed to come from the library below. It might have been just a glass *or* a priceless vase of Theodora's—which would serve her right.

There was only one person under his roof that he was really worried about.

Do not do it.

The warning held his brother's voice—older, wiser, more controlled. *Annoyed.*

Atticus ignored this imitation of his brother. With his palm out and his magic untethered, Atticus thought of her.

Smoke turned liquid. A dark, bitter blood trail of magic dripped from his palm and slithered underneath his bedroom door. He rose from his bed, sliding into shoes and heading into the hallway. The lights in the hall, ancient glass orbs that were mounted high on the walls, alighted as he passed them. The red glow the orbs emitted was easy on his eyes in the dark.

A trail of bloodlike power led away from Maddox's room, cementing his fear that Maddox was the source of the broken glass.

Atticus's magic brought him to the library as he'd suspected, and he dissipated the liquid with a wave. He found the door cracked open and a single lamp lit within. Atticus eased inside carefully, only opening the door as much as he absolutely needed.

Maddox swayed in front of the first bookcase, a blanket wrapped around her shoulders. A vase against the wall was turned over, the top half broken and scattered across the floor. Luckily, it appeared as though Maddox had avoided walking over the mess. Atticus approached her, watching as one by one, Maddox pulled books from the shelves, flipped through the contents, and then tossed them over her shoulder.

What the hell was she doing? Maddox would never knowingly treat a book that way.

How should he wake her? He didn't want to startle her. Atticus whispered to her, adopting a tone he often used with upset students. "Maddox? Can you hear me? It's cold down here. Let me—"

She paused, a leather-bound book clenched so tightly in her hand that Atticus could see her fingerprints denting the cover. Maddox gazed up at him, her eyes wide open and pale. They were too dreamlike, too unfocused. Utterly unlike the woman he loved.

"You're *beautiful*," she said, her fingertips lifting to graze his jawline. His mood soured, and Atticus turned away from her.

Trapped in her dream—or nightmare—Maddox wouldn't recall this event. Atticus returned her compliment with a wry smile. "I am not beautiful, only a very skilled liar."

Her eyes flashed in anger before dulling again to that hazy, open stare. Maddox didn't miss another beat, only resumed discarding books that failed to meet her standards.

Atticus caught the next book she tossed, replacing it on the shelf as his other hand clamped down on Maddox's shoulder. "Maddox." He sighed, wincing when she jumped at his touch.

"What..." Her hands pulled the blanket tighter across her chest, a shield against the cold and her uncertainty. "Why am I in here?"

"I couldn't tell you," Atticus admitted. She must be freezing. "Let's get you back into bed." Though he had no doubt that she was capable of walking herself back, Atticus placed his hand on her waist and tucked her against him. Maddox shockingly accepted the help, leaning heavily against him as they left.

"Do you have a history of sleepwalking?" If she did, there were many safety issues in his home Atticus needed to address.

Maddox rubbed her eyes as she considered. "No? I don't think so?"

"You've been overworking yourself. You finished the write-up alone, and I should have—"

"I'm perfectly fine. I'm not some spoiled princess or a stranger to hard work."

"I know," he said as they approached her bedroom. He entered with her, helping Maddox into her bed unnecessarily. He tucked her in and for some reason, she let him. "I need to know if this happens again. There are things in this house that are dangerous."

Atticus recalled the open book he'd caught sight of before they left the library. This book hadn't been cast aside—it had been laid flat on an end table.

He'd read the book twice as a bored adolescent— *The Evolution of Insects.* The text had been left open on a two-page image spread. A ghastly photograph in black and white of a *strepsiptera* larva burrowing into its victim—a bee that was now doomed to carry and care for an intruder until the host was eaten from the inside out.

Atticus didn't want to spend his time bothering with the party—he wanted to help Lochlan as the exorcist tested Maddox in ways she would not suspect. So far, Lochlan said Maddox passed every test with flying colors. *Of course she did.* And though this information made doubt creep under his skin, Atticus remained unsatisfied.

However, there was no time to focus on Maddox and her possible passenger—Rami had arrived.

There was always a large amount of guilt and wishful thinking whenever Atticus met up with Rami. If Theodora hadn't had Atticus wrapped around her finger, he might have chosen to live with his father, and perhaps he might have had a chance at a normal life. Atticus also knew Rami, though he hid it very, very well, had been slightly hurt that his sons had *both* chosen to live with their mother.

"Atticus!" Rami waved at him, weaving through the mass of caterers and decorators. His assistant tailed him, apologizing to the workers Rami accidentally shoulder-checked on his way to his son.

Hugging, always with the hugging. Atticus cringed at the *crack* his back made before his father released him. Rami slapped him on the shoulder, flashing him a winning grin as he looked Atticus up and down. "The beard is new. Trying to take after me, are you?" Rami rubbed his own facial hair with a laugh before tousling Atticus's hair. "You forgot to trim the rest of you, though."

Atticus smoothed his hair down with a sigh. "It's nice to see you, Dad." Hades, had it been that long since his father had seen him in person? He'd had this beard for ages, hoping it would make him look less gaunt.

Rami, with his good looks and dashing smile, was someone everyone wanted to meet, and he enjoyed the attention. "I know I'm not supposed to speak poorly of your mother in front of you, but that witch isn't coming, is she?"

Atticus scoffed. He hadn't seen Cynthia in years, and he preferred to keep it that way. "Absolutely not."

"Thank Anubis." Rami whistled as he watched the chandelier in the grand entrance lowered to be dusted. "This place has held up better than I thought. I bet it drove your mother crazy that your grandmother left this all to you."

"She wasn't pleased, no, but it's hard to argue with Theodora. Even when she's dead."

"I remember that." Rami nodded at his assistant who was trying to wave him over, a tablet in her hand. "I'll catch up with you later, Atticus. I sort of rushed this event, and there are a few R&D things I'll have to take care of while I'm here. But after the party, I'll take your team out for dinner." Rami gave Atticus another back-breaking squeeze. "Thanks for including me in this. I'm really proud of you."

You don't know what a mess I've made of it. There are so many things I should have told you. Emotionlessly, Atticus watched his father leave and began his search for the exorcist.

Lochlan was in the ballroom, speaking with the Master of Ceremonies to verify he would not have to speak a word in front of the public. Atticus rolled his eyes. While Atticus was doing the majority of the speaking, the MC wanted someone to introduce Atticus. Lochlan had shamelessly volunteered Maddox for the job.

Atticus didn't like it—Maddox introducing him as if he was the most vital part of their trio. All he had contributed was the damned artifact and a few chemicals. Maddox had done all the real work, but she claimed she'd rather chew aluminum foil than give the speech so here they were.

"Did she pass the last test?" Atticus didn't bother with a greeting, and he knew Lochlan would hardly mind skipping pleasantries.

"She did." Lochlan led them to an empty portion of the ballroom, standing behind a table that held an exhibit of their research. "I think she's fine, Atticus. I've finalized my report to the Commission and reported that all is well."

"You're *sure* you've tried everything—"

"Twice. Some of them three times."

Did a test exist that would satisfy Atticus's anxiety? He didn't think so. The idea that he hadn't ruined Maddox was unfathomable. And if Maddox was wholly herself, then he had refused her affection without reason.

It had been hard enough to accept her forgiveness. Could he ever accept that she wanted more from him? That she could ever trust him with the most fragile parts of her?

Lochlan looked like he might touch Atticus's shoulder before he thought better of it. "Relax. She's okay. And you have other things to worry about."

"Like what?" Lochlan had better not mean the damned gala.

"I had to tell the Commission what your grandmother did. I don't know what the consequences will be. I'm sure they'll be in touch with your family's legal team soon."

Atticus put Lochlan's worries to rest. "If that happens, they'll be dealing with my brother. I'm more concerned for *them* than for me."

"I'll do what I can on your behalf," Lochlan offered as he walked away.

Atticus wished he could care more about the Commission, but his mind, as it always was, was occupied by Maddox.

A few hours before the gala was to officially begin, Atticus finished dressing and headed to meet up with the Master of Ceremonies. Atticus wore all black tonight, letting his accessories stand out. He adorned his tie with a small golden bee, complimenting the two pins that sat on both corners of his collar, a small chain hanging between them. His watch and earrings matched as well.

The ballroom was polished and brighter than it had been in years. The black and white marbled floor shone, and the light grey walls were spotless and decorated with wreaths of roses.

The rest of the décor and table setup was still being completed, but Atticus could imagine how grand it would look in the end.

"Now, Maddox will introduce you using the microphone on the podium," the MC, William, said as Atticus scanned the room for Maddox. William continued as if he didn't notice Atticus's wandering attention. "Since you can't keep still while you speak, you'll wear this microphone on your collar. Maddox will clip it on you after she turns off the podium mic."

"Sure, sure." Atticus numbly repeated back William's instructions. "I'm not worried about the speech. I'm quite the artist when it comes to..."

"Your dramatic pauses are leaning a little too far on the dramatic side," William said, frowning.

Atticus never gave him a reply. He couldn't. Maddox had finally entered the ballroom.

CHAPTER 38
WITCH

Maddox's sisters convinced her to buy a corseted blouse, and the outfit aided and exposed her chest in a way that was new. The top was well structured and black, with long sheer sleeves that came to a pretty cuff at her wrist. Her bee necklace dipped low, a last-minute addition to her outfit that she instantly regretted when she saw what Atticus was wearing clipped to his tie.

Maddox's black skirt flowed down to the floor, the soft material caressing her legs, except where a slit bared her left leg, the cut running nearly to her hip. Any higher and her panty line would show. Yes, she was baring much more skin than she usually did, but tonight she only felt powerful. She felt like the dark witch she was, thankful that her sisters had been there to tame her hair into soft waves and to apply her makeup.

Atticus caught her eye, staring at her while the Master of Ceremonies, William, tried to recapture his attention. She paused at the ballroom's entrance, suddenly uncertain, but her family was at her back and Daphne pushed her forward while barking at her husband to find her a chair.

There was only an hour before the official start of the gala, and while Maddox wanted to avoid Atticus, she needed to check in with the MC.

William greeted her before Atticus could even make an attempt, going over the microphone situation with her again and showing her on the podium where her introduction for Atticus was written on a few discreet notecards.

"Thanks, Will," she said, checking over the notes before putting them carefully back into place.

"Don't be late!" William demanded, turning to scold Atticus as well, but the man had already slipped away.

It was easy to find Atticus again—even in all black, Atticus stood out. Oh,

Hades help her. Atticus was tying Colter's tie while her sisters surrounded him. After what Maddox had confessed to her sisters, the warlock didn't stand a chance.

What were they saying to him? Maddox started for her family when someone softly gripped her elbow.

"Maddox! Why haven't you returned any of my calls?" Angeline's glasses slipped down her nose as she scowled at Maddox. "Or any of my emails?"

Angeline's early arrival to the gala was an unwanted obstacle. Maddox tightened her jaw. This was not where she wanted to have this conversation. "I saw the email. You found someone more qualified. I understand. I've been away for a long time."

"What? Why are you so focused on that?" Angeline dropped her grip, laughing. "What's your response to the *other* job we offered you?"

"Other...job?" Maddox's voice went up a notch, and she was beginning to feel very small as her former professor gave a prolonged sigh.

"Lucille, *Mrs. Tuttle*, wants you to take over the head librarian position for her. She's been trying to retire for years, but hates every candidate we present to her. For some reason, she liked you, though I'm not sure if you should take that as a compliment." Angeline plucked a glass of champagne off a tray as a waiter strolled by, ignoring his protests that the party had yet to begin. "Did you not read the entire email?"

Maddox felt foolish and immature and had no idea how to hide those feelings from Angeline. She lied, "I've been busy with the write-up and—"

Angeline interrupted her after chugging her champagne. "Well, I'm glad I decided to be nosy. The Academy thought you were trying to negotiate for a higher salary by not answering right away."

"I'll call them first thing on Monday."

"Good. Gaia will be ecstatic when I tell her. We've been quite worried about it, you know. We thought Atticus might have scared you off again."

Atticus! Maddox whirled around to find him, but he was no longer haunting her family. She excused herself and approached Daphne.

"Where did he go? What did you say to him?"

Daphne rubbed her already swollen ankles before Rob took over the massaging for her. "Dove told Atticus the truth. She said you're coming back with us after the gala and that you didn't get that job. She added a few colorful adjectives, but—"

"And where is he now?"

It was clear Daphne wanted to ask why Maddox even cared, but she only shrugged. "He seemed upset. He left the ballroom, and that's all I know."

Maddox's heels clicked loudly against the marble floor as she checked the rest of the house for Atticus. The study was empty, as was the kitchen, and Maddox actually didn't know which bedroom was his, so she tried the library next. Velvet ropes sectioned off this portion of the house, and she ducked underneath them to enter the library, pushing open the double doors with much more force than was necessary.

What are you even going to say when you find him? Why even look for him at all? Let him pout, let him confuse another foolish girl, and leave him behind for good.

The library doors slammed shut behind her, echoing throughout the room. "Atticus!" she shouted, checking down each line of bookshelves for the man. Was he hiding from her, or was he already back at the gala where she should be?

Atticus stepped out silently from the next row of books, nearly scaring her to death. Maddox held a hand over her thumping heart, noting the bourbon in his hand. *At least he's using a glass, I guess.*

What she had sought him out for, she didn't even understand, so all Maddox could think to do was chastise him. "Say something next time before you just jump out at me! You nearly scared me to death."

"You're leaving." Atticus's crimson glasses made it hard for her to read his emotions. "Were you even going to say goodbye?"

"Of course, I—" She stepped toward him before stopping herself. No, he was the one who pushed her away. If he was really so upset that she was possibly leaving, *he* could chase *her* this time. "What right do you have to be upset with me? You've lived just fine without me."

"I've never been *fine* without you, Maddox."

He always said her name like that—so filled with regret. How she tired of it. "What do you want from me? You tell me you love me one minute and the next you push me away! What am I supposed to think? Is the idea of me *that* much better than the real thing?"

Why did she even start this? All it would lead to was ruined mascara, and she spent forty dollars on the one she was wearing now. Another stupid mistake.

His silence told her volumes. "Atticus," Maddox whispered, "I called for you all those years ago, and you didn't answer. I suppose that should have shown me how this would end."

Now Atticus moved for her, blocking off her exit, his drink left forgotten on some side table. "Called for me? When? What in Hades are you talking about?"

It was her shameful secret, a lapse in her judgment at twenty-one. "That potion brewing competition we entered. Our hotel rooms had that connecting door, and I knocked and I called for you and—"

"I thought I had *dreamt* it." His posture was crazed and poised for action. "I heard you call my name, but I thought it was a dream. If I had known—"

"It wouldn't have changed anything." She shrugged. Why did she even bring this up? Just to spread her pain to him? "Your family wouldn't have allowed us to reconcile, anyway."

"No! I had it under control then, I could have..." He pulled at his hair, mouth pinched shut as he shook his head.

Maddox frowned and prompted, "Under control?"

Atticus skirted around her question. "I would have answered had I known you called. You *must* know that."

No, she didn't know that. "Are you ashamed of me?"

Hysterical laughter escaped him. "Ashamed? Of *you*? Ashamed of myself, if anything," Atticus assured her. "Never have I looked at you and once thought you weren't enough for me."

Her sneer wasn't pretty. "You've always been full of lovely, empty words. You're good at it. I don't fault you for your skill. It just hurts some of us who take them as the truth."

"Look at me!" His hands gripped her face, and he stared down into her eyes. He was hunting for something, and while Maddox could easily break his grip, she allowed his search. If only to bask in his attention one last time.

She really was pathetic. This weak heart of hers had only longed for one person, and Maddox was helpless against him. If she didn't walk away now, she would break.

"Lochlan was right. Your eyes are clear. I—I made a mistake." His hands fell. "I'm sorry. When you kissed me, I thought some part of the artifact had affected your behavior. *That's* why I stopped you, and that's the *only* reason. It was easier for me to believe that you were possessed than to believe you had honest feelings for me."

Her blood ran cold at the accusation. All of Lochlan's last-minute tests suddenly made sense. Maddox stared at her hand, pinpointing on a scar on her index finger, but her mind went blank when she tried to dredge up the wound's source.

"I can't believe you. Whenever I get too close to you, you ignore me." She took a step back, hugging herself to hide her quivering. "All you've ever done is love me at arm's length. If I don't leave you, that's where I'll stay. Close enough to keep me, but too far for me to love you back."

"Love me back?"

She had revealed too much. Maddox had wanted to hurt him, yes, but not enough to stall his breath and stutter his pulse.

Atticus haunted her as he always had. He demanded, "Maddox, do you *love me?*"

No, he did not deserve that information. Even if she wanted his pain, Maddox could not cause that much devastation and walk away feeling good about herself. "It doesn't matter," she hissed. "It never mattered!"

He reached for her before dropping his reckless hands, eyes wild. "That's the only thing that's ever mattered to me!" Atticus was panicking, and she was the cruel cause. Her heart felt like it was twisting, and with any more tension, it would snap.

"Liar!" she snarled, shoving at his chest to get him out of her way, but he caught her hands easily. That proved how rattled she was. She half-sobbed and half-sighed as his hands released her and wrapped around her waist.

Atticus pressed a kiss to the top of her hair. "Yes, I am a liar and worse, and you deserve so much better. But you were kind to a man who has known little kindness in his life, and now his affection is your burden to bear."

"This can't work," she argued but made no move to fight his embrace. "I'm still angry with you."

They were so close Maddox felt his breath hitch. Atticus swallowed. "I thought you had forgiven me?"

"For your past transgressions, yes! But I—" Her tears were hot and overflowing. "—can't forgive what you *will* do to me!"

Atticus pulled back to look at her with dry eyes, but his words trembled. "What I will do to you is love you as best as I can. Until death has mercy on me, I will love you. Whether you stay or leave me behind."

Maddox thought, though she couldn't be certain, that she kissed him first. Who started the exchange became unimportant. Atticus's mouth was hungry and needy on hers, harsh and perhaps more demanding than even he wanted to be.

She hated him for breaking them apart. She loved him for how he looked at her, a powerful man she could shatter with a word.

Atticus took one of her hands in both of his, breaking her focus. "When I'm around you, sometimes I can't fucking breathe, and when I'm not around you, I don't want to." His grip tightened almost painfully before he realized his mistake. "I love you. I'm in control now. Please don't go."

Her answer wouldn't come. Fear trapped the words in her throat, keeping her from risking her heart again. She leaned against a bookshelf, the shelves digging into her back as she avoided his probing stare.

Her hesitation raised his brow. "What combination of pretty and pathetic prose would convince you of my sincerity?" He kissed the back of her hand, smirking against her skin. "Would you have me *grovel*? Should I beg?" Atticus dropped to the floor before her. "Do you want me on my knees to earn back your affection?"

Maddox blinked, a blush climbing across her nose. Atticus's tone had changed. It was soft, but dark somehow, and it drove home the fact that while Maddox had little experience in romantic affairs, that was not the case for Atticus. He may have been the one on his knees, but Atticus was completely in control of their situation. He knew it, too. That sly look he gave her underneath his lashes said it all.

Atticus waited for her answer, her hand still in his warm grip. There wasn't much time before they were needed at the gala, but for once Maddox couldn't care about being late.

For years she had watched her sisters fall in and out of love, worrying that she'd never experience that ache for another. That worry was now gone, pushed aside by a feverish unraveling. She had waited for Atticus for so long, and here he was, offering her everything she had ever wanted.

She felt light-headed in her anticipation, and some stubborn part of her hated to be the one off-balance. *Don't try to compete with him right now,* she thought before her body disobeyed her.

"I want you *lower,*" she demanded, her voice unforgiving and rasping. Maddox gripped his tie just below the knot, tearing it free and using it to yank him down further. Atticus fell forward, catching himself with his hands. Maddox dropped his tie, but pinned the cloth to the floor with her heel.

Atticus glanced up at her, stunned but enthralled.

"Before you touch me, tell me *exactly* what you want to do to me." Her words were foreign to her, escaping before she could think them through, but that didn't make them any less true. She needed to know what he had planned for her. Maddox, though she was doing her best impression to appear otherwise, was anxious. Her competitive side didn't want her inexperience to show. Not in front of her former rival.

Atticus kissed her ankle. His voice was just as shaky as her own. "I want you as *desperate* as I am."

"Be more specific."

He stared at her, catching his breath in the heavy silence. "I want whatever you'll allow me—"

"That's not what I asked." Maddox knew her blush was obvious now. Atticus thought she was purposefully taunting him when all she wanted was to know his intent.

"I want..." Atticus said, trailing off as he struggled to express himself. "I want you *drenched*, and I want *my* tongue between *your* legs to be the reason for it."

Finally. Though, even with the information, Maddox only felt marginally more prepared. But no longer could she stand having only pieces of memories of Atticus. Maddox wanted all of him, and she needed it now. "Now *show* me how you want me." She stepped off his tie, allowing him to rise.

Atticus returned to kneeling before her and twisted her skirt so the high slit now bared her front. His hands slid up her legs and exposed the sides of the thong her sisters had insisted she buy for this outfit. Maddox wondered if getting her in this position was the first thing that had crossed Atticus's mind when he saw how she was dressed.

She looked down at him, wondering why his movements, seconds ago so rushed, had paused. Atticus caught her eye, and once she gave him a tiny nod, caught her thong in his teeth.

Her imagination had never conjured an image as seductive as *this*. Atticus slowly eased her thong down her thighs, and Maddox tore her gaze to the ceiling.

Once she was freed from that annoying scrap of material, Atticus lifted one of her legs and hooked it on his shoulder, turning his face to softly kiss her thigh. He kept up those tortuous kisses, working a path toward her center.

"Love." Atticus's kisses stopped just shy of their target. "Watch me."

"Watch you?" she echoed dumbly.

When Maddox didn't meet his eye, Atticus nipped at her thigh teasingly. "I *kneel* for you, and you can't give me this? I want you to watch."

Maddox obeyed, tilting her head downward. He looked *perfect*. Atticus smiled under her attention and worked his mouth against her center.

Maddox gripped the edges of the bookshelf she was braced against, doing her best to remain upright while Atticus drew out her sighs and whimpers with his tongue. She was coming undone quickly, and Atticus had to help keep her standing.

He tore away only once, moaning, "*Fu-uck,*" in two syllables before he returned to viciously suck where his tongue had previously worked.

Her vision shattered. Though her legs nearly gave out on her, Atticus refused to let her fall. She could somehow feel Atticus fighting a grin while he mercilessly lifted her other thigh and left it over his shoulder.

Maddox was trapped, both feet off the floor, her arms fighting to keep her upright as she pushed down against the bookshelf. If Atticus noticed her balancing act, it didn't slow him down. He worked her like an experiment, watching her reactions, savoring them, and noting what unraveled her best.

It didn't take him long to gather a theory and test it. At the next stroke of his tongue, Maddox, whimpering, arched her back and knocked three books off a shelf.

Her own attempts at pleasuring herself, when the mood so rarely struck her, were nothing compared to *this*.

It was involuntary—completely involuntary. Her hips bucked, nearly threatening her already precarious balance, and Atticus moaned in pleasure.

"Sorry," Maddox whispered, but her body didn't share her shyness and thrust forward again.

"Never apologize to me," Atticus snarled, breaking away to catch his breath and correct her. "Especially for *that.*"

Maddox rambled while Atticus forced her bliss to continue. Nothing she said made sense. She claimed to love and hate Atticus at the same time, and wasn't that just like them?

Maddox cursed him, but her hexes failed to find their mark as her body, her will, couldn't stand to harm him. Her spells, interrupted by her own breathless exaltations, only amused him. When one of her accidental hexes flew a little too close, Atticus bit her thigh hard until her magic fizzled out.

He soothed her skin, kissing what was sure to become a bruise. "*Behave,* my dear. Tonight isn't about *punishing you.* There's time for that later."

It could have been his half-smirk, or his burning eyes, but the next time Atticus touched her destroyed her dying resistance. She lost all control, having to trust Atticus to keep her suspended as she came undone clamped around his face.

After her shaking and trembling quieted, Maddox's legs were jelly. Atticus slid her gently to the floor, hovering over her. He gripped the back of her neck as he kissed her deeply.

"We'll continue this later." Atticus tapped his Rolex while Maddox fought to regain some of her senses. "*Unless* you want me to tell everyone to get the fuck out of my house so I can taste you again."

Her thoughts were too scattered to tell what was a joke and what wasn't. "Considering most of my family is among the crowd, please do not do that."

He laughed, burying the sound in her neck. Not ready to be apart again, Maddox slipped her arms around his back. She kept them pressed together until her heartbeat matched his. It was here that she found her courage.

"I love you, Atticus."

He shuddered, his heartbeat racing away from hers. "Then stay."

"I'll stay."

Atticus sprang up, propping himself up on his elbows. "Really? That's all it took?"

"Now's not the time to pretend to be humble."

"Be serious." His smirk was gone, and Maddox knew it was time to confess.

"I didn't get the job I applied for, but Angeline just told me the school wants me to train to be the next chief librarian." She pushed some of his hair behind his ear so it would stop tickling her face. "I'm afraid you'll be seeing much more of me in the future."

His expression was furious and relieved all at once. "You wicked little witch! You might have mentioned that before!" He scowled and swooped down, biting onto her neck.

Maddox yelped, prying him off her. "Did you just give me a *hickey*? We're not teenagers anymore!"

"It serves you right for leaving me in suspense like that."

"I don't even own any concealer," she complained as Atticus stood and helped her to her feet. She found her underwear and hid them behind her back, flushing. "This is so embarrassing."

"I have something for that bite," he said, leading her out of the library and up a side stairwell. "Let's freshen up before we return to the ballroom. Actually, you *could* just have one of your sisters heal your neck."

Are you insane? "I'm not showing them this!"

"Suit yourself."

He led her to his bedroom, which was impeccably tidy, and into his master bath. Her mind wandered to unfamiliar places as she took in the black clawfoot bathtub and the rain shower. Who knew where her imagination could go after just one hookup?

After adjusting her clothes, she slipped her thong back on, wincing at the discomfort. Her makeup was only a little messed up, and Maddox fixed what she could. While she was combing out her waves with her fingers, Atticus returned.

He slipped a thick, black lace choker around her neck, effectively covering his bite mark. "This belonged to Theodora. It was the least gaudy thing in her jewelry box."

That was the first time she'd heard him insinuate Theodora was anything less than perfect. "Oh. It looks nice."

"I agree." Atticus took over the sink to rinse his face. He showed her the time on his watch, which nearly sent her into a panic.

" *We* can't be late! We're the guests of honor!"

Atticus kept his leisurely pace. "That means they can't begin without us."

She snapped, "Well, hurry up and—"

Ignoring her scolding, Atticus advanced toward her, rather than the door. He placed a foot behind hers and tipped her back on the bed, moving to stand between her legs and nuzzle her neck.

"We made it five feet," she complained.

"You're lucky we made it this far. Did you buy this outfit just to torment me?" Atticus gripped her wrists and pinned them above her head. When his hands moved away, his red magic took over and kept her wrists in place. "I have half a mind to never let you leave this room. I could chain you to this bed and work to please you all night. Damn the party."

Maddox couldn't muster an answer quickly enough. Atticus had taken to kissing her neck, and it scattered her thoughts to the wind.

"Tell me to do it, my dear, and I will," he whispered against the tender skin of her throat. "Order me to do anything, and I'll obey."

She protested, though part of her wished to go along with Atticus's wild requests, as overwhelming as they were. "Atticus, that is the opposite of what I want."

Maddox meant staying here and playing his game was the opposite of returning to the party, but he took it entirely differently.

"Oh?" Atticus tensed, and she felt it in every inch of his body that pressed against hers. "I didn't think you'd want to do that, but I *would* like it." His magic left her wrists, allowing her full movement again. "If you wish to tie me up," he murmured, "don't let anything stop you."

That information had to be stored away for later examination. Maddox shook her head while another confession fell from her lips. "No, Atticus, you're misunderstanding me, and I have to tell you something."

His disappointment flashed briefly before Atticus rolled his eyes. "If you go on about being late again—"

"No. It's something important." She waited for his pestering to cease, beginning when his hand left her hip and began stroking her hair. "I—I have to be in love before I want to have sex. Without it, I have absolutely zero drive." There. It was out there, though Maddox doubted that would be explanation enough.

He was unfazed. "And you love me, right? I don't see an issue." Atticus gripped her hips and pulled her forward against him, the slow friction torturing them both.

"Atticus," she whispered, casting her gaze away from his. It was as if a dam had burst. Years of secretly dreaming of Atticus, of being under him like this, and subsequently hating herself for it, made it nearly impossible to resist him. But she had something she desperately needed to say. "I've only ever loved you. Do you see the problem now?"

"No, I don't. I have many faults, as you know, and jealousy happens to be one of them. So, it suits me just fine that you've...only...ever...loved *me?*"

"Are you getting it?" She was usually so good at reading him, but tonight Maddox felt completely blind. "Are you?"

"So, this is *all* new to you?" Atticus moved back enough to let her sit up on the bed.

"I've been on dates before," Maddox countered, feeling as if she needed to prove something to him. "It just didn't feel anything like what I felt for you. I used to think I only wanted you because I hated you. I know now that the opposite is true."

Atticus sat next to her, placing a gentle hand on her knee to keep it from bouncing. "Thank you for telling me. I hope I didn't overwhelm you in the library."

"No, I wanted that. Which you should well know, considering your up close and personal position a few minutes ago," Maddox said. Atticus laughed at her answer, the sound startled and delighted. Maddox continued, "And you were very gentlemanly until you bit me."

"Wasn't going for *gentlemanly*, and I can't promise I won't bite you again," he admitted. "I will, however, promise that we'll go whatever speed you need."

Maddox sighed in relief. "Thank you. I—" She flushed. "—want you, but I am afraid my drive won't be as, um, consistent as yours."

Atticus nodded. "As long as you communicate to me what you want and when you want it and when you don't, I promise I'll do my damnedest to make this work between us."

His vow nearly made her cry. This exact conversation was something Maddox had worried about for years, and Atticus had accepted her without even blinking twice.

Atticus filled in the empty space, allowing her time to catch up with her emotions. "Regardless, it might be best to wait to go any further until *after* your entire bloodline is out from under our roof." Maddox giggled until he whispered, his teeth nipping at her earlobe, "Because I don't want anything to hold you back when I'm trying to make you scream."

"Atticus!" Maddox jumped from his bed, slapping her hands over her cheeks as if she could pat away her flushed skin. "I had no idea you were like this."

"Isn't it a pleasant surprise?" He rose, taking her hand in his and heading for the door. "Come. You've kept us from our party long enough."

CHAPTER 39
WARLOCK

The party hardly seemed to have missed them, Atticus thought as he led Maddox into the Blackwells' ballroom. Though she tried to untangle them, Atticus stubbornly kept her hand tucked in his arm as they entered.

He would not let her go again.

That was something Maddox needed to know without question. There was work ahead of him, tedious work, but Atticus could not let her down. He had tired of digging his own grave.

Every head turned to look at them. Atticus hardly needed to guess why. He knew he looked good, and Maddox, well, words were not enough to describe—

"Do I look like what just happened happened?" she fussed, pressing closer to his side.

"Yes," Atticus quipped. "But only because I slapped a sign on your back that reads 'I begged Atticus Blackwell to eat my—"

"Do. Not. Finish. That. Sentence!" Maddox nearly shrieked, fighting to keep her voice down to a whisper. "And if anyone was begging, it was you!"

"When it comes to *you*, my dear, I'm more than happy to beg if it gets me what I want."

It took very little to make Maddox blush. This would be fun.

Atticus and Maddox wound through the crowd as he fought back memories of parties thrown in Theodora's time. She so loved attention, and her guests had adored her. Just like he used to.

Theodora would always joke that she hated to be alone, even for a moment, and it was only now that Atticus believed her.

Atticus, as Theodora would have done, announced to the horde, "Good evening, I sincerely want to thank everyone for attending this celebration. It's not every day a lost piece of necromantic history is restored."

Maddox pinched his arm. "Could you warn me before you do something that's going to make everyone stare at us?"

Atticus continued loudly, "I particularly wish to thank Blackened Salt's Research and Development department for funding the expedition to recover this artifact. I'm also grateful to the American Academy of the Dead for allowing the use of its laboratory, and to the Commission for supplying an exorcist."

Polite applause echoed throughout the room. Theodora had always ended her welcome speeches the same way, and now it was his turn. Atticus lifted a hand to the ceiling, snapping his fingers once. Magic shot from his arm in rolling waves of smoke and traveled up into the grand ceiling. It clung to the rafters, and small red orbs of light formed, illuminating the party in pale waves of light. Someone flipped a switch, probably William, and cast the gala in darkness with only his witch lights left. Storm clouds pushed across the ceiling, dimming the red orbs as the clouds swallowed them. Thunder boomed and lightning cracked from rafter to rafter, creating quite the light show.

The applause this time was less polite and more honest.

This simple trick had once impressed Atticus, too. When he was happy to stay at Theodora's side as she made the rounds of whomever she entertained that night. Every weekend, Theodora invited strangers to invade their home for séances, rituals, or simple cocktail parties.

At these events, Atticus was personable and obedient. He was Theodora's loyal little *pet.*

"Hey, are you okay?" Maddox asked, a gentle hand turning his face to hers.

"Don't worry about me," he assured her. "Worry about the angry exorcist storming our way."

Lochlan hunted Atticus and Maddox down, pushing aside any well-wishers who tried to congratulate him. "You two! I've been looking everywhere for you! They almost made *me* give the speech!" Lochlan eyed the way Atticus tucked Maddox tighter to his side with mild amusement. His tone relaxed. "Well, it's about time."

"About time for what?" Maddox echoed.

Lochlan ignored her, raising an eyebrow at Atticus instead. "How many lines of Byron did you recite before Maddox took pity on you and agreed to date you?"

Atticus adjusted his collar with a sneer. "She took pity on me *before* I had to resort to Byron, thank you."

Maddox squeaked, "Pick a new topic!"

"Gladly." Lochlan steered them both toward the podium where the Master of Ceremonies glared at them.

"You're both late!" William gestured to the party. Dozens of guests were already mingling and snatching up the free drinks. "Maddox, go introduce Atticus right now!"

Maddox nodded, slipping out from Atticus's grasp to do her part. "Excuse me, everyone," Maddox said, tapping at the microphone until it made an earsplitting whine that got the party's attention. She was graceful when it came to swordplay, not wordplay. "I'm Maddox Abernathy, and I was part of the team that translated a portion of the missing Tome of the Undying. The project wasn't easy, and we had a few setbacks, but Atticus kept us on track and safe." She looked down at her notecards before casting them back down, unneeded. "He kept *me* safe. I will always be grateful for him, even when he started to irritate me with his, at times, excessive worrying."

Maddox waited for the soft laughter to quiet. "Mr. Atticus Blackwell, professor at our esteemed American Academy of the Dead, will walk you through the finer details of the project." She clicked off the podium's microphone and walked over to him, a lapel mic in her hands.

Atticus met her halfway, allowing her to clip the microphone onto him. Her brow knitted as she worked. She *hated* public speaking, as was apparent from her Valedictorian address so many years ago. Now Atticus was determined to distract her from her post-speech anxiety.

"I love you, too," Atticus said softly, and his words echoed throughout the ballroom at a volume that horrified him and Maddox both.

Atticus glanced about the party, his brain too shocked to realize what he had just done. He saw his father first. Rami patted his jacket dry with a handkerchief as if he'd just spat out his drink. At the other end of the room, Colter Abernathy looked to be doing the same.

"Your mic is obviously ready for you, Atticus," Maddox whispered as she covered his lapel microphone with her hand, her eyes wide. "Good luck."

What a way to begin his speech. Atticus didn't dare make eye contact with any of the Abernathys. Or Angeline, who would have the biggest "I told you so" grin on her face.

His practiced speech left his mind. There was damage control needed, and Atticus saw a way out—lie. He'd announced to everyone, at an incredible volume, that he was in love with Maddox. It would be easy to sweep it under the rug and turn it into a joke, but...

"Sorry for starting things off so personal." He laughed, taking a position behind the podium for now. "If you knew Maddox Abernathy at all, and you're very lucky if you do, you'd understand why I couldn't keep that to myself."

The crowd tittered good-naturedly, most of them smiling at Maddox while she stood next to Lochlan and turned bright red. It was such a pretty color—he'd be sure to tease her about it later.

One of William's assistants set up a large map of the Paris catacombs. Atticus moved a pointer around the map, explaining the path he had taken to find the Tome's missing page. What a *horrid* experience that had been. Unless Maddox was dragging him through them, he would not traverse those disgusting, unstable tunnels again.

"Now, I will admit the expedition was the majority of my contribution. Miss Abernathy and Dr. Rhodes translated the page together, and I'd like to take this time to talk about *them*."

Though Atticus could talk about himself for hours, a trait that was all Theodora's genetics, tonight he focused on his colleagues. Even Lochlan, stoic as he was, looked somewhat touched.

Atticus finished his speech, turned off his lapel mic, and placed it on the podium he'd wandered away from. William wasted no time, and the string quartet they'd hired began to play.

Maddox looked past him as Atticus approached her, staring at her shocked family, no doubt. "Well," she said with a grimace, "everyone knows."

Doubt crept in, and honestly, it should have happened earlier. With their troubled past, it would make sense if Maddox wanted to keep their new relationship under wraps until he proved himself. He tried not to let that anxiety show as he playfully asked, "Were you planning on hiding me away?"

She didn't consider it for a second. "No, but I also wasn't planning on announcing it with surround sound."

"You know my penchant for theatrics." Atticus held out a hand to her, his smile hopeful for the first time in years. "I have a way to avoid them a little longer if you'd like."

He expected excuses and protests, but Maddox accepted his offer with a shy grin. "Don't let me look foolish out there."

Atticus tugged her to the center of the ballroom. "I could never."

They danced, and never had Atticus been so grateful for his mother's meddling. He'd been in dance lessons since he was six, when his mother had dreamt that he'd one day be on the board of Blackened Salt Apothecary.

Atticus had been happy to disappoint her.

It was as if they had turned back time. The ballroom, restored—mostly—to its former glory, sparkled as he led Maddox across the floor. Theodora would be pleased, though Atticus banished that idea as soon as it appeared. He focused on Maddox, who was finally back in his life and giggling as each misstep she took sent her tumbling into him. Atticus was happy to catch her every time.

Aware that her family was watching, Atticus kept his hands in appropriate places, as frustrating as it was. Maddox stumbled through the first dance but was soon enjoying herself too much to care how they appeared. The free champagne also helped shake her anxiety. He and Maddox made it through three songs before Atticus felt a tapping on his shoulder. Turning to glare at whoever was hoping to cut in, Atticus quickly smoothed his expression. "Mr. Abernathy. I—"

Colter jerked a thumb over his shoulder. "Give her back, Blackwell, and try to stay away from any more microphones."

Atticus released her, worry constricting his heart. Maddox tiptoed, though she hardly needed to, to kiss his cheek before she let her grandfather lead her back to her family. Atticus didn't care to hear what they'd be discussing, so he made for the opposite end of the room.

Rami dogged his escape, catching Atticus at the Tome project exhibit, a cocktail in his hand.

"That was certainly a surprising speech," Rami said, his tone light. Atticus kept his father in the dark about his life, and Rami was treading carefully before asking the inevitable. "You always insisted the two of you were just friends. Did something change?"

Atticus *himself* had changed. If he hadn't put in years of working on himself, of bettering the Academy, he wouldn't have had a chance with Maddox. "We had a falling out, years ago. It was my fault, but she forgave me."

Rami looked delighted. "It looks like she more than forgave you."

It was hard, even now, to let his father into his life. There were too many years of watching his words, of hiding, for Atticus to feel at ease now. Rami was a good father—he deserved better sons.

Atticus shrugged. "I can't explain that, I'm afraid. I can only count myself lucky."

"So many changes in your life, and I'm finally here to see it." Rami sipped his drink while Atticus swallowed down his guilt. "I wish Giles could have made it."

"Giles is busy." Atticus, desperate to leave it at that, asked his father about the team dinner he'd mentioned earlier. Rami was happy to prattle on about that, listing a few possible venues and the pros and cons of each location.

When Maddox returned to Atticus, her face flushed, Rami congratulated her quickly before giving them some space. Atticus couldn't believe his father possessed such restraint, or perhaps Rami was saving his interrogation for a later time. This future team dinner would surely be uncomfortable.

There was time to worry about that later. "What did Colter have to say?" Atticus meant to keep his tone calm and undemanding and, in his panic, failed.

"He gave me *the talk.*" Maddox covered her face with her hands. "I never cared about dating when I was a teenager, so no one ever bothered to—and now he—oh, Hades, I could just die!"

Maddox never failed to startle Atticus into laughter. "I'm so glad to hear that. I thought he'd try to convince you I'm trouble."

"You *are* trouble! My neck is purple!" She hid her neck with her hands while shaking her head. "He also gave me a list of tinctures and tonics to make for you. Said he doesn't care for your pallor."

It was difficult to keep a neutral expression. Atticus knew he was failing. He felt the tension knotting between his brows. "Oh, did he?"

His flat tone gave away his unenthusiasm. Maddox noticed the shift and latched onto his arm. "One more dance?"

Atticus relaxed, flexing the fingers of his left hand to ease the ache of an old wound. "You never need to ask."

CHAPTER 40
WITCH

Would her heart ever cease this infernal racing? Maddox pressed her hand against her chest, shivering at the look Atticus threw her over his shoulder. Once the celebration died down, Atticus led her out of the ballroom and back upstairs, skipping the main hallways her family may have been utilizing. He revealed a hidden elevator, a black iron monstrosity she severely doubted was up to code.

His house was a maze. Maddox wondered how many years it would take her to discover all its hidden passages.

She wished she could blame the noisy elevator for her nerves. Her skin felt like fire, her head light and giddy. Was this how love was supposed to feel? When would it end? She'd never get any work done if she couldn't focus her foggy, distracted mind.

Atticus's bedroom was cold, and desperate for a distraction, for anything to force her love-sick brain to concentrate, Maddox stacked logs in the fireplace. Satisfied with the wood's orientation, Maddox stepped back and snapped her fingers.

Her magic *stuttered.*

"What the hell was that?" she murmured. Maddox gathered herself and tried once more, and this time a flame flickered brightly into existence.

While the logs crackled and popped, Maddox stared at her hand, her wounded finger calling to her. There was something important she needed to recall, something vital...

Atticus slipped his arms around her, his chest against her back, and his face tucked into her shoulder. "There are *other* ways to keep me warm, Maddox."

She turned in his arms and eyed his clothing. He'd changed into sleepwear while she'd worked. "That's what you wear to bed?"

"Were you expecting nothing?" Atticus pulled at the hem of his Academy sweatshirt.

"I was expecting you'd wear something someone about to be haunted by three Christmas ghosts would wear."

"Wicked," he deemed her again, removing her lace choker. The itchy fabric slipped away, baring the mark he'd made on her skin. "I know *my* family has a sinister reputation, but I think *you're* the true villain here."

She winced as his lips pressed against her bruise, gently, as if in apology. Maddox sought a new topic. "What am I going to wear? We didn't grab my stuff."

"That's because you insisted on avoiding your family after we left the gala."

"I still agree with that, but I need clothes."

"I beg to differ." Atticus tossed her another Academy sweatshirt, though this one was black and worn, a style that released their senior year. Maddox couldn't say why it flustered her. "I hope you're feeling full of school spirit."

"Be right back." Maddox slipped into his bathroom to change out of her dress and wash her face. She groaned as she realized her mistake. She hated sleeping in her contacts, but she'd rather have dry eyes than face her sisters' teasing.

"This sweatshirt barely covers my butt," Maddox whined as she emerged from the bathroom.

"The perks of dating a tall girl." Atticus smiled, though he seemed suddenly unsure of himself.

"Are we..." Maddox gathered herself, pausing at the side of his bed. Atticus sat on the opposite half, the covers pulled back as if he'd contemplated getting in and then changed his mind. "Is that what we're doing? Dating?"

"That word seems insufficient to describe what I want," Atticus admitted. "But we can start with dating. If you'd like."

"Yes, I'd like that." Maddox slid into bed, mostly to stop exposing her butt, but also to move things along. The more they stalled, the more awkward she'd act.

Atticus wasted no time. He reached for her, drawing her close and kissing her slowly, each slip of his tongue tortuous.

"Was this what you meant by taking things slow?" he asked teasingly.

"If that's what you think I mean, you weren't listening at all." He would drive her mad if they kept this up. Maddox turned on her side away from him, rushing a quiet, "Good night!"

"Good night, enchantress." Atticus gripped her hips and pulled her back toward him so he could loop an arm over her.

She squirmed, but he only tightened his hold on her. "Enchantress! Oh, you embarrass me!"

"I'll think of something better," he yawned.

"More like something worse."

"What about *temptress*?" he asked.

"No one told me romance was going to be this mortifying."

CHAPTER 41
WARLOCK

The next morning was chaos.

Atticus had expected an ambush from the Abernathy sisters, or to endure the probing stare of Maddox's father and grandfather, but this? *This* was unforgiveable.

Flour covered most surfaces in his previously pristine kitchen. Maddox's mother utilized every burner on his stovetop. Diedre stirred gravy, cracked eggs, and generally made a mess wherever she went. Her daughters were no better. Atticus saved his fruit bowl from being covered with flour, and he sneered at the smell. Inside, three pomegranates had rotted, the juices flooding the bottom of the bowl. He dumped the bowl and its contents in the trash.

Jinx loomed in the kitchen doorway, meowing at full volume and appearing as an ally against this disorder until Dove tossed the beast a sausage. Jinx's loyalty was easily bought, Atticus observed glumly.

Maddox tried to step in, putting away perishables as the rest worked, and mopped up spills. Atticus merely wondered if it would be childish if he sat still and covered his eyes until it was over.

Colter's fingers pinched his shoulder, and considering the state of his beloved kitchen, Atticus was almost grateful.

"Let's take a walk, Blackwell."

"Granddad!" Maddox snapped, abandoning her mop to advance upon her grandfather with a vengeance. "Leave him be!"

Atticus raised a hand. "Maddox, it's *fine*. We'll be right back." *I hope.*

Colter lifted a chin in his direction. "Take us to the greenhouse. This place is a damn maze."

With everything that had been going on—the gala, the research project, the possible possession—Atticus had left his conservatory a tad neglected. He felt embarrassed to allow a green witch to see its current state but led the way.

While Colter went straight for the conservatory's soil, Atticus took the time to clean his apothecary workbench, ensuring each ingredient was hidden away in the proper cabinet. As he took stock, he realized he was running low on things he should never allow to dwindle. Where the hell had his head been?

Colter interrupted Atticus's tidying. "This garden... You do all this work yourself?"

"Yes. I take care of this and the graveyard." Atticus nervously watched as Colter scanned the conservatory's fauna. He felt as if he was being tested somehow.

Colter nodded. "You've done well. Don't let Maddie take the greenhouse over. She'll definitely try, and this place will be dead within a week."

Botany had never been a skill of Maddox's, though she tried so hard. Atticus, though he loved her so, would not trust the woman with a cactus. "I won't," Atticus promised. "Are you not surprised by our relationship? I know it's sudden, even to me, and I assume you're aware of our past."

That latter bit was ignored. Venenum dropped from a tree branch, curiously flicking its forked tongue at Colter. The green witch ignored the snake's pestering.

"No one," Colter deadpanned, "is surprised by this. You invited her four sisters, her parents, and her grandfather to stay in your home. You weren't exactly subtle. *Desperate* is the word I'd used."

"That's..." Atticus sighed loudly. "That's accurate."

"She told me how you took care of her while you dealt with the artifact. Well, Maddox complained, is what she did." Colter inspected a few plants as he spoke, checking the leaves and buds.

Atticus squirmed under the positive attention. "I'd rather you didn't compliment me, sir."

"I'd rather you didn't call me that." Colter left the plants alone, and Atticus released a breath of relief that the green witch hadn't found his work lacking.

"Is it promises you want?" Atticus dreaded this stalling. Whatever Colter needed, Atticus was happy to give it. Unless it was a breakup. "Maddox will want for nothing. I won't stand in her way again."

Colter eyed Atticus for a long time. "I want you to take your vitamins."

"Excuse me?"

"Vitamins. Tonics. Whatever brews I tell Maddox to make for you. Drink them down with a smile. I know you're suffering from...*something*." Colter grimaced, arms folded across his chest. "As long as it doesn't affect Maddox, I consider that situation your own business, but don't refuse her remedies. Though she has a bad habit of making them far too bitter."

A lifetime of bitterness was nothing to Atticus. He nodded.

"I'll send you a copy of the family tree," Colter said, and Atticus nearly laughed at the statement. "I have a few cousins whose names I can't even remember."

Atticus chuckled until Colter added, "You're taking on more than you know, Blackwell. Maddox's sisters are making their Christmas lists as we speak, and they suddenly have expensive tastes."

Atticus's return to the kitchen interrupted the sisters' gossiping. As he and Colter rounded the corner, he overheard Dove interrogating Maddox. "Explain why that man speaks like he was written by a Brontë sister," Dove asked loudly.

Maddox defended him. "He was raised by a two-hundred-year-old witch. It's not his fault!"

If only Theodora's overwhelming nurturing had only affected Atticus's speech.

Atticus ignored the glance Colter shot him before they stepped inside the kitchen. Maddox blushed at his return, no doubt feeling guilt over the conversation that had died in Atticus's presence.

She shouldn't worry. Atticus did speak like a Brontë romantic lead. He just hoped he'd have a cheerier end.

"Did you hear anything?" Maddox whispered when Atticus made it to her side.

Maddox's tension eased from her posture the second Atticus placed a hand against the small of her back. He smiled down at her and told another lie. "Didn't hear a word."

"Then you missed my perfect impression of you!" Amber piped up. "Reset the stage."

"No!" Maddox yelped.

Poppy twirled and fell back into Amber's arms, throwing a hand over her face. She adopted a falsetto. "Oh, Atticus. I'll curse you if you dare leave me again!"

Amber growled, "Living without *you* would be the true curse."

"Grandad, make them stop!" Maddox elbowed Atticus. "Blackwell, defend your dignity!"

"How can I?" Atticus asked, laughing in shock at how quickly Maddox's sisters included him. Teasing, he knew, was the Abernathys' way of accepting someone. "That sounded exactly like me."

CHAPTER 42
WITCH

Night brought a new mixture of anticipation and a small dash of anxiety.

Maddox knew this latter feeling would vanish with time. Already she was more comfortable with Atticus's soft touches, though his grand declarations of love still made her tongue-tied. *But those will fade with time, too, won't they?*

While Atticus and Maddox had agreed to wait until her family went back home to have sex, Atticus didn't restrain himself when it came to other forms of affection. The man kissed her senseless whenever they found themselves remotely alone. And the dancing! He twirled her around the estate and was less cautious of intruders while they danced. Twice her sisters had caught Maddox being dipped and spun to no music.

Could a person develop a permanent blush?

The hardest thing to get used to was their sleeping arrangement. Maddox had gone her whole life without sleeping next to such a clingy man—or any man, for that matter. Atticus insisted on spooning her, rendering her unable to move throughout the night.

And tonight, she needed to move.

A rapping sounded upon their window, an etching of claws on glass. Edgar must have slipped outside during the daylight and decided the night air was too frigid for an overnight stay. The raven was quite the spoiled corvid.

Maddox squirmed and wiggled until she slid underneath Atticus's left arm. He huffed once in his sleep but remained lost in his own dreams.

Her feet hit the cold hardwood floor, and she winced, grateful she had her own pajamas tonight. Maddox hugged herself as she went to the window. She drew back the floor-to-ceiling curtain, exposing the darkened glass window.

How odd to stain glass so intensely—no other room contained such glasswork. With the blackened glass, no light could shine through. Did Atticus have insomnia?

Maddox opened the window, and Edgar flew inside, landing with a flutter on the only desk in the room. Papers shot into the air with each wingbeat, and Maddox struggled to capture them all. Unlike herself, Atticus was obsessively tidy, and a mess ruffled his temper. As she snatched the last sheet, Maddox caught sight of Atticus's sleeping form bathed in moonlight.

It was a full moon tonight, and the gentle rays lit upon Atticus and his exposed left arm. From his fingers to his elbow, there was no skin, muscle, or sinew. His forearm was nothing but bone—a skeleton held together with shimmering red magic. His finger bones dug into the comforter and at the sudden movement, Maddox released a shrill, but hushed scream.

To a skilled witch, full moonlight revealed simple enchantments.

Maddox dropped her papers as Atticus sat up in bed, his head whipping in her direction and concern slashed upon his features. The motion brought his visage abruptly into the moonlight, unmasked and afraid.

She only saw his face for a few moments, but that was long enough to make a horrific connection.

Atticus quickly realized what had happened. He covered the left side of his face with a hand, cursing her as he turned away. "Don't look at me," he ordered and repeated his request, though this time Atticus was pleading with her. "*Don't look.*"

Maddox felt her every muscle tense. Fear, grief, and pity each fought to control her actions. Edgar squawked as Maddox backed into the desk, disturbing his perch.

She stammered, "What are you?"

His tone turned cruel, but she understood it was merely defensive. "Don't play stupid now. You know what I am."

Maybe Maddox knew *what* he was, but she'd never understand *why* Atticus would turn himself into...

Hades, the man was a *lich*. A soulless, undead warlock who could raze their entire town to the ground if he wished. But something was off about his transformation—it didn't seem complete. Was Atticus mostly a lich? Or mostly human? Had he been this way the entire time she had known him? *Why, Atticus, why?*

Before she could organize her thoughts, Atticus flew to the window to snap the curtains closed. He remained there as Maddox stumbled toward the bed, trying to sit down but falling to the floor instead.

She attempted to understand what she saw, a half-ruined man. Aside from Atticus's left arm, the rest of his flesh was intact, though there were other oddities in his appearance. His skin held a grey tone, visible even in the pale light, and something like a bone-formed crown adorned his head. Her vision of his true form had been too brief to note anything more.

Atticus's back was bare and tense as he shook, keeping the curtains shut with both hands.

"You prying, little witch. You won't forget this, will you?" His laughter was hysterical. "You *saw*. You *know*."

She fought to find her voice, but Maddox refused to fall silent when Atticus needed her. And, by the gods, did he need her.

"Atticus, what *happened* to you?" She leapt to her feet, shaky as her legs were, and carefully made her way to him. It was easy, despite what had been revealed, to slip her arms around his back. Hades, she wished he'd stop trembling. "Talk to me so I can help you."

"*Help* me?" His trembling ceased, replaced with a stony anger. "There is no helping this, only containing it."

"But—"

He was harsh, snapping, "No. That's it, Maddox. There's no mending me."

Maddox tightened her grip on him. "We don't know that for sure, but if it's true, that doesn't mean it's the end of *us*."

With the moonlight hidden, he would have almost seemed himself again if it wasn't for that furious expression he now bore. Atticus snarled, "Don't give me *hope*. That's too cruel a punishment, even for me." His hands fisted in the curtain. "Hades, I had hoped we'd make it to at least one anniversary before you discovered my hideous truth."

Maddox sought to distract him. "Does this have anything to do with why you pushed me away all those years ago?"

He grimaced. "I wasn't lying. I said I abandoned you because of my family and that was true. But it was also my fault." Atticus held a hand out, palm up, and let his magic overflow from his fingers. It was thick, like a liquid, and Maddox fought her instinct to flinch as it spilled onto the floor and crept toward her.

It spiraled up her leg, like a snake, and stopped at her neck. The cold weight felt familiar somehow.

Atticus pulled the magic back to him quickly. "*This* was the other reason. I don't know if I kept any part of my soul, but when I slept, it didn't matter. I would dream of you, long for you, and this disgusting magic would try to hunt you down."

Maddox preferred her previous assumption—that his family had thought she wasn't good enough for him.

"I was able to control it, eventually, but until then, I had to ignore you." There seemed to be more he wanted to say, but Atticus swallowed and finished with, "It's your turn to do what's best for you and ignore me."

"I'm not walking away from you." Maddox tried to cool her own temper, but she hated how Atticus spoke about himself.

"It's a matter of *when*, not *if*." Atticus moved away from the window and out of her arms, and though he barely glanced at her, Maddox felt it. Felt his *hate*.

No, not hate. It was loss, she realized. Though Maddox was still with him and hadn't run for the door at his secret, Atticus refused to consider what was right in front of him.

Maddox was staying.

But it would take everything she had to convince him of that. This rising panic of his, it was not something new. This was a collection of *years and years* of lying, hiding, and fearing he'd be discovered. She could not simply kiss away something of this magnitude.

Atticus barely met her stare. "*Stop* looking at me. I can't fucking stand it."

She had so many questions. Maddox could only imagine the level of despair welling in Atticus's veins. "How do you hide it?"

Atticus shrugged. "My family is skilled at potion brewing. My mother, my brother, and I created a brew to help me blend in. Cynthia said I was like a chameleon. A wolf in sheep's clothing is more accurate a title."

"How long have you been like this?" she asked, following him around the room as he paced. "Tell me everything, Atticus. It would have come out eventually—"

"No, it wouldn't have." His words were more of a growl than anything human. Atticus stopped running away and faced her. He looked as he always did, devilishly grim and handsome, but Maddox could not shake the moonlit memory superimposed over his skin.

"You wouldn't have kept this from me forever," Maddox scoffed.

"I would have tried," Atticus countered. He was shaking, though a manic grin crossed his lips. "I could have lived with the lie, but I can't live with you knowing the truth."

Her next argument failed to pass her lips. Maddox, in a moment of weakness, felt her faith in him falter. She shook that damning instinct away. This was Atticus. He was *hers*, and he was hurting. "You wouldn't have hidden this. Not forever. Not from me."

Her certainty made him chuckle. "I think you still underestimate what you mean to me. Love and obsession go hand in hand, and I've never been able to separate the two. Not when it comes to you."

That emptiness, that unbearable loneliness that had been repaired only days ago, ripped open. Maddox couldn't catch her breath. "No," she said, though it was more of a plea. "I don't believe it. You would have told me. What if we got married?" she begged, reaching for him. As Atticus backed away, shaking his head, she added, "What if we tried to have *children*?"

"Then I would have disappointed you."

The words were simple and emotionless, and it was the first moment since she threw open that curtain that Maddox believed him.

Why had it taken so long? He lived in a house full of secrets. Lying was like breathing to Atticus.

Love. She'd barely had a taste of it, had spent mere hours feeling finally complete. And now Maddox shattered.

"Something terrible was done to me," Atticus sighed. "I'm sorry to be the terrible, rotted thing to happen to you."

CHAPTER 43
WITCH

*T*his shouldn't surprise you. You've always known Atticus Blackwell was a coward.

The words echoed in her mind, sounding a little like Aegis, but not quite. Maddox's brow furrowed. Atticus loomed before her, but Maddox retreated inside her mind. What else could she do? Atticus wouldn't let her near him.

Alarms went off as her logic demanded that she focus on her own safety, but her thoughts were only of Atticus and the voice.

He's going to leave you alone again. And, like the last time, it's not your fault.

No, that couldn't be Aegis. Her sword was too far away to reach her mind. Then who was speaking to her?

We should punish him, the voice tried.

"No," Maddox muttered aloud. That wasn't what she wanted, was it? Even if Atticus had lied again, no part of her wished to harm him.

Then we save him? We'll need the Tome for that.

That made no sense. The Tome was in tatters. It would take years to bring it back together, if they could even find the rest of it.

It's just one page at a time, and isn't he worth it?

Of course Atticus was worth it. He needed help. He—

He needs a healer. He needs you.

No, no. Maddox was no healer. That was Daphne. All Maddox could do was hurt.

You're the only one who can undo what's been done to him. What else would that make you? BUT WE NEED THE BOOK.

Where would she even start looking?

There's a part of the Tome inside this house. How else could the warlock become such a wretched thing?

But would that section have information on saving Atticus's soul? Necromancers rarely thought about the consequences of their actions. Maddox doubted—

Does he need doubt or does he need action? Don't you love him? What are you without him? Everything you've done in your life was because of him or done in spite of him. If you lose him, you'll lose everything you are.

You will never be complete without him. You'll go back to the farm, and you know you're nothing more than a burden there.

Save him. Save yourself. Find the rest of the book.

CHAPTER 44
WARLOCK

It was over.

It was always going to end this way. Atticus, as adept as he was at hiding, couldn't do so forever.

He saw the break, the moment Maddox realized that his love for her did not prevent him from hurting her.

Maddox held her tongue for a long time, her hand clutched over her heart as she stared at the floor. She drew in one deep breath, and then another, and looked into his eyes.

He saw the shadow, so small he should not have noticed, flash across her face.

Maddox's magic pushed out from her body, *it exploded*, and Atticus flew backward until his back hit the side of his writing desk.

He slid to the ground, rubbing his face as he moaned. When he could see again, Maddox was gone.

The smart thing to do would be to flee. Giles had prepared him for this. Years ago, Giles had sat Atticus down and they developed a getaway plan should anyone discover Atticus's secret. Atticus liked to think that Maddox wouldn't alert the Commission about his condition, but he couldn't count on it.

He should leave. Just run. Grab his bugout bag and go.

It was just that damned shadow in her eyes. No matter how many times Lochlan insisted Maddox was clean, that there was no parasite haunting her, Atticus worried.

You deserved that pain. Her violence was only because of you and nothing else. You are more than enough to cause such hate.

Atticus cast those thoughts aside. He desperately wanted to run. As he dressed hurriedly, half his mind worked on his escape route, choosing halls that were less likely to be occupied at this hour, and the other half was consumed with Maddox.

He left his luggage and passport on his bed before he left his bedroom. The raven tried to exit with him, but Atticus slammed the door before the bird made it out. That thing would surely alert its master of what had happened, and Atticus needed all the time he could buy.

If Maddox's violence was due to a parasite's influence, Atticus presumed she'd be back where her sleepwalking had first taken her—the library. If he found the room empty, he would leave. A simple ultimatum for himself, at least when he took emotion out of the picture.

The library brought to mind those precious, desperate minutes before the gala. There would be no better heaven for him than Maddox's leg hooked over his shoulder.

And no greater hell than what he was living right now.

Inside the library's entry, something caught his foot, and Atticus backtracked to stare at the book flat underneath his shoe. Once again, he was presented with a picture of that gruesome parasitic insect, though he was certain he'd already cleaned up Maddox's mess.

"Where is it?!"

Atticus followed her hysteric voice until he found Maddox on the library's second floor, tearing out books again. This time, there was no doubting she was awake.

"Maddox, what are you doing?" Atticus blocked her access to the bookshelf and found himself promptly shoved aside.

"There's another piece of the puzzle here, isn't there? I can *feel* it. Another part of the Tome somewhere in these halls." Maddox ripped the book she was flipping through in two. Both halves were thrown down to the first floor. "You're hiding it," she accused, her eyes as foggy as they'd been the other night.

There was no way she knew about the portion of the Tome his grandmother had kept for herself. It wasn't included in her grimoire, and Atticus and Giles had both searched for the section and failed. Atticus pleaded with her, "Maddox, stop this. I can help you—"

"*Help* me? All you do is keep things from me!" She stamped her foot and screamed, "I need to be whole! Let me be whole!"

This was more than he could, or should, handle alone. Atticus slid a hand into his pant pocket before sliding his phone out and hiding it behind his back. "You're not acting like yourself. I'm going to *call Lochlan.*"

Atticus's voice command started a call to Lochlan, but Maddox didn't listen to anything he said. She snarled, "Don't get in my way. I have to track down each page, every precious word, so I can help you! I have to, Atticus." She wore her sword at her side, her magic running down the sheath like lightning.

Atticus's phone finished quietly ringing, and he heard Lochlan's confused greeting. If Maddox was in her right mind, she would have realized what Atticus was doing. But now she only focused on the family ring he bore.

"Perhaps your grandmother's grimoire will be more helpful," she decided and snatched his hand before Atticus could recoil.

There was not a moment of contemplation—Maddox tried removing his ring and when Atticus resisted, she broke his finger.

He shouted, though the pain was secondary for a moment. Atticus had been right all along. Something was hitching a ride within Maddox's magic, and now was strong enough, or believed itself to be, to reveal itself.

Maddox tried tearing off his ring again before the swelling made it impossible. Atticus hissed in pain, fearing he would have to fight her and knowing that he, unarmed, would lose. But a flash of dark fur leapt down from a shelf above them and Jinx hissed as she gracefully landed at their feet. Before either of them could react, Jinx bit into Maddox's ankle. The possessed witch yelped and released Atticus's hand.

That crazy cat—one day it was eating his garbage, and the next it was saving his life. Thank Hades his rescue was orchestrated by the cat and not by Venenum.

It was cowardly, but Atticus took the chance to escape, grabbing Jinx on his way to the only entrance and exit to the library. He slammed the double doors shut, pressing his back against them as he fumbled for his phone.

Once the device was pressed to his ear, Atticus heard Lochlan yelling from the other end. "What the hell is happening? I heard you shouting! I swear, if this is a butt dial and you and Maddox are up to something kinky—"

"She's possessed," Atticus said numbly.

Atticus knew Lochlan was rolling his eyes when Lochlan snapped, "Not this again!"

"Lochlan, Maddox just broke my fucking finger. Does that sound like foreplay to you?"

There was a long moment of silence. Lochlan swore and promised, "I'll be there as soon as I can. Contain her and wait for me!"

Wait for Lochlan to do *what?* Lochlan had failed to prevent this possession, and Atticus wouldn't count on his next attempt faring any better. Atticus ended the phone call, releasing a frustrated sigh. Atticus fretted while Maddox threw herself at the other side of the doors. Her escape attempts made enough noise that the Abernathy clan showed up—Colter leading the pack.

Atticus hoped the raven was still trapped in his bedroom, and that the Abernathys remained unaware of his dreadful little secret. He would help Maddox and then leave. He just needed to keep the Abernathys oblivious to what he was for a few more hours.

Maddox's father spoke the first words Atticus had heard from the man. "What's going on here?"

There was no sugarcoating this. Atticus explained, "Maddox has been influenced by the page we translated. The exorcist cleared her, but something lingered that we failed to detect."

"What. Do. We. Do?" Colter's inquiry was a bark, each word precise and mad as hell.

Atticus motioned for Maddox's sisters to take his place barricading the door. Once he was free, his shoulders drooped as he continued. "Keep Maddox contained. The only other way out of the library is through a few windows on the second story. Maddox isn't herself, so you need to watch those windows in case she—"

"Understood." Maddox's father grabbed his wife's hand, and they ran outside.

The Abernathys wanted more instructions, but Atticus was wrapped up in perfecting his own task. He sprinted for the conservatory and his tools, unaware Colter was right behind him.

Atticus stopped in his study to retrieve Theodora's grimoire, glad he still had his ring. Gritting his teeth against the pain, Atticus removed his family ring and slid it on another finger before the break swelled further.

A little more instruction would have been nice. Theodora's notes on this particular potion were irritatingly thin. Atticus supposed such a sacrifice would not have appealed to her, hence the lack of guidance.

With such a poor recipe, anyone else would have struggled. But there was no better motivation than a combination of love and guilt.

Colter joined him at the apothecary bench without even asking what they were brewing. Atticus was barely aware of Colter's assistance until the old man suddenly grabbed Atticus's wrist. Green light spiraled up from Cotler's grasp and surrounded Atticus's swollen finger. A few painful moments later, Atticus's broken finger was healed.

"Oh." With Maddox in danger, Atticus had forgotten he was in severe pain. "Thank you."

"Next time *ask* for help, son. You have a house full of healers. Utilize it." Colter released his wrist and gestured to the apothecary. "Tell me how to help."

After Atticus gave him a few simple instructions, the green witch prepared ingredients and managed the flame roiling underneath the small cauldron that sat on Atticus's stone lab table. Together, they had the solution completed before Lochlan burst into the sunrise-lit greenhouse.

"Mr. Blackwell," Lochlan seethed, hovering over the lab table and sniffing the air. "Is that brew what I think it is? I thought we discussed this. I won't stand by while you damn yourself."

"What took you so long?" Colter demanded of the exorcist, sweeping a hand toward the glass walls of the greenhouse where the morning sun had appeared. "We've been at this all night!"

"Colter," Atticus interrupted, ladling the green potion into a round glass vial. "This brew will allow me to remove Maddox's possessor and transfer it to another host. Might I request your help containing Dr. Rhodes here? He'll get in my way."

Lochlan stepped toward them. "Wait a minute, Atticus. You don't know what you're doing."

"This potion..." Colter glanced between Atticus and Lochlan. "This will help Maddox?"

"It's fucking untested!" Lochlan argued while Atticus grimly nodded.

Atticus had brewed hundreds of different potions throughout his lifetime—he wasn't blindly following a recipe. He *knew* this potion would work.

Colter didn't hesitate another second. Each plant in the greenhouse seemed to wither as strong, white roots burst from the ground and bound Lochlan within their grasp.

"Don't crush him," Atticus advised as he watched the roots coil like a python around the exorcist. He shuddered, recalling being trapped within those roots himself. "You'll need him after this."

Colter finished with Lochlan and grabbed Atticus's free wrist. "What are you going to do, kid?"

Atticus knew without question that if he asked any of the Abernathys to be the parasite's next host to spare Maddox, every single one of them would volunteer. He also knew he would never give them the option.

"It's a simple trade, and I'm the only one that can make it. This will force the parasite to jump hosts." Atticus swished the glowing potion in his hand, waves of viridescent liquid licking at the glass vial. "Maddox will understand the parasite more than I could. She's better at research—better at fixing things. And I am better at suffering."

There was more to Atticus's plan, and there were parts he was certain the Abernathys would protest, but he would save those troubling details for Maddox—*after* he saved her.

CHAPTER 45
WITCH

A heaviness settled in her bones. A frenzied itch crawled right underneath her skin, like a millipede that ran from her head to her toes, and Maddox scratched madly at her flesh until Dove and Amber held her arms against her bed.

They had dragged her kicking and screaming from the library, forcing her into the comfort of her bed while she fought them all. Aegis, her sword, rested on her dresser, just out of her reach. Daphne stood shaking in the doorway, Rob standing defensively between her and Maddox. Maddox felt warm, healing magic caressing her, and it *burned*.

Part of her lingered. That part dug her nails into the bed, as if two handfuls of blankets could hope to ground her.

Her magic was poisoned. This possession had been a slow thing, nearly unnoticeable, though now that Maddox looked back, she could easily read the signs. Her spells sputtered and struggled, and even the simplest of tasks had taken more energy than they should have. As if something was leeching on her power.

Why couldn't Lochlan cast this parasite out? And why had it chosen now to take her body over? Lochlan had said she was okay. He had promised.

Liars, all of them. Her sisters who soothed her and said everything was going to be fine—liars. That useless exorcist—Judas.

And the worst traitor of all was Atticus. How many times was she expected to forgive him?

Maddox was *certain* the Blackwell estate held part of the Tome. Theodora hadn't scattered every piece of the Tome of the Undying to the wind. She'd kept part of it for herself. That—that *parasitoid* had sensed it. And it wanted it still.

If Maddox could only control her voice, she could tell Lochlan and Atticus what she knew. The author of their page had left his magic, his parasitoid, on their artifact. One goal was embedded into that leech—protect the book.

Poppy pried open Maddox's bedroom window, exposing them all to the frigid, damp air. While Dove held Maddox down on the bed, Amber's skillful hands guided in roots and vines through the window from the outside. The bedroom became a jungle, and Maddox's unwelcome guest tried to force her to flee.

Maddox's sisters wound their family's white roots around her arms and legs. Maddox stopped thrashing. Even that parasite could sense a lost cause.

The whispers dropped off suddenly, the silence broken by a creak of a neglected door. Maddox sensed Atticus before she saw him.

"Can we have a moment alone?" he asked, that deep, demanding voice now soft and pleading. "It's dangerous to have another body in the room while I work."

Work? How unspecific. So, there was something Atticus didn't want her to know. Whatever. It didn't matter if Atticus hid one more thing from her. Maddox wouldn't let him get in her way again.

Panic fueled her escape attempts as she watched Atticus move between her sisters.

"What are you doing here?" Maddox pressed deeper into the mattress to give her a half-inch more of space between them. Her mind was unfocused, but tears flooded her vision, anyway.

"I'm here to help you," Atticus said, approaching her bed.

What a joke. There was no use addressing such an obvious lie. "How many pages of the Tome did your grandmother keep for herself?" Theodora Blackwell's hypocrisy made Maddox want to laugh. "She really told you she tore apart the Tome out of concern for her fellow witch? How many years did it take you to see through that bullshit?"

"Too many." Atticus lifted a vial to her lips. "Are you thirsty? You were screaming for quite a while."

"What is it?" Maddox pursed her lips after rushing out her question. "Poison?" Now that she knew what he was, she should expect anything. Maddox wanted to despise him—maybe if Atticus tried to poison her, she finally could.

"Something to help you sleep," he promised, trying to help her drink again. His left hand tilted her chin upward, his fingers cold and rough.

He looked as broken as she felt.

Something was wrong, but Maddox was exhausted. That leech inside her protested, but she fought it and opened her mouth enough to drink.

The liquid burned her tongue, but Atticus's gentle grip turned fierce, holding her mouth open until the vial was drained.

"You'll feel better soon."

Another lie. She wanted to spit in his face, but her throat had gone painfully dry. Maddox coughed with such force that her family roots loosened their hold on her arms and legs, allowing her to sit up.

"There's so many things I should have told you," Atticus began, sitting on the bed next to her and taking one of her hands.

"What the hell did you give me?" His words were meaningless. Only the pain in Maddox's throat felt real to her.

Atticus's thumb brushed over her knuckles, despite the fact her fingernails dug viciously into his palm. "I failed you. Lochlan and I—we didn't know how to help you. I let myself believe everything was fine, even though I knew better."

He turned her wrist over, hissing when he saw a bulge crawling under her skin. "It's grown more than I thought. I'm so sorry, my dear. This is going to hurt."

That parasite begged Maddox to scream for help, but it was too late for that. Pain set her magic aflame. That bulge frenzied and a jaw pierced her flesh from the inside, tearing and biting until some demented insect ripped through her wrist.

Maddox screamed the terrified wail of a child.

The rest of her family tried to break back into the room, but Atticus had dead-bolted her door. "STAY THE FUCK OUT!" he yelled, thrusting a hand toward the door. Magic flew with the movement, liquid and dark, and encased the door in a shimmering substance. Atticus brought his own wrist to his mouth and bit into it.

The creature that had crawled out of her screeched, lifting its legs uncertainly. Half of its bug-like body remained underneath her skin like it was prepared to crawl back inside her to safety. It nearly slipped back under before Atticus presented his bleeding wrist to it.

The warlock's offer was considered for a moment before the creature flew out of Maddox and tore into Atticus's open flesh.

Why doesn't he scream?

Cradling her wrist against her chest, Maddox whimpered and pressed against her fresh wound. She felt her wrist knitting itself shut. With that thing gone, her mind cleared, and Maddox realized what had triggered the parasite's sudden takeover.

It wanted to be *complete*. The author of their page, Warlock Kaspar, had created a parasitoid, applied one goal to it, and trapped it in the Tome of the Undying. That parasite's sole purpose was to protect the Tome, and it had failed.

Now it longed to be whole again, something Maddox felt deeply. The leech was weak. Lochlan might have been able to cast it out if Maddox hadn't desperately wanted the same thing. It hid inside her, her own wish to feel complete masking its presence while it fed on her magic and waited. It waited for her to feel as it did—to feel deficient. And Atticus's damning admission had given that leech exactly what it wanted.

Atticus suffered the parasite's weight now. How willingly he suffered for her. Maddox's anger and heartbreak settled, twisting into something new.

He took on Maddox's burden, and that was a terrible mistake. Atticus, who appeared as a half-human, tortured thing, must wish to be whole more than anyone.

Lochlan would *never* be able to cast the parasite out of Atticus, not while the parasite and Atticus both wanted to be complete. Demons were complex and held their own desires—many of them—and their own twisted personalities. If it was a demonic possession they were dealing with, Lochlan would have no problem separating the two personalities of the demon and the host. But this parasite was so single-minded that it easily merged with the host, becoming impossible to remove.

Warlock Kaspar's colleagues had laughed at his simple leech. Maddox wasn't laughing.

Atticus held his bleeding wrist and hissed. The parasite crawled under his skin until the bulge eventually disappeared, the torn skin closing together after it.

What had he done? He wouldn't last long against the parasite's whispers, surely he knew that. Atticus was sacrificing himself for her. After all his lies and after trying to leave her again, he still...

All that mattered now was that Atticus needed her. How long had

Maddox sat on the sidelines as the rest of her family healed and nurtured? This was her chance to do the same. To mend something no one else could.

"Just one more request." Atticus took her hand and squeezed hard. "After what I've done to you, this might be easy. Let me go."

He stood, wavered, and tried to leave her again. Maddox launched herself out of bed, grabbing onto his shirt. He tore out of her weak grasp, a hand on the door, and was about to exit until the tip of her sword, stolen back from her dresser, pressed into his back.

Atticus paused, half-turning to roll his eyes at her. "There's no need for that, Maddox. I'll make myself, and this parasite, disappear. Where I'm going, I'll never hurt anyone again."

"I don't care about that." Maddox kept her blade trained on him as she circled him. Her back was at the door as she used her sword to move him away from the exit. "You're not going anywhere. I'm going to help you."

"Help me?" Atticus laughed, pushing her sword away with a finger. "I failed you. Lochlan failed you. What do you even plan to do—"

"Lochlan couldn't find the parasite because it's so simple. All it wants is to be put back together again. I wanted the same just as desperately, and that's why Lochlan failed to oust it." With that leech no longer influencing her, Maddox understood it all too well. She could use her new knowledge to defeat it. "But now we have something to work with."

"No." Atticus didn't give it a moment's thought. "It's too dangerous, especially when you account for what I am. It could take years to remove that leech. Let me leave. Let me do that for you."

He walked closer, so sure she'd never use her blade against him. Aegis cheered as Maddox struck, tearing a long gash in Atticus's shirt.

He was left gasping, holding his hands against the rip until Maddox pried them away. She slipped a hand inside his suit jacket, sliding out the silver flask he kept inside.

"You cut me," Atticus said in disbelief.

"Just your shirt, but don't test me," Maddox assured him. She held up his flask. "This is the brew you use to hide your appearance, isn't it? I've seen you take it since we were in school. Back then, you took it daily." Maddox twisted open the lid, sniffed the contents, and dumped it out onto the floor. Atticus watched the liquid pour out, fists clenched and eyes wide as if she had just thrown away gold. "You've had *years* to grow accustomed to it. It must have lost some potency. How many times a day do you need this now?"

"You..." Atticus rubbed a hand over his face. "You're going to *force* me to stay? I'm not your little science project. I won't be poked and examined like a lab rat."

"I wasn't asking," Maddox said.

Atticus hid his pain with a dark chuckle. "Lochlan can't cast out this leech on his own. He'll involve the Commission of Magic Management, and it won't take them long to find my other oddities. They won't let me go. *Ever.*"

"I'll be honest with you, and maybe you'll learn to follow my example." Maddox tilted her sword, letting the dim light catch on the edge. "I'm going to save you. It doesn't matter to me how long it takes or what I have to sacrifice. You can hate me by the end of it, and it will be worth it. You call your affection a burden, but Atticus, I've only ever wanted *you.*"

How could he *ever* think she'd let him walk away to suffer the consequences of her own mistake? She released this parasite into the world. Never would Maddox allow Atticus to take her place and leave to find somewhere to quietly lose himself.

Maddox unlocked and opened the bedroom door by reaching back with one hand. Her eyes never left his.

"I think my love can be just as terrible as yours."

CHAPTER 46
WARLOCK

The Abernathys filed inside Maddox's bedroom with Lochlan in the lead. Lochlan stopped short when he saw Maddox's sword and the gash in Atticus's shirt.

"So, Maddox remains possessed," Lochlan assumed, his attention fixated on her blade.

Maddox shook her head, pointing to Atticus. "No, we've switched places, he and I. But I'm going to help him. I have a few ideas on where to start."

What the hell was wrong with her? Atticus glared Maddox's way. This. Was. Pointless. Even if Maddox found a way to strip this parasite from him, it wasn't like they could resume their normal lives. She knew his secret. How disgusted she must be.

Though, if that was true, why did she keep looking at him like *that*? Why did she insist on making him stay, on trying to fix him?

She hates losing. That's why. Such praise and recognition she'd earn for catching a thing as wretched and unnatural as you.

His chest ached, and Atticus fought the urge to collapse onto the floor and weep over all he had lost. He only had a few hours before he needed another dosage of *Chameleon*. The ingredients required weren't easily sourced, either. Without that potion, no airport would allow him entry.

There were parts of himself that Atticus could hide without the potion, but there were others he could not.

Well, Maddox already knew his secret and had glimpsed his wretched visage in the moonlight. What was one more revelation? He'd been foolish to think things could ever end otherwise.

After one last glance at Maddox's determined, blue-sky gaze, Atticus raised both hands above him and let go.

CHAPTER 47
WITCH

There was more to Atticus's condition than some superficial traits—there was power in the harm that was done to him.

Maddox, Lochlan, and her family were swept out of the room in a literal wave of molten magic. Atticus's spell took on a more physical form than the usual smoke, churning out from him in a chest-high tidal wave of blood-like power. Maddox lost her footing, struggling to keep her head above the sudden ocean that surged against her and her family. It threatened to drown them all.

Maddox's feet went out from under her after the second wave overcame her. Her head went under the liquid magic, and she pinched her eyes and mouth shut. She was pushed backward, left pinned against a wall in the hallway.

Only Daphne had been spared, kept safe in a corner of Maddox's bedroom. By the time Maddox made it to her feet after the bloody magic had dispersed enough, Atticus was gone. Daphne had tried to contain him with the roots that had been used against Maddox, but they were left sliced to ribbons.

Maddox unleashed a furious scream, spinning on her heel and running to Atticus's room. "Lochlan! With me!"

Atticus needed that potion to disguise himself. He'd surely have more of it stashed away. And—ah, there it was. Sitting on his bed, half-unzipped was a simple black duffel bag. Maddox tore into it, tossing out clothing and toiletries until she found three flasks. She removed them and dumped them into the adjoining bathroom sink.

She bumped into Lochlan on her way out of the bedroom. Maddox didn't explain herself, just pulled Lochlan along as she raced for the conservatory.

The apothecary station was empty—Atticus hadn't made it there yet. Maddox sat on the stone bench, crossing her arms while her legs dangled. She waited for the rest of her family to find her, ignoring Lochlan's demands for information.

Colter filed inside first. "What the hell was all that? His magic—it wasn't like yours."

Maddox nodded. "It *isn't* like mine. Atticus is something new. Something different." She jumped off the bench. "I need everyone to guard the greenhouse. In order for Atticus to walk among us unnoticed, he needs a certain potion. I hope I destroyed all his spares, but he might try to brew a new batch."

Daphne tried to slow Maddox down. "Hey, can we all take a minute here? None of us understand what just happened. Maddox, you were *possessed*, and Atticus did something to save you, and now—"

"Lochlan, don't you need to call this in? A possessed man is on the loose. We need the Commission to alert the airlines, though I doubt Atticus would try to board a plane without his potion." Maddox ignored her sister and motioned for her grandfather to follow her. If she kept talking, no one would have time to stop her. "Grandad, we'll need your help. Come with me and Lochlan." To Lochlan, she asked sharply, "You can walk and talk, right? Do you need to borrow a phone?"

Lochlan frowned. "No, I—"

"Good. Let's move."

Maddox led them outside the mansion, taking the broken stone footpath through the Blackwell family cemetery.

"What are we doing out here? Do you realize all you're wearing is fuzzy pajamas and a scabbard?" Colter stood by as Maddox found a toolshed and kicked in the wooden door. "Maddox! What the hell are you—"

Maddox tossed a crowbar to her grandfather and kept one for herself. She released an exhausted laugh. "I'm getting *answers*. Finally. I've had enough of lies. I'm digging up the truth, once and for all."

Lochlan struggled to keep up with them and also explain to the Commission what was going on. Maddox didn't wait for him. She approached Theodora's tomb, tapping her chin. Atticus had used a spell to open the tomb, but she assumed it was a family spell. Even if she knew the incantation, she'd be out of luck.

"Granddad, do you think your roots can pry this open for me?"

Colter was, for the first time, hesitant to give his grandchild exactly what she wanted. "I think we should take a step back and evaluate our situation."

"I don't need you to do this," Maddox snapped. "Atticus has enough ingredients in his apothecary that I could blow this tomb into pieces. I'm only asking for your help because I don't have time to clean the mess I'd make."

The Abernathy family roots burst from the grave dirt and attacked the tomb's doorway. Slowly, the roots opened the tomb's double doors and Maddox slipped inside.

Rest in peace was engraved above Theodora's coffin. *Not for long,* Maddox thought.

Her crowbar slid underneath the coffin lid and Maddox huffed and worked the lid until it slid a few inches. All that heavy lifting on the farm didn't seem so useless now. Colter joined her as she dropped her crowbar and, together, they pushed the lid halfway off the coffin.

"Fucking hell," Colter breathed, taking an involuntary step back. "What is *that?*"

Lochlan pushed his way inside, finished with his phone call. He remained next to Colter, frozen and transfixed as Theodora's corpse creaked and groaned as it sat up in its bed.

Theodora shouldn't have already been awake.

Maddox. Had. Fucked. Up.

"I—I didn't know," she sputtered, backing away from the coffin.

There was doubt in his tone as Lochlan said, "A lich? A fucking *lich?*"

The men were utterly confused, but so many small, seemingly insignificant things fell into place for Maddox. Atticus wasn't responsible for his undead state— *Theodora was.*

She made him like her. Theodora had forced her own grandson to become a lich. It would explain why Atticus had panicked when Maddox discovered what he was. He never wanted it in the first place.

Theodora Blackwell must have been quite the sight when she was alive. Now undead, Theodora was terrifying, and yet Maddox couldn't help but find her strangely and grotesquely beautiful.

Theodora's eyes had rotted away, a black pit with a red glowing center that drew the eye within the dark tomb. Some skin on the left side of her face was gone, pristine, white bone underneath. The rest of her face and her throat were still mostly intact. Her hair was bleached, though Maddox wouldn't know if it had been white before her undead transformation. The Blackwell estate didn't boast a single portrait of Theodora, and now Maddox knew why.

Maddox finally felt cold, unable to battle the chill with adrenaline alone. Why hadn't she seen this coming? Atticus wouldn't have done that to himself—he must have had a guide, someone pressuring him to perform such forbidden magic. Or someone that tricked him into it.

Peeking out through the locks of Theodora's waist-length, white hair were spikes made of bone. They formed a foreboding, imperious crown around Theodora's head. While Atticus seemed to have had his transformation interrupted, judging from his still-mostly human appearance, Theodora must have completed her ritual. She was more creature than human.

Maddox wished death could touch that evil bitch.

Theodora brushed back a few strands of her hair, both of her hands completely skeletal. She laughed, a dry thing, and said, "Atticus, when he deigned to visit my tomb, told me enough about you to recognize you, *Maddox Abernathy.* I can guess why *you're* here. Though, I can't say why a priest and a cowboy would wish to visit little old me. Did any of you bring me flowers?"

"I don't understand," Maddox spat, knowing if the crowbar was still in her hands she would strike Theodora with it. "I don't understand how Atticus can stand to speak to you."

Aegis awoke, radiating fire and bloodlust in its sheath.

Take me out! Are you insane? Don't talk to that thing unarmed!

Aegis was right, of course. And Maddox would allow her blade its moment. But for now...

"What did you do to Atticus? Is he fully a lich, like you?" Maddox doubted Theodora would answer her without something to gain. Right now, the lich was inspecting her body and the black velvet dress that hung so tightly over her that Maddox could count every single one of her ribs.

Lochlan grabbed Maddox's elbow, trying to tug her backward. "Atticus is a lich? *And* carrying that parasite?"

"Possibly." Maddox tore out of his grip. "Theodora? Care to chime in? Atticus needs our help. Anything you can clarify would—"

"Clarify? The only thing I now know for sure about my grandson is that he's *weak.*" Theodora began climbing out of her coffin, swinging her legs over the side and dropping with a click of her heels. "I wish I'd noticed it sooner. What a waste of my time, including him in my ritual."

Maddox ignored the slight, pushing on with her questions. "Can you tell me anything about Warlock Kaspar? He created the parasite that has Atticus."

"Kaspar." Theodora snorted. "That fool cursed any artifact remotely of value. The Academy library used to find one of his enchanted trinkets every decade. He cursed a teapot once with a parasite that always desired the perfect cup of tea and burned anyone who failed. He was a lunatic. The Tome of the Undying would have been far better literature without his rambling."

"He cursed the book itself," Maddox said, hoping Theodora would be intrigued enough to pay attention. Maybe even offer insight. "He left this...parasite."

"I *know*, dear. It was simply one of many layers of protection cast upon that book. The parasite tried to possess me while we dismantled the book. It failed, of course. Kaspar gave it one duty, keep the Tome whole, and it was too weak to do it."

Maddox wasn't surprised the parasite had failed to capture Theodora. It had possessed Maddox easily, partly due to her slipup in the lab, but mostly because Maddox had, ever since Atticus had left her, failed to feel complete.

Theodora wanted for nothing her entire life. There was nothing she lacked—not money, or power, and Maddox doubted the woman desired love. Maddox once thought that Theodora had at least loved Atticus, but it seemed obvious now that she only loved his obedience.

That pinprick of red light in Theodora's eye sockets brightened. She chuckled behind her bony hand. "If that's what has my grandson, it'll consume him quickly. He's never been sure of himself, always hunting, begging, for validation. And, though he didn't complete the ritual with me, what raw power he has. I'd say you're doomed."

Before she could ask more, Lochlan pulled Maddox away from Theodora who was confidently, though stiffly, making her way to the only exit. "That's *enough*, Maddox!" With a single outstretched hand, Lochlan called forth his pure fire, the Latin he whispered hitting the back of Maddox's neck like bug bites. Lochlan formed a wall of fire between them and Theodora.

Theodora waited on the other side of the flame, eying it curiously. She reached a hand into the fire, hissing and quickly snatching it back. Maddox couldn't ignore Lochlan's sudden intake of breath and the pain that flickered briefly in his eyes. Keeping something as strong as a lich at bay would wear on him.

Honestly, she was impressed he managed it at all. Liches were the reason necromancers were so carefully watched and trained.

They were soulless, all-powerful, and lived forever unless destroyed. Destroying them required their phylactery, the vial they kept the remains of their soul in, and that was usually hidden away.

Maddox unsheathed Aegis, who uncharacteristically advised her to run.

"Lochlan, let me through." Maddox approached the wall of flame, stopping when the white fire tickled the toes of her boots.

"Absolutely not," Lochlan and Colter said in unison.

"I'll step through, regardless. If I burn, I burn." Maddox didn't give them a moment to stop her. She walked, Aegis in her tight grip, and Lochlan allowed her passage through his fiery wall at the last second.

Theodora observed her approach. "What shall it be, dear? A little chat between us girls or a duel? I'm afraid my ungrateful grandsons buried me without my sword."

"Atticus needs our help. We need the parasite out first, and I'll deal with what *you've* done to him later."

"Good luck," Theodore said with a shrug. She smoothed out the dark purple of her velvet gown. "Unless Atticus has drastically changed in the last however many years, you'll never separate the two. He was never the most confident boy. I'd suggest a good therapist, but I've been buried, well not *alive*, but buried for several years now. I'm sure my contact book needs updating."

"I'm glad his plight amuses you." Maddox hadn't truly thought Theodora would be of any help, but she needed the witch to confirm her suspicions about Atticus. And she needed one more thing from her.

Maddox flexed, flicking Aegis to the side. Theodora grinned, her teeth perfectly preserved. "Ah, it's to be a duel then?"

"Not exactly." Maddox felt Aegis begin to warm, her blade knowing her next move. "You ripped the Tome apart for your own gain, not for whatever self-righteous drivel you sold Atticus. The curse Kaspar laid on the book, that destruction made it worse. It wants to put that entire damned book back together."

Theodora held out her hand as if she was inspecting nails she no longer had. "What's your point?"

"I know you kept some of the Tome for yourself. The parasitoid could sense it. I suspect that's how you ended up this way." Aegis's excitement was stifling. Maddox had never been more thankful that Aegis could only communicate with her and only telepathically. Her blade was simultaneously damning her and giving her pre-battle advice.

Maddox asked her final question, aware she was testing Lochlan and her grandfather's patience. "Where's the part you kept?" Without Lochlan, Atticus wouldn't be able to retrieve the part of the Tome locked away in the Academy. But if they possessed Theodora's stolen part of the Tome, perhaps they could use it to lure Atticus back into Maddox's arms.

The lich gave no answer. Theodora raised both of her palms, facing them toward each other, and let sparks of deep red electricity run between them. Just the sound of it was painful.

At Aegis's command, Maddox dropped to a knee and rolled forward. Theodora's spell hit a wall behind Maddox like a lightning strike, blasting through Lochlan's shield of fire.

Aegis turned red-hot in her hand, the metal melting and reforging from its thin blade into a butcher's chopping knife. She's read more than one text concerning liches, but nowhere did it care to mention how damned quick they were.

Theodora caught Maddox's shirt before she could twist away. But that didn't matter. Maddox clamped her hand on Theodora's cold wrist, ignoring the shreds of flesh left on the bone, and slashed her reformed weapon down hard.

Aegis slid through the lich's bone like butter, severing the arm at the elbow. As Theodora stared in disbelief, Maddox caught the hand as it fell.

Maddox was no hero. She took her skeletal prize and scrambled away from Theodora, pulling the other men out of the tomb with her after Lochlan dropped his wall.

Lightning chased their heels. Lochlan raised another wall of his white flame to cover the exit, though Maddox could sense it was more for show than anything else.

Theodora's tomb began billowing red smoke from its entrance. The protective runes, the ones normally meant to keep out grave robbers and not contain all-powerful undead creatures, sparked and sputtered until one by one they cracked.

"We can't let her in the cemetery!" Lochlan shouted, jerking out of Maddox's hold. He widened his stance, faced the open tomb, and prayed. His second wall of fire went out in a wave of pure power that blasted from the tomb.

With all protections broken, Theodora was free to leave the confines of her tomb. Her first step outside came down on green, trimmed grass. It died, curled and grey underneath her heel. She raised a hand over her face, shielding it from the abnormally harsh sun. Theodora smiled before reaching into the sky, a claw trying to snatch the light.

Clouds gathered, pulled in quickly by a whipping wind originating around the lich's body. Maddox ripped Theodora's ring from the hand she'd stolen and cast the bones aside. Aegis had reformed into a rapier and was ready to spill blood, or whatever vile liquid was pumping through Theodora's wretched remains.

Around them lay the corpses of the Blackwell family—Theodora was going to raise the dead. Necromancers were buried with their blades. Theodora was about to have an armed army of her family, and Maddox had to stop her.

Maddox charged, Aegis ready and shouting war cries, until a white root wrapped around her waist and flung her backward. She skidded as she fell but scrambled to her feet just in time to be hit by Lochlan's flying body.

They both tumbled backward, Lochlan apologizing as Maddox shoved him off of her. "Grandad! Let me go!" she howled, fighting to make it to her feet as more roots wrapped around her ankles. Lochlan received similar treatment, though he accepted his capture without protest. Aegis was ripped from her, dragged away by Colter's green magic.

Her heart pounded, soon becoming the only sound she could hear. As powerful as Colter was, liches were feared for a reason, and he was walking headfirst into a battle he didn't understand.

Colter stood his ground, tipping his hat back as he regarded Theodora. "I can't say I understand everything that's going on here, but it sounds to me like you tried to make your own grandchild into a corpse."

The lich turned her head to the side as she laughed at him. "You wouldn't understand even if I explained. I offered Atticus power. I would have given him *eternity.*"

"That's not what children want," Colter said. He held out his hands, palms down toward the earth. "They want consistency and security. They don't want whatever the hell you are."

"That's enough from the cowboy." Theodora strode toward him, confident and menacing, and tripped, landing face-first in the dirt. She sputtered, lifting her head and glancing behind her to glare at the white root coiled around her ankle. It bit into her skin, shredding her weakened flesh and pulling her back to her tomb.

Thorns sprouted from the roots at a snap of Colter's fingers. Maddox felt the pull of his magic, tugging at her own reserves of power, and she gasped.

Lightning cracked from the reddening sky—just a taste of Theodora's power. Storm clouds rolled in to shade the estate, casting them all into an unnatural darkness.

Theodora's rotting jaw sprang open, and Latin poured out of it. A spell Theodora never finished.

A flock of birds descended from the sky, previously hidden by cloud cover. The birds were mostly crows, but some sparrows and cardinals joined the group. They flew straight for Theodora, a cardinal clawing its way into her mouth and choking out her spell.

The lich shrieked and tore out of Colter's wrapping roots. Maddox felt another tug on her power, this time strong enough to make her fall backward. Lochlan caught her, tugging her protectively against his chest as he watched Colter and Theodora, the green of Lochlan's wide eyes small against the white.

Colter stood his ground, unblinking, and twisted more and more roots around the lich. Her advance slowed, the roots and the swarming birds leaving her unable to do anything but scream.

The plant life rooted Theodora's ankle to the ground, with more and more white branches snaking their way up her leg.

The pure power it took to contain Theodora was draining Maddox, and she knew the rest of her family must be collapsed inside the estate. While Maddox was the only necromancer in the Abernathy coven, Colter could use a similar type of magic. The green witch's patriarch could pull from his family's combined life force to fuel his spells.

How fascinating Atticus would find us if he knew. Though, the Commission would find it more threatening than fascinating.

Lochlan tried to help Maddox stand, but her limbs were not cooperating. "Maddox, what's *happening* to you?" He spoke to her, confused and fearful, but he kept his eyes on Colter.

The roots fused as they twisted around Theodora's bones. They poked in and out of her open ribcage and fought their way to her throat. They now resembled a tree more than mere roots, forcing her arms up into the air to form branches. Her defeat was imminent, and still, Theodora thrashed and squirmed until she became a terrible thing—half tree and half witch. Leaves sprung around her hair and eyes before withering and falling to the ground.

Maddox's sight went in and out. If Daphne wasn't a beacon of power and life right now, Colter might have failed to stop the lich. And it would be Maddox's fault for risking Theodora's release, just because she hoped beyond hope it might help save Atticus.

Colter turned to them with a cocky smile. He didn't see Theodora's remaining arm spring free of his trap and point a bony finger at him.

Maddox screamed, but it was too late. Colter's body jolted as a thin bolt of red lightning shot from Theodora's hand and hit Colter's back. Theodora cackled in triumph, even as more roots shot from the ground and recaptured her arm.

"Grandad!" Maddox lurched out of Lochlan's grip, half-crawling and half-running to Colter's fallen form. Never had her grandfather looked so small. His hat lay a few feet away, and his mirthful, teasing eyes were closed. His chest was still—too still.

Even if Colter hadn't drained her magic to power his own spell, Maddox couldn't have helped him. The only thing her hands caused was death. All her magical knowledge and there wasn't a damned thing she could do.

After her grandmother had passed, Colter had spent more time with Maddox than with the other grandchildren. He made sure she never felt out of place for being what she was. For being unable to heal like her sisters could.

You can mend just as well as any other Abernathy. You just have to go about it a different way.

Maybe Colter's words could have been true, but Maddox knew that now, *right now*, she was useless. Maddox knelt next to Colter's body until Lochlan shoved her out of the way. Lochlan began chest compressions on Colter, commanding, "Go get your sisters!"

Maddox sat frozen, muttering, "I *swear* I didn't know what Theodora was. I swear I—"

"Dammit, Maddox! Now!" Lochlan shouted, cutting off her stammering.

Maddox stood on trembling legs. What had she *done*? If she had only taken a moment to think, her grandfather wouldn't be...wouldn't be...

Maddox turned and ran back to the manor, her guilt nipping rabidly at her heels.

CHAPTER 48
WITCH

"**I**t felt like the time I tried to fix the dryer and you *promised* me it was unplugged." Colter rolled his eyes at Rob's stupid question of what being hit by lightning felt like. "But a thousand times worse."

Maddox felt Lochlan stare at her. The two shared an armchair while the Abernathys crowded Colter's bedframe. It had been so close. If Lochlan hadn't started compressions immediately, and if Dove hadn't sprinted out to the graveyard in time...

They could have lost Colter.

Maddox twirled the ring she'd stolen from Theodora. The light glinting off the silver piece distracted her from her family's chatter. Theodora's family ring was thin with small red jewels covering the band. It was tasteful, unlike the one Atticus had placed on Maddox's ring finger just a week before.

It burned just like the first ring had, but whatever spell Atticus had whispered to Maddox as he'd kissed his ring still worked on Theodora's band. Maddox felt the ring accept her and knew she'd be able to read a Blackwell grimoire again.

There was no time to waste, and Maddox couldn't take another second of watching the rest of her family lay a healing hand on Colter while she sat back and did nothing.

Necromancers only brought death—it would be better for them all if Maddox stepped outside.

Maddox rose and left the room without a word. Lochlan followed her out and stepped in front of her, blocking her access to Atticus's study. Maddox fumed but remained silent. She understood they'd all have questions, but right now Lochlan was nothing to her but another obstacle keeping her from saving Atticus.

Lochlan didn't mince his words. "What is going on, Maddox? That lich could have killed us all. She still might."

Maddox knew Lochlan would not care for her answer but gave it anyway. "I didn't know what she was. I just wanted answers. Atticus loved Theodora. I never imagined she would do that to him."

"We need to move slowly and share information, not run around blindly in our pajamas." Lochlan pinched the skin between his brow. "Dammit, Maddox. I'm trying to be considerate here, but you keep fucking me over. *Talk to me.*"

No, Maddox couldn't take that risk. Lochlan worked for the Commission of Magic Management. That was where his loyalties lay, not with the two necromancers he had briefly worked with. She shook her head. "It's better if you leave now. Report what you have to, Dr. Rhodes. I have a lot of work to do and little time to do it." Maddox shoulder-checked Lochlan and made her way into Atticus's study. "Be sure to come back with a warrant."

"So, you're just going to shut me out? After all we've been through?" Lochlan followed her inside the study, stopping in front of the oak writing desk as Maddox dug through it. "I care about what happens to Atticus, too. And, whether you believe it or not, my first loyalty isn't to the Commission. It's to my community. I may be only an exorcist, but I've taken vows that are dearer to me than some government mandate."

Maddox ignored him, though Lochlan's earnest tone pricked at her heart. He continued, "If the Commission finds out about Atticus, I doubt they'll bother imprisoning him. It would have been kinder to let him disappear, just as he wished."

Maddox slammed her fist down on the desk. "If you want to keep discussing the morality of my decision, find someone who gives a fuck. *I* don't. Atticus—he—" She wrung her hands together until the pain cleared her thoughts. "He was prepared to run off somewhere remote and *wait to die.* Like an animal. Just to keep us all safe. And you think I should have let him do that?"

Lochlan blanched. "I didn't mean—"

"I know what you meant. I know I'm making a mess of everything." She sunk into the desk chair and covered her face with her hands. Muffled, she continued, "The odds of success aren't in our favor. I might fix Atticus. I might make him worse. But I absolutely won't leave him."

"I understand, but you need to understand the position you've put *me* in.

If that lich hadn't spent a decade trapped in a tomb that drained her powers, none of us would be standing here. Now, there's a second lich loose upon the world, and we don't even know where he is."

"Half-lich," Maddox corrected. "He ages. The ritual must have been interrupted in Atticus's case."

Lochlan huffed at her theory. "That won't matter to the Commission."

"I *know*. Which is why I need to get to work." Maddox wished Lochlan would just leave her be. This was her disaster. Her bloody mistake in the cleanroom had led to all of this. Atticus should have let her rot in obscurity. "Think what you will of me. If everyone hates me for the way I'm handling this, if *Atticus* hates me, it will still be worth it."

Lochlan stared back at her, hovering around the exit. "You're not the only one that feels guilty."

"But I'm the only one that can fix this," she countered, dropping her focus to the grimoire and shutting Lochlan out.

Lochlan left Maddox to her own devices, claiming he wanted to call a few priests he trusted to share information on liches without asking too many questions. Maddox waved him off, her nose still buried in Theodora's grimoire. She was so focused on the text that her entire family had crowded into the study without her notice.

Colter cleared his throat to catch her attention. He leaned on Rob, who helped Colter into a chair. Colter prompted, "Maddie? We want to talk to you."

"I don't really have time..." Maddox blinked at her grandfather's inexplicable presence. "You! You should still be in bed!"

"That's what *we* tried to tell him," Rob muttered.

"I was *barely* unconscious," Colter protested. "Yes, there are some burn marks that won't go away anytime soon, but I have the best healers in the world with me. I'm fine."

Fine? Colter looked weak, and that was a terrible sign. Even when he was dog-tired from a hard day on the farm, Colter never let himself *look* exhausted.

Maddox would bet containing Theodora was what really drained her grandfather. If Maddox had to swallow any more guilt, she was going to get a stomachache.

"You *can't* be fine," Maddox argued. Necromancers' spells, especially their lightning, would never truly heal. Colter would bear that burning pain forever. Maddox pushed the base of her palms into her eyes. "You should all go home. I'll stay—"

"You want us to *leave*?" Dove scoffed. "If we go, Madame Skeletor will be free in no time. Face it, Maddie. You're stuck with us. Now focus on saving your spooky boyfriend."

Maddox could think of nothing to say that would convince her family to save themselves. She scowled and pointed around the study, counting her family members. "Please tell me Amber and Poppy are watching the conservatory like I asked." If Atticus was still nearby, he could be waiting to sneak back in to make the potion he used to conceal himself.

Hell, depending on what the potion required, Atticus might try Redhollow's local apothecary, a Blackened Salt-owned little shop, to steal the ingredients he needed. She hoped his potion needed more than what they stored in local shops and that it took ages to process. If not, he could already be in disguise and on his way out of the country.

And all of this would be for nothing.

"They're guarding the conservatory, don't worry," Dove answered, concern turning her normally bossy tone gentle. "You should worry about yourself. You're acting crazy."

Maddox shrugged. "Necromancy isn't the prettiest of magic. I'm doing what I have to."

Her mother came up next to her, resting a soft hand on Maddox's shoulder. Diedre asked quietly, "You have a plan to help Atticus, then? Dr. Rhodes says we won't have much time. That *thing* in the yard won't stay contained forever."

"I have an idea," Maddox replied carefully. "But I'll have to talk to Theodora again."

"If you're going to do that," Colter said, arms crossed, "I'm going with you. You need to include us in your plans, not whisk us along in the dark."

Maddox kept her mouth closed. She didn't want to do as he asked because she didn't want anyone to impede her victory.

There was too much at stake. *Atticus was at stake.*

"We can all see what you're thinking," Daphne huffed. "But if you want our help, you need to be open with us."

She wanted—no, *needed*—their help, but Maddox was reluctant to ask her family to risk so much for her and for a man she'd spent a long time convincing them to despise.

"Abernathys don't work alone," her grandfather huffed. "We don't work blind, either. Now, bring the rest of us up to speed, and let us help. As conflicted as the exorcist is, I don't know how long he can keep the Commission from stepping in."

Maddox leaned back in her chair, considering what she felt safe asking them to do. "I need help finding Atticus. If I had a sample of his blood, I could do it myself, but—"

"Don't worry about that." Colter pointed at Daphne and her husband. "You two stay with Maddox. The rest of us can head outside and work with the roots to search for Atticus."

"Right now?" Diedre held her hands up. "You took a lot of power from all of us, Dad. We need time to recharge, and you're not at your best, either."

"You're right," Colter agreed. "We should eat and rest. Even me."

The family dispersed, wishing Maddox luck and reminding her to rest herself. It was kind of them, but there was absolutely no time to waste. Maddox skimmed Theodora's grimoire cover to cover, tabbing what might be useful to come back to later. She ate and drank only when Daphne forced her, shoving food in her face at regular intervals.

After hours of reading with bleary eyes, Maddox's messy notes were just beginning to make some sense when Lochlan reappeared. He loomed in the doorway a long time, unnoticed by Maddox until her brother-in-law nudged her.

They were short on time, so Maddox prompted gruffly, "What's the bad news, Lochlan?"

"The Commission is sending more agents to help find Atticus. They won't be as gentle as I, but I can't refuse them." He paused, examining her expression carefully. "Like I said, I have a responsibility to the community first, and that parasite is too dangerous to leave unchecked. The parasite is all they know about. For now."

Ah, that was better than she thought. The Commission wouldn't panic over one possessed warlock. A loose *lich*, however... They'd shut down the entire county for that.

Lochlan recaptured Maddox's attention. "I'll have to tell them about the lich soon. There's no avoiding that. Who knows how long that tree will last?"

"I understand." Maddox stood, gathering her books and notes into her arms. "I need to reference the library. After that, you'll find me in the Conservatory."

"I need to keep a watch on the lich," Lochlan said, frowning. "That's my top priority. I won't be much help to you otherwise."

"I think that might be best," Maddox replied. "I work better alone, anyway."

"You're not alone!" Daphne snapped, sighing as she slowly rose from the study's couch with her husband's help. Daphne was due in *two weeks*. She should be back home, not all the way across the country. Abernathy babies always arrived late, but still, Maddox worried. She also knew Daphne would ignore her sister's concerns and stay right where she wanted.

"Sorry," Maddox whispered, running a hand through her hair. "I have a lot to do and multi-tasking was never my forte." She had a bad habit of abandoning a task halfway through simply because she forgot it as soon as she began a new chore.

"Apology accepted, but only because you seem to be going through a quarter-life crisis." Daphne tapped her chin. "I guess for you it's an eighth life crisis, though, isn't it?"

Just what Maddox needed. A reminder that she would outlive her sisters by *a lot*. "Just meet me in the conservatory. I'll be right there after I finish in the library. I don't want you wearing yourself out, Daphne."

Daphne grumbled in return, but she waddled toward the conservatory without further protest.

As Maddox headed to the library, Jinx tailed her steps while keeping a few feet of space between them. Maddox could hardly blame the cat. Though she was not herself at the time, Maddox still attacked Atticus and forced Jinx to defend her obvious favorite. Typical. Maddox brought the cat in from the cold, saved her from a life of eating Atticus's garbage, and Atticus was her favorite.

The Blackwell library was well stocked, and Maddox found most of what she wanted. After carefully stacking her books and documents, Maddox noticed a single book left out in the open. Had she done that? She barely recalled the possessed tantrum she'd thrown earlier—was this stranded book a casualty of that event?

Maddox abandoned her stack of books and lifted the lonely text, the spine revealing it as a worn copy of *Jane Eyre*. She nearly missed the gilded stationary poking out of the yellowed pages.

Was this a forgotten bookmark? Maddox eased out the paper, hoping to save the spine some wear, and blinked as she read her own name written on the folded stationary.

Should she read this? Perhaps this was some old letter Atticus had written her and thought better of sending. Would it be an invasion of his privacy to take a peek?

She traced her name, still envious of his artful handwriting, *and the ink was still wet.*

Her heart caught in her throat, and Maddox ran through every aisle and peered in every corner of the library. "Atticus?" she whispered, and then she shouted his name.

Her fingers trembled as she unfolded the letter.

My dearest and most troublesome Maddox...

CHAPTER 49
LETTERS FROM THE DEAD

My dearest and most troublesome Maddox,

I solved the problem of what endearment to call you. You were correct. Enchantress is not right, though it makes you no less enchanting. I considered "my love" and while that is close, I have decided on "my dear" instead. Why? Because it has always been true. Despite the trials of our relationship, you always remained dear to me.

So, my dear, what have you done to me?

I have underestimated you, which I did not think was possible. I always, even when I abandoned you so harshly at the Academy, held you in the highest regard. Your skill in magic and swordplay have always been unmatched. And how beautiful you are, and never more so than with your blade at my throat, smirking at me in triumph.

I could write of your beauty for pages, and I think you would forgive me. And not only because I am quite deliciously drunk.

No, Maddox, I mean I have underestimated how damned insane you are.

Your actions must surprise your family—they have never seen how vicious you can be. But I know. And still I was caught off-guard when you swore to never let me go.

My escape is ruined, thank you very much. Months of planning, wasted. With this ghastly appearance, I won't be accepted anywhere, except in your arms. How you must enjoy that! You've trapped me so completely. I suppose all I can do is accept it.

How do you plan to cure me, I wonder? I've looked into it myself. I've even asked my grandmother for answers, which she promised to provide if I would only release her from her tomb. I declined her offer, but I see you could not resist.

How is Colter able to contain her? It must be draining him. I feared him before, but now... Will I end up in one of his trees, Maddox? If so, I think a weeping willow would be a most fitting prison for me.

Would you do me a favor, Maddox? Stop guarding my apothecary. Let me make my potion, my Chameleon, and let me go. I was telling the truth (for once) when I said I would have kept my secret from you forever. I would have let you love a corpse. Let you marry one.

Remember that I was prepared to do that and let me rot somewhere that's quiet and far away from you.

This is the only way I can love you honestly, in the way you deserve. Let me go.

Yours forever,
Atticus

CHAPTER 50
WITCH

Maddox longed to tear Atticus's letter to pieces and throw the remains into a fire. Instead, she pressed the letter against her lips once before folding it carefully in her pocket. She gathered her books once more, returning to the conservatory with hastened steps.

Atticus was still here.

If Maddox had only been a little faster, she might have caught him stashing that note.

"I'll find you eventually, Atticus," she announced to the empty air. Jinx meowed in encouragement. Maddox flashed the cat a smile over her shoulder. Perhaps the stray had already forgiven her. Or, more likely, Jinx considered tailing her the fastest route to finding its preferred master.

Once she made it to the conservatory, Maddox checked and double-checked the apothecary set up, seeing if any of the stored ingredients had changed in volume.

Daphne waved at her from the padded chaise lounge she was occupying. "Maddox? Hello? Care to bring the rest of us up to speed?"

"Atticus is close. I think everyone should rest for today and start fresh in the morning. The sooner we're able to locate him, the better." Maddox turned to Daphne's husband, Rob. "Hey, can you help me move a bed in here? I want to sleep here for now."

"You're going to sleep in the *greenhouse*?" Rob questioned, but he followed Maddox to one of the guest rooms, anyway. Daphne stayed behind, frowning.

Once Maddox and Rob finished struggling to push a metal bedframe and its mattress into the greenhouse, Maddox sent Daphne and Rob off to their own beds. She promised to explain more in the morning, though Daphne was dissatisfied with that. But what else could she do? Maddox had to succeed where Atticus and Lochlan had failed, and she had no idea where to begin.

Theodora's grimoire was a good start, but Maddox needed something…more. She had knowledge, but no plan.

Maddox sat at the tall stone table Atticus used to brew his potions. She consulted her notes and the grimoire, moving on to a few texts on possession she'd found in the library. The Academy would have better references, but Maddox wasn't about to leave the property with a temporarily trapped lich fighting to free herself.

She studied for hours, shooing away her parents when they tried to force dinner down her throat. When night cast her in shadow, Maddox conjured a few red, floating orbs to provide enough light to keep reading.

Dawn arrived through the tinted greenhouse glass, stinging her tired eyes. She did not sleep. She did not stop. Maddox kept working until the words blurred and her hand ached from taking notes.

Her cell phone vibrated, and Maddox only lifted it to check if it was Atticus calling her. When she saw Daphne's name, she set it back down until Daphne called her a third time.

"What is it?" Maddox demanded as she answered the call. Her leg bounced as she waited for Daphne to get to the point.

Daphne huffed once, probably annoyed with Maddox's sharp tone, before replying, "Someone just opened the gate and is tearing down the driveway. I don't know cars, but it looks expensive."

"Cover the conservatory for me," Maddox said before she ended the call.

As soon as Daphne and Rob entered the conservatory, Maddox jumped up, leaving her phone on the table and clipping Aegis onto her belt. Daphne shouted after her, but Maddox shut her out and ran to the foyer, tying her messy hair up as she stumbled down the main stairway.

She was nearly at the tall double doors when someone threw them open.

He wasn't as tall as his brother, but Giles was broader and more filled out. Most of his appearance was the same as Maddox remembered from his time at the Academy. His black hair was still short and perfectly arranged, and that same scar trailed from his eye to his jaw. Giles shared his brother's red eyes but kept his uncovered. He dressed just as well as Atticus, but Giles's suit, though it looked slept in, was much more modern.

Giles's gaze darted about the foyer until it trailed up the entryway stairs and stopped on Maddox.

"Where the *fuck* is he?" Giles threw out his right arm and shouted, "Umbra!"

Shit. Shit. Shit.

Maddox stumbled down the rest of the stairs, throwing herself to the ground when she reached the bottom. Overhead, she heard a rushing noise like a javelin and glanced up to see Giles's sword fly into his hand. He adjusted his grip and lowered the blade, glaring down at her. Darkness pulled in around him, curling over his shoulders like tentacles.

He advanced upon her before she could rise. Giles grabbed a fistful of her hair and yanked until Maddox stood up. " *What* have you done to my brother?"

She hurried to respond. "He contracted a parasite—"

"Let's pretend that I already know everything the Commission knows. It's what I pay that whistleblower for. So," Giles said as he pulled her hair until she was eye to eye with him, "explain to me how *Atticus*, who was not supposed to touch the fucking page at all, is the one carrying a traveler? Why—" He tore at her hair again. "—isn't it *you*?"

Tears blurred her vision as Aegis demanded to be unsheathed. As fucked as it was, Maddox didn't mind the pain spreading on her scalp. Atticus's situation *was* her fault, and if Giles was her consequence, she would accept it.

"It *was* me," she admitted after the pain in her scalp subsided. "Atticus took it on when the exorcist failed to destroy it. He saved me."

Giles released her hair, looking at her in disgust. "Of course he did. That love-sick idiot. Why couldn't you stay in fucking nowhere and leave him be?"

She hated that he was right. If Maddox was stronger, she would have had some self-respect and turned Atticus's offer down. And things wouldn't have turned out so fucked.

"Tell me where Atticus is," Giles spat. "And then stay out of my way."

"I—I don't know where he went," she said, stepping away from him. She had never fought Giles before, but Atticus had always admitted his brother was a better duelist than him.

Giles rolled his eyes. "Give it *up*, Abernathy. You're useless to him. I'm the only one that can help him now."

"She's telling the truth. We don't know where he is." Lochlan appeared at the top of the stairs with Colter close behind. Unlike Maddox, Lochlan had taken the time to shower and make himself presentable. His white collar looked authoritative. "Now put away your sword."

"Tell me what to do in my own fucking house one more time." Giles's magic misted around his body. "You're one of the Commission's exorcists, aren't you? You can keep your hands off my brother and get the hell off my property."

"Maddox," Colter said, his tone even. "Come upstairs."

Putting more distance between an unhinged Giles and herself was a smart move, but Maddox ignored her grandfather's command.

"Giles," she pleaded. "We want to help him. We know about Atticus's peculiarities. What your grandmother did was terrible, but it doesn't mean he's past saving."

"What do you know about *that?*" Giles's left eyebrow twitched. "Atticus would never—"

"It was all an accident!" It was hard to think clearly. Passages from all the books she'd read last night rolled through her mind, distracting her. "I saw what Atticus is, and we had a fight, and that triggered the parasitoid." Maddox avoided meeting her grandfather's questioning glance. "The parasite was meant to protect the Tome of the Undying. When the Tome was torn apart, I think it affected the parasite as well. It's desperate to feel whole. That's why Lochlan couldn't exorcize it from me. I share too much of that same emotion. So, Atticus—"

"*That's* what's inside Atticus?" Giles covered his mouth with his free hand. "Are you fucking kidding me? Atticus is absolutely the worst warlock to deal with something like that."

"I know—"

"But you let him do it!"

Lochlan descended the stairs quickly. "Enough. This isn't getting us anywhere. Not only do we have to worry about Atticus, but that lich still needs to be put back in her tomb."

Maddox had never felt a quiet so threatening.

Giles sucked in a breath, a vein popping on his neck. "What the *fuck* did you say?" Giles turned from Maddox to Lochlan. "You let that thing OUT?"

"I wasn't aware of what we were releasing." Lochlan glanced Maddox's way, and she flinched. "I thought Maddox was raising a corpse to speak with it, not that she was unleashing hell upon earth."

Giles's grip on his sword trembled. "What have you done? Where is it?"

Colter answered, "She's contained for now. I can't guarantee it'll last forever. Outside that tomb, she's getting stronger."

Laughter, sharp and cruel, exploded out of Giles. "Do you have any idea how much work it was to deal with it the first time? I only succeeded because I had Atticus on my side."

Before Giles was aware of it, Colter caught his wrist. "Let's put the sword away and sit you down. There's a lot to talk about."

Giles always had a volatile nature, but the news about his grandmother's near escape had shaken him. Giles let Colter tug his sword away from him and shakily led them to one of the estate's many sitting rooms.

They all brooded in silence for a long time. Giles stared at the carpet, unmoving, until Diedre joined them and placed a cup of tea into his hand.

Giles took a sip before speaking. "Where are you keeping it? In a tree?" He said it as an insult, but Maddox merely sighed and nodded.

"A tree? Honestly?" Giles set his cup down and dropped his head into his hands. "You green witches are insane."

"It may be unconventional," Lochlan said, shrugging. "But it's working. Though, I wouldn't count on it becoming a permanent part of the landscaping. She's fighting it."

"We're lucky she wasn't buried with her sword," Maddox admitted. "We wouldn't have stood a chance."

Giles frowned. "Atticus uses Theodora's sword. Does he have it with him? It's vital Theodora doesn't get a hold of it."

"Oh." Maddox cringed. How could she have overlooked that? "I'm actually not sure..."

"I know where Venenum likes to hide. Let's walk and talk." Giles took his tea with him and motioned for Maddox to follow. He shook a finger when the rest of her family and Lochlan stood up as well. "I only want to speak to Abernathy."

Lochlan quipped dryly, "There's nine of them in this house alone."

"I mean Maddox."

Maddox waved her family away. "It's okay. I'll be fine." Well, that might be a lie. Giles hadn't exactly greeted Maddox calmly when he first arrived home.

Giles carried his tea carefully, stopping in Atticus's study to grab a bottle of whiskey hidden behind a set of witch-specific encyclopedias. Giles gave his tea a healthy shot of liquor before offering her some. Maddox declined with a shake of her head. She was already exhausted—she didn't need alcohol affecting her judgement as well.

Also, it was seven in the morning.

"I flew here as soon as I heard," Giles explained, tugging at his crumpled suit. "I have a man inside the Commission that alerts me for any unusual activity in Redhollow." He stopped walking to take a huge gulp of what Maddox assumed was now ninety percent whiskey.

Maddox tried to cut in. "I have a lot of questions—"

"I told Atticus to leave that damned book alone. Look what it turned our grandmother into. But, no, he was so persistent." Giles opened a gold trimmed door for her and ushered her inside the room.

Maddox fumed. How casually Giles was speaking to her! As if he hadn't fought her and pulled her hair just an hour before.

Like Atticus, Giles didn't need anyone to help him carry a conversation. He continued as he walked through what appeared to be a weapons gallery. "I should have known you had something to do with it. Atticus wouldn't have been so obsessed with the project otherwise."

Maddox made a humming noise to signal she was still listening. The room they'd entered was covered wall to wall with weapons. Each rapier hung artfully against a black, red, and white wallpaper. She itched to test the weight and edge of them all, but waited patiently instead as Giles quickly scanned the blades.

"It's not here," he said, rubbing his temples as he turned back to her. "It might be in his study or the Conservatory. Atticus let the thing roam free."

Maddox would not admit to Giles that she'd been so focused on making sure Atticus couldn't leave her that Maddox had forgotten about securing his blade. Giles might not agree with her actions, and she didn't care to repeat their tussle in the foyer. It would be better for Atticus if she and Giles could work together.

Giles touched her shoulder, jerking her out of her thoughts as she flinched. "Relax," he said, annoyed. "I'm not trying to be your fucking friend. Just tell me what's going on and how you plan to fix this."

She gave him a brief rundown as they walked throughout the manor, explaining how the Tome of the Undying's page had been booby-trapped and the parasite had first latched onto her. She told him that since Lochlan could not remove the leech from her, Atticus had taken it upon himself.

The worst part of all was revealing *how* she'd discovered Atticus was a lich.

She'd barely had time to talk to anyone about her relationship with Atticus, and now she had to explain it to his brother.

Giles didn't remark on Maddox's revelation that she was sleeping, and it really was only sleeping, with his brother. "How the hell did Atticus run out of Chameleon?"

Chameleon? Giles must have meant the potion Atticus used to disguise himself. She hesitated. "Um..."

Giles waved a hand. "It doesn't matter. He can't have gone far. The ingredients needed for that won't be easy to find. I doubt even the Academy could supply all that's needed. And the chemical process is far from simple."

"So, we have time to come up with a plan."

"Ha! We have no time. The Commission will bring in the calvary once they find out about *it*." He stopped them outside Atticus's study and pushed her inside. Giles said, heading straight for the desk, "I'm shocked they're not already here. No, the best thing we can do for Atticus now is find him and get him out of the country. If the Commission's calvary arrives before we can, then we'll have to kill him."

Aegis was out before Maddox could control herself. Giles sneered at the blade poking his chest as he asked, "Are you out of your mind? You know what he is. If the Commission gets their hands on him, they'll *dissect* him." He lowered her blade with a finger. "Get that feyrie shit out of my face."

He's right, you know.

Now even Aegis was on Giles's side.

He's an asshole, but he's right.

Maddox ignored her sword's advice. "How did Atticus end up like that? What did she do to him?"

Giles seemed unable to answer, his mouth twisting into a scowl whenever he tried to speak. He picked up the human skull from the desk where it still sat on display and shook it, presumably to see if Venenum was hiding inside. Nothing came out, and Giles gave in to Maddox's questioning. Perhaps he needed to talk about it to someone as badly as Maddox needed to hear it.

Giles's smile was self-deprecating. "She pretended to love him. And he fell for it."

CHAPTER 51
ELDEST

Necromancers lived for roughly two centuries. Theodora had turned two-hundred and six this past year, and all the signs pointed to it being her last birthday.

Giles couldn't care less.

Atticus was devastated.

Though Giles recalled how it felt to be Theodora's favorite, he never wanted to be under that fickle witch's thumb ever again. He'd tried warning Atticus about Theodora's mercurial affection, but there was no saving him. Atticus admired their grandmother above all else, and Giles didn't have the patience to convince him otherwise.

Giles didn't have to question if that made him a terrible big brother. He already knew that answer.

Theodora led Atticus down the hall, her thin, long fingers clamped onto his shoulder. Giles watched them whisper conspiratorially to each other and scoffed. Whatever they were up to, it didn't concern him. Cynthia had enrolled him in yet another night course, and he had already bribed an extension from the professor once.

Giles shoved his grandmother's concerning scheming out of his mind.

Sneaking back into the Blackwell estate was simple. No one cared where Giles went, no matter the hour. He'd celebrated his latest victory with the other dueling team members, and it had involved much more alcohol than usual. The American Academy of the Dead hadn't won against the Royal Necromantic Magistry in years. Giles, however, had overheard his mother planning to leave the family behind for a job at England's Magistry, and he had been *fucking motivated* to see them lose.

His head spun as he locked the old metal gate that surrounded the Blackwell estate, slipping the key into his pocket. He was going to be so hungover in the morning.

Umbra, his blade, thumped against his leg as he jogged up the driveway, using the garage to creep back into the house. As expected, he met no one on his way back to his bedroom.

Giles met no one, but he definitely *heard* someone.

The Blackwell manor was sprawling and well-insulated. If Giles hadn't been right above the basement stairwell when Atticus screamed, he might not have noticed it at all.

His brother's terror cleared his head, fighting through the fog alcohol had wreaked upon him. Giles curled a hand on Umbra's hilt and descended the stairs.

Had Theodora summoned something? Giles knew she had helped tear apart the Tome of the Undying, but he had never believed that she hadn't kept a part of it to herself.

Magic was sticky in the air, choking each breath he took as he advanced further into the basement. He swept past the shelves of wine his ancestors had hoarded, pausing before the tight corridor that led to the largest part of the basement—an open room with a large drain. Giles used to dare Atticus to see how long he could sit in that room, alone and in the dark.

Giles thought that tonight, Atticus would have preferred to be alone.

He discovered Theodora and Atticus inside the room, hovering around the drain. A podium held some loose papers, and Theodora leafed through them as she read in a language that made Giles want to scratch until he ruptured his eardrums. Occasionally she twisted some bone-colored device in her hands before reading further.

Near the drain, standing between Theodora and Atticus, was a large iron spike. The spike was around five feet tall and pierced through Atticus and Theodora's left hands.

Atticus's hand was below Theodora's, and it held up the rest of his body which was slumped to the ground. Viscera spilled across the stone floor, its origin something Giles refused to think about.

"You're too late to join us," Theodora said, her tone cool and even. "And Giles, you weren't invited, were you?"

Her free hand ceased turning pages and threw magic out at him. Giles attempted to dodge and slipped instead. He landed on his back, the wetness that had thrown off his balance soaking his shirt. He dipped a finger in it, rubbing the substance between his thumb and forefinger.

Blood. Atticus's blood.

Atticus caught his eye, struggling to lift his head so he could mouth, "*Run.*"

Giles rolled to his feet, unsheathing his blade. Theodora released another wave of magic, this time in the form of sharp, red discs that he ducked, letting them impale the brick wall behind him.

Anyone else would have hesitated. Giles lunged forward and drove his rapier through his grandmother's chest, just missing her heart.

Dammit. He cursed, though the string of swears was drowned out by Theodora's sudden wail. Giles withdrew his sword, sheathed it, and kicked her feet out from under her, watching Theodora fall to her knees. Simply out of spite, Giles kicked her podium and sent her papers and gadgets flying off the stand. Lifting Theodora's hand off the metal spike, Giles pulled Atticus free after. He used Atticus's good arm to pull him onto his back. Atticus, that lanky fucker, was heavier than Giles had thought.

The stairs were the worst. Giles struggled up them, slipping twice on the blood dripping from Atticus's wounded hand. The thought of Theodora reaching from below and wrapping that bony hand around his ankle helped Giles keep going.

"I'm so sorry. I didn't know what she meant," Atticus muttered, drawing in a shaky breath. "I didn't know what she was going to do. I swear, I—"

Giles shook off the rambling apology. "I believe you. That witch is fucking batshit."

Atticus fell silent as Giles dropped him at the top of the stairs. There was no use locking the door—there was a second entry into the basement outside.

"She won't come after us right away." Atticus stared at the hole in the center of his palm. "She'll finish what she started."

Giles sprinted to the kitchen, returning with a towel to tie around Atticus's wound. "Yeah? What exactly did she start?"

"Grandmother said she found a way to live past her expiration. I *thought* she meant she found a way to add on a few years." Atticus gasped as Giles tightened the makeshift bandage. "She meant *forever*."

"Forever?" Giles repeated, jerking Atticus up to his feet. "Lean on me. We need to get the fuck out of here." *Wait, did he really say "forever"?* Giles's heart stopped, and he couldn't move.

Oh, gods no.

Atticus wiped at his eyes, smearing blood across his face. "She's turning herself undead—into a lich. She tried to make me one, too."

They were absolutely fucked.

"We're fine," Giles snapped, helping Atticus limp toward the garage. They'd grab one of the cars, drive to the hospital, and report Theodora to the Commission on the way. They'd be okay.

"Fuck," Giles muttered, settling Atticus into a leather chair in a sitting room. He had situated Atticus in a dark corner, next to a tall window they could break through if needed. This room also held a small elevator that led down to the garage. "Fucking *Cynthia*."

Their mother was still in the house.

They should just leave her. It wasn't as if she was Mother of the Year. Nannies and, until the divorce, their father had raised them, not their mother.

"Mother." Atticus sighed, but he looked at Giles as if he was ready to accept whatever his brother decided.

"I'll get her," Giles groaned.

Atticus pleaded, "Don't leave me alone down here. If Grandmother finds me, she won't let me go."

Lightning suddenly struck. Through the window, the night turned bright as day as dozens of bolts of lightning touched down.

At the same time the lightning hit, Atticus screamed.

Giles hated himself for jumping like a child. He demanded, "What the fuck is wrong with you?"

Atticus pulled off his bandage, holding his left hand aloft as it caught the moonlight that filtered through a large arched window. Flesh dropped from his arm in tatters. The sound his skin made as it hit the wooden floor was unforgettable.

Giles grabbed the nearest book he could, a thin hardcover, and he shoved it in Atticus's face. "Bite down on this," he ordered.

Only Atticus would hesitate, checking the title of the book before setting it between his teeth. His shouts were muffled enough for Giles to think, to truly take in the horror his brother was becoming.

Atticus's left hand dripped muscle and matter until only bone remained. The bare bone was coated in a shimmer of red magic. It held the appendage together.

Would the rest of his body suffer so? What could even be done about it? Giles fought to recall a potion that might help, but anything that came to mind only helped with the symptoms, not the cause, and would take days to brew.

Forcing himself back into action, Giles grabbed a blanket off a couch and re-wrapped Atticus's arm. "Don't look at it."

If only that was the end of it. Atticus's hair was changing, the dark color replaced with white, and something seemed to grow from his skull, spiking through his fading strands.

"ATTICUS!" Theodora's voice, magically amplified, boomed throughout the house. "Are you changing at all? You ran away before we could finish. I must admit, I am curious."

"We need to move now!" Giles tugged at Atticus, but his brother curled up on the floor, shaking, and ignored him.

"What the hell is all this noise for?" Cynthia entered the sitting room, a chilled bottle of wine from the kitchen in her hand. She shook her head at her sons and spat, "Giles, did you dye Atticus's hair? What the—" She lifted Atticus's chin and cursed. His left eye, the white of it, had darkened like a bruise.

There was no time to explain, and there was no longer any need. Theodora had crept into the room, her transformation further along than her grandson's.

Both of Theodora's arms were only bone, and the rest of her skin was sloughing off. She grabbed a handful of loose skin at her throat and cast it aside. Cynthia gagged and covered her mouth with a hand.

Theodora laughed at her daughter's dry heaving. "Oh, Cynthia. You're a necromancer, for Hades's sake. Have some composure."

"What have you *done*?" Cynthia spat. "What did you do to Atticus?!"

"Why are you so shocked, dear? Did you think I was going to let myself die of something as mundane as *old age*?" Theodora's tone took on a daydreamy quality. "And don't start fretting about Atticus now. I've given him *eternity*. I've given him the *family* you all denied him. He'll never be alone because *I* will always be with him."

Cynthia turned her head to the side to retch. She wiped spittle from her mouth and said, "You've finally lost it, Mother."

Giles had no intention of staying and observing their mother-daughter chat. He ran for the elevator, reaching for the door's open button until lightning hit the center of the metal doors and welded them shut.

Theodora cackled, her fingertips steaming from the lightning she'd conjured. She turned her attention to Atticus, raising his left arm and examining it while he cowered.

"Don't touch him!" Cynthia, her magic forgotten, tackled her mother. Theodora, surprised by the physical violence, toppled to the ground. Cynthia raised the wine bottle in her hand, bringing it down to shatter against the lich's skull.

Taking advantage of the situation, Giles sprung forward to unsheathe Theodora's sword from the belt that held her decaying waist together. She screeched at him, wine and glass marring what remained of her flesh.

Giles lifted Atticus off the ground, pulling him further into the manor. There were plenty of places to hide, but none that Theodora didn't already know about.

The closest exit was through the kitchen. Giles dragged Atticus outside until Atticus pushed him away.

"I can walk," Atticus said, proving it by dropping the blanket covering him and breaking into a run for the tall metal gate that enclosed the estate. He stopped before the exit, arms limp against his sides as he waited for Giles to catch up.

The old-fashioned lock was melted—unusable. Giles's stomach sank with the realization that the key in his pocket was rendered useless. Theodora had ensured none of them would escape her clutches.

Giles turned back to the house. The windows flashed with crimson light from the spells the mother and daughter were throwing at each other.

Conducting the ritual to become a lich was illegal. Theodora has torn out her soul in exchange for immortal life and at the cost of a normal one. And she'd done the same to Atticus.

How much of Atticus's soul had left him? Giles considered the worst possibility. Would Atticus turn on him and join Theodora? What else could Atticus do, really? The Commission feared liches above all else—they'd call in the calvary and level their entire town if it meant they'd destroy a lich.

Giles knew what he'd do in Atticus's place. And he had never been so grateful that they couldn't be more different.

Giles studied Atticus in his defeated posture. "Fuck this. Come on."

"Wait." Atticus caught the back of Giles's jacket. "Maybe I can give you a boost over the fence. Grandmother wants me, not you. You have a chance of escaping, but me? She'll hunt me down wherever I go. If not her, the Commission will."

Giles didn't bother judging the distance. "The fence is too high. Shut the fuck up and keep moving." He started for the family cemetery. After a long pause, Atticus followed.

The tool shed contained shovels, crowbars, and everything else necessary for a family reunion. Giles broke out a shovel, tossing a second one to Atticus. Giles rested the shovel's blade on his shoulder as he walked along the gravestones, reading off the names of his ancestors until he found the one he was looking for.

Giles Thaddeus Blackwell.

His namesake, a great-great-great-great uncle who had been burned at the stake, was thankfully buried in a shallow grave. The brothers silently dug, Atticus doing so without question, until they heard the dull thud of a shovel meeting a coffin lid.

Giles Thaddeus Blackwells coffin was in pristine condition. The Blackwells spelled their coffins to be impenetrable. The brothers lifted the coffin lid free, unveiling a rather well-kept corpse underneath.

Atticus's magic shouldn't be trusted at the moment, Giles decided. Not until they were desperate. He barked at Atticus to move back as he gathered his sword and lifted it high.

Clouds rolled in above them, blocking out the moonlight. Giles directed a bolt of red lighting down from the sky, a single, perfect bolt that hit his great-whatever in the chest. The corpse spasmed, jolting about in its supposed eternal resting place.

With an unending moan, Giles Thaddeus Blackwell sat up straight. The corpse cracked its neck, one way and then the other, and swept a hand over its cranium as if it expected hair to still be there.

Giles raised a hand to stop Atticus from speaking. They wouldn't have much time with the now-living dead, and Giles didn't want to waste it asking irrelevant questions.

"Uncle Thaddeus," Giles said, deciding that would be the least confusing way to address him. "I'm your descendent, Giles Thaddeus Blackwell—*the third*."

"*Another* Giles Thaddeus?" Thaddeus laughed, and the hollow sockets of his skull filled with a twinkling amber light. "I thought *I* was so bad that it would prevent another. Appears not. Are you giving me a chance to try again?"

"No, we need your help." Giles glanced back at the house. The home had gone quiet, the spells having stopped for a few minutes now. "Our grandmother, Theodora, has turned herself into a lich and made my brother into some half-creature."

"I'm guessing there won't be any more Theodoras!" Thaddeus stroked his chin. "I'm not sure why you chose me to assist. Have you already tried running away and screaming?"

"We can't get over the fence," Atticus explained.

"It's not so bad—" Thaddeus waved a hand at himself. "—being dead." He pointed at Atticus. "It may be different for you. You seem *odd*."

"I know we're asking for a Hail Mary here," Giles tried again.

"I have no idea why you think *that* would help. Have the Blackwells turned to religion? If so, would you mind bashing in my skull, so I won't be summoned by you lot again?"

"No, it's an expression. Never mind!" Giles pinched the bridge of his nose. "If you can think of *anything* that would give us a chance, just the slightest chance, tell us."

"No, thanks. I may have nothing to lose but my bones, but I'm not pissing off a lich for you." Thaddeus began scooping out dirt that had fallen into his coffin. "Now, *Junior*, put me back to—"

"I'll bury you," Giles said, his voice cold and sounding much older than his nineteen years. "I'll bury you, but I won't put you back to rest. You'll spend eternity staring at your own coffin lid, unable to even claw out your eyes to make it stop. I'll leave you there, *awake*, until you go insane, and even that won't be a comfort."

Thaddeus was silent for a long time. "I see now why they named you after me," Thaddeus hummed. "If I were unlucky enough to be you, I would try...but there's no way she'd fall for *that*."

"I said we'll take anything," Giles reminded him sharply.

"The founding Blackwell's tomb has had protective runes carved into it by every Blackwell after him. They can drain magic—"

"Right." Giles already knew all of that. He'd placed his own runes there at age sixteen, and Atticus's turn was next year. "How does that help us?"

"If you can get the lich in that tomb, you may have a chance. Once she's in there, activate the wards from the outside. Three centuries of wards may be enough to have a chance of containing her."

"And how the hell are we going to get—"

"You said give you the slightest chance! I held up my end of the bargain. Lay me to rest before the lich gets here!" Thaddeus snuggled back into his padded coffin and snapped his fingers at them. "Be quick about it!"

Giles hated being snapped at. He considered ignoring his ancestor's plea but didn't care for the possibility of Thaddeus clawing his way out of the earth and coming after him later. "Fine."

Thaddeus lowered himself back into his coffin, lying back and crossing his arms over his ribcage. Atticus picked up one side of the coffin lid, waiting for Giles to grab the other end.

Well, there *was* another option.

Giles picked up his shovel and drove it down hard and fast, cleanly separating Thaddeus's skull from the rest of his skeleton.

Thaddeus howled as his skull rolled around in the coffin, "YOU BASTARD! YOU PROMISED ME!"

"You should have done what I asked the first time," Giles said with a shrug. He snapped his fingers, putting Thaddeus to rest and ending that horrid complaining. Giles reached down and picked up the skull, tossing it aside for later.

Atticus stared at the skull as it bounced on the ground and stopped. "Giles..."

"What if we need more information later? I hate digging fucking graves," Giles said. "It's not like the corpse has anything better to do. I think he'll make a fine mantelpiece."

Giles stretched his sore muscles, preparing for the fight to come. He handed Theodora's blade over to Atticus. "Can you use that hand?"

Atticus flexed his finger bones and grimaced. "Yes, as disgusting as they are, they still work."

A plan, though hopeless, formed in Giles's vision. "I'll need your help. If it's really *you* she wants—"

"She doesn't want to be alone. That must be why she made me like this, too." Atticus tested Theodora's blade without enthusiasm. "My magic feels strong, but it's different. I'm afraid—"

"There's no time to bother with that," Giles said as he approached their family founder's tomb. "We've work to do."

Was their mother still alive? Giles wondered as Theodora, alone, walked out to the graveyard. Her steps were puppet-like—as if her changing body threw off her balance.

Giles doubted Cynthia had survived. Theodora was without a soul now—there was nothing to stop her from killing her own daughter. Hell, she'd *had a* soul when she destroyed Atticus's life.

There was no warning. Once Theodora spotted Giles, she struck. Her power shot toward him, a crimson lightning bolt that he adsorbed through his sword, swinging the blade behind him and letting the lightning fly free. His arm tingled after, but he had avoided disintegration.

"Why didn't you go with your father when he asked?" Theodora whined. "You would have lived like a prince, and you would have stayed out of my way."

Her next strike wasn't as easily redirected. Umbra was shuddering under the power, even though it was only contained for a few moments.

Giles gasped, resting his free hand on his knee as he caught his breath. Distracting Theodora was easier said than done. The lich threw lazy lightning bolts at Giles, but she really focused her attention on scanning the graveyard for her favored grandson.

He'd left it up to Atticus to figure out how to get Theodora into the tomb. What kind of *Looney Toons* trick would work on the lich, Giles had no idea, but—

What the fuck.

Raising a corpse entailed a myriad of work. Dig up the coffin, pry open the coffin, call down the right amount of lightning to animate the corpse and not fry it, and then you had to deal with the corpse's *personality*.

Thaddeus had certainly proved that not all corpses were grateful to be awoken.

What Atticus was doing, though, wasn't the same.

His shovel lay abandoned as he raised his hands high and drew forth bolt after bolt of lightning down upon the graves of their family. The bodies became feral things, clawing their way out of the ground with a ferocity that made Giles shiver.

The living dead were completely under Atticus's control. Their own thoughts, their own being, had been left in their grave.

"Impossible," Giles breathed, forgetting all about his grandmother.

Theodora swept past him, heading for Atticus. "My perfect boy! What strength! I knew you wouldn't abandon me—"

There was a moment when Theodora and Giles both thought Atticus had surrendered to his new power.

Then Atticus directed his loyal army to march upon Theodora, their ratty arms gripping the lich around her arms and legs. They lifted her off the ground and carried her into Ivan Blackwell's final resting place.

One of her arms broke free and Theodora grabbed on to the frame of the tomb's entrance. Her words were almost lost in her screech.

"Atticus! I did this for *you*! I coddled you, reassured you, and this is what—" Atticus's undead yanked on her legs, trying to free her grip on the frame. "—what I get in return? You selfish brat! You're going to leave *me alone?* Your mother will throw you to the wolves! I am all you will ever have. You're doomed, you fucking—"

Her hand popped off the frame as her ancestors dragged her inside. Giles ducked inside the tomb, watching as the corpses slid the lid off Ivan's sarcophagus and threw Theodora down in it. She fought them as they tried to push the heavy stone lid into place.

Giles raced forward, pushing the lid alongside the dead. Theodora's arm popped out of the small opening, swinging and catching Giles underneath his eye. He backed away before she could scar him again and watched the living dead overpower her. As soon as the lid was closed, Giles slapped his palm on the lid, activating every rune at once. A wave of power radiated from the coffin, knocking Giles off his feet.

Giles crawled outside, accepting Atticus's bony hand as he helped him to his feet. Together, they slammed the tomb's doors shut. They stared, panting and waiting for those cursed doors to reopen and for Theodora to emerge.

Every second felt like a lifetime.

Atticus finally spoke. "Those things I made...I felt them crumble. The tomb's wards are working."

"But are they working on *Theodora?*" Giles asked, never taking his eyes off those aged double doors.

"We can only hope—" Atticus suddenly fell to his knees, his hands cupping the swirling, white light that emerged from his stomach. It was a wisp of a thing, Atticus's soul.

Giles limped to the toolshed, searching the building until he found what he wanted.

Giles returned to his brother with an opened urn and ushered Atticus's soul inside of it. They'd transplant it later and hide it from Cynthia—if she was still alive, that is.

Giles wished Atticus would stand up. He was pitiful, kneeling in the mud like that. Giles sighed. He was so fucking tired. "It's okay. We'll find a way to hide your appearance. You'll live, Atticus."

"But..." Atticus's fingers dug into his knees, his head falling to touch the earth. "For how *long?*"

Giles ignored his dramatics. If he fed into Atticus's despair, it would only strengthen it. "We tell no one what you are. *No one.*"

Atticus agreed, though Giles didn't care for his reasoning. "I have no one left to tell."

CHAPTER 52
WITCH

"**N**ow you know what she did to her *favorite*, to her family." Giles sneered. "You let it out. If that thing gets loose, what do you think it will do to us?"

"I fucked up," Maddox agreed, not knowing what else to say. "But Atticus—"

"He's just as much of a problem as Theodora! Do *you* want to see what a possessed lich can do?" Giles folded his arms, disgust muddying his good looks. "I sure as fuck don't."

Maddox threw up her hands. "So, what are you saying? That we should give up on him? Kill them both?"

"We need to be prepared for it, yeah. And don't fucking look at me like that. Atticus is *my* brother."

Maddox rubbed her forehead, smoothing out the wrinkles her agitation caused. She should have known Giles would be a threat, but she'd let him help as long as he remained on her side. But if Giles tried to end Atticus before she decided he was truly lost, Giles would find their next duel wouldn't be so one-sided.

"Before we make a decision about Atticus," Maddox pleaded, "please look at what I've found so far."

Maddox presented a heavy stack of notes she'd gathered from Theodora's grimoire and the Blackwell's extensive and dangerous library. Maddox had found ten books already in the collection that the Commission would have the Blackwells arrested for simply possessing. Not that she was going to snitch.

Giles spread her notes out on the desktop and tapped the mounted skull. "Uncle Thaddeus, care to have a look?"

Giles's magic coated the skull and reanimated it. Thaddeus cracked his jaw, the pits of his eyes burning with a red flame. The flames danced, focusing first on Maddox and then finding Giles.

"Bastard!" the skull screeched. "Grave defiler! I asked you to put me back in my coffin, not keep me as a knickknack!"

"If you don't shut up," Giles said emotionlessly, "I'll take you to the pound and let the dogs fight over you."

"Change your name!" Thaddeus cried, chomping at Giles like a piranha. "I no longer wish for you to be named after me!"

Giles rolled his eyes. "So you're not in your eternal resting place. Who gives a fuck? Shut up and look at these notes."

Thaddeus continued to howl until Giles drummed a pencil against the skull. Maddox snatched the pencil from Giles. To Thaddeus, she vowed, "If you help us, I promise I'll return you to your grave. Deal?"

Thaddeus fell silent, and the flames in his eyes ran back and forth. "Deal," the skull sighed, and he set his gaze on Maddox's work.

"You're trying to *fix* the half-lich?" Thaddeus wondered and laughed hysterically. Giles held up a permanent marker threateningly, and Thaddeus snapped his jaw closed.

Ignoring the strangeness of her new situation, Maddox pointed out a few sections she'd highlighted to the skull. And as much as she disliked Giles, it was good to talk about this with someone who understood necromancy. "Your grandmother doesn't have many details on liches. I think she has a separate grimoire hidden, and I bet there's a portion of the Tome of the Undying tucked away with it."

"We knew she used the Tome to turn herself into that thing, but when we looked for it after she was trapped the first time, it was already gone. Atticus has spent years searching for it. It's lost, so forget about it." Giles lifted one of the sheets and tapped on a paragraph. "We need to deal with the parasite first. Atticus is too dangerous to be around when he can turn on us at any time."

Thaddeus butted in. "Let's say we succeed in separating the parasite from the boy. What then?"

Giles frowned. "We can't trust the exorcist. He knows Atticus is a lich. If he knows, the Commission will know. Atticus will have to assume the identity I had made for him and leave the country."

Maddox's nerve wavered. Had she done the right thing by stopping

Atticus from leaving? She'd torn through his bugout bag—Atticus had been trying to follow Giles's escape plan before she'd lost herself to the parasite. He'd stayed to help her, and then she'd trapped him.

Maddox had spent so long fixating on being right about everything, that it hadn't occurred to her that her first instinct might be terribly wrong.

Maybe she had made a mistake, but the thought of Atticus sequestering himself somewhere to lose his mind alone...

Atticus had spent enough time alone.

"How *exactly* did Atticus take the parasite from you?" Giles scowled at her, hate burning in his eyes.

Maddox shrugged off Giles's red-hot glare. "He used a potion. Once I consumed it, the parasite clawed its way out of me and Atticus presented himself as an alternative." She showed off her bandaged wrist.

Thaddeus asked, "Does the potion *have* to be consumed? Can it be applied in other ways?"

Maddox took Theodora's grimoire and opened it to the section that covered the brew. Giles studied it carefully, threading a hand in his hair as he concentrated.

"It just says it needs to enter the body," he surmised, groaning. "What a mess. Even if Atticus *could* take the potion, that parasite won't leave him. I don't think any of us would be as tempting as a lich. As simple as the parasite may be, it's clear that Atticus is the stronger host."

"You're right," Maddox agreed, her shoulders sinking. She recalled how that devious bug had taken the time to consider Atticus before jumping over to him. "If only—"

Maddox slapped her hands over her ears and closed her eyes to block out all distractions. She needed to think, to rearrange this horrific puzzle. Maybe, just maybe...

Her thoughts finally settled, forming a somewhat clear picture. "We need to speak with your grandmother."

The words that left Giles's mouth when Maddox suggested they speak to Theodora were, to put it mildly, nasty.

But he followed her outside, after retrieving his sword, and together they entered the graveyard. Lochlan was resting on a stone bench and rose to greet them.

Lochlan began, "She's—"

"*It,*" Giles interrupted.   He had carried Thaddeus's skull with him, keeping it at arm's length as Thaddeus tried to bite him.

"The lich," Lochlan tried again and ignored the chattering skull, "has been moving her fingers. Other than that, there's nothing to report."

"There wasn't much progress on our end, either," Giles reported.

Maddox let the two share information while she approached Theodora. The lich's prison was a maple tree, the bark and branches twisted around her skeletal body. Those fingerbones were twitching, just like Lochlan had said.

The lich's eyes still burned, tiny pinpricks of light in a hollow void. This light focused on Maddox, flickering in and out. A branch had grown out of Theodora's mouth. Maddox summoned her magic, burning the branch until ash flew from Theodora's slack jaw.

"*This* prison," Theodora said as she coughed, "isn't as comfortable as the last one."

"The next will be worse," Maddox promised, her lips tilting up into a smile. "At least out here you get a pleasant view of the landscape. The Commission will give you nothing but white walls forever."

Theodora strained against her cage, the wood creaking until she gave in, panting.

Maddox knew she shouldn't taunt the lich, but the vicious side of herself, the one she hid from her family, couldn't help it.

"Why did you involve Atticus in your insane attempt at immortality?

Maybe you were at the end of your life, but his was just beginning."

Running through their limited options with Giles had helped Maddox form the barest ghost of a plan. But she needed something confirmed first.

Theodora didn't answer. The wind whistled through the branches containing the lich, and the women watched a few leaves fall to the ground.

"If you help Atticus," Maddox prompted, "I'll keep the Commission from finding you. I'll bury you somewhere nice and quiet. That's better than an eternity of Commission scientists experimenting on you, right?"

There it was. In the decayed state Theodora was in, it was almost impossible to notice slight changes in her expression. But there was nothing slight about the fear that raked the lich's body.

"Is it the dark?" Maddox laughed, stepping forward until she was face to face with the lich. With the branches halting her movements, Theodora could not look away. "Is it the quiet? What could make a *lich* tremble? It's being alone, isn't it?" Maddox's fingers curled into fists. "That's why you made your own grandson into a horror. So you wouldn't live like this, live forever like this, *alone.*"

Aegis shone brightly as Maddox tapped Theodora's exposed ribcage with it. There was still some flesh clinging to her ribs and some organs, too. Perfect. "It's good to know," Maddox sang, "that you're just as incomplete as the rest of us."

Maddox returned to where she left Giles and Lochlan, her jaw set and determined. "I have a plan," she announced, though truthfully it was missing a few key pieces.

"Thank Hades," Giles grumbled. "Though, it better be good if it's going to fix this shitshow."

"I'll need everyone's help," she added, nodding to the manor. "Giles, come with me—"

Lochlan gripped Maddox's arm before she could run away. "I'll help in any way I can, but it might not line up with what you want," he admitted. "Maddox, if we don't find Atticus tomorrow, I'm telling the Commission everything. I'm sorry."

She had expected to have this talk a lot sooner. "I understand," Maddox replied, giving Lochlan's arm a squeeze back. "Do what you need to."

Lochlan's guilt was written all over his face, but, hey, he was Catholic. Perhaps that was his default state.

Maddox and Giles headed back inside, and she found her family in the kitchen. It was time to open up and share her plan. It was time to face their judgment.

She asked for no questions until the end, and Maddox relayed each step in excruciating detail. Everyone had their part to play, and all were willing, but Daphne wasn't happy to be sidelined.

"I'm the most powerful witch here!" she protested. "Except maybe the *liches*, but it's not fair to count them!"

"You also have the most to lose," Rob reminded her.

Daphne scowled down at her stomach and the teacup and saucer that rested on it. "Well, whatever happens, I'm not leaving. Without my power, Grandad won't be able to contain that lich for another minute."

Colter grimaced, scratching his hair as he admitted, "Unfortunately, she's right. I've had to call on Daphne's power more than I've wanted to."

"You share power with each other?" Giles asked, his brow knitted.

"It's more like our lives are tied together. The head of our coven can call upon our magic reserves to aid his own," Maddox explained. "Or he can use our life force."

"That is..." Giles clicked his tongue, and this time he seemed to look at the Abernathys with respect. "Almost necromantic."

"Don't lump us in with you!" Dove scoffed. "We don't make zombies or use our magic to harm."

"Sounds boring," Giles said, but his tone was nearly joking.

Maddox interrupted before her family could distract them more. "Have any of you been able to find Atticus?"

Her mother volunteered the unhappy information. "We've searched the grounds but have found no sign of him. The family roots are working through the town now, but nothing so far. If he touched the earth, we should have been able to detect him."

"Maybe Atticus was too quick. Maybe he had more *Chameleon* squirreled away," Giles offered. "I'd prefer that scenario."

"Let's still work on the assumption that he's nearby. We stick with the plan," Maddox said, her jaw aching from clenching. "We have one more day before the Commission ends it for us. We can give up later."

Everyone else could give up. Maddox never would, and she needed to leave before her family realized that.

To Giles, she said, "Show me where it is."

Maddox paced in the greenhouse, waiting for Giles to return. She wrung her hands until they hurt, but if she stopped, she'd start biting her nails again, and it had taken her *years* to break that habit.

Thaddeus sat on the lab table, humming. Maddox brought him with her to stand guard over the cooling cauldron. Her plan required a potion, and Giles and Thaddeus had both been happy to boss her through the process.

Giles entered the conservatory, sneering at her. "Don't look so happy to see me. It freaks me out."

Maddox took what he offered, the heavy collection of horror stories a familiar weight. *Frankenstein* was the cover title, and when she opened it to the title page, she was able to trace her own words.

Thanks for being my friend.

She hugged the book to her chest, not caring that Giles could see how pathetic she was. Wait...

The balance of the book was all wrong. Maddox opened the book to its center and revealed a large section of the pages had been cut out. Tucked in this gap was a small, flat vial with a silver skull-shaped stopper. The vial held a silver vortex inside, and the glass was hot to the touch.

Maddox held what remained of Atticus's soul.

CHAPTER 53
WITCH

The sound of a cauldron on the verge of bubbling over woke Maddox in a panic. She clutched at her heart, cursing herself for still having anxiety dreams about her lonely school days. She was too old for nightmares like that. Failing a potions lab was not the end of the world, and why had she ever thought it was?

Wait. Something *was* boiling. Maddox wiped the sleep from her eyes as she staggered out of bed. She had only attempted sleep because Giles had demanded it. Her family had attempted the same, though much kinder, but only Giles's threat to "put her to sleep so she'd actually be some use to Atticus" was the only thing that worked.

The Conservatory was the warmest room in the house. She should have slept there ages ago. Though, when she was in Atticus's arms, the drafty mansion wasn't an issue.

Oh, Atticus. I'm always missing you, aren't I? Wait. Atticus?

Maddox froze before the apothecary table, watching the cauldron steam as Atticus precisely added another solution to it. He kept his back to her, uncaring that she had discovered him.

She had wandered over to his apothecary station with her blanket wrapped around her shoulders. Now Maddox let her makeshift cloak fall to the floor as she ran to him.

Her arms slipped around his waist, holding him from behind, though she could not forget the last time she'd done so he'd pushed her away.

Her panic threatened to send bile up her throat. If she had slept any heavier, Atticus might have left before she even noticed a thing. She should have kept Thaddeus with her, if only as a guard dog, but Giles had insisted on using the skull to help him search the library for any information they may have overlooked.

"Where have you been?" Maddox pressed her cheek against Atticus's back. He smelled freshly showered with a dab of his normal cologne. While he was the possessed one, he seemed more put together than she was.

"I left you a hint." He laughed dryly. How relaxing she found that sound. "When I slipped your letter inside *Jane Eyre*, I half-expected you to storm up to the attic immediately. You must have been so frazzled."

"Oh, I didn't even stop to think..." Maddox shook her head. This whole time, Atticus had simply been hiding in plain sight, making use of the Blackwell manor's secret rooms and servant halls that Maddox couldn't keep track of.

"Stop messing with the potion," she said, glaring at the cauldron as he played with the flames below it.

"I'm working, my dear," Atticus chided her. "You've put me in quite a difficult position. I haven't much time left."

"But you don't need it." Atticus didn't need to hide, not around her. Maddox let him go only to try for the stove's dial. Atticus caught her wrist before she could extinguish the fire, his gloved left-hand pinching into her skin.

He scolded her while avoiding her gaze. "Leave it on. This needs to simmer for another hour. If the temperature drops—"

"Dammit, Atticus! Look at me!" Maddox tore out of his grip and pushed him away from his cauldron. She reached up to take his face in both of her hands, fighting to see his expression clearly through her tears.

His glare cut into her. Atticus snapped his fingers and the lights in the conservatory blinked out.

No, she would not let him hide from her any longer. Maddox willed her own light into existence, throwing a half-dozen red orbs into the air and casting Atticus in their red, wavering light.

His gentle, love-struck gaze was gone. How imperious he seemed, staring furiously down at her and allowing her to see the full effects of his grandmother's insanity.

Like Theodora, a crown of skeletal spikes stabbed through his hair. The white of his left eye had turned black, though his right eye remained normal. His overall complexion had a grey tone to it. Grey and white streaks wove through his thick, dark hair, nearly taking over. Maddox wanted to stroke those pale locks but kept herself still. Atticus had his left hand hidden underneath a black leather glove.

Maddox scanned him again but found no more afflictions. She wanted to weep for him. Hades, how that must have hurt! Pain a fifteen-year-old boy should never have had to endure.

"Giles told me what Theodora did to you. I'm so sorry."

Her pity furrowed his brow. Atticus scoffed. "I'm sure Giles's rendition was fascinating. I hope you took notes. Would you like to take a sample of my blood before I go? It might do your research more good than staring at my abnormalities." The sneer he shot her broke Maddox's heart. He thought she was staring because she found some *scientific merit* in it?

Well, it was easy to prove him wrong.

Maddox brought his mouth down to hers, kissing him between apologies. He stilled underneath her affections, frozen like stone beneath her kisses.

"Maddox, what are you—"

She could not stand his disbelief. He had to know how easy it was to love him. "Atticus, please stay with me. I'll save you. I promise."

"That may not be a promise you can keep." Atticus moved out of her arms. He seemed terrified of her, his hands raised before him to keep her at bay. "Even if you can remove the parasite somehow, I will forever look like this." He ran a hand over his face as if to accentuate the oddities of it. "What I am will never change. An undead *thing*, a *lich*, and what remains of my humanity never balked at lying to you. I wanted to keep you. At any cost."

"You have me!" Maddox protested. "You will always have me. I'll keep helping you, even if it destroys us both."

"Then I have lied too well."

Atticus was a damned fool. If they had to spend the rest of their lives fleeing from the Commission, Maddox would do it for him. If he lost himself, really lost himself to that leech, and she saw no other way out, Maddox also knew she'd do what was best for him. Even if it killed her.

So how could Atticus write her off like that? As if she had already left him.

Atticus kept distancing himself from her with his words. "It's kind of you to worry, but you're not responsible for what happened to me. Stop feeling guilty. I was ruined long before that nasty little parasite came into our lives." Atticus started for her but halted his steps before he closed any space between them. "I think, my dear, it's better this way. I would have chained you to *this*.

Now, at least, my actions will let you hate me, rather than miss me, when I'm gone."

She marched up to him, her fury unable to be contained for another moment. "Stop deciding things for me! How dare you!"

Maddox hated how easily Atticus dropped to his knees before her. He held her hands, bringing each one to his lips to kiss her knuckles, one hand at a time. "The parasite is strong. It fed off you just as it's feeding off me. But I have much more to offer it, and I struggled against its whispers. Don't let me hurt you."

"Please stand up," she pleaded, tugging at his hands until he rose. "And stop talking like this is the end. Giles and I, we have a plan. I can't share it with you as I don't want that leech aware of it, but—"

"One of us has to face reality, and I've been ignoring it for too long." Atticus gave her a sad smile. "You own what's left of me, and if you must destroy it to protect yourself, I beg you to do so."

No, no, no! Maddox worried her lip, searching for the right thing to say so that he would end his self-sacrificial loathing. "I can't do that to you!"

Why not? It's not like you're killing a person, just slaying a monster."

"Stop calling yourself that!" Her pain made her reckless. She threw her arms around his neck, lowering his mouth until she could capture it. "If you insist on chasing me away—" Maddox slid her tongue against his. "—then I must convince you I'm telling the truth."

Atticus, despite all he had just said, could not refuse her. He desperately returned her kisses until Maddox pushed him, guiding him to the bed she'd just left. Another shove and he fell back onto the tangled sheets.

"I will rip that parasite from you, Atticus. I'll send it to hell for what it's done to us." She climbed onto the bed, straddling his waist. "But first I will love you."

She unbuttoned his shirt slowly before working on removing her own. It seemed silly to feel self-conscious, even if it was only for an instant. Maddox banished the thought and dropped her sweatshirt onto the floor.

"I don't..." Atticus clicked his tongue. "I mean, you don't have to do this. I know what I look like." He swallowed, turning his head to the side so his "good" side was all she could see.

"All you look like to me, Atticus, is mine." Maddox lowered herself so she could trail kisses up his bare chest and up to his neck. "That's all you've ever been to me. *You're mine.*"

Atticus sat up suddenly, bringing her face back to his to deepen their kiss. His hands found her hips, his fingertips digging ruthlessly into her skin as he moved her slowly against him.

The friction was delicious and not nearly enough for her. Her logic fought against her lust and, for the first time ever, her logic failed. This wasn't the right time for this. There was a parasite, a lich, and a whole damned government agency to worry about. Maddox did not care. She loved Atticus, and for the first time, she understood a little how foolish sex could make someone.

With his lower lip caught in her teeth, Maddox bit down until Atticus released her hips. She dropped off the bed just long enough to rid herself of the rest of her clothing.

"Beautiful," he whispered, staring openly as Maddox crawled back into bed. Atticus pinned her by her shoulders, settling himself between her legs. His hands were all over her, cupping her curves and threading into her hair. "If we had time, I would kiss every *inch* of you."

"We'll have time later," she sniped. There would be no more talk of deadlines or endings. If Atticus tried again, Maddox had more than a few ideas on how to shut him up.

Atticus shot her a sly look. "For now, I'll have to focus on my favorite part instead."

Oh! Maddox closed her eyes, prepared for that infuriating man to kiss her somewhere inappropriate. She blinked a few moments later, confused about why he had gently kissed her forehead.

"I've wanted to do that for years," he confessed. "You're at perfect forehead-kissing height for me."

Why did something so uncharacteristically sweet make her so wild? "That doesn't matter when we're in a bed," Maddox huffed.

"You're right." Now he moved between her thighs, kissing and biting her gently. "*This* was what you wanted, wasn't it?"

She fought the urge to tug his hair until he stopped dancing around the edge of her. "I—I didn't say that."

"You enjoyed it last time. You *did* say that."

Well, that was true.

Maddox tried to protest. She had started this to comfort *him*, not to make Atticus—Hades below, he was so good at that. She could hardly think straight with his tongue between her legs.

"All the conservatory's foliage makes for good insulation," Atticus said, letting her trembling legs relax for a moment. "Be as loud as you like, my dear."

There was no need to convince her. Maddox whimpered as he returned to his work. "Please," she moaned, trying to slip away until Atticus braced an arm across her stomach to keep her still. "I need you."

"Be more specific. You currently have *all* my attention. What more do you need from me?"

Perhaps Atticus needed to hear her say it. He'd proven how uncomfortable he felt about his looks, and there was no need for it. Maddox, though inexperienced, was prepared to do whatever he asked of her.

Maddox nervously bit on her pinky nail as she answered, "Fuck me."

Atticus's breath stopped. "Again."

Maddox shifted her body until she was as exposed as she could physically be. "I want *you*, Atticus. Fuck me, *please*."

CHAPTER 54
WARLOCK

Gently, Atticus had to remind himself as he clamped a hand on each of her knees. He wanted to do this easy, *slowly*. Atticus wouldn't be able to stand it if he hurt her.

He'd done enough of that already.

"I want to prepare you," Atticus said, bringing his hand between her legs. He placed a finger against her apex and waited. "I want to start with this and work our way up to more."

She sighed in quiet relief. Maddox nodded and Atticus slid a single finger inside, cautious and attentive to her reactions.

He asked softly, "Have you done this before? To yourself?"

"Yes, a few times. Not many," she amended.

Atticus kept his strokes shallow and testing. "Tell me about the last time," he said, hoping conversation would help her relax.

She flushed brighter, biting back a moan. "It was...last spring, I think? I dreamt of...you," she finished shyly.

"Of me?"

"We were seniors and you found me in my study room," she admitted. She gasped as Atticus added a second finger and quickened his stroking. Maddox rocked against his hand, her panting and whimpering spurring him faster.

Maddox's movements thrust him further inside. "You grabbed me and told me you missed me."

Atticus groaned. "I did. Gods, I missed you every day."

They both moved in a frenzy, each hunting for Maddox's release. She cried, "You said you loved me!"

"I *did*, I *do*, I *will forever.*"

Atticus removed his fingers, and Maddox nearly sobbed at his absence.

His hands traveled again to her knees, moving them apart until he could settle himself against her. It was *agony* to wait. To see her open and waiting to accept him and to *hesitate*? To give her a final chance to change her mind, to see him for what he truly was.

Liar, coward, monster.

Lich.

Maddox reached for him and pleaded, "Atticus, please!"

And with that, he was lost. What could he refuse her? Nothing.

Atticus eased inside her in stages until Maddox hooked her legs around him and used her heels to drive him all the way in.

As a chronic overthinker, Atticus could not remember the last time he had felt such mind-numbing bliss. *Such quiet.*

He had paused too long. Maddox reached up to cradle his face with a hand, allowing him to turn his head to kiss her palm. Atticus sighed. He had thought Maddox would never look more beautiful than that she had the night in the library, but now...

"You look perfect, you taste perfect, and you feel *fucking perfect.*"

Maddox flushed, or maybe it was just those damned red orbs she had conjured. Atticus had considered extinguishing the light but knew she'd protest.

How could she stand to look at him?

They moved together, Maddox setting the pace. Atticus let what little remained of his secrets out. "I've only ever thought of you. It didn't matter if I was alone or with someone else—you're all I could ever think about." He buried his face into her neck. "Does that make me fucked up?"

There was no pause. Maddox actually seemed pleased that she occupied every lustful thought he'd ever had. "No, it just makes you mine."

She spurred him on faster. Her nails raked down his back, and Atticus loved the idea of her marking him. He only wished he could see the damage she'd done to his back.

Maddox grabbed a fistful of his hair, knotting it around her fist and pulling his face down until she could nip his earlobe with her teeth. She whispered in his ear, "Every time I touched myself, it was because of you."

Atticus stopped only to have Maddox bite his neck until he resumed driving into her. *Slow down*, he chided himself. But Maddox wouldn't allow it. If he slackened his pace at all, Maddox bit down where his neck met his shoulder and viciously so.

"Occasionally, I'd remember you," she continued, her voice low and making it so *fucking hard* to stay focused. "I'd think about you, though I tried not to because I was still so mad at you, and I'd—"

He couldn't believe the filthy words she whispered into his ear as Maddox recounted the vivid details of what his memory did to her. Atticus stared at her, watching her blush deepen as she shyly described the image of him she liked to replay in her mind while her hand worked between her legs. Atticus couldn't hold back another second.

Atticus quickened his pace and used a thumb to play with her, just as Maddox had described doing to herself. The added pressure turned her into a writhing, babbling mess.

He grinned. "All those languages you speak, and yet, the only thing you can think to scream is my name?"

Maddox fisted her hands into the sheets. "I think—I think I'm—"

"My dear, don't interrupt me unless you *know* I'm about to make you—"

His teasing stopped instantly as Maddox's core clenched around him. Atticus chased her ecstasy, needing to experience his bliss alongside her. He caught up with her and, after, fell against her panting chest.

He could have stayed there forever, but Maddox must have been sore. Atticus rolled off her to retrieve her discarded underwear and help her slip them back on.

She wiggled into her clothing, and her plotting brain restarted and was ready to boss him around again. "In the morning, we'll gather everyone and try my plan."

"Don't forget to use the bathroom," he reminded her. Maddox flushed, gathering the rest of her clothes to dress fully. Atticus waved her off when she hesitated. "I'll be here when you come back. Don't worry."

Maddox left the conservatory for a few minutes, giving Atticus just enough time to slide the lid on his bubbling cauldron just a little off the pot. Waves of purple smoke rolled from the potion, and Atticus extinguished Maddox's red orbs one by one. In total darkness, the soft lavender smoke was invisible.

Maddox came racing back, raising a brow when she found Atticus in bed. "We shouldn't sleep. We need to get to work right away."

"I can't tempt you?" Atticus teased and lifted the covers for her to slide under. He asked, "Do you need anything? Water?"

She yawned and crawled into bed with him. "No, I'm fine. I'll lie with you just for a few minutes."

Atticus complied, tucking her back against his chest and kissing the top of her head. With her expression now hidden from him, Maddox murmured, "I'm sorry. I trapped you here without caring what you wanted or what was right for you."

"It's okay. I didn't handle it well, either."

"You just ended us. You didn't give me a chance to prove you wrong." She shook until Atticus tightened his hold on her. Maddox continued, "If this doesn't work, I know we'll have to run. Lochlan kept your nature from the Commission, but we can't expect him to lie forever." She repeated firmly, "If this doesn't work, I'll run with you. I'll keep trying, and I'll stay with you. No matter what happens."

What had Atticus done to earn such loyalty? "Is that a promise?"

"Yes." Maddox placed a hand over his. "We won't leave each other ever again."

She was drifting, but Maddox fought the potion's effects. Her eyelids fluttered as Atticus slipped out of bed. "Hey, where are you..." Maddox's yawn interrupted her question.

He was running out of time. Atticus opened the bottom cabinet of his apothecary bench and removed a gas mask. He donned it quickly while Maddox used the last of her strength to light the room in red once more.

Atticus watched her struggle against his sleeping potion, his stomach roiling with guilt. But it would be better for her to sleep through everything he needed to do.

"The parasite got me, Maddie," Atticus confessed. "I didn't last very long at all. I *need* you to know that. I need you to know that before I walked into this room, *it was already too late to save me.*"

CHAPTER 55
WITCH

A haze settled over her mind, willing Maddox to keep sleeping. It would have been *so* nice to sleep in—she couldn't recall the last time she had the chance to. What let her fight the unusual and overwhelming need to rest was an absence. Maddox didn't feel Atticus's arms around her.

She rose groggily, her head throbbing, and glanced around the bed. Empty. Maddox jumped out of bed, but her knees gave out as soon as she touched down. The floor of the conservatory was cold, rough stone, and Maddox tried to stand and failed.

During her third failed attempted to pick herself up, Maddox noticed the lavender fog creeping across the floor. She blinked, her eyelids becoming heavier and heavier by the second. *What the hell is this? What happened to me?*

Someone lifted her up and placed her back into bed. Maddox struggled to sit until Atticus's hand cupped her chin.

"Rest, my dear. I'll take care of everything."

Why did his voice sound muffled? Maddox argued, "There isn't time to rest anymore." Hell, they shouldn't have slept at all. As soon as Atticus had revealed himself, Maddox should have woken the house and enacted her plan. She blushed at her own foolishness. "We only have one day until Lochlan calls in the Commission—"

"I have a plan of my own."

"You didn't mention that last night," she said with a yawn. Why was it so hard to stay awake? And why was it so dark in here? She could barely see Atticus, though he was hovering above her. Maddox pushed off the blanket he was trying to cover her with. "I don't want to sleep, Atticus!"

"It will be easier if you stay in bed." He stubbornly tucked the blanket around her again. "I need to find the rest of the Tome, the section Theodora used to make me this way."

"Find the rest of the..." Maddox shook her head, covering her mouth to hide her gasp. "Giles said you've already tried searching for those pages. We don't have time for that. They'll require translating, most likely, and there's no guarantee that..."

Hades, no. Maddox knew what had brought this on. Atticus smoothed her bedhead back from her face.

The parasite had tempted her with the same thing, claiming the Tome was the key to saving Atticus. Though the memories of her possession were still foggy, Maddox remembered what had caused her to fall.

"What are you going to do?" she asked.

Atticus moved away from the bed, and Maddox could finally see the cauldron on the stovetop, bubbling over and releasing those purple clouds that made it so hard for her to concentrate.

A sleeping potion.

Her magic sputtered from her exhaustion, but she was able to cast a soft, red light that illuminated her love and the gasmask he wore. His eyes were wild and so far away, though he never broke her troubled gaze.

"I'm going to tear this house apart, brick by brick. I'll find where Theodora hid those pages, even if I have to dig up every inch of earth on the property." Atticus patted the blade at his side, the sheath humming with power. "My family got me into this mess, and they *will* get me out of it. We'll be together, Maddox. Like we should be. Like normal witches, not with me being a freak of nature."

Maddox dove to stop him, but fell, landing face-first on the bed. Her hand dangled over the side as her eyelids drifted closed.

She barely felt Atticus gently squeeze her hand before he left her.

Someone pinched her shoulders and shook Maddox awake. Her first instinct was to throw them off her, but she took a moment to breathe before she lashed out.

It was Rob who hauled Maddox out of bed and forced her to stand. Maddox saw Daphne behind him at the stove, the cauldron that put her to sleep now covered.

Rob shook Maddox's arm lightly. "Maddie, did Atticus make that sleeping draught?"

Even half-awake, Maddox defended him. "Atticus is possessed. He's not in control of himself, not really. He was trying to keep me out of the way. Out of danger."

Daphne waddled over, her face pinched. "Your weird boyfriend is doing something weird in the cemetery."

Rob helped Maddox to the nearest window. "Look."

The entire manor was cast into shadow, dark grey clouds gathering in the sky above them. Electricity cracked, the sheer power in the air sending a shiver down Maddox's spine.

"What is he doing out there?" Rob asked, pressing a palm against the windowpane.

"Atticus is gone." The words were almost impossible to say. "That parasite is in charge now, and it wants him to find every piece of the Tome of the Undying and bring it back together."

"Is he heading to the school?" Daphne gasped.

"Not yet." But he would. After Atticus found the pages Theodora had hidden, Maddox was sure the Academy would be his next destination. "We need to stop him *here*."

Reaching under her bed, Maddox pulled out her luggage. She tore through it, searching for clothing she could move around in. "Rob, let everyone know we need to enact the plan and to meet me in here."

"Got it."

Maddox changed quickly and was braiding her hair when the rest of the household arrived. Giles entered last, cutting through the Abernathys' conversation. "I already tried to speak with Atticus and nobody's home. I stayed out of his way, so he mostly ignored me. Once we start interfering, however, I doubt he'll play nicely."

Maddox revealed, "Atticus said he'll tear this place apart if that's what it takes to find Theodora's part of the tome."

"Atticus *was* digging through her tomb when I approached him," Giles admitted. "The exorcist is watching him now."

"Wait, Maddie, you *spoke* with Atticus?" Diedre questioned. "When was this?"

What a horrifying moment. Maddox stilled, unable to speak, and it was Giles, surprisingly, who saved her. He looked from her disheveled appearance and to the bed's twisted sheets and cocked a single, incredulous brow. He interrupted Deidre's interrogation. "What does it *matter*? Did Atticus say anything else important?" Giles pulled at his clothing. "I'm wearing another man's clothes and shoes right now, and I'd love to move things along—"

Giles suddenly shouted, stumbling away from Daphne. Daphne hugged her stomach, nearly in tears as she stepped away from the pool of water at her feet.

"At least those were another man's shoes I ruined," Daphne huffed.

"Now?!" Rob cursed, pulling at his hair for a moment before running around Daphne in pointless circles.

Deidre halted Rob's spinning with a hand on his elbow. "Rob, *relax*. I've done this a dozen times. Daphne and the baby will be fine. We'll help her to your room."

Dove added imperiously, "Daphne should go to the hospital. It's not safe here. Actually, she *should* have left as soon as the lich showed up."

White roots snaked out of the greenhouse's soil and knotted into a rather foreboding throne. Daphne sank into the seat with a groan. "Fuck off. If I leave, that lich will break free. You *need* my magic."

Colter cut in, "Not *that* badly, Daphne."

"Maddox said Atticus is going to tear the house apart!" Poppy argued.

"Then leave me be and stop him!" Daphne was nearly howling. "And just because my water broke, it doesn't mean—fuck, that *hurts*!"

"She started having what she said were SMALL contractions this morning," Rob revealed.

"Snitch!" Daphne snapped.

Maddox couldn't take any more. "Daphne, *please* listen to Dove. I couldn't bear it if something happened to you because of me."

"Piss off." Daphne reached for Rob's hand and squeezed it until he yelped. "I have *my* job to do, and you have your own. You were the best student in that creepy school, and I have yet to see a *fraction* of your gift. You can't hide it from your family any longer."

The foliage in the greenhouse began to blacken and transform. Dark green vines with finger length thorns sped across the stone floor to curl protectively around Daphne's chair.

Daphne waved Maddox away. "I'm not leaving. If you want to protect me, Maddox, go out there and do it."

CHAPTER 56
WITCH

Giles and Maddox sprinted to the graveyard, her family promising to catch up once they settled Daphne. Maddox ran until Giles caught the back of her shirt and tugged, nearly sending her spinning to the ground.

"Why is the *gate opening*?" Giles yelled, skidding to a halt outside the graveyard's entrance.

Maddox followed Giles's line of sight. Around the corner of the manor, a compact sedan was crawling up the driveway. Gaia's head poked out of the passenger window, and she waved enthusiastically.

"What *day* is it?" Maddox asked, paling.

"Tuesday," Giles answered.

"I think Atticus's coworkers came to check on him," she moaned.

"You're fucking with me." Giles rubbed his face, hiding his sneer for a moment. "You're absolutely fucking with me."

Maddox ran up the drive to Gaia's car while trying to signal with her hands for Gaia to turn around. Gaia did not. Instead, she parked, hopped out of the car, and met Maddox halfway.

Gaia looked serious for once. "Hey, Atticus isn't answering my calls, and he's missed a whole day of classes."

"He's been preoccupied," Maddox lied. "Gaia, he'll get in touch tomorrow, just—"

Angeline appeared next, exiting the passenger seat as she complained about Gaia's driving skills. "I'm not *waiting in the car*, Gaia. It's not dignified. Now, what are we—"

Giles stabbed a finger toward the gate. "As you were cruising past the no trespassing signs, you never stopped to think, hey, maybe that applies to us?

Get the fuck out."

Angeline whipped in Giles's direction, her hair floating as her magic plumed around her. "Watch your tone, Giles Blackwell. It'll be a cold day in hell before I let you talk to me that way."

"Dammit, Professor!" Giles snarled. "I'm trying to—"

Lightning struck again and again and again. Their small part of the world was lit by so many bolts of electricity that no detail, no matter how small, was obscured. Their terrible situation was crystal clear. Maddox turned toward the graveyard and saw Atticus, arms outstretched and his stance wide. The sky directly above him was black and red and thundering. His magic whipped around him, a cyclone of pure, dark power. All beneath them, the earth rumbled and hands burst forth from the ground, sending chunks of dirt and grass flying.

Rain suddenly fell in cold, heavy drops, turning the upturned earth into mud.

The buried Blackwells needed no help to leave their graves. The corpses tore out of the earth while their screams flooded the skies. They watched the birth of a horrific dead army, and while Lochlan, already at the graveyard, managed to send a few crawling back into their graves, there were far too many for his celestial powers to turn.

The Blackwell corpses were in varying states of decay, though all exceedingly well-dressed. And they were *armed*—their swords clipped to their belts, true to necromancer tradition.

Lochlan sprinted away from the edge of the cemetery, catching Maddox by her shoulders. "I *had* to tell them, Maddox. The Commission—they know about Theodora and, if he's still here when they arrive, they'll find out about Atticus, too."

"What in Hades is going on?" Angeline demanded. Gaia asked no questions. She fled to the trunk of her car, popped it open, and removed her sword from within.

"Atticus is raising an army of the dead," Maddox explained. She unsheathed Aegis, who muttered "*It's about time,*" and held the blade out in front of her.

"They won't be the usual shambling corpses. The ones Atticus raises are fast, strong, and a real pain in the ass. They bite, too." Giles pushed on ahead without another word.

Lochlan clasped his hands together. "I can try to keep them away from the house, but it will take all of my attention."

"That's fine. Just do your best," Maddox said. "Daphne's in labor, and she won't leave. Lochlan, if things go south, can you promise me you'll get Daphne out of here?"

"I'm not looking forward to telling a woman what to do with her body, but I'll try," Lochlan returned dryly.

Lochlan would do the right thing, even if he didn't want to. Maddox would just have to focus on doing her part and worry about the aftermath if she failed later.

"We're going to need a more substantial blade here," Maddox warned Aegis. She placed the sword on the ground and stepped back. Her blade answered silently, the metal melting and reforming until it resembled a longsword, rather than a rapier.

"Neat trick," Gaia quipped. "I don't know what's going on here, but if the zombies equal the bad guys, I know enough to help."

The right thing would be to refuse her help and send Gaia back home, where it was safe. Maddox settled for a *thank you*, instead.

Angeline volunteered as well. "I'm too old to run around with sharp objects, but I'll help Dr. Rhodes."

Lochlan nodded, and Angeline followed him to the side of the house. A few mumbled prayers later, and the shambling corpses nearest to the exorcist burst into flame. Angeline dealt with any corpses that slipped through Lochlan's prayer.

"If you're sure about this," Maddox said to Gaia, "then let's go!"

Maddox ran for the cemetery and a second later, Gaia followed. The women caught up with Giles, brandishing their swords as the three of them hit the first wave of the dead.

Hacking through human flesh and bone was a harrowing experience. The sounds were the worst—these servants of Atticus's ranged from recently deceased to a pile of bones barely held together. The smell was not something Maddox would forget soon.

OH, FUCK YEAH!

At least Aegis was having fun.

How many Blackwells were buried on this property? Maddox lost count of how many corpses she hacked through. She and Aegis never rested. Her blade changed shapes depending on the battle they found themselves in. Right now, Aegis swapped form from a one-handed axe and a shield.

The first time Aegis changed into a round, metallic-red shield, Gaia had pouted, yelling across the battlefield, "No fair!"

Gaia hardly needed a shield. She was a master at work, her sword never missing her target. Protecting the exorcist as he kept the corpses from tearing apart the home, Angeline called down her own lightning and blasted the living dead apart with her brutal magic.

The corpses, however, were the least of their worries. With magic splitting the air and chaos ensuing, Theodora tore at her prison, peeling bark from her dying skin. And there was Atticus.

Now that Maddox and his friends were directly interfering with Atticus's plans, he pivoted his attention toward them. Atticus sent a bolt of lightning Maddox's way, which she dodged by throwing herself behind a tombstone. Metal shields were useless against such attacks.

Giles reached his brother before Atticus could throw more spells. Atticus and Giles battled, their swords clashing angrily. Darkness enveloped the brothers, encasing them in a whirling shadow. Black tentacles whipped out from the darkness, sending the corpses flying backward.

But Giles's darkness wasn't enough. The shadows vanished in an instant, revealing Giles lying back on the ground, his sword a few feet away. Atticus loomed before him, tall and with his unnaturally pale hair whipping behind him. His eyes were unseeing, his movements like those of a puppet.

He was going to kill Giles.

But how had Giles failed? Atticus had always claimed Giles was the better swordsman, and after seeing Giles in action, Maddox had to agree. Was Atticus that sociopath's only weakness?

How inconvenient.

Maddox jumped in front of Giles, raising her shield to meet Atticus's blade as he swung downward. She blocked his attack and hurried to drive Atticus back, forcing him away from Giles.

"Giles, stand up and go help Gaia!" Maddox barked, hoping Giles could hear her over the battle's din. "I'll handle Atticus from here!"

There was no need for the frightened tears threatening her vision. Maddox had bested Atticus dozens of times—this would be no different.

But it was. It was heartbreaking. She was the same failure she always was, and the point was driven home *hard* every time her blade connected with Atticus's.

Atticus pushed off her shield, and Maddox stumbled backward as Aegis returned to a rapier shape. Atticus said, eerily dream-like, "I don't understand. I'm doing this all for you, my dear. *Everything* I do is for you."

Maddox chanced a glance backward. Some of the shamblers broke through Lochlan and Angeline's defenses and tore planks, one by one, off the manor.

"I know," Maddox began, lifting her blade to keep some distance between them. "I know what that leech is telling you. It sold me that same hope. But, love, the Commission is coming. You need to call off this spell and leave with me. Take my hand."

Maddox reached for him but kept Aegis ready. "*Please.* We're running out of time."

Aegis shouted a warning too late. Her blade snapped back into a shield, blocking Atticus's downward strike. Atticus's blade only connected with her shield for a moment before Venenum shimmered and returned to its viper form. The snake slithered over her shield before Maddox could swing her arm. The viper reared, eyes glinting red, and struck.

"Paralyze her," Atticus commanded as his viper's fangs sank into Maddox's left shoulder. The venom pulsing through her veins was burning, and it drove Maddox down to her knees.

"She's had enough," he said. Atticus let Venenum crawl up his arm to rest on his shoulders, head raised and ready for another strike should it be ordered.

Maddox bit back a scream and then immediately failed to hold back the next. Her pain ripped her throat into a raw, aching mess. The venom spread quickly, carving a burning trail through her body.

The only thing still going in her favor was that she'd managed to keep Aegis on her arm.

Maddox slunk forward. She could barely wiggle her fingers, let alone stand and face him. "Atticus..." she moaned, grateful she could still speak.

Atticus lowered himself, kneeling in the mud with her. "It's temporary," he promised. "You'll have your grace and strength back soon enough." He lifted a hand, his right, and cupped her face. "The parasite isn't your fault. I don't have a soul—how could I fight against its poison?"

"The...Commission is coming." Maddox shuddered. "They'll destroy you if they see what you've done. We can run away *together.*"

It was as if Atticus didn't even hear her—or the leech wasn't allowing her words to hit home. He placed his other hand on her waist, keeping her upright. Atticus had removed his glove for battle, baring his full, skeletal form for all to see. "I can undo this. I can make us whole. I can—"

Aegis warmed, and Maddox suddenly had a very bad idea.

"Kiss me," she begged, forcing her fingers to move despite the venom. She needed to buy herself some time. Venenum's bite was already wearing off, something she didn't really understand. Snakes could control how much venom they used. Had Venenum deliberately shown her mercy? Could the viper sense its master wasn't himself?

Her request drew Atticus's brows together. "*Now?*"

"Atticus, *please—*"

A single 'please' was enough. Atticus brought her face into his hands, the skeletal tips of his left hand lightly scratching her skin and kissed her. It was a heady, breathtaking kiss, and it distracted Atticus long enough for Aegis to melt down from its shield form and into a long, thin dagger.

With her wound and her fading strength, Maddox had to act NOW. She slid her tongue against Atticus's, his pleased moan a strange vibration, and unhooked a potion from her belt. She unstoppered it and poured the vial's green liquid on Aegis until the blade glittered.

Atticus's kisses paused, and he tried to look down at her hands. Maddox bit down on his bottom lip hard, and then she struck.

As her blade shot forward, her wound suddenly throbbed, the poison in her veins throwing off her thrust. Maddox still made contact, but not exactly where she'd been aiming.

It *shouldn't* have been so easy. Aegis slid into Atticus's chest like butter. It should have been the hardest thing she'd ever done. Failure sank into her stomach. She had struck too close to his heart. *His heart, my heart, it's all the same. If this kills him, I'm sure it will kill me, too.*

Maddox didn't want to know what killing Atticus felt like. The memory of it would live forever in her bones.

Atticus slumped against her, his forehead hitting her shoulder, and Maddox slid Aegis out and sheathed it. Before the sheath silenced Aegis, the blade whispered, *I'm sorry, kid.*

Atticus's hands trembled as they covered his wound, blood spilling between his fingers. He glanced up at her, eyes suddenly clear.

"Oh." Atticus's hands pressed further into his chest. "I see."

"I'm sorry," Maddox whispered, the wind consuming her words.

She caught him as he wavered, each gasp he took a heartbreak, and watched his wound carefully. Atticus caught sight of her shoulder despite his own pain. "You're wounded, too," he realized, his voice trailing off. "It's *poisoned*. I did that, didn't I?"

"You didn't mean to," she countered. "And I broke your finger when I was possessed, remember? We're even now."

Atticus groaned as she hauled him to his feet, one hand still against his chest. If he were fully human, Maddox knew he would be dead by now, and she swallowed that information and the guilt that accompanied it.

"It's okay," he said, the love she'd missed honeying his tone. "It's *okay*. I wanted you safe. If I pay the price, I don't care. Whatever it takes."

"I'm not leaving you behind," Maddox snapped. "Shut up and save your strength." She pulled him along until her destination became clear.

Giles screamed as he fought off two corpses, though the magic puppeteering the beings was fading along with Atticus. Giles demanded, "Get him the fuck away from there! Abernathy, what do you think you're doing?!"

Atticus didn't falter as Maddox led him before his grandmother. The lich's arms had wiggled free, and Theodora pushed down at the roots still ensnaring her legs.

This was it. Maddox had excelled at the theory, but now it was time to see if she truly deserved to be valedictorian.

Maddox released her hold on Atticus, and he dropped into a kneel. She stepped in between Theodora and her love, blocking out the wind, the rain, the battle, and her surely disappointed family.

For the first time since she lost her grandmother, Maddox completely unleashed her magic. Her red smoke whipped around her as she called down her own lightning, sending bolt after bolt into the surrounding earth.

The ground exploded into large chunks, cascading down into a dark void that slowly appeared beneath them. Giles had fought off his attackers and made to intercept them, falling back to avoid running straight into the bottomless pit Maddox was forming around her.

There was so much electricity in the air and running through Maddox's body that her hair lifted.

Atticus caught her pant leg. "Maddie, what are you—"

"We stay together," Maddox vowed, lifting his chin with a finger. "I promised you we'd never be separated again. I *meant* that."

"Don't let me take you down with me," he begged.

"We all go down together. The Commission won't have any of us." Maddox turned to Theodora. The lich had ceased her escape attempts, opting to stare hopelessly into the deepening pit growing around her.

"What are you planning?" Theodora asked, her rasp bordering on panic.

"A more permanent tomb for you—for all of us." Maddox let her emotions run wild, throwing sobs between her words. It was all true, after all. This spell came at a cost, all spells did, but none so high as this one. To form a bottomless grave, the caster had to be willing to fall in themselves.

Her balance wavered. Maddox planted her feet and shouted to Theodora, "I released you. I won't allow such a mistake again."

"You're throwing me down there?!" Theodora shrieked. The Abernathy roots had retreated enough that Theodora could use her magic again, but it was no use. She might have been able to destroy Maddox, but there was no escaping the bottomless pit threatening to swallow them all. They stood uncertainly on a small island in the middle of the darkness Maddox had created.

"Yes, down there. *Forever.*" Maddox watched the lich unravel. A decade trapped in a tomb had already worn on Theodora's psyche. Maddox just hoped it would be enough.

Maddox spun, reaching down to tear open Atticus's shirt. His chest was soaked in blood. Though she'd shrunk Aegis's blade before stabbing him, it didn't look like it had helped.

Did she use enough of the potion? Maddox hauled Atticus upright, pushing him until he was only inches away from Theodora. He fought it, of course, but Maddox trapped his arms behind his back and shoved.

His wound suddenly split open even further. Atticus threw his head back and screamed while Maddox kept him standing.

Dammit, that parasite had grown so much. Feeding off Atticus's power had nearly tripled the parasitoid's size. Now the grotesque, beetle-like insect was the size of a bird. Its pincers dug and tore until its body hung halfway from Atticus's chest.

Seeing his pain like that would live on in her head forever.

She used one arm to hold up Atticus and the other Maddox used to unsheathe his sword. Venenum slid through its former master easily, tearing open Theodora's dress and her stomach. The rotted organs that tumbled out made room for the parasite as it jumped, propelled forward on blue and green wings like stained glass, from Atticus's chest and into the lich's stomach.

"Like I said," Maddox shouted, watching the horrific takeover with wide eyes, "you're just as incomplete as the rest of us. But you've got your wish, Theodora. Now you'll never be alone."

The lich's bony hands pushed and dug at the beetle scurrying into her stomach, but it was no use. She cursed, flinging hexes until, all at once, Theodora fell forward, bending at the waist, her head and arms dangling to the ground.

When the lich looked up, Maddox knew what was in charge now.

Their small, teetering island wavered. Maddox reached for Atticus, certain they were about to fall to their death. If they were to fall forever, Maddox wouldn't let Atticus spend that deathless eternity alone. She'd hold him until her muscles could bear it no longer.

Instead, something snake-like wrapped around her waist and yanked Maddox across the gap to drop her back onto solid ground. One of the Abernathy roots had snatched her up and tossed her to safety. Maddox skidded across the grass, her slide eventually halted by a rather uncomfortable tombstone.

A second later, Atticus was thrown, too. He landed silently and curled up on his side.

Maddox crawled to him, turning him to lie on his back. What could a lich survive? The wound she'd caused was now larger and less clean. His breath was shallow and growing fainter. Her adrenaline spread the venom throughout her body, muddying her vision.

Atticus spoke, and Maddox squinted, trying to read his lips. "What?" she prompted.

His voice raised a notch. "I said, did you really make a bottomless grave?"

Maddox fought to stay awake. The venom and the power she'd unleashed threatened to put her to sleep. The black pit called to her, ordering her to throw herself to its depths. "I found the spell in the forbidden section of the Academy's library."

"Of course you did." Atticus's quiet laughter seemed to exhaust him.

Maddox tucked herself next to him, resting her head against his shoulder. "I'm so sorry. I think I killed you, Atticus."

CHAPTER 57
WARLOCK

The sky faded from the dark red storm Atticus had summoned to a soft grey-blue. The light hurt his eyes. He wished he'd been in the right state of mind to remember his glasses.

Maddox mourned him already, her tears mixing with the blood that already stained his white shirt. He didn't try to convince her he didn't need her tears. Everything was okay. Theodora was falling, a fate that would never end, and she'd gotten what she wanted. What she had hurt him for.

She wasn't alone.

And he would get to rest. It had been his greatest fear—immortality. The worst part of becoming such a terrible thing had been the threat of living forever. Feeling pain, feeling his end coming...it was a fucking godsend.

Atticus would tell Maddox it was okay. She'd never believe him, but he'd leave her with only gratitude and love.

"MOTHERFUCKER, NEXT TIME I WANT AN EPIDURAL!"

Maddox's sobbing stuttered as she raised her head, searching for her foul-mouthed sister. Atticus didn't see Daphne until she was hovering directly over him, clearly in labor, with her husband at her heels and begging for forgiveness.

Daphne was ethereal. Though she was holding her stomach and cursing like a sailor, Daphne shone with a soft, green light. Her golden hair was shimmering and growing before their eyes, now ending at her waist.

Was Daphne the one who had saved Atticus and Maddox from falling into the pit? Her aura of power burned his skin.

Daphne sucked in a breath and released a fresh stream of swears—several of which Atticus had never even heard of. With Rob's help, Daphne slowly and carefully sat down before them.

"Give me your fucking hands," she ordered, snatching Atticus's right hand when he hesitated. With Atticus on her left and Maddox on her right, Daphne let her power go. Without Theodora to worry about containing, Daphne's magic seemed limitless.

Atticus hadn't expected it to *hurt*. The skin around his wound stretched until it nearly closed, and Daphne's green magic seared it shut. It left a long, red scar too close to his heart for comfort.

"It's going to get much, much worse," Daphne promised, and it took Atticus a moment to realize she wasn't talking about her own situation.

Maddox's bite healed after his sword's black poison poured out of her gash. What Daphne commanded, her magic made so.

Daphne's will turned back to him, this time as black, thorny vines that encased his body. Her hand squeezed his like a vise.

This time, her magic didn't feel like a warm spring day. It was rebirth, the battle the earth faced rebuilding after a forest fire. His bones ached. *Nothing* brought him relief. Neither screams nor tears made any difference.

His left eye burned, his head throbbed relentlessly.

But though it killed him, Atticus felt, above all else, *alive*.

Daphne's thorny vines retreated when it was over. Atticus struggled to sit up, fighting to fill his lungs.

"Atticus," Maddox cried. "She *healed* you! All of you! Your eye is clear, and your complexion, and your crown..."

As Atticus lifted his left hand in front of him and found it unchanged, Daphne explained, "There wasn't anything left of the arm to *heal*. Even like this, I can't—Rob, after our daughter is born, REMIND ME TO NEVER LET YOU TOUCH ME AGAIN."

Rob settled himself between Daphne's legs. He nodded, eyes on his stopwatch as he timed her contractions. "Anything you want, sweetie."

Maddox twisted her belt, pulling out another vial Atticus hadn't seen in years. Maddox bit off the stopper and released his soul. It hovered, dreamlike and silver, before slowly drifting over to him. Daphne's green magic appeared behind it, guiding it along until it vanished into his chest.

Atticus waited for it to reject him, for it to exit his body again and this time disappear forever.

It settled somewhere by his stomach and *stayed*.

If he didn't count the fact Daphne was crushing his good hand, Atticus hadn't felt this alive in years. Atticus brushed a hand over the top of his hair.

The bone spikes that crowned his head were gone.

Around them, the corpses he'd raised had stopped fighting. Atticus watched them shamble off to their perspective graves, climbing inside or digging themselves a better entrance back into their casket.

Giles limped over, stopping a few feet away as though Daphne's condition was contagious. "That monster isn't going to climb out of *that*, is it?" He indicated the void behind them as Lochlan inspected it.

"It's bottomless—Daphne, why are you Abernathy women so damned *strong?*" Atticus attempted to yank his hand free from her. "Thank you for performing a miracle, but, and no offense, I don't want to be a part of this."

Daphne howled and only crushed his hand harder.

Atticus appealed to her husband. "Robert, could you—"

Rob had absolutely no sympathy for Atticus. "Sorry, bro. Your plight means nothing to me. I have to catch the baby, and believe me, you don't want to trade places."

"WHAT DOES *THAT* MEAN?" Daphne sniped. "And Atticus, I just performed a godsdamned *miracle* on you, and now I'm having my firstborn in a *cemetery*. I'd like a little more appreciation from you, asshole!"

Wincing, Atticus looked to Maddox next, but she was shaking. Was it from Venenum's poison? No, the black streams of venom spidering from her wound had vanished, thanks to Daphne.

Atticus reached for Maddox, wincing as the only hand he had available was still only bone and magic. She accepted him, anyway.

Without pause, Maddox offered him a quick kiss on the knuckles of the ruined hand she held.

"Oh, gods," Daphne moaned. "We didn't decide on a name!"

Rob blinked slowly, casting his gaze about the graveyard. "Uh, what about Dahlia?"

"No, that's too..." Daphne chewed her lip, considering. "Actually, I like that. Baby Dahlia."

Atticus nearly mentioned he'd had a long-deceased Aunt Dahlia but caught himself. He looked behind Daphne, noticing the name on the tombstone behind her. Atticus glanced at Rob, who now shook his head and mouthed, "*Don't say a damn word.*"

Like Atticus would risk pissing off Daphne with his good hand in her grip.

"Time to push!" Rob announced, sounding much more confident than he looked.

The rest of the Abernathys appeared and crowded behind Daphne's head. Diedre knelt down next to Rob while the rest of the family stayed a few feet away and cheered Daphne on.

Atticus thought his hand would break under Daphne's stress. He shut his eyes once the pushing started and still kept them closed a long time after he heard the shrill cry of both mother and child.

Both of his hands were suddenly freed, and Atticus backed up until he had enough room to stand. He let the Abernathys coo over the mewing newborn, stumbling over to the still-open pit. He placed a heavy hand on Giles's shoulder, needing the physical support more than anything.

"I hoped I'd be able to see her falling." Giles stared into the darkness, his grip on his sword tight. "Do you think it's truly bottomless?"

Atticus had no doubts. "If anyone could do it, it would be Maddox."

"It better be. I won't sleep otherwise." Giles spared him a quick glance. "You look good. Well, better. Wouldn't kill you to eat some carbs occasionally. Took me ten minutes to fit into your pants."

"Why are you wearing *my* pants?"

"I'm not fighting the living dead in *my* clothes."

Atticus stepped away from Giles and from the edge of the pit. He thought, though it may have been his imagination, if he leaned over the grave, he could almost hear Theodora scream.

Lochlan didn't wait for permission. The exorcist threw what Atticus could only assume was holy water into his face.

Atticus ran his right hand down his face, shedding water as he did so. "What...the...hell...was *that* for?"

Lochlan cocked his head. "Just checking. I can't believe I didn't realize you were undead before. I just thought you were strange."

"How kind of you to say. Now, stop inspecting me." Atticus shoved Lochlan's hands away. "You saw what Daphne did for me."

"And yet a reminder of it remains," Lochlan said, pointing to the bones of his left hand.

"There wasn't anything left to heal," Atticus replied, unable to keep his disappointment hidden.

Lochlan softened his tone. "The Commission will be here any minute. We need to disguise that hand before they arrive."

"Let me see." Dove broke away from the rest of the Abernathys, confidently butting into their conversation. As she snatched up Atticus's "bad" hand and examined it, she decided, "Yes, I can do something about this. It'll be temporary, but I can make you a proper prosthetic when I'm back home."

"A proper prosthetic?" Atticus echoed.

"Yes," Lochlan agreed. "You'll need it if you want to re-enter society."

The two of them and their belief that Atticus could simply return to his previous life was baffling. Atticus considered the idea. A prosthetic would be a fine solution. He'd never have to brew his *Chameleon* again, not to mention he was growing more and more tolerant of the potion. Eventually, it would have ceased to conceal his undead features.

Atticus questioned, "But the *Commission*... Lochlan, didn't you tell them what I am? Was?"

Lochlan adjusted his collar, a shameful blush coloring his pale cheeks. "They know about *Theodora*, and I'm certain they'll spend quite a bit of time examining her new grave. But you? I didn't tell them about you. Other than the possession, I mean."

"Why?" Atticus couldn't help but question his good luck.

"How little you must think of me." Lochlan laughed dryly. "I know who I work for. I know the good the Commission can do, but I know the bad far more intimately."

What did Atticus *really* know about the exorcist? Maybe not enough, he realized. Atticus added, "You're putting your reputation at risk if you do this for me. Omitting information like this—"

Lochlan guided Atticus away from the others. "I can tell you this since I have so much leverage over you. I *hate* the Commission."

Atticus had always thought Lochlan had a rather overenthusiastic approach to exploring the darker arts, particularly for a man of the cloth. But he hadn't expected *this* response. "You *hate* them?"

"The Asylum is only one of many horrors the Commission orchestrates. This—" Lochlan tapped on the white cloth on his collar. "—is necessary if I want to see my father. He's been held in the Asylum since I was young, and he's never getting out. This position gives me unlimited access to him. Otherwise, I'd never get to see him."

That only made Atticus feel worse. "That's even *more* of a reason not to lie to them about me!"

"Do yourself a favor," Lochlan insisted. "Shut up, but thank me first."

Atticus stuttered through a few responses, before settling with, "*Thank you*, Lochlan. Truly. I don't know how I could ever pay you back for this."

"I'll cash in on what you owe me eventually, so don't worry about it."

"Well, I *wasn't* worried before you said that." Atticus held out his arms. "Do I hug you now?"

"Don't be ridiculous."

Atticus ignored him, squeezing the man around his shoulders. Lochlan suffered the embrace for a full minute before he pried Atticus off of him.

"Ugh. Enough. Go inside and take care of that hand." Lochlan pushed Atticus toward the house, where Dove was waiting impatiently outside the back door.

Atticus did as he was told, but paused outside the doorway, staring back at the graveyard and the mess it had become.

Giles and Gaia had broken out a few shovels from the toolshed and were helping the remaining dead back into their graves. Angeline rested against a tall tombstone, bossing the younger folk around. Lochlan circled the bottomless grave, his cell phone a foot from his ear as someone yelled at him about proper procedure.

The Abernathys crowded around Daphne. Colter tried to pass the baby to Maddox, who protested and claimed she was too covered in dead-people juices to hold her.

Colter gave her no choice, nestling the baby in Maddox's arms and backing away. With healing gifts like what Daphne possessed, the Abernathys didn't seem to worry about germs.

Atticus lowered his eyes, a heavy yearning burning his chest. It was an odd feeling, looking at Maddox like that. Flustered, exhausted, and uncertainly cradling a baby while the mother rested. It was not something Atticus thought he could ever give her, but maybe, after what Daphne had done for him...

His melancholy musings were cut short as Dove yanked Atticus inside the house as sirens pierced the air.

CHAPTER 58
WITCH

The main sitting room of the Blackwell estate swarmed with Commission agents. Some used strange-looking devices to sweep the house, sporting large headphones and waving around sensors from wall to wall. Atticus sat in the midst of it all, with wires and electrodes stuck to his temples as an unfamiliar agent interrogated him. The Commission's people examined Atticus thoroughly, though they passed over his heavily bandaged left arm after the warlock pretended it pained him to be touched. Maddox watched the Commission work on Atticus, her hands twisted together until it was over. The agent finally moved on, returning to berating Lochlan and his lack of control of the situation.

Maddox felt for the exorcist. Her own interview had been deeply unpleasant—Lochlan's must have been downright brutal. None of this would look good on his record. He'd failed to notice Maddox's initial moment of possession, didn't exorcize the parasite (though it truly wasn't his fault), and nearly let a lich loose upon the world.

And they didn't even know about all the lying he'd done and was still doing.

Lochlan took it passively, possessing the appropriate amount of chagrin for his situation. Maddox went to him the moment Lochlan was free.

"Are you okay?" she worried. "Did they fire you?"

He was too somber to laugh, but Lochlan awarded her a half-smile. "They can't really fire an exorcist. They can only control whether I continue working for the Commission or if I go back to the Church." He shrugged. "To answer your question, the Commission still wishes to keep me. The Catholic Church doesn't have enough exorcists as it is. It may be a year before they give the government another."

Maddox wanted to cry with relief. "Thank Hades."

"They have, however, assigned me...*a partner*. I'm no longer allowed to work alone." Lochlan pulled a face, and Maddox might have thought he would have preferred losing his job to having to work with someone. "Anyway," Lochlan continued, "stop using me as an excuse and speak to Atticus before he hexes me. The look he's giving me over your shoulder is downright villainous."

"I will," Maddox promised, though the mere thought of approaching Atticus now had her stomach in knots. "Could you do me one more favor? Gaia and Angeline are still being interviewed. The Commission is having a hard time believing they really had no idea what was going on before they jumped in to help fight an undead army."

"Of course."

Maddox turned around, keeping her eyes on her feet as she crossed the carpet to stop in front of Atticus's seat. The points of their shoes were nearly touching. The rest of the Abernathys, thankfully, were at the hospital with Daphne. Good. Maddox didn't need more witnesses to her awkwardness.

Just look at him. Give him something.

Atticus quickly stood, the motion almost throwing her off balance. He gripped her elbow, his bandaged fingers rough on her skin, and dragged her inside his study. His magic brushed against the door, locking them away from everyone else.

"Look at me," he ordered, waiting only a moment longer before cupping her face in his hands. "*Please, just fucking look at me.*"

Maddox raised her chin, though her bottom lip quivered as she fought the emotions welling up from her heart. "I almost *killed* you. If my family hadn't been here, if Daphne wasn't in labor, she wouldn't have had enough power to save you. In the end, I couldn't help you at all."

"That's what your family does," Atticus countered. "*They help each other.* It doesn't make your effort worth any less."

Your power is different, not less. Atticus had said that to her before. Maddox wanted to believe it. She wanted to forget what it was like to be in his arms and feel his life slipping away and know there was nothing she could do to stop it.

"My strike should have been surer," she argued. "If you weren't half-immortal or half-undead or whatever, you wouldn't have survived."

"But I did survive. I'm right here, and you can't even look at me." Atticus took her hand and settled it on his chest. "My life was irreparable before I met you. If you hadn't befriended a stranger, one who'd given up on *everything*—"

"Don't pretend like I'm some perfect—"

"Maybe you *aren't* perfect," Atticus snarled. "But I'm not grading your performance. I don't care if you're perfect because you are *everything* to me. You're my vengeful fucking goddess." He hooked a finger in her belt, pulling her along to his desk. After clearing the surface, sending books and ink everywhere, Atticus lifted her by her waist and dropped her on top of the desk.

It was clear what Atticus wanted. Maddox watched the door, nervously fidgeting with her hair. "Atticus, there's so many people right on the other side of us. We can't—"

"Then do your best to be quiet," he snapped. "You can't perform such terrifying, spiteful magic and not expect me to want you."

His words were so sure, but his breath grew ragged as Atticus waited for her to encourage him.

Maddox knew what was wrong with her—what was wrong with her *at the moment*. She was panicking. It was way after the fact, but Maddox was fairly certain of it. She wanted to curl up in her bed, stuff her face in her pillow, and scream until she stopped feeling. But they'd just been through so much, and Atticus needed reassurance. After some self-reflection, Maddox knew she wanted it, too.

Maddox copied his earlier move, pulling Atticus forward by his belt. Instantly, his hands were in her hair, lightly twisting as they kissed. Her fear wore away, soothed by his ferocity.

He broke away to fumble with her clothes. "Never tell me you didn't do enough for me again. My dear, you *avenged* me. You conjured a fate worse than death."

Once she was undressed, Atticus switched from complimenting her magic to lavishing her body with sweet words Maddox couldn't even focus on.

Most of his clothes remained on. Atticus pressed himself against her waiting for Maddox to guide him further. She made him enter her slowly so she could savor the strange push-pull of pleasure and pain.

They felt so damned good together.

"I couldn't have done it," she whispered. "I thought that in the end, I could do whatever was best for you, but when I stabbed you..."

"Hey," Atticus murmured, freezing and resting a hand on her hip. "Do you need to take a break?"

"Don't move away," she begged, locking her legs around him. "I just wanted you to know that I couldn't have done it. Killed you. Even if I needed to do it to save myself."

"That's okay. We don't need to worry about that anymore." Atticus moved his hands to grip the edges of the desk. "Just be with me."

She wanted that, an end to her anxious hyper-focusing. "Then I want you faster, harder. I don't want to feel anything but you."

His eyes brightened. "I wouldn't give you anything less."

They weren't very discreet. Maddox muffled her cries by biting on a knuckle, though anyone passing close by would have heard the heavy desk sliding across the floor.

Surely, there was a spell that could help, but Maddox couldn't form a single coherent thought.

Atticus slowed his movements once her cries quieted. "Was that enough?" he asked, giving her hips a brutal squeeze. "Or are you still convinced *you* didn't save me?"

Maddox protested, "I didn't—"

"How can I convince you to see this *my* way?" Atticus questioned. "Do I need to fuck this out of you?" He pulled away, separating them.

Maddox instantly missed their closeness. Her hands chased after his retreat. Atticus gripped her hands and tugged her forward, pulling her right off the desk.

Her feet touched down only for a moment. Atticus turned her around and gently pressed down on her back until Maddox understood what he hinted at.

As Maddox settled herself to rest her upper body on top of the desk, Atticus asked, "Do you *want* me to convince you?"

"*Yes.*" It was embarrassing how quickly her answer came.

Atticus kicked her feet into a wider stance. He reunited them and gave her a moment to adjust to the new position. This time he moved tortuously slow.

"Faster—"

"No." Atticus resumed his leisurely pace. "Not until you understand that you're the one who saved me. Not today, but years ago." His hand threaded into her hair, pulling on it until Maddox looked back at him over her shoulder.

His longing was written all over his face and sparkled in his eyes. "When you befriended a broken boy who was determined to lock himself away forever, *that's* when you saved me."

Her heavy tears hit the desk. Maddox responded the only way she could. "I love you."

Atticus's relief relaxed his brow. "I know. If I ever need proof of it, I can look at the bottomless pit in my backyard."

Maddox laughed and cried again, exhausted but happy to be so loved. Atticus finally relented, taking on a brutal speed that she begged for. His fingers dug painfully into her hips as they worked toward each other's bliss until they came together.

Together. She wanted to do *everything* together. Maddox worried she'd become the clingiest partner ever until she realized Atticus would surely be twice as bad.

After, Atticus dressed and lifted Maddox in his arms. He carried her to a narrow bookcase where he directed her, "Grab the top of the Edgar Allen Poe collection and tilt it forward."

Maddox complied, rolling her eyes as the bookcase slid to the side, revealing a hidden and grandiose bathroom.

"I see how you hid from us so easily," Maddox muttered, frowning. Typical Blackwell move. Even their architecture was over the top.

Atticus smiled softly, setting her naked body down beside a claw-footed tub that took up most of the bathroom. He turned on the tap and helped her step inside.

"I'll get us some fresh clothes," he promised, ducking out the door.

Atticus returned quickly, moving to set their clothes by the sink and blinking at the fluffy feline curled up in the bowl. "How the hell did Jinx get in here?"

"No idea." Maddox laughed, sinking in the bath until her chin touched the water. "I closed my eyes for a second and suddenly there she was."

"Sneaky, little trash cat," Atticus said, shaking his head. He scratched the back of his head. "Venenum is hiding under my bed and won't come out. I think he feels bad about biting you."

Maddox pitied the vicious little thing. "Tell Venenum I forgive him. Actually, I think he went easy on me."

"I should have known if I let an Abernathy into my home, it would fill with animals," Atticus grumped. "There's feathers and cat hair everywhere."

Maddox snorted. She knew Atticus secretly liked to see the Blackwell manor filled with people and animals, as much as he tried to convince everyone otherwise. She couldn't imagine how lonely it must have been, living in the empty, echoing house by himself. Her own life was always filled with noise and too many bodies in too small a space.

Well, she wouldn't let him isolate himself again. Not that her family would give him a choice. Atticus might not be ready for an Abernathy level of smothering.

Atticus knelt at the end of the tub, unhooking a handheld spout that he used to rinse her hair. As Atticus worked in shampoo, Maddox protested, "I thought we were bathing together!" The intimacy of someone washing her hair made her blush harder than their earlier activity.

"We will. After I wash out any remaining bits of my desecrated ancestors." He gently touched her chin to catch her eye. "It's important to me that I take care of you after being not so gentle with your body."

Atticus certainly wasn't *shy*. Maddox allowed him to work and shivered as he drained the tub and refilled it. As she sank back into the hot water, Maddox wanted to relax but couldn't forget about the Commission agents still on the property. While Lochlan had convinced them that Theodora was only awoken for her expertise on the Tomb of the Undying, and no one had realized what she was until it was too late, Maddox had the feeling the government hadn't fully bought it.

She pondered, "Should we be out there with everyone else?"

"While they tear apart my house?" Atticus huffed. "They can do that without me. It's better if they deal with Giles, anyway. They won't get anything useful out of him, and his attitude might make them leave sooner."

Perhaps he was right. Atticus nudged her forward and slid into the tub behind her back. While he adjusted, Maddox updated him on Daphne's condition and how long the hospital wished to keep her and the baby.

"But everyone's healthy?"

Maddox nodded and leaned back against him. She felt him sigh and mutter, "*Thank Hades.*"

"I know," she agreed. "It's hard to believe everything turned out as well as it possibly could have."

"It's even harder for me," he confessed. "I feared I'd live forever as a soulless—"

"You did pretty well on your own," Maddox interrupted.

"I could reason my way through most moral situations. Though I fear I failed when it really mattered." His arms wrapped around her, pulling her close. "I'm so sorry I lied to you."

"*You* have an excuse. I drew my sword on you and wouldn't let you leave me."

"Well, that was quite flattering, actually. I forgive you."

Maddox whispered her fear. "Do you think we can move past what we've done to each other?"

"I don't want to even think about the alternative," Atticus swore. He was silent for a long time. "Move in with me."

Maddox nearly slipped further underwater, but Atticus tightened his hold on her. "*What?* Isn't that a big step?"

"You threatened to stab me if I tried to leave you. I think moving in together is the next logical step."

Well, that made the offer much less romantic. Maddox pretended to mull it over, even though her heart was screaming her answer. "My family's going to be shocked."

"I don't think so," Atticus said, tucking his chin in the crook of her neck. "Colter wasn't surprised when we first got together. He said you used to talk about me *all the time*. You aren't as subtle as you think."

Her grandfather needed to mind his own business for once. "I only talked about you that much because you were so aggravating!"

"I plan to become even more so."

Atticus made good on his vow immediately, showering her neck with kisses and nips until Maddox promised anything he wanted if she could have a moment of peace.

EPILOGUE
WARLOCK

Whoever said farm life was a quiet one was an idiot.

Everywhere Atticus went, bugs flew against his ear, buzzing and biting and making him relive those horrific moments of possession. The animals were loud, the tractors were loud, and the Abernathys themselves were the worst noisemakers of all.

"Try to keep up!" Colter barked, walking ahead down the field of lavender they inspected. Colter's magic trailed behind him and rejuvenated any plants that were in need of extra help. Atticus's magic followed Colter's, strangling and decimating any weeds that threatened the crop.

Some summer vacation this was. Atticus doubled his speed, noting on his clipboard which section they were inspecting and Colter's proposed plan for it. Hades, it was *hot*. Washington wasn't supposed to be so sunny, he thought gloomily. If Maddox hadn't forbidden it already, Atticus would have stood in line with the sheep and allowed his head to be shorn.

Venenum's presence didn't help Atticus's body temperature. The snake curled around his neck like a scarf and happily drank in the sunlight Atticus so despised.

When they reached the end of today's plot, Atticus slid the clipboard into his bag and pulled out his water bottle. As he chugged half its contents, Colter crossed his arms. Colter lectured him, "You need to wear a hat. It's hot enough out here, and that prosthetic can't be comfortable."

"I'm not a hat person," Atticus argued. He returned his bottle to his bag and rolled his sleeves. The silver prosthetic on his left arm was Dove's second iteration. Since he could still use the bones of his left arm with a small amount of magic, the prosthetic was mostly cosmetic. She'd offered to match his skin tone, but since the Abernathys dragged him into the sun so often, Atticus knew that would always be a moving target. Anyway, a silver prosthetic impressed the students. Atticus had convinced them that the new head librarian had chopped off his arm with her feyrie sword.

Maddox had not been amused.

Colter thought Atticus's excuse was bullshit, which it was. "You're an Abernathy. That makes you a 'quit being an idiot and do what you need to do' person."

Atticus blinked. That was the first time Colter had used his new last name.

Colter cringed. "Don't get sappy on me. You still can't hold a flashlight still for shit."

Atticus turned in his paperwork to Diedre and walked quickly, fighting the urge to run, to the farm's beehives.

Maddox was finishing up her own chores and slid out of her beekeeper suit. She sidled up to him when she noticed his impatient stance and tucked her arm into his.

"You've survived another day," she teased him.

"When you said you wanted to visit your family every summer, you didn't mention hard labor would be involved."

"It's good for you." Maddox jumped up to steal a quick kiss as they walked.

Atticus couldn't hold back his good and shocking news any longer. "Colter called me an *Abernathy* today."

"You know," Maddox said, turning shy, "when Grandad told you all the men who marry into our family take on our last name, he was kidding."

A bee flew into her hair and Maddox froze. After the parasite, insects bothered her. Atticus used his left hand to gently remove the bee.

They both watched it fly away, heading back to the hive. Maddox pressed closer to Atticus's body, possibly unaware she was even doing so.

"I know Colter was teasing me." Atticus shrugged, pressing a harsh kiss on Maddox's head to replace the phantom presence of the bee. "I really wanted to be a part of your family. It's nice they're starting to feel that way, too."

"If *Grandad* called you an Abernathy, everyone feels that way already," Maddox assured him.

"Now if only the little ones would stop calling me *Uncle Zombie*," Atticus pouted. Maddox's laughter only made him double down. "It's not even accurate. I was never a zombie! I'd never let *our* child be so disrespectful!"

They stopped walking.

"You...want a baby?" Maddox stared up at him like he was an alien. "You know kids are always dirty, loud, and covered in jam, right?"

He pointed out the gaggle of Abernathy children who were currently carrying Jinx around the backyard as if she were a queen. "If I didn't know that before, I definitely know it now."

Maddox scrunched her nose. "Is *that* why you asked my aunts about fertility charms? Now, whenever they see me, they giggle and whisper to each other!"

"I was going to speak with you first," he defended himself. "I was simply curious. With my past condition, I feared it may not be possible."

Atticus's secret wish had surprised him for a long time. He'd spent years alone in a manor built to house multiple generations of family. He thought he liked the solitude until Maddox had filled their home with her laughter and stray animals. That was what he wanted forever. A home full of life and love.

"I see." Maddox resumed walking. "Okay."

Atticus raced after her. "Okay to *what?*"

"To a baby. But I have some conditions." Maddox counted off on her fingers as she spoke. "One, I want to wait quite a few years. Two, I want to keep working."

"I accept!" Hades, why was his voice suddenly so loud? "I can stay home with the baby."

"I wouldn't sound so enthusiastic. I've babysat for *years.* It's not easy." Maddox's words were sharp, but she softened quickly. "And three, I want us to go on an expedition of our own next summer. I'm still a little peeved you explored the Paris Catacombs without me."

That one took a little longer to think over. "As long as we're not hunting down any more cursed books, I accept that term as well."

She held out her hand to seal their deal. "Then it's settled, though I'm not sure how I feel about *Giles* being an uncle."

"I'm sure he's even less pleased with the thought." Atticus swiped her hand away, grabbing her waist and squeezing her in a tight embrace instead. "I love you."

"And I love you," she whispered back, holding him just as fiercely. She pulled away to give him her shy smile.

Atticus took her hand and resumed their walk to the main farmhouse. "Now, my dear, let's see if our family will let me rescue dinner."

Atticus stirred a sauce one-handed while the other cradled a squirming toddler. The second time the toddler's foot threatened to dip into the sauce, he yelled, "Whose baby is this?!"

Colter sauntered into the kitchen, grabbing a hot roll from the pan and tearing into it. He squinted at his great-grandchild. "I have no idea who that baby is."

Atticus passed the toddler to Colter. "Take her. I need to fight Aunt Olive on the right seasoning for her summer squash pasta."

"Oh no, you don't!" Aunt Olive swatted at Atticus with a wooden spoon. "Mind your own dish!"

By the time the Abernathys all sat down for dinner, the sun had fully set. Atticus had a middle seat at the table with Maddox on his right. On his left was a new Abernathy every night, all fighting to get to know him.

Daphne stuffed pasta into her mouth at hyper-speed while Rob juggled their infant. Colter waved at her to get her attention.

"Daphne!" Colter snapped and silenced the chatting table. "Daphne, I have an important announcement regarding you."

Daphne stopped shoveling in food, letting her fork drop with a clink. "Yes?" she asked, bewildered.

"Rob, you should pay attention, too," Colter demanded.

Rob nodded, passing baby Dahlia over the table to Atticus. Atticus held the child, tension rippling through his arms, but he was slowly becoming more comfortable with infants. Dahlia cooed and reached for his beard, yanking on it mercilessly. Atticus let her. After all, it was partially thanks to Dahlia that he was no longer undead. It was why she was currently the only Abernathy with a trust fund.

Colter stood, holding a hand out to Daphne. "We had a busy year. Maddox has a new job, and a new husband, but the journey there wasn't easy. Mostly because the newest Mr. Abernathy is hard-headed."

Diedre scoffed, "*All* the Mr. Abernathys are hard-headed!"

Colter ignored her. "Daphne, you performed some of the strongest magic I've ever seen. And it wasn't all thanks to little Dahlia over there."

The baby squirmed in Atticus's arms while Colter continued. "Daphne, I want you to be the next head of our coven. It's time for another Matriarch to lead the Abernathys."

Daphne closed her eyes for a long time. When they flickered open, she was *pissed*. "Are you out of your mind? I just had a baby! Like I don't have enough things to do!"

Colter lowered the glass he'd just raised in Daphne's honor. "Uh, that was...unexpected."

"*Really?*" Daphne returned to eating as if Colter's grand gesture was nothing but an inconvenience. "Ask me again in twenty years, Grandad. Until then, sorry, but you're not retiring any time soon."

Colter slowly sat back down, confusion flitting across his face. He grumbled, "You'd think being electrocuted would buy me some sympathy around here!"

"Nope!" Daphne quipped.

A few more awkward seconds of silence passed before the table erupted with laughter.

Only Maddox seemed as eager as Colter for Daphne's appointment as the new Matriarch. She squeezed Atticus's hand underneath the table, her grin impossibly wide.

Atticus knew what fueled her excitement. When Daphne became the new

Matriarch, her life would be extended through her family's magic. Maddox would still have a sister to turn to after she outlived the rest.

The table resumed eating and bickering, and, as always, Atticus was included. Tonight, Aunt Olive sat next to Atticus, but she had simmered down from their earlier spat in the kitchen. After Atticus passed Dahlia back to Rob, Aunt Olive looped necklaces with fertility charms strung through them over Atticus's head until he looked like someone who had *a lot* of fun at Mardi Gras.

Maddox turned ten shades of red as she watched it happen. "How many babies do you think we're trying to have?!" she shrieked. "Take some of those off him!"

Atticus laughed, lifting Maddox's hand from underneath the table to kiss her knuckles.

Maddox scowled at the table. "Rami is visiting next week! Can we be less embarrassing, *please?*"

"Oh, I want my dad to get the full Abernathy experience," Atticus joked. "No family secrets."

Maddox understood he was being gravely serious, despite his light tone. "No family secrets," she grumbled.

Maddox leaned against Atticus's shoulder as she picked at her food. With her loud family, she was able to discreetly whisper to him, "I've won it *all* this time. I've won *you.* How lucky our future child will be."

There was no part of Atticus that cared to argue. If Maddox wished to view him as a prize, he was happy to let her do so.

"Yes, my dear. How lucky we all are."

CAST OF CHARACTERS

Maddox Abernathy: The only necromancer in the Abernathy coven of green witches, Maddox has spent the past five years on her family farm recovering from academic burnout. Demisexual, neurodivergent, and embarrassed to admit she missed Atticus Blackwell.

Atticus Blackwell: Necromancer and professor of potion-making at the American Academy of the Dead. He was friends with Maddox before they became academic rivals. Dramatic, secretive, and forced to admit he missed Maddox Abernathy.

Elden and Avalon Cavanaugh: The married feyrie couple are both redcaps and the Abernathys' only neighbors. They run a magical inn together. Elden grew up alongside the Abernathys.

Daphne Abernathy: Maddox's favorite sister and a very powerful and very pregnant green witch.

Angeline Boleyn: A professor at the American Academy of the Dead. She taught Maddox and Atticus curse-breaking.

Colter Abernathy: The patriarch of the Abernathy coven and blessed with long life. Maddox's grandfather has a fantastic sense of humor when he's not in a grumpy mood.

Deidre Abernathy: Maddox's mother and a green witch.

Dr. Lochlan Rhodes: A skilled psychologist and exorcist, Lochlan is a quiet man who's just strange enough to get along with Maddox and Atticus. Allergic to chocolate. Loves running.

Gaia Proctor: A former student of the Academy of the Dead that dropped out to be homeschooled due to bullying. Gaia is now a professor at the Academy and a skilled duelist.

Rob Abernathy: Daphne's doting husband. Married into the Abernathy coven and took his wife's last name.

Dove, Amber, and Poppy Abernathy: The Abernathy triplets are all very loud and very blonde. They are the oldest siblings in Maddox's family.

Giles Blackwell: Atticus's elder brother. Not nice. He has layers, but underneath each layer is an asshole, except for the layer that reluctantly cares for his little brother.

Theodora Blackwell: Atticus's grandmother. She lived a too-long life as a tomb raider, explorer, and had a stint as the Academy of the Dead's master librarian.

Cynthia Blackwell: Mother of Atticus and Giles. Daughter of Theodora. Works in England as the Dean of the Royal Necromantic Magistry.

Rami Alsharif: Father of Atticus and Giles. Lives in Dubai and heads the research department of Blackened Salt Apothecary. Rami is what would happen if a Golden Retriever was given power over death.

Thaddeus Giles Blackwell: A talking skull and reluctant ally.

Aegis: Maddox's magic sword, forged by a feyrie blacksmith, has the power to change shapes. Aegis can communicate telepathically to Maddox, an unusual trait.

Venenum: Atticus's sword, his grandmother's former weapon, can coat itself in poison and take the form of a snake.

Umbra: Giles's sword can call upon a creature formed of darkness to aid it.

GLOSSARY

Necromancer: A type of witch specializing in death magic. Powers include raising corpses for interrogation, creating zombies, draining life, and ability to conjure lightning for attacking and for resurrection. Necromancers live for two centuries and, in exchange for their soul, can become a lich.

Commission of Magic Management: The government entity responsible for maintaining a good relationship between the humans and the supernatural or fantastic. They have several branches and investigate any supernatural crimes.

Green witch: A type of witch specializing in nature related magic and healing.

Coven: A community of witches.

Feyrie/Fey: Feyries are magical creatures that travel between Earth and the fey realm. There are many types of fey, and they are split into the Seelie and Unseelie. They are known for tricking humans into unfair bargains.

Redcap: A type of ill-tempered feyrie that's known for dipping their hats into the blood of their enemies. They possess razor sharp teeth and are part of the Unseelie.

Lich: A soulless undead creature that was once a witch or warlock. Liches will live on forever unless their soul is found and destroyed.

Exorcist: Someone trained to expel spirits or other unwelcome entities from a person or place.

Parasitoid: A special sort of entity designed with a single purpose. Leeches off the magic of the item or person it is bound to.

Zombie: A deceased human who was supernaturally reanimated.

Undead: A being that is no longer alive but was reanimated by a supernatural force.

ACKNOWLEDGMENTS

If I don't thank my very patient husband first, I think he'll go insane. Jeff, thank you for giving me time to be creative while we both try to achieve our dreams together. Our family will always be the most important thing to me, even if I seem a little daydreamy when I'm writing. I love you.

Thank you to my sister for beta reading and illustrating the epic scene breaks for me! Also, I'm sorry for trauma-dumping my characters' sad backstories to you.

Thank you to my beta readers. C.K. Andersson, Sara Bee, Sabrina, Kelley, Erika, Alexus, and Nikki—you helped bring The Academy of the Dead to a better place. And some of your comments were hilarious.

Rashed AlAroka, Kateryna Vitkovska, and lepetitghostcat—you all created amazing illustrations for this book. Thank you all!

To everyone reading this—thank you for giving my spooky book a chance!

Check out the first standalone in Vermilion H Baine's
Haunted Creatures, Haunted Places series!

A mysterious inn, hidden away on the western coast of Washington, has asked for help.

In a world where the modern meets the magical, Avalon has learned to assume danger is lurking around every corner. As a seer, she often uses her power to ease her paranoia, but she fails to foresee that Elden, a grumpy and handsome innkeeper and her new employer, is much more than he claims.

Elden only wants to restore his late mother's inn to its former greatness, not to deal with the bossy woman he hired to do the actual restoring. He has other duties to deal with—like guarding the entrance into the feyrie realm that hides behind his inn.

Avalon and Elden both have their secrets. Unfortunately for them, they accidentally learn what the other is hiding and are forced to work together to not only to save the inn, but to save everyone they've grown to love.

ABOUT THE AUTHOR

Vermilion H Baine is an indie fantasy author based in the American Southwest. After a tour as a nuclear electrician's mate in the US Navy, Vermilion now works as a field service engineer in the semiconductor industry. She writes fantasy, low and high, and tries to sprinkle in humor between the extreme bouts of angst. If she isn't hyper-focusing on writing, she is hiking, reading, or replaying *Morrowind*. She lives with two very codependent rescue dogs, her grumpy, can-fix-anything husband, and her Viking-sized son.

The Academy of the Dead is her second novel.

instagram.com/author_vermilion_h_baine

tiktok.com/@authorvermilionhbaine

www.authorvermilionhbaine.com

SIGN UP FOR MY AUTHOR NEWSLETTER!

Find me at

www.authorvermilionhbaine.com